Bruce Venables was
Tasmanian Police F
Kong Police as an Inspector. He served in the Hong Kong Marine Police as a Launch Commander and in the Tactical Unit as a Platoon Commander.

In 1984 Bruce took up residence in Sydney and began his career as a writer of film and television scripts. He is also very well known to Australian stage, film and television audiences as an actor.

He is the author of a collection of poetry, *The Spirit of the Bush*, and four other novels: *A Necessary Evil*; *The Time of the Dragons*; *Two Tigers, One Mountain* and *Scattered Monkeys*. He also co-wrote, with Richard Fidler, the stage play *Flying Solo*.

Bruce lives in Sydney and is married to bestselling novelist and actress Judy Nunn AM.

Also by Bruce Venables

A Necessary Evil
The Time of the Dragons
Two Tigers, One Mountain
Scattered Monkeys
The Spirit of the Bush (poetry)

EUREKA RUN

BRUCE VENABLES

BANTAM
SYDNEY AUCKLAND TORONTO NEW YORK LONDON

A Bantam book
Published by Penguin Random House Australia Pty Ltd
Level 3, 100 Pacific Highway, North Sydney NSW 2060
www.penguin.com.au

Penguin
Random House
Australia

First published by Bantam in 2017

Addresses for the Penguin Random House group of companies can be found at global.penguinrandomhouse.com/offices.

National Library of Australia
Cataloguing-in-Publication entry

Venables, Bruce, author
Eureka run/Bruce Venables

ISBN 978 0 14378 239 1 (paperback)

Historical fiction
Eureka Stockade (Ballarat, Vic.) – Fiction

Cover images: cart © Delmas Lehman/Bigstock; burnt grass © Marina1408/ Bigstock; horse © aaltair/Shutterstock.com; flames © Kesu01/Bigstock
Cover design by Josh Durham/Design by Committee
Internal design and typesetting by Midland Typesetters, Australia
Printed in Australia by Griffin Press, an accredited ISO AS/NZS 14001:2004 Environmental Management System printer

Penguin Random House Australia uses papers that are natural, renewable and recyclable products and made from wood grown in sustainable forests. The logging and manufacturing processes are expected to conform to the environmental regulations of the country of origin.

To the memory of Judy Greaves

AUTHOR'S NOTE

The exact location of the Eureka Stockade is unknown. I say this with some authority because I asked half the population of Ballarat its whereabouts and after much finger pointing and directional advice their replies invariably finished with 'sort of' or 'I think'. Of course, I'm joking, but the precise location of the Stockade is still a bone of contention for many in Ballarat. There is a memorial to the battle erected in the suburb of Eureka and most people say the Stockade was there, 'or close by, probably within a couple of hundred yards, one way or the other'. Unlike Americans, who can tell you the precise location of the Battle of Bunker Hill and the Battle of Yorktown, or the British, who can take you to Hastings, or Bosworth Field, Australians are slightly more relaxed with the geography of their political history. It's the way of Aussies. It's the way we are.

Fortunately, *Eureka Run* is a work of fiction, so my description of places and events is whatever I want it to be. Therefore, I can claim the Eureka Stockade was precisely where I say it was, 'or close by, probably within a couple of hundred yards, one way or the other'.

I have made slight adjustments to the times and dates of specific goldfields events to suit my characters' purposes, but only by a few hours here and there. Furthermore, I have mentioned real characters and events to give an historical perspective to the narrative and in doing so I hope readers will gain a heightened sense of that turbulent time in Australia's history, when we were a heartbeat away from revolution.

PROLOGUE

London, December 1852

'Gentlemen, it is incumbent upon me to ask, for a third and final time, can this matter between you be settled without the shedding of blood?'

On a cold winter morning in St James's Park opposite Horse Guards Parade, two officers of the 3rd King's Own Dragoons faced each other, pistols in hand. Both shook their heads in response to the question.

'So be it,' Regimental Sergeant-Major Wilson continued. 'You shall stand back to back.' He paused until they turned and their shoulder blades touched. 'I will now count to ten. You will each respond to my count with ten paces, then turn and fire in your own time. One. Two. Three . . .'

John Farrington's jaw muscles tightened as he began the walk. When the count reached seven, his gaze briefly caught the eyes of his second, Lieutenant Harry Bellamy. Something was wrong. Bellamy's look was one of shock, his mouth open as if to call out.

John began to turn, when he felt the ball of shot hit him in the back. He fell to the ground, his face registering the chill of frost on the grass, and he watched two sets of spurred Wellington cavalry boots running towards him.

'Major Bingham!' he heard the RSM roar. 'That, sir, was the act of a coward!'

'Captain Farrington!' The voice seemed to come from far away. Hands rolled him onto his back and he looked up into the eyes of the Regimental Surgeon, Major Fraser.

'Sergeant Geary, bring the hearse,' the doctor called to the dragoon in charge of the cart referred to as 'the hearse' in military duelling circles.

I'm dying, John thought, as the doctor's face faded in and out of focus.

'It's a nasty wound,' Fraser continued. 'It's best we get him to hospital as quickly as possible. He won't last a night in the barracks.'

John looked beyond the medical officer at the dark, surly clouds above; faces swirled within them, mocking him. 'You fool,' he heard one hiss, or was it the surgeon who spoke? 'You should have known better than to trust Roger Bingham.'

'The count was ten, Sar'nt-Major!' John heard Bingham reply. 'I heard you distinctly. The count was ten.'

'The count was *seven*, Major,' the RSM answered. 'You turned prematurely and shot Captain Farrington in the back!'

A surge of anger rushed through John Farrington, revitalising him instantly. Despite the fierce pain in his back and shoulder, he pushed Fraser away, seized his firearm from the frozen ground and rose unsteadily to his feet.

'Sar'nt-Major Wilson?' he called as the doctor put a supportive arm around his waist. 'By my reckoning, the duel is unfinished.'

'Can you stand unaided, Captain Farrington?' the RSM responded.

'I can indeed.' The surgeon dropped his arm and backed away.

'Then, by the laws of honour agreed to, the duel is unfinished. Major Bingham, you will stand your ground. Captain Farrington, the shot is yours.'

Farrington looked across the short distance separating him from Roger Bingham. The man's face lost all colour and he dropped his duelling pistol to the ground. 'Farrington,' he called, raising his hands defensively. 'Farrington! I have a family, children . . .'

John Farrington raised his weapon and took aim, but his target began to blur. The Wogdon duelling pistol seemed suddenly too heavy for him. His arm sunk to his side, his vision faded to black and he fell unconscious to the ground.

CHAPTER ONE

Carrick House, London, April 1853

'Spring is by far the most beautiful time of year. Would you agree, Captain?'

'I would indeed, Nurse Chalmers,' John Farrington called. He didn't bother turning in his chair to greet her. He could hear the clip of her highly polished black brogues approaching as he sat on the wooden verandah outside his room. Nurse Chalmers arrived each morning at precisely nine o'clock and invariably remarked on the state of the weather. The banter that always ensued had become their standing joke. 'As I'm being discharged from your care today, I would say today is probably one of the most beautiful days of the year. Would *you* agree, Nurse Chalmers?'

'I would indeed, Captain Farrington,' she replied with a smile. 'In fact, because your convalescence here at Carrick House is complete and you're being discharged from my care, I would go so far as to say it is *the* most beautiful day of the year. Gainsay me not, sir.'

'*Gainsay me not*?' Farrington smiled. 'My dear Chalmers, you never cease to delight me!'

Gwyneth Chalmers, a handsome woman closer to fifty than forty, laughed girlishly. Oh, how I wish you would delight *me*, Captain, she thought. Then, immediately shocked by her indelicacy, she blushed. Stop it, Gwyneth! You're old enough to be his mother.

'I gleaned the phrase from a book of poetry given to me by my aunt Felicity,' she answered. 'The poems are by the

Reverend Lancelot Pringle, a Wesleyan minister from Wales, and, in my humble opinion, an uncompromising exponent of the art of appalling verse.'

'Oh dear, a poetaster!' John exclaimed. 'God save us all from inferior poets.'

'Not inferior; inferior suggests a level of ability, be it howsoever low. Lancelot Pringle has no ability whatsoever, well, for poetry at least, which leaves one to contemplate what he does to the word of God. I can't help but imagine Our Lord sitting on his cloud every Sunday morning, reduced to tears.'

'Stop, stop!' John laughed and clutched his chest wincing. 'Damn it, Chalmers, will I never be rid of this ache?'

'You were shot in the back, Captain. The bullet passed through your right lung. You're lucky to have survived. Mind you,' she patted his shoulder, 'if it weren't for Surgeon Fraser's decision to get you straight to Guy's Hospital you would have succumbed to infection. Army barracks are notoriously unsanitary places.' She wrinkled her nose in disgust.

'Yes, I'm very grateful to Major Fraser, but it's been three months since I was shot and I still can't walk fifty yards without the need to rest.' He looked at her and she could see the fear in his eyes. 'Will I be able to return to the regiment and resume my duties?'

Oh, my God! He doesn't know. A shiver ran through her. 'A duel of all things!' Her voice was shrill as she forced a change of subject. 'Only men would behave in such a fashion.'

'An officer in my regiment insulted my family's honour by inferring my father reneged on a land sale. When he did no such thing.'

'Oh!' she responded, exasperated. 'Sticks and stones may break my bones.'

'It was a matter of honour!' John snapped.

'Honour! Anyone who fights a duel cannot possibly explain the word honour!' She wagged her index finger before his nose.

'Now, steady on, Chalmers.'

'This man *you challenged* to a duel, Captain,' she went on, 'did he have a family?'

'Yes,' he replied evenly. 'But he cast aspersions upon my father's honour.'

'Be that as it may, if you had killed him, you would have destroyed their lives too, and the lives of his wider family, not to mention your *own* family had *you* died. I ask you, sir, where is the honour in such behaviour?'

'But he besmirched the good name of my family! Had I not challenged him . . .'

'You foolish boy.' She looked down into his beautiful young face and all the fight suddenly went out of her. God, he looks all of ten, she thought.

'. . . I would have been branded a coward, Chalmers,' he finished.

She shook her head and smiled at him. 'Not by a woman, Captain Farrington.' She reached out and stroked his cheek with the back of her hand. '*Never* by a woman.'

Why had he not been told? The question made her angry. John Farrington was a fine young man, a credit to his family and most certainly to his regiment. Gwyneth had read his Record of Service, which had arrived at Carrick House Sanatorium six weeks previously. He had returned from the North-West Frontier of India, where he'd been involved in the Anglo-Sikh Wars. He'd fought in the disastrous Battles of Ramnagar and Chillianwala, and then the magnificent victory at the Battle of Gujrat. His service record revealed he had been Mentioned-in-Dispatches an incredible five times for acts of gallantry and promoted in the field to brevet major by General Sir Hugh Gough, Commander-in-Chief, India. Upon his return to England he'd been congratulated personally by none other than the Queen herself. Gwyneth had read of it in *The Times*; Captain John Farrington, the Hero of the Punjab, the paper had called him, was summoned to Buckingham Palace for a private audience. It was also rumoured he'd been rewarded for his gallantry by Her Majesty's husband, Prince Albert, with a personal gift. It really was the stuff of dreams.

Until this had happened. She sighed. It's just not fair. But it's not my place to tell him.

Her thoughts were interrupted by a clack of boots on the verandah and she turned to see two army officers striding towards her. She recognised young Lieutenant Bellamy and the handsome, moustachioed Regimental Sergeant-Major Wilson. The same two men had brought Captain Farrington to Carrick House for convalescence six weeks before.

'Ah, my escort back to the barracks has arrived.' John rose to greet them, smiling warmly. 'Bellamy, Sar'nt-Major.' He shook hands with both. 'How good it is to see you both. I'm entirely sick of convalescence. My bag is packed,' he indicated the door to his room, 'and I'm ready to depart.' Before the visitors could reply, John continued excitedly. 'Oh, Harry, I can't tell you what it's been like cooped up in this *zoo for the infirm*! No offence meant to you, Chalmers.' He beamed at her. 'You've been wonderful all the way through my nightmare, but,' he turned back to his friend, 'I must say, Harry, I can't wait to get back to duty with the regiment. Then I can –'

'For God's sake, will one of you tell him!' It was Gwyneth's voice.

'Tell me what?' John's smile faded. He looked at Bellamy and Wilson in turn. 'What am I supposed to know, chaps?'

'You've been discharged from the army,' Bellamy said. 'That was three weeks ago. I thought you knew.'

'Is this some sort of joke, Harry?' John sat abruptly in his chair.

'Allow me to explain.' RSM Wilson stepped closer to John. 'There was a Board of Inquiry, Mister Farrington.'

Mister Farrington?

'It was conducted by Royal Order.'

'The Queen?' John was completely dumbfounded.

'When Her Majesty heard there had been a duel fought practically on her front doorstep, in St James's Park, she was furious.'

'Apparently she detests duelling,' Harry Bellamy added. 'She won't tolerate duelling in any form among either civilians or the military.'

'Surely someone in the regiment must have been aware of this. Had I known I would never have entered into the duel.'

'Major Bingham knew, sir.'

'What?' John rose and stared at Wilson. 'Bingham knew? Why in damnation did he not say something? He must have realised his fate would be the same as mine.' Another silence followed. 'His fate *was* the same as mine, was it not?'

'He was transferred to the Far East,' Wilson said. 'A dreadful outpost in China called Hong Kong. The Home Secretary, Lord Palmerston, described it as "a barren rock with nary a house upon it", which sounds like just the place for Major Bingham.'

'Actually, his circumstances are considerably worse, RSM,' Bellamy chimed in. 'He's stationed in China itself at Canton International Settlement on the Pearl River. He's been appointed British Army Liaison Officer to the Viceroy of Canton. It's the worst posting a man could be given.'

'Still, a better fate than mine, wouldn't you say, Harry?'

'I suppose so,' Harry conceded. 'But his family has great influence, John, and they wielded it. Half of them are in the House of Lords, including his father, Rupert Bingham. And his maternal uncle is Sir Horace Bolitho, Private Secretary to the Chancellor of the Exchequer.'

'And let's not forget his mother, Lady Catherine,' Nurse Chalmers added. 'A more vindictive woman you're never likely to meet.'

'So,' John said softly, 'Bingham gets transferred and I get cashiered.'

'Not likely, old boy!' Harry Bellamy exclaimed.

'That may have been the order from the Board of Inquiry,' the RSM continued, 'but the officers of the regiment informed the colonel of their intention to refuse any order to parade as witnesses to your cashiering.'

'Really?' John was surprised. 'They refused to fall in?'

'To a man, John,' Harry added. 'If we were ordered to fall in on parade to watch you be cashiered, we officers agreed to remain on the edge of the square and turn our backs.'

'The Lieutenant's right. The officers were determined not to see you humiliated. The whole matter has been kept hush-hush of course,' the RSM added. 'For the sake of the regiment, you understand, Mister Farrington?'

'Yes, of course, RSM, for the sake of the regiment.' John looked at Nurse Chalmers, whose sad smile did nothing to help his situation. How did it come to this? he wondered. What will I do without the army? The regiment was my home, my family, my friends. What on earth do I do now?

'Anyway, fortunately it's not relevant anymore,' Harry said, 'because someone with a great deal of authority intervened on your behalf and new instructions came down ordering that you be honourably discharged.'

'Really.' John was surprised. 'Who was it, do you know?'

'No.' Harry shook his head emphatically. 'No-one's got the slightest idea. And all efforts of investigation have met with stone walls. All I can say is, old boy, you were damned lucky.'

'Lucky?' John snorted. 'It's not the word I'd choose to describe it.'

'With all due respect, Mister Farrington,' the RSM said evenly. 'Have you ever witnessed an officer cashiered?'

'No, never.'

'Well I have. Cashiering is the most degrading and humiliating experience a soldier can ever know. He is paraded in front of the assembled troops, his epaulettes are ripped from his shoulders, his badges and insignia are stripped, his sword is broken, his cap is knocked away and his medals are torn off and dashed upon the ground. Then, as the entire regiment watches in silence, he walks in disgrace from the parade ground, out of the gates and out of the army.'

'An honourable discharge means you can *sell-out*, John,' Harry added. 'You can sell your commission and get your money back.'

'Never mind the money – my life is lost.'

'Oh come now, my dear fellow,' Harry chided.

'The regiment has been my life since I was seventeen.' The desperation in his voice was apparent as he looked into the stern face of RSM Wilson. 'I know nothing but soldiering.'

'You can't return to the regiment, Mister Farrington.' The RSM gravely shook his head. 'Colonel's orders are you can't set foot in the place.'

'That's very kind of him,' John sneered.

'He means no offence, Mister Farrington. The colonel's on your side in this matter. However, he's suggested you get out of London before any of Bingham's relatives, of which there are many, attempt to avenge his humiliation.'

'*His* humiliation,' John scoffed. 'That's a bit rich, wouldn't you say?'

'Believe you me, John,' Harry said, 'even now, three months after the event, rumours of the duel are still being discussed and those few in the know are on your side. It's become a scandal for the Bingham clan.'

'It's a miscarriage of justice, is what it is!' Nurse Chalmers announced with force.

John looked at her gratefully, and then at his friends. 'I think that may be a signal for us to depart, gentlemen.'

RSM Wilson handed John a small leather folder. 'Regimental papers and discharge certificate, Mister Farrington.'

John could only nod as he took the folder.

'We'll take you to Euston Railway Station.'

'Euston, eh? I take it I'm being shipped home to Warwickshire?'

'The colonel, mindful of your situation, purchased a ticket for you.' He passed John a bright blue ticket. On it were the words London & North Western Railway – London to Coventry One Way. The Farrington family estate was situated halfway between Coventry and Rugby.

John chuckled humourlessly. 'First I'm discharged and now I'm being sent to Coventry. What next, Sar'nt-Major, transportation to Van Diemen's Land?'

RSM Wilson picked up John's bag and he and Harry Bellamy started off along the verandah. Gwyneth grabbed John by the arm and held him back.

'Get out of London as your colonel suggests, John.' The sense of urgency in her voice was palpable. 'The Binghams are a ruthless lot, especially the matriarch, Catherine Bingham, she's evil. There's nothing but misery for you here. Go and live your life to the fullest and enjoy whatever it may hold in store. And find a good woman, one who will teach you the *real* meaning of honour.'

'I loved a good woman once, but I lost her.'

'Then go and find her again.'

John took her hands in his and kissed them both. '*You're* a good woman, Gwyneth,' he murmured suggestively, trying to make light of the conversation.

'I am indeed,' she laughed, reading his tone, 'but unfortunately far too old for you, more's the pity.' Then her smile faded. She pointed to the exit and looked him in the eye. 'There's a good woman waiting out there somewhere in the wide world, John. You'll find her.'

John's reply was cut off by the sound of horses' hooves on the cobblestones and a gleaming black Brougham landaulet, drawn by two magnificent greys, rolled into the courtyard. Its curtains were drawn but there was no mistaking the livery worn by the coachman – it was Royal Household. A Guards officer on horseback accompanied the carriage, and as it halted he dismounted.

'By gosh!' Harry exclaimed.

'Atten-shun!' the RSM barked and all three of them stood rigid, backs straight, feet together.

'Thank you for that, Sergeant-Major,' said the officer, a major in the uniform of the Grenadier Guards, returning a salute. 'Stand easy, gentlemen.' He regarded the three of them with an experienced eye.

John recognised the man immediately. One of the equerries from the Royal Household, he recalled. He was on duty when I visited the Palace. He conducted me to the Royal Suite. Of course! Grenadier Guards; Prince Albert holds the colonelcy to the Grenadier Guards. Now what's his name? Vallance? Yes, Vallance.

'Captain Farrington,' the major said.

'That's Mister Farrington these days, Major Vallance,' John replied evenly.

'Yes, quite. As the Queen's Equerry I am, however, one of the few people aware of the circumstances surrounding your discharge. My sympathies are with you, sir.'

'Decent of you, Major.'

'Your transportation to Euston Railway Station,' Vallance said, waving a hand at the landaulet.

'How did you know I was going to Euston?'

'No time to waste, eh?' Vallance indicated the landaulet again.

'Well,' John indicated his friends, 'actually, these two gentlemen were about to oblige me with just such . . .'

'I would strongly advise the use of this landaulet, Mister Farrington,' the major murmured, leaning in to John's ear. 'I would *strongly* advise it. You gentlemen,' he snapped officiously, 'may offer your farewells to Mister Farrington and return to your duties. That's an order.'

'Yes, sir!' The two soldiers saluted smartly.

'This is it then, old boy.' Harry Bellamy offered his hand to John, who took it firmly. 'God speed, John. Stay safe.'

'And to you, Harry.' He turned and took the RSM's outstretched hand. 'Sar'nt-Major, the regiment was the great joy of my life; make sure you look after it.'

'You can be assured of that, *Captain* Farrington.'

John registered the errant protocol from the veteran. 'Thank you for that.' He looked the old soldier in the eye. 'Thank you very much.'

'Mister Farrington.' Major Vallance opened the door of the landaulet; John climbed in without a backward glance and the door slammed shut behind him.

'I'll take that, Sergeant-Major.' Vallance took John's carpet bag and threw it up to the coachman. He then saluted both men and mounted his horse. As the greys responded to the coachman's command, he fell into line behind the carriage and followed it from the courtyard.

The two dragoons watched the landaulet cross the courtyard and pass through the arched entrance.

'I say, Sar'nt-Major,' Harry Bellamy drawled, 'rather odd that, what?'

'What's that, sir?'

'Major Vallance riding his horse and leaving Johnny all alone in the carriage. Rather rude, wouldn't you say?'

'I don't think he's alone, sir.'

'Who?'

'Captain Farrington, sir.' Wilson's eyes flickered briefly skyward. 'I don't think he's alone.'

'Then who's . . .' The penny suddenly dropped. 'I say! . . . I say! . . . *I say*!'

'I say indeed, sir,' the RSM muttered, as he thanked every god he'd ever fought alongside that he was not endowed with the brains required for officer rank.

Inside the landaulet John was momentarily sightless; it was pitch black until a brief ray of light breached a curtain and lit upon a pair of tiny, highly polished boots. He froze and, as his eyes adjusted, he realised who he was sitting beside.

'My husband sent me.'

There was no other voice like it. John was paralysed, unable to move a muscle, even though his brain was aware his thigh was touching her thigh, *her thigh*! Oh God, oh God, his mind screamed, as he managed to force one of his knees to the floor in an effort at obeisance and then his chin hit one of her knees. Sweet Jesus, take me now! he prayed.

'There is only one seat in a Brougham landaulet, Mister Farrington; it is designed to accommodate three people at most.' A long pause ensued before the Queen sighed. 'Will you sit down, sir!' Her irritation flared momentarily but she checked it. 'And for your own sake, compose yourself.'

John did as he was commanded, but speech was beyond him.

'As I was saying,' Victoria continued, 'my husband Prince Albert sent me. He insisted I get into this wretched dog cart and deliver you to Euston Station.' He caught her eyes in the gloom; they were cast straight ahead. 'He is the only man from whom I will ever take an order and on this particular occasion he has demanded I humiliate myself. He insists it is for my own enlightenment.' A long pause followed as the Queen of England awaited his acknowledgement. 'Have your wits deserted you completely, Mister Farrington?'

'N-n-no, Your Majesty,' he managed to stutter.

'I am to deliver you a message.' Queen Victoria gave a slight clearing cough. 'As you must realise, my husband is in awe of you; indeed, he sees himself in you. Your dash and gallantry on the North-West Frontier, as reported by *The Times*, enthralled us all, but none more so than my husband.' She paused again. 'You were his champion in India. That is why, at his insistence, I summoned you to tea.' Another pause. 'My husband believes it is I who am responsible for your recent misfortune.'

'Oh, no, Your Majesty.'

'Silence!' A very long pause. 'I must say in my defence that I believe duelling to be a breathtakingly stupid endeavour; only a man could conceive of it. Despite what men may think, including Albert, the act is without honour and serves no purpose other than to satisfy male pride, at whatever cost to his kith and kin, *and*,' her voice rose, '*diminish the ranks of my finest officers!*' John Farrington's heart shrank as her supreme authority washed over him. '*Do I make myself clear, Mister Farrington!?*'

'Indubitably, Your Majesty.'

'*Good!*'

A long period of silence ensued as the carriage rattled over cobbled stones, turning this way and that as it negotiated London Town. John's mind was in such a state of shock he remained at a loss for words. What does one say to one's monarch on a carriage trip through London? Thank you for driving me to the train station, perhaps? Oh God. Is there anything one can say? I hear the Isle of Wight is beautiful in the summer, Ma'am; will you be taking the children to Osbourne House? Stop it! Do you get to Scotland much these days? Stop it! His head rattled with questions, but his instinct for survival won out and his mouth remained closed.

'You must be vigilant, John Farrington.' Her voice was soft. 'The Bingham family regard revenge in much the same way as the Plantagenets, who made it an art form. I know the family well – they never forgive and they never forget. They will stop at nothing until the person who brought about the humiliation of one of their own is no more. And I can do nothing for they have done nothing.' She paused. 'Therefore protocol forbids my intervention.'

'Yes, Your Majesty.'

'My husband's message to you is this, rise above the tribulations you have suffered and seek your fortune like the warrior you are.' Yet another pause. 'He wants you to succeed, Mister Farrington. He sees himself in you and he wants you to seize the day, as he would do, and make it your own.'

'I understand, Your Majesty.'

'Do you still have the gift he gave you?'

'Of course, Ma'am! I'll treasure it until the day I die.'

'And he insists I give you this.' She handed him an envelope, which he nearly dropped as the landaulet came to a stop. 'It is a money order. The Prince believes it will give you independence until you discover your new vocation.'

'I don't know what to say.'

'Honesty. A rare commodity. I wish there were more at my court so endowed.'

'Yes, Ma'am.'

'If word reaches me concerning this meeting or our conversation, you'll regret it, Mister Farrington.'

'I shall be the soul of discretion, Your Majesty.'

'I know you will.' For the first time her eyes met his and he felt a rush of indescribable happiness. 'You're a good man, Mister Farrington. My husband believes it and so do I.'

'Thank you, Your Majesty.'

'Now,' she straightened in her seat and looked directly ahead, 'that's all the humiliation I intend to suffer for one day, or indeed any day. Goodbye, Mister Farrington.'

The door swung open to reveal the doric propylaeum of Euston Arch, the magnificent seventy-feet-high stone entrance to Euston Station, modelled upon the original Propylaeum that served as the entrance to the Acropolis in Athens. John alighted and was about to say farewell to Major Vallance when the Queen's voice from the carriage called to him.

'May the road rise up to meet you, Mister Farrington.'

It was the first line of an old Irish farewell, for some long forgotten reason so familiar and much used by men in the military. Wherever he'd served, men had used the verse to say goodbye.

'May the wind be always at your back, Ma'am,' he called the second line. She continued to gaze directly ahead, but she smiled and it was a truly genuine, womanly smile, the warmth of which reminded him of Gwyneth Chalmers.

'May the sun shine warm upon your face.' Major Vallance added the third line as he closed the landaulet's door, shook John's hand and mounted his horse. Then he moved off after the carriage.

'And the rains fall soft upon your fields.' John said the fourth line softly, to himself.

A cracked Cockney voice behind him added, 'And until we meet again . . .'

John turned to face an old soldier with a red coat, tarnished medals resplendent and a tin cup in his hand.

'. . . may God hold you in the palm of his hand,' they chorused together and laughed.

'It's been a while since I 'eard that one, sah.' The old soldier doffed his cap.

'Let me see those campaign medals.' John reached for his chest. 'Peninsular War, Spanish campaign and Battle of Waterloo. Am I right, soldier?'

'Righ' on the money, sah,' the old man chortled. '2nd 3rd Foot Guards, wiv Wellington at Wa'erloo. Corporal Douglas George Usher at your service!'

John searched his pockets and hauled out a coin. It was a sovereign, which he dropped into the old soldier's cup.

'Oh my word! Fank you, sah.' He looked into his cup to confirm his extraordinary luck. 'A sovereign, oh my very word!' He exclaimed again. It was more money than he'd seen in a long time. 'A sovereign!'

'Yes, a sovereign. And had you seen the one in that carriage, Corporal Usher,' John laughed and patted the old soldier on the shoulder, 'you would not have believed your eyes.'

CHAPTER TWO

Warwickshire, England, spring 1853

The train journey north-west on the London–Liverpool line exhausted John. No matter how he tried, he could not get comfortable. The muscles in his back and shoulder ached continually, reminding him his body was nowhere near healed. Walking up and down the almost empty carriage seemed to ease his discomfort, but then his breathing got the better of him and he was forced to sit down to recover. Looking out the window did him no good, either. As tiny villages, hedgerows, copses and green fields rolled by, a sense of self-pity engulfed him.

You were wronged, his mind kept repeating, spurned and cast aside by the only real family you ever had. He felt the rush of blood pounding at his temples. Ten years of my life, his mind raged, *ten years*.

'Damn it all!' he said aloud, drawing the attention of a mother and daughter, the only other occupants of the carriage.

In 1843, as a seventeen-year-old, he'd purchased the rank of cornet, the lowest grade of commissioned officer in a British cavalry troop, and had fought his way to captain and even brevet major on duty abroad.

Damn it all, his mind screamed, upon my return home to England I was invited by the Queen to a private audience with Prince Albert, who thanked me on behalf of the British nation!

He took a deep breath and exhaled slowly. As quickly as the anger rose, so it subsided. Listen to yourself, Johnny lad, he thought. So, you lost your commission, so what? You'll just have to choose another path in life. Stop feeling sorry for yourself. You're lucky to have led the life you've had so far. You've been abroad. You've proven yourself in battle. You've known the *camaraderie* and the *esprit de corps* of a mighty regiment. You've known beautiful women. And you've known love. Yes, he reminded himself, you've known love. Unrequited it may have been, but at seventeen you knew the ecstasy and the agony of first love. Theresa Lacey. He couldn't stop the smile spreading across his face. Tessa, as he'd called her. The most beautiful creature he'd ever seen.

He'd arrived in London as a young lad with six pounds, a loaf of bread and a block of cheese. Within forty-eight hours he'd learned one of life's greatest lessons: never wander around Limehouse and Stepney after dark.

Tessa had found him in the gutter outside the gates of the Jewish Burial Grounds in Bethnal Green. By then he had neither bread, nor cheese, nor money. He did, however, have a broken nose, broken ribs and three inches of split skin over his right eye. Tessa lived in Green Street behind London Hospital off Whitechapel Road and she'd managed to get him to her house and fill him with brandy before inserting seven stitches in the gaping wound.

'John Farrington,' she'd said after she'd bandaged him up. 'That's a hard name.'

'What is?' He'd had no idea what she was talking about.

'John Farrington is a hard set of letters to make out in Jumble. You know – the game where you make new words from the letters.'

'Aah, I see.' Jumble was a game he'd played at school. 'How about Jofn Harrington?'

She laughed. 'Jofn's not even a word, let alone a name.'

'Okay, how about Jingo Hartfroon?'

'That's pretty silly too.'

'My name was never much good as an anagram.'

'I love playing Jumble.'

From that day on they'd played it regularly over a glass of wine. Tess had given him shelter, fed him, clothed him, taken his virginity and lined up a commission for him in the 3rd Dragoons via Lord Dunford, a favourite among her many benefactors.

'Can you ride a horse?' she'd asked one morning at breakfast.

'Of course, I was raised on a farm,' he replied, taking the cup of tea she offered.

'The army would be a good career for you.'

'The army?'

'Why not? A commission could lead you anywhere. You've obviously had a good schooling and you speak like an aristocrat.'

'But I'm not any such thing.'

'You went to Rugby School, didn't you say?'

'Well yes, but only for two years.'

'Your father's a squire, isn't he?'

'Yes, he's quite a wealthy landowner, but that hardly makes me aristocratic.'

'So? Who's to know that but us?' She clapped her hands in delight. 'I'm attending the opera tonight with a senior officer in the army. I think he's in charge of the horses, or guns, or something like that.'

Tessa, she of the honey-blonde hair and beautiful green eyes, was only nineteen, yet already established as one of London's most sought-after courtesans.

One week later she'd loaned him the incredible sum of eight hundred pounds to buy his entry into the Dragoons as a cornet-of-horse.

On the night before he joined the regiment, and after she'd taken him to her bed, she'd told him she'd been 'on the game', as she put it, for four years. But she'd soon be off it for good. 'I'll be a woman of independent means, my love,' she laughed. 'I'll have a country estate and a small townhouse in Belgravia, or perhaps even Mayfair. And,' she snuggled closer to him, 'I'll have my very own dragoon to escort me about the town.'

She told him of her bourgeoning bank account and boasted she already owned the house they were in and another one besides. 'In Red Cow Lane off Cambridge Street,' she'd said proudly. 'Bequeathed to me by a wealthy suitor who died suddenly.' Her accountant, a Mister Charles, managed the rental of the terrace house for her, and she insisted its rooms be leased to girls in similar circumstances to her own.

'In other words, you're not just a whore, you're a brothel keeper.'

He'd said it in a rush of jealous anger which, he realised in hindsight, he'd had no right to do. It had been a childish response. She'd hit him and ordered him out of her bedroom. He'd heard her crying in the night. The next morning, dry-eyed and in a voice as cold as ice, she had told him to leave.

My beautiful Tessa, he now thought. What would have become of me without you? He'd searched for her three years previously when he'd returned from India with two hundred pounds, which he meant to give her as part repayment. No-one knew her whereabouts or what had become of her. He'd inquired around the theatres, especially in Drury Lane where he knew she'd sometimes worked as an actress. He even tracked down her accountant Mister Terence Charles, and her speech coach Madame Carlov-Dalton. But the result was the same. She'd disappeared.

'Excuse me, sir?'

'Sorry!' John sprang upright at the touch of the conductor's hand on his shoulder. He'd fallen asleep. 'Sorry, sorry.'

'That's all right, sir, trains can have that effect on travellers. Your stop is just minutes away. Brandon Siding, I believe you said?'

John dropped his bag and stood at the gateway to Farrington House, his ancestral home, looking down the two hundred yards of carriageway. It was no less a forbidding structure than it had been when he'd left in the dead of night ten years before. Red-brick English Baroque style, built in 1709 during the reign of Queen Anne, it would once have been a beautiful sight. But his father, a miserly man, had neglected its maintenance. Farrington House remained just as John remembered it – a dirt-stained, dilapidated and unhappy place.

He picked up his bag and began the walk to the front doors, gazing left and right at the lush spring greenery, but no fond memories of childhood rose to meet him. Images came of his father beating him and his brothers; the slightest mistake by any of them would see his father drag them to the stables and thrash them until they lay, sobbing wrecks. He remembered being deliberately locked out of the house as an eight-year-old, forced to sleep in the hay loft above the horse stalls. He remembered being denied food for two days when his father heard his mother scolding him for forgetting to say his prayers before bed. And he remembered the looks when his father's eyes would fall upon him, looks of pure loathing, which made John wonder what he'd ever done to offend the man.

Turn and go the other way, his brain kept urging him, but he continued, his feet crunching on the gravel drive.

He had to admit the fields of Farrington Vale were as beautiful as ever, but he felt no sense of belonging. A herd of dairy cattle dotted one paddock, several horses grazed in a grassy enclosure near the main barn, but every which way he looked there were sheep, mainly Southdown and Oxford breeds. His father was also a renowned breeder of Rambouillet Merinos, the wool of which was highly sought after by the weavers of Coventry.

''Ere then, who be you, eh?'

The distinctive tones of the West Country accent struck his eardrum like a stone from a slingshot. Turning, he saw a burly man walking towards him from one of the outhouses. He held a blacksmith's hammer in his hand and wore heavy boots with a leather apron covering his worn hemp shirt and thick woollen trousers.

'My name is John Farrington.'

'Ah, Wa'ter's boy, eh?' The man pronounced Walter as if saying water in a drawn out fashion. He reached John and circled him, inspecting his clothing and bag.

'Well,' he squinted at John, 'my name's Clem Norton.'

'I assume,' John looked at the steel hammer, 'you are my father's blacksmith. Would that be correct?'

'An' I assume you're 'ere for the funeral. Would that be correct?'

'Funeral? Whose funeral?'

'Your father's. I sent a letter by post to the army tellin' you about it, but that were a month ago. The Mayor o' Coventry wrote to you as well, or so he said.'

'I've been in hospital . . .' John said. 'I received no letters.'

'Well, you're a bit late. He be well in the ground now.' Norton walked around John full circle again then squinted one eye at him. 'You didn't miss much. No-one came to see him buried. Because he was who he was, a squire and all, the Mayor and some of his Coventry Council cronies attended, but no-one else came. Wa'ter had no friends. There weren't one person hereabouts what liked 'im.'

'Surely my family were in attendance?'

Any further conversation was rendered impossible by screams coming from inside the house. As John watched, the front doors opened and a young woman in a bright yellow dress burst forth and ran towards him.

'Johnny! Joooohnnnny!' The girl rushed at him and threw her arms around his neck. 'Where did you go? Where did you go? Where did you go? Where did you go?' She repeated the phrase as if compelled, almost hysterically.

'Here now, here now,' Clem Norton said soothingly. 'That's enough of that carrying on, Missy. You'll frighten your brother off all over again with that caterwauling.'

The girl jumped back as if she'd been bitten and stood, hands clasped, staring at the ground.

'I be Lily's 'usband these last two years, John.'

'Lily?' John murmured, then smiled. 'Is that my Lily, Lily, Piccadilly?'

The girl looked up, her face aglow. 'I waited for you. I told Mama you'd come back.'

'My, how you've grown! And how pretty you are.' He felt a lump rise in his throat. She was the only joyful memory of his wretched childhood. The last time he'd seen her she'd been ten and she'd followed him to the main gates in the dead of night.

'I'll wait for you, Johnny,' she'd said as she stood at the gate and watched him disappear down the lane.

It all seemed so long ago, he thought, so very long ago.

'I'm a part owner of Farrington Vale now,' Clem said evenly.

'That's ridiculous.' John almost laughed in the man's face. 'My father would not let that happen. Firstly, my father has four sons . . .'

'Your brothers are all gone, John.' It was Clem's turn to be abrupt. 'Of the twins, Mark died of typhus some years ago and Luke were killed in a tavern brawl in Rugby in this year last gone.'

'Dear God. I had no idea.' He'd communicated with his mother by letter for the first two years, but after that she'd not replied. He'd assumed his father had forbidden her to write.

'And my oldest brother, Matthew?'

'Aaaah, the priest.' Clem nodded. 'Arter takin' up Catholicism like he did, he were right out of favour with your ma, her bein' Presbyterian an' all.'

'Where is he?'

'He took up with a woman, name of Hitchens, over in Worcestershire and got 'eld to account in the Birmingham Assizes for tupping her daughters. Only little kiddies they was.'

A surge of disgust ran through John as he remembered Matthew, a self-obsessed mother's pet with a penchant for whisky and young girls. 'What happened to him?'

'He's gone to the demons!' Lily declared.

'She means Van Diemen's Land. Transportation for life, he got. They wouldn't hang him 'cause he was of the church, so it was reckoned, but a lot of the local lads was all for stringin' 'im up.'

'Where is my mother?'

There was a notable pause before Clem answered. 'I think you better come along inside and set down your load. Perhaps a cup of tea might be in order.' He patted Lily on the shoulder. 'You run on and set the kettle to boilin', lass. There's a good girl.' Then he looked John in the eye. 'Ten years is a long time, John. There's a hell of a tale I've to tell you.'

As John entered the kitchen at the rear of the house, long-forgotten memories once again poured into his mind. He remembered the housekeeper-cook they'd had, Missus Watney, who sometimes fed him bread and lard, strictly against his mother's instructions. He'd liked her, she was kind to him. She'd also, once, given him a Christmas present of a carved wooden cat, nothing particularly artistic or special, which his mother had confiscated, calling it ungodly. His father had dismissed both Missus Watney and her husband, who'd worked as the stable hand, for some trivial reason John could no longer recall. He could still see her waving goodbye to him as they left the farm. With tears in her eyes she'd called God's blessing upon him.

'Sit down, John,' Clem Norton invited him, indicating a chair at the kitchen table.

He did as he was bidden and watched Lily scamper around the kitchen setting the table with plates and cutlery, then slamming a cup and saucer in front of him before rushing to the stove to get the boiling kettle.

'Slow down, Lily,' Clem called to her across the huge kitchen. The pretty simpleton obeyed instantly and walked to the table, kettle in hand.

'Yes, Clem.'

'Slow but sure wins the race, eh? Be like the tortoise. There's a good girl.'

'I'm married to Clem now, John.' Lily beamed happily at her brother.

'Yes, so Clem said. I'm very happy for you, Lily.' She's happy, it's obvious, he thought. If Clem Norton makes her feel that way and cares for her as he seems to, far be it from me to interfere.

'Your father reckoned no-one would have her 'cause she's simple in the 'ead, see?' Norton watched like a doting father as Lily poured the tea into cups before he continued. 'I don't believe it was ever possible for him to see into 'er 'eart. To see what a wonderful person she is. I knew it the moment she first spoke to me. There's nothing but goodness in 'er. If all in the world were like my Lily, it'd be a much better place.'

John declined the sugar Norton offered him. 'I'm pleased to see she found someone to love her for who she is.' He shook his head as Lily offered him milk. 'She has nothing but love to give. You're a lucky man.'

''Ere, don't I know it.' Clem patted her on the buttocks and she laughed, skipping away to the sink where she promptly commenced washing dishes. 'She might even be a mum come next spring, ain't that so, Lil?'

Lily nodded furiously and smiled at John. 'I'll be twenty-one and that's the right time to be a mum.'

Norton looked at John and whispered, 'It wouldn't 'ave been fair of me to burden 'er with it when she were younger. She's a lot stronger now and she'll 'andle being a mother without any fuss or bother. You mark my words, she's a grand lass.'

John sipped his tea and placed his cup on the table. He needed all the bad news in one hit and he knew the worst was yet to come. 'I take it my mother is dead also?'

Clem nodded. 'She's been gone a year now, John, I'm sorry to say.'

'There's only me and Clem and you now, Johnny,' Lily called.

Clem coughed. 'Over the last couple of years, what with Mark dying, then Luke killed in that brawl, she didn't 'andle it too well. Then Matthew, blast 'im, didn't help neither! What with him gettin' at Widow Hitchens' kiddies like he did. The scandal was awful. Your ma went from bad to worse in a matter of days. Lily found her on the upstairs balcony, passed on.'

'She's in heaven now, John,' Lily said as she came to him and stroked his arm. 'She's with the angels.'

John stood at the far end of the upstairs balcony and imagined Mary Anne Grace Farrington, nee Bailleau, standing there gazing out over Farrington Vale as she had so often when he was a boy. Her hair had been lustrous, honeycomb blonde, and her complexion faultless; such a rare beauty. He used to press against her and smell her skin whenever he had the opportunity, which was not often. Mary, by nature, had never been an affectionate mother. She cared for him and his siblings, taught them right from wrong, fed them and made sure they were well dressed and well schooled, as befitted the children of landed gentry, but she never exhibited any affection for any of them except Matthew.

She'd been obsessed with religion; she'd called her boys Matthew, Mark, Luke and John and she'd instilled in them the truth of the Bible and the meaning of the Lord's wrath if they transgressed the thousand and one sins she told them to expect on the rock-strewn road to Christian enlightenment.

Matthew had been her shining light. Matthew – the very thought of his name filled John with disgust. He was the one who should have died. How many times had she compared John and the twins to Matthew and announced them wanting? How many times had she hurt her children by showering her eldest with kisses and affection? She offered some degree of fondness to Lily, but she always prefixed her remarks with 'of course, she's simple and can't be expected to understand', or 'the Lord will take her into his house for the deformed and unnatural, for they are his children too'.

John had hated her when she pontificated, which she did regularly. She floated across Warwickshire in its entirety, knocking on doors and spreading the word of God, which she had no authority to do and, when so doing, dragged her hapless children along to experience what she called 'unity with our Lord, as disciples of his love'. John and his brothers remembered the occasions as embarrassing and humiliating.

But there was one time, burned into John's memory, when, after he'd been savagely beaten by his father and cried himself to sleep, his mother had awoken him and lay down by his side. She had bared her breasts and pressed them against the flayed skin of his back and hummed lullabies to him until the sunlight had peeped through the window. Then she'd hurried back to her husband's bed, lest he become aware of her act of compassion.

'I made it to London, Mother,' he said aloud, 'and I walked all the way.' He began to talk at length about the life he'd led since leaving. 'I met a beautiful girl called Tessa who I fell in love with, but I misjudged her and I lost her friendship. I joined the Regiment of the King's Own 3rd Dragoons. You would have been proud of us, Mother; like peacocks on parade we shone and glittered. We advanced in review order and presented our colours to the Queen. And then we went to war – to India, where I saw elephants and even a white Bengal tiger in the wild. I saw the Himalayas, mountains so high they're said to be the roof of the world. And then we fought, oh how we fought. In a place called the Punjab known as the North-West Frontier. It's a wild, beautiful place full of mountains and passes and lush green valleys and all types and races of people dwell there.

'When I returned to London, I was invited to Buckingham Palace . . . to tea with the Queen, Mother dearest . . . Prince Albert gave me a gift . . .' John's voice faded as he realised he was talking to thin air. He turned and walked off the balcony and down the stairs, back into the land of the living.

'Your prospects for advancement were diminishin', you say?' Clem Norton asked with a frown, in response to John's evasive reply to an earlier question of why he'd left the army. 'Well that would do it for me too, I dare say.'

They sat at the table in the formal dining room, just Clem, Lily and John at a table which could seat twelve. Lily had cooked the dinner of duck and vegetables followed by pound cake, cream and a port-wine sauce. 'Suffice it to say, Clem, I enjoyed soldiering, especially my time in India, and the British Army and I parted ways amicably.' John hoped that would put paid to any further inquiries.

'Did you ever see an elephant?' Lily asked.

'I certainly did.'

'Tell me about the elephants?' Lily asked.

John laughed. 'The elephants, eh? Well, Piccadilly, elephants are wonderful animals, strongest of any on earth, and big! Why they're as tall as the ceiling we're now beneath.' He pointed upwards and her eyes followed, while her jaw gaped. 'I once rode on one, for three days. I sat astride her neck and her big ears kept the rain off my legs.'

'Her neck,' Lily repeated, her eyes still gazing upwards as she tried to imagine animals so tall.

'India must be wonderful . . .' Clem began.

'What gift did Prince Albert give you?' Lily interrupted as her gaze returned from the ceiling. 'What did Prince Albert give you? What did Prince Albert give you?'

'Well now, that be one a' the questions I might be after askin' 'im myself, Lil.' Clem stroked her arm gently, calming her. 'Everyone 'ereabouts knows you was given somethin' by the Prince, because it were in the newspapers, a gift they said, but them newspapers never found out what it was, so we was all left none the wiser.'

'What did Prince Albert give you, brother John?'

'I've never told a living soul, sister Lily,' he smiled at her, charmed by her wide-eyed innocence, 'but I suppose I could tell you.'

'Yes!' she squealed in delight. 'Yes!'

'As a matter of fact, Piccadilly, I might even *show* you.'

'Yes!' she whooped again.

John rose, leaving the dining hall. He took the stairs two at a time to his room. He'd vowed he'd show no-one the gift, a personal exchange from a man he admired greatly. To show it would, in his eyes, somehow demean it. 'But for Lily,' he said aloud when he'd found what he was looking for and was heading back down the stairs, 'for my beautiful Lily, why not?'

He re-entered the dining room and sat, placing the rosewood box on the table before him.

Lily's eyes opened wide and she stared intently. 'What is it?'

John opened the box, and there on blue satin it lay, gleaming in the light of the chandelier above.

'Ooooh!' Lily purred. 'It's a gun.'

'Aah, but not just any gun, Lil. This is a very special revolver made for Prince Albert by Robert Adams, a famous London gunsmith. It was put on show at the Great Exhibition of the Industry of All Nations two years ago, just after I returned from India. The Exhibition was Prince Albert's idea and this very gun was Robert Adams' gift to him.'

'And the Prince gave it to you for your appreciation.' Lily nodded, satisfied with her deductive reasoning.

'Yes.' John laughed. 'Something like that, Piccadilly.'

'It's very beautiful.' She put her face to the shining weapon and ran her nose along the barrel. 'What's its name?'

'Do you know, I've never thought of naming it?' He paused. 'Why don't we call it Mister Adams after the man who made it?'

'Mister Adams,' she murmured reverently. 'I think that's a splendid name.'

'Very well.' He lifted the gun from its case. 'Mister Adams it is then.'

For the next two weeks John noticed a distinct improvement in his own physical wellbeing. He'd been helping Clem with the running of the farm. He'd rounded up sheep and goats, milked cows, stacked kitchen firewood and done several shifts in the forge, heaving on the bellows while Clem manufactured horseshoes. And he'd cleaned harnesses and collars, polishing them until they gleamed, reminding him of his first years as a cornet-of-horse in the cavalry. By the fortnight's end he was putting in a full day and his lungs were working to capacity.

His mind dwelled often on the duel.

What if the shot in my back had killed me? Would Bingham's punishment have been the same? Probably, he answered himself, given the powerful family that surrounded him. And what if I'd turned at ten paces and killed Bingham? I'd probably be languishing in prison, or on my way to Van Diemen's Land to join my brother in that Godforsaken penal settlement called Port Arthur.

Over the coming weeks John avoided invitations to attend various events in Coventry. He knew those with influence were hoping he would follow in the footsteps of his ancestors and give himself to being John Farrington Esquire, Master of Farrington Vale, and as such a City Alderman, plus the newest member of the judiciary at Coventry Assizes, but to do so would merely advertise his whereabouts to the Bingham clan. Furthermore, he could think of nothing worse than presiding over a court full of drunken illiterate loom-weavers, as half the working-class population of the town were, and middle-class malcontents and vexatious litigants who spent their lives suing each other to assuage their dissatisfaction and boredom with life in a provincial textile town.

He had ventured into Coventry on only two occasions. Once to seek the services of Keating and Johnson, the Farrington family solicitors, in making a last will and testament and having his money from Prince Albert banked confidentially.

The second occasion had been at Lily's request for his company to attend the first ever performance of the newly created Coventry Dramatic Amateurs, who performed *The Irishmen in London* at the Theatre Royal for the benefit of the Freemen's Seniority Fund. Lily's love of theatre had been instilled in her by her mother, who had taken her to production after production as companion in the absence of her husband Walter. And although, over the years, Lily had never understood the plays themselves, she adored the lights, costumes and sense of the dramatic a night of theatre could create.

On a night John was desperate to forget, seven hundred Coventrians, full of fun and rum, had fought throughout the production. And one couple had fornicated so loudly John had been forced to get Lily out of the theatre into the morally safer environment of Smithford Street, a thoroughfare renowned for its prostitutes, whereupon Lily had thought it necessary to explain the act of copulation to her seemingly ignorant brother.

'It's perfectly normal behaviour.' She emphasised each word, imitating the schoolteacher tone her husband had used when explaining it to her. 'But Clem says it must be done in private. And,' she'd raised her index finger as Clem had done to emphasise the point, 'screaming like a mare, or squealing like a sow, although fine and capable of enhancing the moment, must not be done loudly.'

'Thank you, Lily,' John had muttered, as he'd hustled her around the corner to the courtyard that held their trap and horses.

'It's all right for farmyard animals to –'

'All right, Lily!' He thrust her onto the trap's seat and took hold of a bridle, then walked the pair back into Smithford Street before climbing aboard and setting off for home. Fortunately, Lily soon fell asleep against his shoulder and he was left in peace to smile at the moon.

It was a week after the Coventry Amateurs failed to hold the attention of their audience at the Theatre Royal that a letter arrived from the Honourable Samuel Newsome, Lord Mayor of Coventry. It was an official invitation to be guest of honour at a mayoral dinner at St Mary's Guildhall.

'They've got you this time, John.' Clem Norton laughed and thumped the table.

'They've got you this time, John.' Lily repeated her husband's words and laughed along with him, making John smile.

John and Clem sat at the kitchen table being served breakfast by a very busy and talkative Lily, who thumped the table, without knowing why, and laughed anew.

'You can 'ardly knock 'em back,' Clem crowed gleefully. 'It'd be a right royal insult to the whole town of Coventry, it would, if you don' go! That Lord Mayor, Sam Newsome, he's a smart one, 'e is. That there is the seal of Coventry City,' he said, pointing at the official envelope on the table. 'He's invited you as a guest of the city itself. You daresn't refuse, or there'll be 'ell to pay. And,' he pointed his gnarled finger at John, 'half of those people you'll be a dinin' with are the people who buy our Farrington wool. And our milk, and our cheese, and our beef, and our lamb, and our mutton.'

John nodded metronomically as Clem mentioned each product. 'I know, I know, I know.'

'But especially our wool, the Rambouillet Merino wool in partic'alar. That be the cream on our cake. You mark my words.'

'I understand what you're implying, Clem.' John could only keep nodding, abjectly. He knew he'd been out-manoeuvred and another trip to Coventry was unavoidable, but the thought of being drawn into and included as one of Warwickshire's landed gentry was anathema to him.

I'm only twenty-seven, he thought miserably. He imagined himself as a fat-bellied, red-faced, jovial Squire Farrington, pipe smoking and laughing gutturally from one county sheep and cattle sale to the next, or sitting bewigged and benign as a judge on the courtroom bench at Coventry Assizes, dishing out punishments and distress warrants against the poor and downtrodden.

'God help me,' he moaned.

'Another sherry, John, or would you rather a pint of ale?'

The speaker, Willoughby Barfoot, was the proprietor of the Golden Cross, a Tudor-style inn located at the intersection of Bayley, Hay and Cuckoo Lanes in the medieval heart of old Coventry.

'God grant me strength, Will,' John answered his boyhood friend as his glass was refilled. 'I should have you make that a pint of whisky given the fate that awaits me in the Guildhall.'

Will Barfoot laughed good-naturedly. 'It won't be that bad. I'll be there to hold your hand.'

'How so?'

'I'm not merely an innkeeper, I'll have you know. I'm an alderman on the City Council and I'll be on your side tonight.'

'I don't want to be a judge, Will.' John sipped his sherry. 'I don't want to be an alderman. For the love of God, I don't even want to be Squire Farrington!'

Willoughby Barfoot guffawed. 'Don't talk nonsense, John. They want to appoint you the youngest judge ever to sit at the Assizes.'

'I don't know the first thing about the law . . .'

'Neither do the rest of them!' Will interrupted.

'I don't want to be rich, Will.' There was a hint of desperation in John's voice. 'I don't want the money. I don't want the responsibility. I don't want the prestige.' He downed his sherry and slammed his hand on the bar. 'I want my commission back. I want my life as a soldier back.'

'Come on now, old fellow,' Will said, 'why on earth wish for a life like that when you can be a man of great wealth and influence? There's even Parliament to consider in the future. Listen to me; I'm speaking as your friend.'

Will and John had been schoolmates at Brandon Primary School and then for two years at Rugby School until John's father had demanded he shoulder his family responsibility and begin work at Farrington Vale. But they'd continued their friendship, hunting on Will's father's property and in the Forest of Arden until John had taken off for London.

'And friends we are, Will.' John gave up. 'And friends we'll always be.'

'My word, Farro,' Will shook his head and smiled, 'I never thought to see you back here in Coventry. Hero of the Frontier, tea with the Queen and the gift from Albert the newspapers went into a flurry about. What was it, eh?'

'That's a secret that will remain between me and the Prince.' And what's left of my family, he neglected to add.

'Fair enough.' Will Barfoot grabbed his three-quarter coat and long top hat from a peg and stepped out from behind the bar. 'I'll prise it out of you on the way to the Guildhall.'

Together they walked down Bayley Lane in the moonlight, John answering Will's endless questions. Their feet clattered on the cobblestones and echoed off the wall of the great cathedral of St Michael's. The edifice towered so far above them on their left John was forced to tilt his head back to see its spire meet the night sky, while on their right old stone buildings frowned down as if to ask their purpose for being in the narrow lane. They passed Bayley House and arrived at the ancient building that was their destination.

The view of the Guildhall from the outside was deceptive. At first sight, it could be dismissed as just another medieval building. The stature of the place was not immediately obvious and it would be easy to walk past the semi-concealed courtyard and not give a second glance.

However, as they passed through the arched entrance and entered the well-preserved courtyard, John began to sense its history. He'd never before set foot in the place, but he immediately envisaged kings, queens, knights and noblemen and women, all dressed in their finery and gathered on the very stones he now trod, living out the grandeur, intrigue and dangerous times that painted the pages of English history.

He saw the Lord Mayor, in his cloak and chain of office, striding forward to greet him and at the same time heard his name called.

'*Farrington!*'

The voice, coming from the archway he'd just passed through, rattled around the courtyard. Then a shot rang out.

John heard Will Barfoot grunt and fall to the ground. He spun around, the gun he'd named Mister Adams already in his hand, and ran back towards the entranceway. He heard the sound of feet running on the cobblestones and gave chase. As he turned into Mary's Lane, he caught sight of a man attempting to mount a horse. John stopped, took aim and fired. The bullet found its mark. The horse bolted and the man toppled forward onto his face, dropping a flintlock pistol as he fell. John approached cautiously, his revolver still trained on its fallen target.

The bullet had struck directly between the shoulder blades. He rolled the body over and knew instantly the man was dead. There was already a pool of blood on the cobblestones and the exit wound caused by the massive .44 calibre bullet was a blood-drenched, gaping hole in the man's chest.

In less than a minute the Lord Mayor and others were gathered around the dead body.

'It's Lester Poots!' someone exclaimed.

'Who's Lester Poots?' Sam Newsome asked as he removed his mayoral chain and wound it around his hand. 'Apart from the scoundrel who ruined our civic dinner?'

'A bad piece of work, is who he is,' another answered. 'A villain for hire.'

'Why would he shoot poor Barfoot?' Edmund Cooper, alderman and Chief Police Magistrate, asked.

'He wasn't after Barfoot, was he?' Mayor Newsome turned to John. 'He was after you, Farrington, was he not?'

John nodded. The Bingham family, he thought. Just when I thought it might have been forgotten. I should have known better. 'How's Will?'

'Shot in the leg, flesh only,' Newsome answered. 'He'll be all right. Doctor Cranston's with him.'

'Thank God.'

'Amen to that,' the Mayor muttered. 'Excellent shot by the way,' he added as he poked the dead man with his foot. 'Cooper?'

'Yes, Mister Mayor?'

'You're the Police Magistrate. Better see to it that the constabulary are summoned and have them get this body off to the mortuary. I don't believe this matter needs any further investigation. Open-and-shut case, what? Oh yes, and there's a skittish horse on the streets to be rounded up too, before it tramples someone.'

'Straight away, Your Worship.'

'Gentlemen,' he spoke to his coterie, 'I'm sure you'll agree this calls for a stiff drink. But first we'll adjourn to the hall and check on the state of dear old Barfoot.'

As the group of City Elders walked back towards the Guildhall, leaving the corpse in the street, Mayor Newsome placed his arm around John's shoulders.

'Now look here, Farrington,' Newsome said *sotto voce*, 'bad business this, eh what?'

'It's complicated, Mister Mayor. I'll say that for it.'

'I assume this is a result of the duel?'

'I'm assuming the same, sir.'

'They're a bad lot, the Binghams. I know them only too well. Powerful family, damned dangerous enemy, you understand?'

'I do.'

'Royalists!' Newsome spat the word. 'During the war, you know?'

What war? John wondered. God's grace, he means the Civil War, two hundred years ago. I should have realised; my father never shut up about it either.

During the Civil War Coventry had been a walled fortress and the great majority of its population rabid supporters of the English Parliament and the Church of England. John remembered his father explaining with great glee how captured Royalists were sent to Coventry to be confined and the locals refused to speak to them and even turned their backs on them. Then with the Restoration, Charles II had ordered the Coventrians to pull down the old city walls, at their own expense, so it could no longer be used as a prison. Faith in the monarchy had been even thinner on the ground in Coventry ever since.

'The Binghams were bloody Royalists,' the Mayor went on, 'the lot of them! And Catholics to boot! You mark my words, John. They're a vindictive family, especially Catherine, Roger Bingham's mother – she's the one you must watch out for. This attack tonight would be of her making I've no doubt. She'll have turned this business of the duel into a vendetta. She'll never let it rest until she's satisfied you're dead and buried.'

'I'm afraid you're right, sir,' John said as they turned left back into Bayley Lane.

'I know I am.' Newsome patted John on the shoulder. 'Because I know Catherine Bingham. You're the living proof that her only son Roger is a coward. And she can't deny the fact while you're alive to refute it.'

'I see what you mean.'

'Which means we have much to discuss. Because you, my friend, are at war with one of the most powerful families in all of England.'

It was midnight when John arrived home, yet Farrington House was a blaze of lights. He tethered his horse to a fence some distance from the house and drew Mister Adams. He went to the back of the house and peered through the kitchen window. His sister was sitting at the table, head in hands, and Clem was pacing about, a worried look creasing his face.

He pulled open the door and signalled to Clem with a finger to his lips, but Lily looked up and screamed, then ran to him and threw her arms about him.

'It's all right, John,' Clem said. 'It's all right, man.'

'What's happened?' John sagged with relief.

'A fellow on horseback rode right up to the front of the house and Lily went out to speak to him.'

'Shhh, Lily,' John cooed, stroking her hair. 'Go on, Clem.'

'Well, 'e were nice as pie to start off with and he asked a'ter you.'

'What did you tell him, Lil?' He held her at arms' length.

'You went to the Guildhall,' she sobbed, 'to have dinner with the Mayor.'

'Then what did he do?' John looked at Clem.

'I was in the stables when all this went on, but apparently he told her he was going into Coventry to kill you, then he rode off and Lil came a runnin' to me cryin' and carryin' on. It took me a minute to get any sense out of her.'

'I'm so sorry, Lily.' John guided her to the table and sat her down.

'Why should you be sorry?' Clem asked. 'It weren't none of your fault.'

'It's all my fault.' John sat at the table.

'Did this fellow find you?' Clem sat too.

'Yes he did, and he tried to kill me,' John replied and Lily's mournful wail sent a shiver running through him.

'And?' Clem asked.

'I killed him.'

'Dear God!' Clem exhaled and Lily wailed again.

'Quiet now, Lily,' John said and stroked her hand upon the table top.

'Has things been taken care of, like?' Clem said. 'The constabulary notified and such?'

'Yes, everything's all right.' He looked at Clem. 'But I have to go away.'

Lily sat upright, her wailing ceased and she blinked at him. 'No.'

'I must, Piccadilly. For all our sakes, I must.'

'No!'

'Listen to me now, both of you.'

He sat and stared into the kitchen fireplace and slowly recounted to them the events since the duel. He told them of his recuperation, his discharge from the regiment, of the Bingham family and his colonel's advice to leave London. He told of Lester Poots' attempt to kill him and the wounding of Will Barfoot and described briefly the death of his would-be assassin. Finally, he told them part of the discussions he'd had with Mayor Samuel Newsome.

'Leave England!' Clem declared. 'That's takin' things a bit far, ain't it?'

'This matter with the Binghams will never be resolved until Catherine Bingham or you, or indeed both of you, are dead,' Newsome had said when they were well settled in chairs in the Guildhall and on their third glass of French brandy. 'We had such great expectations for you, John, but you have no chance of a normal life here in Coventry, or even in England for that matter.'

John could only nod in agreement. He'd foolishly believed the Binghams wouldn't go to the bother of seeking him out once he'd left London. But they had, hadn't they? They'd gone so far as to hire an assassin! And he had no doubt their alibis would be secure if they were ever to be accused of having done so. They would be relentless in their pursuit of him and the longer the drama went on, the more people would be exposed to danger. Will Barfoot had suffered a bullet wound that very evening. Lily, of course, his darling sister, would be vulnerable while he was near. And her loving husband, Clem Norton, was a man with enough on his plate already without having to keep watch for assassins. God forbid that anything should happen to Clem! What would become of Lily?

'The colonies, John.' Newsome's voice had shaken him from his thoughts. 'America, or indeed Australia, which is in the throes of a great gold rush. Why, last year alone, fifteen million pounds' worth of gold was exported from the Ballarat goldfields in the Colony of Victoria.'

'There's my family to think of . . .'

'Exactly!' Newsome exclaimed. 'While you're around they'll never be safe.'

'But Australia, it's such a long way.'

'Ten thousand sea miles,' the Mayor nodded thoughtfully. 'But that is ten thousand sea miles of ocean between you and the Binghams.'

'I'll have to give it some thought.'

'Have you not been listening to me, John?' Sam Newsome snapped. 'You've no time to think! You've no time to consider options because you have none! You must get out of England. In fact, get out of the British Isles altogether! I'm sorry. I should not have snapped as I did.' He patted John on the knee. 'But you've no alternative but to run.'

'You're right, Sam.'

'I know I am. It'll only be for a few years I'm sure, John lad. Even Catherine Bingham will probably have mellowed in that time, or better still, died. Then you'll be right to return and get on with your life. Come in to my office here tomorrow morning and we'll sort out your affairs. Then it's onto the express to Liverpool and southward and eastward to the antipodes.'

'I'll hold you to that offer, Mister Mayor. I do need to sort out my affairs.'

'Tomorrow morning my office. I'll arrange a notary public. You bring your lawyer.'

John drained his drink and stood. 'I'll be going home now, while I can still ride.' He looked at Sam Newsome sitting, holding his brandy balloon beneath his nostrils. 'Tell me, Sam, why are you doing this?'

'The truth?' Sam looked up over the rim of his glass.

'The truth.'

'I like you, John. You're the only Farrington I ever met that I do like. I didn't like your brothers, especially the Catholic priest. I didn't like your mother, and I despised your father.'

'Thank you for your honesty.'

'You will succeed, John. You'll come home one day and you will be the Squire of Farrington Vale, and a damned fine one at that.'

'You can't leave England,' Lily whined like a puppy. 'Please don't go away again, John.'

'That'll be enough of that, my girl,' Clem snapped and Lily blinked at him, suddenly silent. 'Your brother John has a great problem to deal with and he'll do it in the best way 'e knows 'ow. Now, you were sayin', John?'

'Tomorrow morning I'll go into Coventry to arrange my affairs and then I'll be off. I may not return for some time.'

''Ave you decided where it is you'll be a goin', John?'

'It's better you do not know, Clem. I've arranged with Mayor Newsome and the Farrington Vale lawyers to transfer another twenty-five percent of the farm to you . . .'

'Oh, no!' Clem interrupted. 'Farrington Vale belongs to you, John. You're the Squire, man.'

'As of this morning Farrington Vale will belong to the three of us. And should anything happen to me, all I have will become Lily's. That is how I wish it to be. You will introduce yourself at the offices of Keating and Johnson, our estate lawyers in Cuckoo Lane; they will expect you. You will be given control of the accounts relating to Farrington Vale. You will make all decisions and if you have any trouble you're to call upon Mayor Newsome or Mister Cooper, the Police Magistrate. They have assured me they will keep your interests at heart and give you guidance should you need it.'

'I don't know what to say.'

'When will you come back, John?' Lily sobbed.

'When it's safe, Piccadilly. I'll come back one day when it's safe.'

CHAPTER THREE

Liverpool, April 1853

The completion of Steers' wet dock, in 1715, with Her Majesty's Customs House at its head, marked the turning point in the fortunes of the City of Liverpool.

Previously, it had languished in the maritime shadow of the Port of Chester in the Dee River Estuary not fifteen miles to its south. But Liverpool's granite docks and warehouses slowly yet surely mushroomed over six miles in both directions along the banks of the Mersey River until by the early nineteenth century Liverpool had become a major centre for world trade.

In the 1840s it became known as the 'city of palaces' because of the opulent mansions built by the wealthy few, mainly canny traders and ship owners, especially those involved in the slave trade. But for the ordinary merchant seamen, the city was no such place; for them it was an iniquitous port full of prostitutes, profiteers and crimps, those cut-throat middlemen who found employment raising unwilling crews for ruthless sea captains.

After staring in wonder at the colossal, and soon to be opened, St George's Hall opposite the Lime Street Railway Station, John Farrington made his way down Hanover Street towards the Liverpool Docks. He had been given directions by Edmund Cooper and he'd been told to follow them with all due caution, 'Liverpool being the den of iniquity it is'. But there was something about the city that caused him to stop regularly and take it all in.

Hanover Street had a bazaar-like atmosphere. As he walked the cobblestones towards his destination, he was surrounded by sailors from all the continents, prostitutes, pimps, beggars and aggressive hawkers, some of whom had set their stalls and barrows up in front of the legitimate shopfronts, much to the ire of those merchants. In the many side streets, John could see warehouses with large iron doors and slate roofs pressed against small residences and tiny office fronts. And all about were children, filthy and unattended, running hither and yon, supposedly playing innocent games, but in reality picking the pockets of unsuspecting citizens.

Finally, above and beyond the roof of a tavern called the Bull and Bear, John glimpsed the sight he'd been told to expect. Four mighty towers atop a brick and stone building reared up into the afternoon sky. He quickened his steps until he stood gazing up at the side of the brand-new Liverpool Sailors' Home, designed to provide safe, inexpensive lodging for sailors, as opposed to the temptations on offer along the docks.

'Good heavens,' he muttered aloud when he turned the corner from Hanover Street into Canning Place and the front of the establishment presented itself.

Decorative architecture gone mad confronted him. The building was an explosion of artwork and a monument to stone and iron workers, some probably of unsound mind, in John's opinion. But it was the front entrance and doors that defied description. When closed, the huge mass of iron would be impenetrable. Indian war elephants wouldn't breach it, he decided. The building was a veritable monument to modern security.

His mouth curved into an ironic smile after he walked through the impregnable fortification, took the remaining front steps, and entered the building unchallenged.

'Excuse me,' he said to a rather shabby looking man in the foyer. 'I wish to speak with Mister Coolidge.'

'That sea scum!' the man declared. He swung to confront John with an ancient mariner's rheumy eyes. 'It were in Porta'geez Macau where it all went wrong, la! Me kit were took and me boots stole clean orf me feet!' He grabbed

John's sleeve in his scrawny hand. 'Me decks was awash, la, understand? And I were sleepin' it orf on the Praya Grande. Clean orf me feet them boots was took, la.'

Mad as an Indian mendicant, John determined. Then the question occurred to him: if the inhabitants were all like the mad mariner he was speaking to, perhaps the massive iron doors of the Sailors' Home were not designed to keep thieves locked out at night, but to keep the sailors locked in.

'Can I help you, matey?' The voice from directly behind him had the depth of an ocean and the boom of a cannon.

John, not short at five feet ten inches, spun on his heel and stared directly into the chest of the biggest man he'd ever confronted. His eyes wandered upward to a big, bushy, grey-bearded face, its cheeks reddened and eyes twinkling mischievously.

'Do you work here?'

'I most certainly do not.' The voice rumbled around John's head like a distant thunderstorm. 'I'm a seaman like Gubby 'ere.' He pointed a finger at the old mariner who'd confronted John and was now staring intently at a potted plant.

'What say yer?' Gubby snapped.

'I said get up to your cabin, la, and get your 'ead down. We be shippin' out on the mornin' tide, Gub.'

'Right ye are, Deucer.' Gubby saluted with two fingers to his brow and wandered off obediently.

'There be no more shippin' out for Gubby, I might say,' the big voice rumbled on. 'He be all the while three sheets to the wind on rum these days, la.' He tapped his temple with his finger. 'His mind's in the doldrums.'

'It's a sad thing when that happens,' John replied.

'Aye.' The big man looked John up and down then seemed to make a decision. 'And only a good man will recognise it.' He nodded his head. 'Now, who was you lookin' fer?'

'Mister Abraham Coolidge.'

'Aah, right.' The giant leaned back and crossed his arms. 'He be a bigwig, that Mister Abraham Coolidge. You'll find him on the next deck, la.' His eyes glanced upward. 'First floor says they,' his eyes twinkled again, 'on the bridge says I.'

'I'm obliged to you, sir.'

'And if you have any other inquiries while you're here, la,' the giant offered a friendly smile, 'you just be askin' after me.'

'Who do I have the honour of addressing?' John extended his hand.

'My name's Small.' The Goliath took John's hand and stared into his eyes, waiting for a reaction to his name, but none was forthcoming. John's face remained frozen. 'James Small,' he continued, 'but shipboard people call me Mister Rhodes.'

'The Colossus of Rhodes,' John nodded. 'I understand; it's a respectable title.'

'And a learned man to boot.' The man nodded back. 'Your name is?'

'John,' he paused for a split second, 'er, Bailleau,' he finished, offering his mother's maiden name. On the advice of Mayor Newsome and Magistrate Cooper, he'd agreed a change of identity might be prudent during his travels.

'Are you sure about that name, John la?' There was the twinkle again.

'Absolutely certain, Mister Rhodes.'

Abraham Coolidge, a man of sixty years, balding with a pot belly and bushy, grey, mutton-chop whiskers almost meeting at his chin, stood in front of the window, sipped his tea and gazed out over the Mersey River Estuary. Huge sailing ships and steam-powered vessels lined the docks and many other ships – schooners, brigantines, clippers and more – lay at anchor on the water between Liverpool side and Birkenhead as the western shore was known. People swarmed over the miles of docks, busy at their various trades and livelihoods: men with horses and wagons loaded and unloaded ships, young girls sold cockles and mussels, boatswains and mates barked their orders, while gulls hovered and cried over the vibrant scene.

'So, how is my dear friend Edmund?' He turned and waved the letter of introduction Edmund Cooper had given to John.

'Oh, healthy and in good spirits and always the ever-vigilant magistrate.'

'That is excellent news. We schooled together at Rugby, you know.' Coolidge returned to the window and continued his observations of the harbour. 'And Samuel Newsome, is he well?'

'In fine humour.'

Coolidge stared out the window for several seconds, rocking back and forth on his heels. 'A journey to the colonies is not to be taken lightly, Mister Bailleau.'

'I've been so informed, sir.' John placed his empty cup and saucer on the beautiful oak table and joined Coolidge at the window. Through it the view was truly remarkable.

'It is quite some distance even across the Atlantic to America, you know. And Australia is much further. Ten thousand miles across seemingly endless oceans filled with storms that batter, winds that howl and doldrums that can break a traveller's heart.'

'It seems to be every man's preferred destination these days.'

'Gold.' Coolidge looked at John. 'Gold, dear lad, make no mistake. And Ballarat in the Colony of Victoria is a Mecca for the world's adventurous men, both young and old, hopeful of striking the mother lode, to use the goldfields vernacular.'

'I'm not without a sense of adventure, sir.'

'Look down there, Mister Bailleau.' He pointed at the docks. 'Those ships can transport you anywhere your heart desires. Are you sure it's to the bottom of the world you wish to go?'

John looked the portly man in the eye. 'I do, sir.'

'I thought as much.' He nodded sagely. 'Then so be it. In my friend Edmund's letter he requests I secure for you passage to your desired destination and give you accommodation until your day of departure.'

'I would be in your debt, sir.'

'Nonsense, it's the very least I can do for Cooper, a fine man, none finer in my estimation.'

'I concur, unequivocally.'

'Next door is an apartment, currently unoccupied, that we reserve for visiting dignitaries such as senior representatives of the British East India Company.'

'The E.I.C. I'm impressed. An illustrious company indeed, sir.'

'Renowned the world o'er.' Coolidge glowed with pride. 'Given a Royal Charter by the Virgin Queen herself in the year 1600. Had dealings with the Company, have you?'

If only you knew, John thought, as he shook his head. 'No, sir. I know of it only by reputation.'

'Two hundred and fifty years of service to the British Crown and still going strong,' Coolidge crowed.

Rather two hundred and fifty years of service to its ravenous investors, John thought. But not for much longer. A hundred years of internecine warfare in India, plus cholera epidemics and bad management, had brought the monstrous monopoly to its knees and the British Parliament, the *Tyrannosaurus rex* of monopolistic regimes, was circling menacingly.

'I'll have fresh linen and towels set in the rooms. Consider it your accommodation until you depart.'

'You have my deepest gratitude, Mister Coolidge.' John extended his hand.

'On Wednesday night we'll dine with Captain Glover, master of the *Maid of Shanghai*, an American chap. I'll secure your passage meanwhile, but I'll warn you it won't be cheap,' he added as the two shook hands.

'That will not be a problem,' John assured him.

'The *Maid* sails next Thursday for the Port of Melbourne. She's the finest ship on the route and the fastest. If I were in your shoes, it would be the *Maid* I'd be on or nothing at all.'

Over the next two days, John walked the length and breadth of Liverpool, but gained no enjoyment from the exercise, because he found himself stopping in front of shop windows, searching their reflections for people who may be following him. The assault in Coventry had stayed with him to the point of paranoia. The awareness that he could be murdered in his own country incensed him. All well and good to be shot or stabbed in India or elsewhere on Her Majesty's service, he thought, but in my homeland? The very idea infuriated him.

In his wanderings he purchased first a travelling trunk, some clothing he would need in the heat of a colonial summer and a fine set of military standard Galilean binoculars. Then at Southey's Gunsmith he discovered two weapons, the likes of which he'd never seen before.

John had stumbled upon the tiny shop in a laneway off Ranelagh Street and, as he'd been advised by Abraham Coolidge to purchase a decent fowling piece, he entered with precisely that intention. He had browsed several racks of rifles and guns before an old man finally appeared from nowhere.

'Alastair Southey,' the man announced. 'May I be of assistance, sir?'

'I've a mind to purchase a fowling piece.'

'Ah,' the old man nodded, 'pheasant or grouse?'

'I don't know.' John stopped his browsing, caught out. 'Are there pheasant or grouse in Australia?'

'Good heavens, are you going to that hellhole?'

'I am, sir.'

'Then it is most fortuitous that you found my door this morning.'

'It is?'

'Yes. May I suggest you arm yourself correctly?' He took John by the elbow and escorted him to a small counter at the rear, beyond which was a beaded curtain covering a door to the back of the premises. 'Australia is no place for the meek, sir. I've been reliably informed that wretched continent abounds with outlaws and brigands. No-one is safe. And the gold discoveries have only added to decent folk's distress.' Southey leaned close to John and lowered his voice, although John had no idea why; they were alone in the shop. 'Money, murder and Irish music.' He glanced about with mad eyes before repeating the phrase. 'Money, murder and Irish music. I'll say no more.'

'Well,' John was a little nonplussed, 'if I am offered the choice I'll take the money, or the Irish music.'

'Australia,' Southey muttered knowingly. 'May I show you something?' Then without waiting for John's response he scurried behind the counter and through the beaded curtain only to return a minute later with a wooden box about five feet long, He placed it on the countertop. 'I received this only yesterday from an American seaman, down on his luck and forced to sell.' The old man leaned his elbows on the polished maple box and, hands cupping his chin, he smiled. 'It's a Sharps rifle. Never been fired.'

'Sharps, you say?' John commented. 'I've never heard of the brand.'

'Christian Sharps,' the old man stated with some reverence. 'He's an American gunsmith, in the State of Vermont, a master craftsman.' He opened the maple box and there, encased in dark red velvet lining, lay a Sharps breech-loading carbine, Model 1853.

John was mesmerised, as any soldier would be, by the state-of-the-art weapon.

'This carbine,' the old man whispered forcefully, 'and a man with shooting eyes, would make a formidable combination. It's pin-point accurate at one thousand yards and with its breech-loading capability you'd get off eight, even ten, shots a minute.'

'What's its calibre?' John realised he had whispered too.

'Fifty. It'll stop an elephant at eighty yards.'

'An elephant, you say?' John coughed to clear his throat then looked at the old codger and smiled. 'There aren't any elephants in Australia, are there?'

'No, sir.' Alastair Southey shook his head, the irony lost on him. 'There's much worse.'

'Such as?' The old man's as mad as a hatter, he decided.

'Humans, especially those mad with gold-fever. They are far more dangerous than any elephant.'

'Yes, I take your point.' John's eyes were drawn to the rifle.

It gleamed in the candlelight and his mind went back to India. Slowly, he felt the rage he dreaded come upon him, the blood rush. He could hear the screams and smell the smoke of cannon-fire and the blood gathered behind his eyes.

The old man snapped the box shut. 'If you buy it this morning, I'll throw in a box of fifty-calibre paper cartridges and this.' Southey placed a sheathed knife on top of the box. 'It came with the rifle and I have no use for it. However, I've no doubt it will come in handy where you're going.'

John unsheathed the weapon and the biggest blade he'd ever seen glittered in the light. Despite the fact he'd never seen one, he knew precisely what it was.

'It's a Bowie knife, so the American said, named after the inventor, a Louisiana gentleman by the name of James Bowie.'

'Colonel James Bowie,' John said, 'a martyr of the Texas Revolution. He died in a battle at the Alamo Mission, a decade or so ago I believe it was.'

The old man grunted. 'Too bad he never had *that* with him.'

'He did. Well, at least one similar to this. In the story I was told he was abed in the infirmary, sick with fever, when a dozen Mexican soldiers burst in and killed him with bayonets.'

'Dear God.'

'But,' John waved the knife in front of the gunsmith's nose, 'not before he sent six of them off to hell ahead of him, using nothing but one of these.'

'It's a tool of the devil,' Alastair Southey declared. He tucked the rifle case under his arm and scurried towards the front of the shop. 'I knew it the minute I laid eyes on it. Come to the front counter, sir, and we'll strike a deal. Then you can take the infernal instrument to the bottom of the world with you.'

'Fourteen thousand, six hundred and eighty-eight miles is the distance from Liverpool to the Port of Melbourne,' declared Captain Winston Glover, master of the *Maid of Shanghai*.

John sighed with relief to be off the subject concerning the benefits of Methodism and the evils of drink. Winston

Glover had been at it since they'd sat for dinner. He'd started by saying grace, which intermittently touched on the doctrine of salvation by faith in Christ's atonement, but for the most part was a diatribe against everything from nude Polynesian natives, Jewish usurers and drunken seamen, to the Church of Rome and finally the questionable morals of Liverpool's female population. When John opened his eyes at Glover's 'amen' the soup, which had been served piping hot, he knew would be lukewarm at best.

'And an extra amen to that, Captain,' Abraham Coolidge added sycophantically. 'You're a good and righteous man.'

'I merely follow Jesus's command to spread the Good News, be of service to all people and treat them as equals.'

Except Polynesians, Jews, seamen, Catholics and the women of Liverpool, John thought.

'How long will we be at sea?' he asked the captain.

'Now that's the question foremost in my mind of late.' Glover placed his elbows on the table and tapped together the tips of his fingers, only to pull his arms away again as the servant set a plate of lamb and vegetables in front of him.

'Why is that, Winston?' Coolidge was desperate to be included in the conversation.

'Well now.' The captain leaned back in his carver and began to expound upon his favourite subjects – himself and his seamanship. 'On my first run to Australia, my ship was a damned sea-cow and the crew a scurvy bunch of wharf rats held together only by my ability to command. The passengers were assorted scum, mostly Irish and all "assisted immigrants" to use the polite phrase for them. One hundred and twenty-eight days we laboured until we made land at Fremantle on the west coast of the continent.' He sighed, reflecting for a moment. 'I'd used the cat o' nine tails liberally, fairly but liberally, and a number of the crew jumped ship. I had to recruit afresh to make Melbourne Town.'

'Hard days, Winston,' Coolidge shook his head. 'Hard days indeed.'

'But to answer your question, Mister Bailleau.' Glover leaned forward and pushed his untouched meal away from him.

Damn it, John cursed. Doesn't the man eat? He was famished, but as Coolidge had not touched his meal either, etiquette demanded John do likewise. 'The *Maid of Shanghai* is a remarkable vessel. She's a steamship, schooner-rigged, thirty-five hundred tons, three hundred and thirty feet by fifty with sixteen feet o' draught, four schooner-rigged masts, two forward and two aft, of a square-rigged main and she's auxiliary steam-powered and propeller-driven. And in a race to Australia nothing that floats will beat her.'

'What about the Yankee clippers?' John had heard them spoken of in the streets. 'I've been told they are the greyhounds of the seas.'

'Being a Yankee myself I must agree, indeed they are, Mister Bailleau.' Glover grinned, warming to his subject. 'But they rely on wind. The *Maid* has auxiliary steam power. Those greyhounds may be slick on the water, in fact they fairly fly downwind, but they invariably find themselves becalmed, if not in the Doldrums then elsewhere *en route*.'

'How long do you anticipate our journey will take?'

'Seventy days.'

'Heavens,' Coolidge gasped. 'Not even the Yankee Clippers have achieved that!'

'Have no fear, Abraham,' Glover announced, pompously. 'My last run to Melbourne was my first in the *Maid* and I did it in eighty-one days. I'll see seventy this time or I'll drop my anchor for good.'

It was nine o'clock by the time John escaped the dining room and decided to take in the evening air.

A walk, he thought, is just what I need, as he strode across Canning Square, which opened onto the docks proper. He turned south into Wapping, taking in the hive of activity around Salthouse and Albert Docks before locating, directly opposite the enormous Queen's Dock, the Sailors' Retreat, an alehouse recommended by the giant Mister Rhodes as one of the more salubrious the infamous docks had to offer.

'The owner be a close acquaintance of mine, la,' the big man had said. 'Just ask fer Tiny Maloney. Mention my name and you'll be welcome.'

John's entrance went unnoticed by the drunken, noisy customers and the loose women, some seated on sailors' laps and three dancing a jig to a single Irish fiddle. The air was a fog of tobacco smoke, and the stench of sweat, urine and cheap rum was intense.

John pushed his way to the bar and ordered.

'I'll have a bottle of Bristol Cream, barkeeper, and I'll open the seal myself.'

'Ooh aah,' the barkeeper, a short, thin individual with a ratty beard, mocked. 'Sherry no less, aren't we the toff?' he continued. 'What's the matter, afraid I'll slip you a dram o' Shanghai sleep juice?'

'That would be the act of a very brave man.' John's icy cold stare connected with the barkeeper. 'And you don't look like a very brave man.'

'I don't be meaning' no harm, Cap'n,' the ratty individual whined. 'One bottle of Bristol Cream comin' up.' He scurried to the end of the bar and disappeared into the tap room.

'Would ye be up for sharin' that bottle o' Bristol with a gifted companion, Bucko?'

The voice was deep, sexy and inviting, but the speaker now standing next to him was a painted harridan, a middle-aged woman tending to fat with bright orange hair and two front teeth missing.

'I would indeed, ma'am,' John replied warmly.

'Maude's the name.' She offered a wide grin that reminded John of an old picket fence with a black gate at its centre. 'It's rare we girls get to drink fine grog. Bristol Cream's a florin a bottle in this place and even more in other places that stocks it.'

'Would you do the honours?' John indicated the sealed bottle of sherry the barman placed before them.

'Ooh la la.' The woman primped her stiff hair and reached for the bottle. 'You are a right gentleman, aren't you?'

'In return for the drink, would you mind telling me where I'd find Tiny Maloney?'

'I'm Tiny Maloney,' a deep Irish voice boomed to his right.

The voice might be Irish, John thought, but the woman who'd spoken and now stood directly beside Maude had to be a Viking. Easily taller than his five feet ten, she was a striking individual. Handsome was the word that came to mind. Yes, he decided, handsome suited the Amazonian creature appraising him.

'How do you do?' John smiled.

'Beat it, Maude,' Tiny commanded, 'and leave the bottle of Bristol on the bar, you thievin' bitch!' Maude's hand let go of the bottle as if it had burned her and she hurried off into the smoky gloom.

'A glass of Bristol, ma'am?' John signalled the barkeeper for another glass.

'If I have to,' Tiny replied, maintaining her frown. 'It's not really my cup o' tea, but I'll drink wid ya.' She leaned towards him menacingly. 'Now, who is it looking for me?'

'I'm passing through Liverpool and was told to look you up by an acquaintance of mine, Mister James Small.'

'Ah, the Colossus of Rhodes!' At the mention of his name the woman's eyes lost their steely glint, her face softened and she offered him a beatific smile, revealing the true prettiness that once had been a young girl from Dublin. 'He's a lovely man, to be sure. If you're a friend of James Small, you're a friend of mine.'

'I'll drink to that.' John handed her a glass of the English sherry and raised his to the toast. 'To the Colossus of Rhodes.'

'And I can vouch for that!' Tiny laughed raucously. 'He has a cock the size of Perch Rock Lighthouse does our man James!' She downed her drink, pulled a face at the sweetness of it and slapped the glass on the bar. 'Jaysus, Mary and Joseph,' she cried, 'but that's a terrible drink. I wouldn't give it to a Protestant on St Patrick's Day!' She spat onto the sawdust floor. 'Seamus,' she signalled the ratty barkeeper, '*uisce beatha*, for the love of Jaysus.'

John knew the Irish phrase *uisce beatha*; he'd heard it in the army. It meant water of life. The Irish fusiliers on the

Indian Frontier had told him the word whisky was actually an Anglicisation of the Gaelic word *uisce*.

'Whisky's your poison then, Tiny?'

'Anything that keeps me half drunk's my poison. There's nothin' worse than walkin' into this fookin' place sober.' She extended her large hand. 'What's your name, Englishman?'

'Oh, I'm sorry. My name's John Bailleau.' He shook her hand. 'Pleased to meet you, Tiny.'

'Call me Eileen. That's what your man James calls me, except when he's sweet-talking; then it's Tiny because he's bigger than me.' The eyelids fluttered and the young girl returned for a moment. 'Seamus,' she called to the barman, 'whisky for the *Sassenach*.'

'That's very kind of you. I wasn't sure whether to order the spirits.'

'Ha!' she hooted. 'Afraid you'd cop a dose of knockout drops and wake up on a schooner to the ports o' China, eh?'

'Well,' he shrugged.

'Not in my establishment, John Bailleau; I've got no fookin' time for the press-gangs. I'll not have any customer of mine pressed into Her fookin' Majesty's Navy ships o' the line, nor shanghaied into service with the merchantmen. It's an appalling thing to do to a man. Who knows if he has a wife or not, or poor little kiddies to feed? To knock a man unconscious or drug him and put him to sea for two years or more is the act of a coward.' She smiled at him, a very genuine smile it seemed to John.

'Here's to you, Eileen Maloney.' He raised his glass. '*Sláinte*,' he attempted the Gaelic.

Eileen laughed at his dreadful pronunciation of the Gaelic toast. 'And may ye be in heaven a half-hour before the devil knows ye're dead!' she answered. They clinked glasses, then she leaned towards him and spoke to his ear. 'Now what are you goin' to do about the two fellas who followed you in here?'

John's face lost all expression.

'Keep smilin', bucko,' she urged him, 'or they'll know we're onto 'em.'

'I didn't realise I'd been followed.' He forced a grin.

'Just keep smilin' like you're havin' the best time ever.' She stroked his face with her fingers. 'Well you *were* followed, lad. And I know those two; they're crimps, press-gangers. Dublin boys and hard men, the both of 'em. And men who, when they're not press-ganging, hire themselves out to do the dirty work of others.' She looked him in the eye. 'Does someone want you done in?'

'Damn.' He cursed himself for having been so careless. I should have known things were going far too smoothly, he thought. And here I am now caught without Mister Adams. He looked at her. 'Don't worry, Eileen, I won't bring trouble to your house. I'll make my exit and take them with me.'

'I'll set the girls onto 'em,' she offered. 'There's not much more I can do, but it'll give you a head start. Keep smilin', keep smilin'.' She raised her glass to him and they clinked again. 'When you get outside, turn right.'

'I know,' he interrupted. 'The Sailors' Home is about half a mile.'

'Fook that!' she hissed. 'It's after ten o'clock. That place is locked down tight and won't open its gates till mornin'.'

'Then I'm done for.'

'Listen!' she hissed. 'Opposite is Queen's Dock, then you'll pass Wapping Dock, then Salthouse. Turn left at Salthouse and head for the river. You'll run onto Albert Dock and that's where your man Rhodes is working tonight.'

'Really?'

'Aye. The *Maid of Shanghai* docked alongside there this afternoon. Mister Rhodes is the Deucer.'

'The what?'

'The second mate; he'll be on the dock overseeing the loading of coal for the steam engine. If you make it that far, Rhodes'll do the rest.'

'Thanks, Eileen,' was all he could manage to say as his mind asked the question, have you got a decent run left in you? His breath was quickening already in anticipation and he could feel his scarred lung tensing for the challenge.

'Give me a moment to set the girls on 'em.' Tiny downed her whisky. 'Good luck, John Bailleau.'

'Thanks for the drink,' he answered, but she'd gone into the foggy air. He turned his face to the bar and contemplated his fate. Why didn't you bring your gun, he chastised himself, or at least the blade? The mere sight of the Bowie knife would be enough to put most men off their purpose. You've been stupid, John. You've been careless. From now on you'll wear those weapons at all times. You will never be caught like this again. Providing of course you get out of the fix you're in now.

It was ten minutes before he heard the caterwaul from the corner of the bar.

'Don't touch what you can't fuckin' well pay for, you dumb Irish cunt!'

It was redheaded Maude, the sherry fancier, who screamed and then punched one of John's pursuers in the face. All hell broke loose. At least four other girls converged on the Irishmen and swarmed over them, punching and kicking.

As the two men disappeared under a coverlet of petticoats, profanities and punches, John made his move. He went through the main doors on the run out onto the docks proper. He ran for his life, dodging and weaving along Strand Street, and reached the end of Queen's Dock without taking a breath, or so it seemed to him. But after three hundred yards or more, halfway along the edge of Wapping Dock, he felt his lung seizing up. The pain was sharp and serious. Where the ball of shot had passed through him an ache began to develop and by the time he'd reached Salthouse Dock he knew he was in trouble. He had never before placed so much pressure on his lung and now realised how foolish he had been to neglect its repair.

He turned left as Eileen Maloney had instructed and headed for the river. He ran alongside the small canal known as Dulce's Dock, which with no ship in it was deserted, and a darker and more sinister place he couldn't imagine. He stumbled on towards the lights at the far end where he could see a flurry of activity taking place. A hundred yards, his mind screamed, one hundred yards. Get to the lights and you'll stand a chance. The pain in his right lung was critical and he was forced to stop and rest against the wall of a tobacco warehouse. It was then, over his stentorian breathing, he heard the sound of running feet. Against the lights of Strand Street, he could see the silhouettes of two men coming his way. Inspired by raw fear he staggered on as the footsteps grew louder until they were a roar in his ears. Suddenly an arm went around his throat and he knew the game was up.

'Who be this pair, la?' a big voice growled. 'Friend's o' your'n I b'ain't be thinking, eh?' The arm released him and he dropped like a stone. 'Come 'ere, you two!' he heard the big voice snarl.

John's pain was so bad his mind retreated into unconsciousness and several minutes later when he awoke, he was on his behind, back leaned against the tobacco warehouse wall and with the face of big James Small frowning down at him.

'Tis lucky for you Eileen sent young Enda, la.'

'Who?' John managed to gasp as his lungs screamed for air.

'Enda, her young son. He come runnin' ahead of you and told me his ma was gonna send you a skitterin' this way with a couple a' pressers on your tail.'

'Ah,' was all he could muster. Speech was beyond him.

'Are your lungs ill, la? Or 'ave you got 'ead damage?'

In between gasps he tried to explain. 'Lung . . . shot in lung . . . duel in . . . London . . . family feud.'

'Is that why those fellows was after ya?'

John gave up trying to reply. He just nodded as his lungs heaved.

'Well it be no good gettin' you back to the Sailors' Home; it b'ain't be open again til morn. And besides, we'll be sailin' tomorra a'ternoon on the tide.' The big man picked John up like a rag doll. 'Might as well install you in your cabin on the *Maid*; you been payin' fer it since she docked this a'ternoon so you might as well use it.'

'Ooogh,' John grunted as he was slung over James Small's shoulder.

'It's company policy with most lines that First Class payin' passengers get charged from the hour their ship comes alongside until the hour they disembark.'

'Oogh, oogh, oogh,' John grunted with each step the big man took as he strode along the dock.

'Well, since you ask, la, it's on account of First Class folk seem to turn up as soon as the ship docks and expect to get on board, even though it might be a week until the ship's loaded and ready to slip 'er moorin's.'

'Oogh.'

'Well, it saves them the cost of taking lodgings until the ship sails. By the same token, when ships arrive at the destination port, First Classers will only get off when they're good and ready. They might take days goin' about it, so the companies charge 'em in advance.'

'Oogh.'

'For a man who can't breathe proper, you're askin' an awful lot of questions.'

The following afternoon, John stood on the weather deck gazing up in awe at the four masts, which seemed to disappear into the low-lying clouds above. The *Maid of Shanghai* was all she'd been described as and more. One hundred yards in length she was a magnificent mistress of the sea, John thought. Every inch of her was freshly painted or polished. From stem to stern, from scrubbed deck to top gallant yards and mast-heads, she gleamed. In John's imagination the *Maid* smelled of the sea and of tropical isles and the Orient and, of course, the ports of the subcontinent he remembered so fondly.

He'd not returned to the Sailors' Home, but remained onboard until the ship's departure. Mister Rhodes had arranged for his clothes and belongings to be brought and stowed in his cabin by the Third Mate, a tall, handsome thirty-year-old man from Boston, Massachusetts, named Theophilus Kittredge. Being American he spoke with deep reverence about the Sharps rifle, which he was reluctant to put down. He insisted John call him Kit.

Now, at four o'clock in the afternoon, John walked forward and up the companionway onto the fo'c'sle deck to stand gazing over the port bow, as the *Maid* slipped her moorings and eased under way on the high tide.

As the ship moved slowly from its berth out into the channel and north towards the estuary mouth and Liverpool Bay beyond, he gazed one last time at the City of Liverpool and the towers of the Sailors' Home soaring above all else on the docks. How lucky was I? he thought. If it had not been for the quick thinking of Tiny Maloney to send her young son ahead to warn Mister Rhodes of my predicament, I'd be facedown in the Mersey with my throat cut. Whereas, here I stand, still alive and on the brink of a great adventure.

'It be a grand feelin' ain't it though, Mister Bailleau?' Mister Rhodes called over the strengthening wind as he joined John on the fo'c'sle deck.

'I must admit, it is just such, Mister Rhodes.' John remembered the big man's statement that when on board a ship he insisted on being referred to as 'Mister'. 'My sense of adventure is much heightened. I'm like to a hound on the leash.'

'Aye, it's that feelin' precisely that makes a man return t' the sea.'

'I can understand that, Mister Rhodes. Tell me,' he pointed at the shore off the port bow, 'what is that on the headland?'

'Well, the stone building be a fort, built about thirty years ago. It's a gun battery to protect the sea port o' Liverpool. And that erection beyond it be Perch Rock Lighthouse.'

John managed to turn his snort of laughter into a cough, as Eileen Maloney's anatomical declaration of the giant's manhood came back to him. 'Ah, yes, I've heard tell of it,' he managed to say.

'Beyond it is Liverpool Bay, then be the Irish Sea proper. The skipper'll call for sail and the mighty *Maid* will be on her run south down the Atlantic. The next sight o' land for you will be the coast of West Africa, most like, or the Canary Islands and they be fifteen hundred sea miles from 'ere, la. Then the Cape of Good Hope be four thousand further on, then Australia another five thousand across the Southern Ocean.'

'The Southern Ocean, you say?'

'Aye aye, la.' Rhodesy shook his head. 'The Devil's Ocean, it be.'

'How so?'

'It's home to the Roarin' Forties, the wildest winds on the globe, freezin' and howlin' all the while; they'll thrust us headlong across an ocean filled wi' icebergs and mountainous waves the size of the Liverpool Sailors' 'ome and 'igher.'

'Good God. It sounds terrifying.'

'It can be terrifyin', indeed. But,' Rhodesy slapped him on the back, 'the *Maid* will take it in her stride; all you 'as to do is 'ang on, la. Your adventure's only just beginnin', John Bailleau.'

Indeed it is, John thought, as excitement rose in him. And the Binghams be damned. Soon I'll be in Australia, the wide brown land they speak of that lies at the bottom of the world.

'And let the dice fall as they may, Mister Rhodes.'

'Aye, la! That's the spirit. Let the dice fall as they may.'

CHAPTER FOUR

The British Crown Colony of Hong Kong, 1853

Chang Lou-shi sat in front of her mirror, her two dressers beside her, one to hold the brass bowl full of warm water and the other to hand her brushes and toiletries. She held a wet cloth over her face and counted to ten and her skin was warm, then she dampened the backs of her hands, once again counting to ten. She covered her face and hands with a mixture of honey and perfume, and applied rice powder until her entire face was snow white. She took particular care to cover the tiny tattoo of a blue nightingale on the back of her right hand, set between her thumb and index finger. She applied orange powder from ear to ear like a bandit's mask, used kohl to darken her eyelids and a charcoal stick to give the mask a lining. Finally, she rouged her lower cheeks and painted her lips a bright red. Then she again counted to ten as she assured herself her efforts were exactly right. Then again she checked her right hand to make sure her tattoo was concealed, before closing her eyes for a final count to ten.

One dresser finished shaping her long, thick, lustrous black hair as the other placed the bowl of water on the floor and, reaching to her left, picked up a jewelled headpiece of green and red satin, festooned with diamonds, rubies and pearls. With great reverence she placed it on Lou-shi's head.

'Oh, Mistress,' both girls gasped in unison, 'you truly are the Masked Princess.'

Lou-shi rose and over her soft clothing of fine linen she drew rich embroidered robes of the finest silk and walked to the full-length mirror in the corner. In the rich red and apricot robes and her magnificent headpiece, her reflection was truly that of Chan Wai-ming, the Masked Princess.

'That will be all now,' she said.

The girls, who also performed in the chorus and needed to prepare themselves, scurried from the room as if commanded by the Emperor Hsien-feng himself, and when the door closed, Lou-shi looked again at her mirror image.

'Tonight may be the last time we shall be together, Princess. The thought saddens me, but you must know the Emperor has declared me a traitor and his soldiers are seeking me. It may be some time before I see you again, if ever, so I will wish you good health, good fortune and double happiness.'

Lou-shi bowed to her mirror image and left the room.

She stood in the wings as Jiao Mun leapt and swung his arms in mock attack. It was the conclusion of Act I when his character, Prince Tsuen, would vanquish the dragon, represented by a huge shadow puppet on a screen behind him.

The cymbals crashed, the drums boomed and the bells rang with a maddening intensity. Then as the cacophony reached an ear-splitting crescendo, Jiao Mun struck the fatal blow, fell into the wings and the lights came up on the audience cheering wildly.

'Lou-shi,' he gasped. 'You must listen carefully. The Imperial authorities are here, in the theatre!'

'Here?' The news terrified her.

'Yes. And they mean business. They have a British officer with them. I will arrange a distraction.'

'You're on!' The stage manager Mister Ho, realising Lou-shi had missed her entrance, pushed her out onto the stage.

'I am a lonely princess,' she sang, as she skipped across the stage, 'and I seek the slayer of dragons.' She pirouetted, somersaulted and crouched to face the audience, who gasped as one at her athleticism. She was a curiosity to the women of Canton and not only because she was a famous opera star. Many had come to see her perform because her feet were not bound, a terrible affliction most women of the middle and upper classes were forced to suffer. 'He will come and help

me rescue my little brothers from an evil dragon who preys on children.'

As she performed, Lou-shi watched several Imperial soldiers enter the rear of the theatre. She looked to the wings and Jiao Mun nodded solemnly then pointed at the ceiling.

A mad crashing of cymbals and ringing of bells announced the entrance on stage of the Dragon King of the Eastern Sea and the children in the audience began calling for her to beware.

Lou-shi was perplexed. The Dragon King is not in the play we are performing, she thought; what is happening?

As she watched, dumbfounded, the Dragon King began to chant a magical mantra and a huge dragon's head suddenly appeared in the air above the audience, smoke issuing forth from its nostrils.

This is not part of the play, she thought; am I going mad? Then she realised Jiao Mun had lowered from the flies the smoking dragon head prop used in another of the operas.

In a matter of several minutes smoke filled the theatre and the patrons panicked, screaming and shoving each other in an effort to get to the exit.

Galvanised into action, Lou-shi fumbled her way off stage through the smoke to the rear of the theatre and out into the laneway. She ran to the next building, a large wooden structure, and entered through the open back door. She scurried between lathes, wooden work benches and large scrap metal bins towards the front doors, which would give her access to Fort Road and a view of the proceedings.

Through a window she could see a large crowd of onlookers in front of the theatre. A number of opera performers and backstage hands were huddled together on the front steps being questioned by both an officer of the Imperial Forces and an English officer in the bright red coat and white trousers of the British Army. She watched in horror as the British officer took his pistol and held it to the props manager's head. He appeared to speak to the Imperial officer then he fired the revolver, putting a bullet through the man's skull.

The crowd gasped as the officer trained his pistol on yet another worker. Lou-shi was horrified to see it was Chou, one of the chorus girls who helped her dress.

'Where is Jiao Mun?' the officer of the Emperor called out over the crowd. 'I want the revolutionary called Jiao Mun!' When no-one responded he nodded to the British officer, who pulled the trigger and shot Chou dead.

'I am Jiao Mun!' the opera star called loudly. He stood in the main street, clenched fists on hips, and then began walking slowly and proudly towards the steps, the crowd parting to allow his approach. He stopped at the foot of the theatre steps and glared defiantly at the officer.

'I surrender. There is no need to shoot anyone else.'

'And where is the girl, Chang Lou-shi?' the officer asked.

'I do not know.'

The British officer then fired his revolver and the bullet hit the dirt beside Jiao Mun's foot.

'On behalf of the Viceroy of Canton,' the Chinese officer snarled, 'I ask you one last time.' The British officer raised the firearm and aimed it directly at Jiao Mun. 'Where is the traitor, Chang Lou-shi?'

'I do not know.'

The officers exchanged a look and the Englishman discharged the firearm and the bullet entered Jiao Mun's heart, killing him instantly. Then he waved the weapon at the crowd as if daring them to respond to his actions.

'Listen, all of you!' the Imperial officer roared. 'Anyone who brings me the traitor Chang Lou-shi, alive, will receive one hundred taels of silver as a reward.' The crowd shifted restlessly. 'Now get about your business or there will be more bloodshed.'

'There is the traitor, Chang Lou-shi!' a man called loudly, pointing straight to her.

She was exposed, standing alone in the street. How did I get into the street? she wondered. I was hiding in the building.

The officers were suddenly in front of her. 'Are you Chang Lou-shi the opera star?'

'No,' she sobbed.

'You are lying!' roared the Chinese officer. 'You are the one they call the Emperor's Nightingale. You are Chang Lou-shi.' He seized her wrist and with his finger he wiped away the make-up, revealing the tattoo of the blue nightingale. 'You are marked as such! You are the Emperor's Nightingale! You are Chang Lou-shi!'

'No!' Lou-shi screamed, as the British officer seemed to grow bigger, taller even than the surrounding buildings.

'You will come with me.' The Englishman towered over her and grabbed her wrist. 'The Viceroy of Canton will make a present of you to the Emperor.'

'No!' she screamed. She tried to break free of his grasp and flee through the streets of Canton.

'You must be returned to the Emperor Hsien-feng.'

'Noooooo!'

'Wake up! Wake up, Lou-shi.'

She sat up in the bed, staring blindly at a wall with a crucifix on it. She clutched at the arm reaching for her.

'You have been experiencing nightmares, Lou-shi.' He held a cup to her lips. *'Here, drink this.'*

'I dreamed Jiao Mun was killed.' She drank from the cup. *'It was awful.'*

'Oh dear, never mind.' He stroked her forehead, checking her temperature.

'Where are we, Master Feng?' Looking again at the crucifix on the wall, it seemed to calm her considerably.

'We are in Hong Kong, the island the Emperor gave to the British,' the old man replied, loosening her grip on his sleeve. *'We are in the house of Father Michael the Jesuit. You must remember him, Father Michael of the American Society of Jesus who came to advise the Heavenly Kingdom on the principles of Christianity.'*

'And he taught me English.'

'That's correct. So you do remember him?' Feng was relieved, satisfied her temperature was normal and her

memory was functioning. He'd been deeply worried about her. She'd been ill for a week, since they'd fled Canton, and he'd thought he might lose her altogether.

'Yes,' Lou-shi nodded, continuing to stare at the crucifix, *'he was the fat father who did not bathe regularly.'*

'Shhh.' Feng blanched at the candid comment although it was one of the things he loved most about her. She made statements on whatever subject occupied her mind, without a thought for the consequences. It was one of several manifestations of a mental condition she suffered. He'd first noticed it years ago in her early childhood. People often thought of her as stupid or retarded, but Feng knew it was more complicated than that. Lou-shi was far more than the talented simpleton people assumed she was. He knew just how brilliant she could be, especially on stage. *'He is our host.'* He put the cup to her lips again and she drank.

Lou-shi looked at her master. *'We are in Hong Kong?'*

'Yes, and much has happened since we left Canton, but you must rest. You have been ill, my child. For a week you have suffered a fever. You have been hallucinating and your body temperature has been far too high, but now it has dropped.'

'We are in Hong Kong?' She yawned and lay back down on her bed.

'Yes, we are in Hong Kong to board a ship that will take us across the ocean to a foreign land.'

'Just like Chi-Chi in The Peach Orchard,*'* she sighed sleepily, referring to a Peking opera she had performed many times in which the heroine is kidnapped by a ghost and whisked away to an enchanted island.

'That's right,' Feng replied. *'Only you will not be kidnapped; you will be travelling as the guest of honour on a fine ship.'*

'Where is Jiao Mun?'

The old man froze; he'd been dreading the question. Jiao Mun had been like an elder brother to her for the last ten years. *'He remained in Canton,'* he lied. Given her condition, he did not dare tell her the truth. She had been terribly traumatised in Canton a week previously when Imperial soldiers had raided the opera company warehouse, and she'd fallen gravely ill. Fortunately, her mind seems to have blocked the memory of it, he thought.

Feng had been forewarned of the raid but had been too late to warn Jiao Mun and the others in the company. He'd taken Lou-shi and escaped to British Hong Kong and arranged for his precious costume trunks to be shipped to an island in the Pearl River called Huang Pu, or Whampoa as the foreigners called it after hearing the locals pronounce it Whang-pu-aaah in their singsong Cantonese tones. Feng had arranged for his old friend, the Yankee sailing master, George Featherstone, to bring the trunks from Whampoa to Hong Kong in his clipper the *China Moon*.

Good, he thought, as Lou-shi's eyelids drooped; the opiate he'd given her was working. He watched as she drifted back into sleep.

Feng Chi-pei looked lovingly upon the sleeping girl. He'd found her, a tiny baby, in a costume trunk backstage at the Peking Opera Theatre twenty years before. No explanation for her being there, no parents ever claimed her. She'd been part of the Green Lotus Opera Company since her birth. He smiled at the thought. She'd brought love back into his lonely life and he'd raised her as his own.

Chang Lou-shi was special; Feng regarded her as unique in all of China. She had a brilliant mind which often left him in awe of her, but he knew she was damaged. Her behaviour could at times be erratic and inexplicable, leading many to dismiss her as a simpleton. And yet, he thought, shaking his head, she was the finest exponent of Chinese opera he had ever known and she was entirely and utterly self-taught.

Since she'd been old enough to walk, Lou-shi had watched from the wings, until she knew the music, words, blocking and dance of almost every opera performed. Blessed with a truly extraordinary voice, she eventually became known as the Emperor's Nightingale, recognised imperially as the rising star of Chinese opera. She'd been solely responsible for the success of Feng's Green Lotus Opera Company. They had travelled the length and breadth of the Middle Kingdom, as the Chinese called their country, and each time they'd returned to Peking the Emperor had demanded she sing for him alone. He'd even offered her the great honour of having her feet bound and declared he'd make her a princess of the Imperial Court. Fortunately, the Emperor had accepted the explanation that Lou-shi's feet needed to remain unbound in order to bring joy to him through her acrobatic performances.

And so it had been, Feng remembered. Their lives had been special and they'd wanted for nothing until two years ago, when they'd been touring the southern provinces and a man called Hong Xiuquan had experienced an epiphany that brought about the greatest rebellion against the Dragon Throne that China had ever experienced.

The Taiping Rebellion, as it was referred to by the authorities in Peking, was a massive civil war in southern China which broke out in 1850 against the ruling, Manchu-led, Ch'ing Dynasty. Hong Xiuquan, after a severe illness, had been given a Chinese translation of the New Testament and immediately announced that he had experienced visions in which he learned that he was the younger brother of Jesus. He established the Taiping Heavenly Kingdom with its capital at Tianjing. His agenda, as dictated to him by Jesus, included social reforms such as shared common property, equality for women, and the replacement of beliefs like Confucianism and Buddhism with Christianity, albeit a distinctly Chinese form of Christianity as dictated by Hong Xiuquan himself.

China, by the mid-nineteenth century, had suffered a series of natural disasters, internecine warfare and defeats at the hands of the West, especially the humiliating defeat in the First Opium War in 1842, after which the Emperor had been forced to hand over the island of Hong Kong to the British. The Ch'ing government, which was a Manchu government and therefore, to the vast majority of the Chinese, a foreign government, was seen as an immoral and corrupt regime, particularly in the south among the labouring classes. It was these disaffected people who rallied around Hong Xiuquan. Huge ethnic groups of southerners, particularly the Cantonese and Hakka peoples, very quickly gave up their former beliefs and adopted Hong Xiuquan's form of Christianity until, by 1853, Hong realised he had not only ten million adherents, but also a possible army of ten million soldiers. A full-scale war with the Imperial Forces commenced with a vengeance.

As in any revolution, the first to fall are the intellectuals, the teachers, storytellers and artists. In this particular case, the opera companies were the initial targets of the Emperor's wrath. His advisors suddenly interpreted every operatic script as seditious and every song a secret message to the rebels. His crackdown on opera companies was immediate and intense, especially upon the Green Lotus Company with the nightingale he now detested for her traitorous behaviour. Feng and his troupe were forced to seek refuge in rebel country at the city of Tianjing. They'd been safe there for two years until a request had come from Canton from the wealthy Hong merchants to do a single performance for them. The money they offered had been irresistible and since the Imperial Forces were not known to be anywhere near Canton, he'd accepted the offer. But it had been a trap; half the company had been killed or arrested. Jiao Mun, his leading man, had been shot, as had Chou, one of the chorus girls, and his props boy. He and Lou-shi had barely escaped with their lives.

And so it was that Feng Chi-pei and Chang Lou-shi were in the house of an American Jesuit in Hong Kong awaiting a ship to take them out of China and away from the clutches of a very angry and malevolent Emperor.

Feng had discussed his dilemma with Father Michael, when he'd first arrived in Hong Kong. Feng's initial idea had been to regroup his cast and crew and take the opera company to Singapore where Lou-shi was known and greatly admired.

'*We will make a fortune,*' he had said in Cantonese to the multilingual Jesuit. '*Once the Singaporeans realise the Green Lotus Opera Company with its principal, Chang Lou-shi, the Emperor's nightingale, is in town . . .*'

'*The Emperor will also know the minute she sets foot in Singapore,*' Father Michael interrupted. '*And he will have her kidnapped and returned to Peking, where he will make an example of her to all who oppose him.*'

'What shall I do?' Feng wailed, suddenly terrified. He'd never taken much notice of the goings-on in the real world. He knew nothing of real political intrigue, revolution or war. In his world such things were abstract philosophies struggled with by heroes and villains on the stage. He had lived his entire life in the theatre surrounded by beautiful painted faces and lavish costumes, where every character, despite their trials and tribulations, ultimately lived happily ever after.

'You must go far away, Mister Feng,' the Jesuit offered. *'You must leave China as soon as possible and go far, far away. Take passage on the first available foreign ship, no matter its destination, and go beyond the reach of the Celestial Kingdom. Find somewhere safe for Lou-shi until this entire rebellion business is a long-forgotten thing.'*

'Beyond the reach of the Celestial Kingdom?' Feng frowned, perplexed. *'Surely there can be no such place.'*

'There are many such places.' The Jesuit smiled. *'There are many people who have no interest in China or the Emperor. Indeed, there are some who have never even heard of Emperor Hsien-feng or his Celestial Kingdom.'*

'And it is to one of these places I must take Lou-shi, true or not true?'

'True. You have no alternative, Ah Feng.' The Jesuit had patted him on the shoulder. *'If the Emperor catches Lou-shi, he will kill her.'*

When Lou-shi awoke, the room seemed to be rotating. No, not rotating, she thought, it is rocking. And although the feeling was not unpleasant, it was distinctly disconcerting. She could not recall having the experience before. Then she noticed the lamp hanging from the ceiling was swaying independent of the room and her mind went into panic mode.

'Ah Feng,' she called and sat up. On the wall next to her was a circular brass plate with a window in its centre and through it she could see nothing but water, a shining blue expanse stretching to the horizon. I am on the ocean, she

thought, not the blue-painted canvas sheets of ocean I've walked through on the stage, but the real ocean.

She lay in a single bed with a small wall around it, obviously to stop people from falling out, she reasoned. Parallel to her bed and three feet away against the wall was an identical bed and at the end of the small room was a chest of drawers with a mirror above it in which she could see her startled reflection. Beside the mirror was a wooden door. The door opened and Mok, one of her maidservants, appeared.

'Ah, you are finally awake,' the young woman said. *'I was afraid you might sleep forever.'*

'Where are we, Mok?'

'We are on a wonderful ship with huge sails on our way to Singapore.'

'How did we get here?'

'Last night you were sleeping so soundly Master Feng ordered you be carried on board and I put you to bed.'

Mok placed fresh clothes on the bunk opposite her mistress. She adored Lou-shi despite the fact the girl was a simpleton. Mok regarded her as her little sister and worshipped the ground she walked upon. *'You must get dressed, Mistress, and if you feel up to it come on deck and see the gigantic sails. They are taller than the Huang Pu Pagoda. They are truly wonderful.'*

Indeed, Mok had been right, Lou-shi thought half an hour later when she stepped onto the weather deck. She was forced to twist her head back as far as it would go to see three colossal wooden masts towering into the sky. The sails were full and the masts and yards creaked and groaned under the pressure from a stiff breeze.

Utterly exhilarated, Lou-shi ran to the railing and looked over and down to the water. It seemed to be racing by the ship when, indeed, she knew it was the vessel's movement that was creating the illusion. The ship was the fastest thing she'd ever experienced. Never in her life had she known such speed, such excitement and such a sense of freedom; it took her breath away. Lou-shi shouted into the wind like a little girl trying to express the sheer joy she felt.

'Be careful you do not fall in,' Feng called, seizing her by the arm.

'Oh, Master Feng,' she exclaimed, *'isn't it wonderful? Thank you, Jesus,'* she shouted into the wind.

Feng was delighted with the intensity of her gaze and her rapturous smile. She is healed, he thought, and gave thanks to the gods, then as an afterthought to Jesus. He nodded in agreement with himself. After having accepted the shelter of the Taiping Heavenly Kingdom and the generosity of its Christians for the last two years it would be mean-spirited of him not to thank Jesus.

Feng had never been comfortable with the philosophy of one god; it made life too easy and, as he knew from experience, life was anything but easy. The myriad gods his people had worshipped for the last five thousand years were real; they had to be. How could there be one god for everything? One single god would have so much work to do he'd probably fall ill from the strain. And besides, gods fucked, didn't they? So there had to be at least two of them in the beginning, one male, one female, otherwise where would the other gods have come from? Everything in existence fucked in order to procreate, so why should gods be any different?

Christian priests weren't supposed to fuck though, he thought, at least not according to the rules of Christianity. He found the concept difficult to comprehend. They were supposed to remain celibate, although no Christian he'd ever asked could explain why. It's God's law, was all they'd ever answered. But priests did fuck! He knew beyond all doubt they fucked, especially the Jesuits – they fucked like rabbits. There were half-breed Jesuit-Chinese children all over the country.

However, he had been told that the god of Christianity, who they all called Our Father, had never fucked, so how could he possibly be a father? That's when Feng's doubt about Christianity had manifested itself. If Our Father had never fucked anyone at all, he asked himself, where had Jesus, who everyone agreed was his son, come from? And more to the point, if all the Christians in the world called themselves children of God, Feng decided God wouldn't have time to do anything *but* fuck!

And to complicate matters even further, Father Michael, the American Jesuit, had told him that Our Father and his son Jesus never fucked anyone, but there was a third deity, the Holy Spirit, who all Christians prayed would enter them!

Did this mean, he wondered, the Holy Spirit fucked everyone on behalf of Our Father and Jesus? And when he'd inquired of Father Michael whether this Holy Spirit was male or female, he had been told it was both! And furthermore, when the Holy Spirit entered a man it was a man and when it entered a woman it was a woman, from which information Feng logically concluded the Holy Spirit was a homosexual. He decided he had no desire to be entered by a homosexual of either gender and gave up on Christianity altogether.

'We must give thanks to the Father, the Son and the Holy Spirit.' Lou-shi crossed herself, calling to him over the noise of the wind in the rigging.

'Most certainly,' Feng called back, not wishing her to know of his disbelief. *'Our Father and Jesus by all means, but be careful of the other one, it's homosexual.'*

'What does homosexual mean?'

'Um, I must speak with the Captain,' Feng replied and took off for the quarterdeck as fast as his ageing legs would carry him.

'Master Feng.' Stupid Ho caught him as he scurried across the main deck.

Stupid Ho was a stagehand who'd been with the company for ten years, ever since Feng had caught him stealing food from the Actors' Room of the Shanghai Opera Theatre. He subsequently learned the boy had been following the company for months as it had toured across China, sleeping under caravans and helping himself to food each night while the cast and crew performed.

Stupid Ho was anything but what his name suggested. An uneducated street thief, he was quick-witted, intelligent and totally loyal to the man who'd given him a home and a sense of belonging. He was Feng's eyes and ears in the company.

Feng had taught him how to act, talk and look stupid and then named him Stupid for a specific reason. He'd made the boy his company spy and his efforts had paid dividends over the years. Stupid Ho was regarded affectionately by the company as a likeable idiot and he wandered among them with impunity, grinning, watching and listening. Stupid knew the desires, expectations, ambitions and secrets of the entire Green Lotus Opera Company and Feng knew better than to ever ignore him.

'What is it, Stupid?'

'The ship is infested with rats, Master Feng.' The little fellow scowled as his eyes searched the deck.

'All ships have a rat population, Stupid. Should I be concerned?'

'These rats have only two legs.'

A shiver ran down Feng's back. Stupid appeared nervous and that made Feng even more so. The young man was prone to melodrama like the rest of the company and, indeed, the Cantonese race in general, who could turn a street argument into a full-scale riot in a matter of minutes. But Feng could sense Stupid was troubled.

'Ho boy.' He patted the young man on the arm. *'If you are aware of some imminent catastrophe, please inform me of it before it happens. Such information is invariably useless after the event.'*

'Master, there are men below this deck who are not honourable.'

Feng sighed. The only drawback to having Stupid Ho as a company spy was the amount of time he usually had to waste cross-examining the boy to glean whatever information he had to report.

'Ho boy.' He grabbed the lad by the ear. *'Don't make me interrogate you. Tell me what you have discovered in one breath, or I will cast you into the sea.'*

'They are Brothers of the Red Pavilion.'

Feng did not like triad societies. He'd made a habit of telling anyone who'd listen that he was a loyal subject of the Emperor and regarded secretive groups, like the Brothers of the Red Pavilion and their ilk, as potential threats to the good order of the Celestial Empire. This was despite the fact that he and his entire company had accepted the protection of armed revolutionaries for the past two years, who were even more paranoid about keeping secrets than the triads.

'How many?'

'Fifty or more, Master Feng.'

'Fifty!' Given Stupid's penchant for exaggeration, he decided ten would be much closer to the mark.

'Or more,' Stupid added, nodding furiously.

'What on earth are they doing on the ship?' he wondered aloud.

'I do not know, Master.'

'You must find out!'

'They are dangerous men.'

'Spend more time with them. Gain their trust.'

'But, Master . . .'

'Become one of them.'

'What?' Stupid was horrified.

'Join their brotherhood.'

'Do you know what they would do to me if . . .'

'Now is not the time for timidity, Stupid,' Feng exclaimed disdainfully. *'We must learn their purpose. Only then, when we know their intentions, will we have the upper hand.'* The old man frowned. *'How do we know they do not intend to seize the ship and cut our throats? They could rape our girls!'* He grabbed the boy's arm as if struck by a seizure. *'We could lose the company wardrobe!'*

'I fail to see your logic, Master.' Stupid frowned. *'If our throats are cut and the girls are raped, would not the wardrobe be irrelevant?'*

Feng slapped the boy. *'Don't be impudent. I was being histrionic.'* He glared at his faithful acolyte. *'It's not your fault. Your brain doesn't think very well, does it?'*

'One thought has plagued me all morning.'

'What is it?'

'It is a very serious thought.'

'What is it?'

'I have given it great consideration.'

'What is it!' Feng was already regretting the fact he'd asked.

'What will the Red Pavilion boys do when they realise the owner of the Green Lotus Opera Company is on board this vessel, departing China . . .'

'Fuck!'

'. . . and the Emperor's Nightingale is on the same ship?'

'A thousand fucks.'

'The very least they would do is abduct her.'

'Ten thousand fucks!' Feng began wringing his hands.

'That may also be her fate.'

Feng looked at his wonderful little Lou-shi playing on the deck with her maid, pointing at the water and up at the masts, her expression one of childlike wonder. If anything happened to her my life would not be worth living, he thought. I really believe I would kill myself.

'However, Master,' Stupid continued, *'it has also occurred to me that Lou-shi was carried on board unconscious, by me, in the dead of night. No-one would be aware of her presence aboard ship. It is unfortunate that she and Mok are scampering around the deck behaving like six-year-olds. Someone will soon recognise her.'*

'Lou-shi!' Feng called as he scurried towards her.

'What is it, Master Feng?' Lou-shi frowned, detecting the note of fear in his voice.

'Get back into your cabin immediately!' He signalled frantically to her maid. *'Mok! Get Lou-shi to her cabin!'*

'Yes, Master.' The young maid was startled into action.

'Lock the door!'

'Yes, Master.'

'Cut her hair and dress her like a boy! Her name is now So Chi-ming.'

'But why, Master?'

'Hurry!' Feng snapped and the two young women ran for their lives. He looked around the deck, but apart from Stupid and the helmsman on the quarterdeck there was no-one in sight. Thanks be to the gods, he thought.

'Dress her like a boy!' Stupid beamed in admiration. *'Call her So Chi-ming! You are a genius, Master.'*

'Go and infiltrate the enemy, Stupid,' Feng said with a wave of his hand and walked off, his mind on other things.

He stopped on the main deck at the foot of the companionway that led up to the quarterdeck. He placed his hands on the railing, gazed out over the vast expanse of ocean surrounding him and prayed he'd made the right decision. Australia, he thought, six thousand miles to the south.

'Oh, Ma-tsu-po, what have I done?' he called out across the open sea. Literally translated from Cantonese, *Ma-tsu-po* meant grandmother, an affectionate name for Tin Hau the Goddess of the Sea. *'I know I have forsaken you of late for the Christian Jesus, but I've given up on him and now contritely return to you through Buddhism, Confucianism and Taoism and all of the lesser gods and the Eight Immortals and any other gods I may have forgotten that you might like me to consider.'*

'Does my limited knowledge of Cantonese tell me that you are praying, Ah Feng,' Captain Featherstone asked, as he negotiated the steps of the companionway down from the quarterdeck. *'Did I hear you call for the help of the Goddess of the Sea?'* The captain's knowledge of Cantonese and many other dialects of Chinese was anything but limited. An old hand of the Orient, he'd sailed the South China Sea and all the ports of the Far East for over thirty years.

'Good day, Captain.'

Feng had known the American for a long time. They'd met up occasionally in any number of Chinese ports from Canton to Shanghai as they'd followed their professions. Strangely for a *gwailo* – a foreigner devil – George Featherstone was a dedicated follower of Chinese opera and particularly the Green Lotus Opera Company and its star, Chang Lou-shi.

'Why would you need the services of Tin Hau? You are safe on board a Yankee clipper bound for Australia with your nightingale concealed in a first-class cabin.'

'She will be safe in Australia, Captain, true or not true?'

'True. I can't think of a better place to hide her, Mister Feng.'

Feng smiled, relieved. *'You are a good man, Captain George. Oh, by the way,'* he dropped his voice and looked about before continuing, *'are you aware this ship is infested with Brothers of the Red Pavilion?'*

'I was just about to inform you of that fact. They paid me big money to take them to Australia.'

'What is there in Australia that would interest a triad society?'

'Gold.'

The wind freshened in the late afternoon and by the time Feng and what was left of his opera company, namely Lou-shi now a boy called So Chi-ming, Mok and Stupid, gathered in his cabin to dine, the ship was rolling and dipping noticeably.

'Aaaiiiyyaaah!' Mok wailed in pure Cantonese fashion as the ship lurched and the bowl of boiled rice she'd put on the table shot to starboard and was brilliantly caught by Stupid Ho.

'Will the entire voyage be as uncomfortable as this, Master Feng?' Stupid asked, as the vessel righted itself and the dining table, suspended on ropes from the ceiling, centralised.

'Believe me, Mok, it can get much worse,' Feng answered, remembering a fierce voyage he'd once taken from Amoy up the China Coast to Shanghai. *'We have two good cabins courtesy of Captain George. Imagine what it must be like below decks where men are sharing berths eight to the cabin. The decks will be awash with vomit by now.'*

'Oh, please don't talk of vomit!' Mok, hand over her mouth, fled the cabin.

'Give that to me.' Feng took the bowl of rice from Stupid. *'Go after her and see she doesn't go overboard. There is a storm approaching and things will get much rougher.'*

Stupid needed no second bidding; he was in a similar state to Mok and seized with both hands the opportunity to get out of the confined space.

'And how are you feeling, Chi-ming?' Feng asked, when Stupid, also with his hand over his mouth, had disappeared.

'Like a boy!' she snapped.

'Ah, my little bird,' he cooed, *'I am so sorry to have subjected you to such a fate, but it is vital no-one knows you are on board. Disguised as the boy So Chi-ming you will go unnoticed.'*

'I like my real name.' She pouted and sat cross-legged on a bunk, elbows on knees and chin in hands.

She does indeed look like a boy, he thought. Mok had created a faultless transformation. Her top locks had been drawn back tightly from her high forehead and hidden beneath a close-fitting cap, from which Lou-shi's long hair emerged in a queue down the centre of her back. Her clothes were that of a coolie, baggy black trousers and loose-fitting top.

'Where is Jiao Mun?' Lou-shi asked, staring at him with accusing eyes.

The usual blunt delivery of her question hit him with the force of a hammer blow.

'Well, I . . .' Unable to answer, his voice trailed off.

'He is afraid of ghosts?' She nodded as if confirming her own statement. *'That is why he did not come, true or not true, ah?'*

Feng nodded as he watched a tear roll down her cheek. The girl was utterly bereft as only Lou-shi could be. There was no middle ground in her being; only the very extremes of feeling would suffice. He wanted to reach out and wrap her in the safety of his arms. But he knew her beautiful, broken mind would neither understand nor respond to the gesture of affection.

'And we are travelling to a land full of ghosts and spirits, true or not true?'

'True, Lou-shi, and we will be forced to live there until such time as you can safely return to China.'

'And when will that be?' She wiped the tear away and, chin up, wide-eyed she stared at him.

'Only the gods can answer that.' He shrugged. *'Until they do, our future and whatever it may hold is in the great land to the south, called Australia.'*

CHAPTER FIVE

Melbourne, British Colony of Victoria, summer 1853

To ten-year-old Jack Shearley the crowds went unnoticed. Great cities and crowds had been part of his life since before he could remember. He didn't recall London, but he had vague memories of New York City and the house on 14th Street. He remembered vividly San Francisco where his mother had owned a fine hotel and the miners, the '49ers, at least those among them who'd struck it rich, had dined à la carte, sipped the finest champagne and settled their bills with pure gold dust. And now he was getting to know Melbourne, a city that would soon rival his former hometowns in size due to the gold strikes to its west.

He leapt onto the front verandah of the Golden Sheaf, a brand new two-storey building. 'Built and paid for by me,' his ma had boasted, 'in the most elegant Victorian style, so don't dirty it up.' He paused momentarily to take off his muddy boots then, after gathering speed again, he burst through the double front doors and in his socks slid across the black-and-white chequered marble floor to the foot of the grand carved black-wood stairway. He grinned at the check-in desk where Dorothy, the receptionist, stood frowning at him. After taking the stairs two at a time he sped along the landing then stopped on a sixpence, adjusted his clothes, entered his mother's private apartment and knocked softly on her bedroom door.

He waited patiently, hoping she might still be asleep, then after more than a minute of silence, he carefully opened the door and went in. Although no direct sunlight entered the room, his mother's bed was awash in a golden glow filtering through the blinds and she lay sweetly asleep.

In all of his young life, his fondest memories were of watching his ma when she was unaware of his gaze. His mother Cate Shearley was an hotelier and a damned fine one in Jack's biased opinion. She'd operated the Grand Hotel on Broadway in New York City for his Uncle Solly, and when he'd died, she'd built and worked the famous California Eldorado Hotel in San Francisco.

He knew something had gone horribly wrong and his ma had needed to get out of San Francisco in a hurry. She'd tried to hide it from him, and he didn't know the actual reason, only that it had something to do with a big Frenchman from Canada called Jean-Baptiste Le Pen, a man to whom Jack had taken an instant dislike.

'Run, Jack, run like the wind,' she'd urged him as she ran holding a towel over her bleeding eye. And so they did, with Uncle Amos, her mother's black retainer, all the way to the San Francisco Docks. He remembered on that terror-filled night having the feeling he was being pursued by all of the demons in hell. They'd taken the first available ship. It had set sail not ten minutes after they'd boarded. His ma hadn't even asked its destination. It turned out to be Melbourne and that's how they came to be in the Colony of Victoria in Australia, at the bottom of the world.

His mother never appeared until after ten in the morning and normally he would respect that, but he had news and he'd been told by Uncle Amos that she must know of it immediately.

Young Jack gazed down at his sleeping parent and the familiar rush of joy washed over his face. She sure is beautiful, he thought yet again. Her face, lying on her right side as she was, looks exactly like the face of Sleeping Beauty, he reckoned. Then she rolled to her left, and without the black patch to conceal her empty right eye socket, the sight made him avert his gaze.

Cate Shearley became aware of a presence in her room and sat up aggressively. 'Jack,' she snapped. 'Jack, what is it? What's wrong?'

'Nothing, Ma.' He raised his hands to assuage her concern. 'I'm sorry to wake you so early –'

'What time is it?' she interrupted, reaching for her eye patch and putting it in place.

'It's coming up for nine o'clock, Ma.'

'Are you all right?' She reached out and clasped him by the shoulders.

'Yeah.' He nodded. 'I got a message . . .'

'I *have* a message,' she corrected.

'No, Ma, you don't have a message, *I* have a message.' He grinned cheekily. 'It's from Uncle Amos.'

'Don't play games with me, young man,' she said sternly, but smiled at him.

'Uncle Amos told me to tell you he's doing the exchange with Captain Alvarez from the *Donna Isabella* and the captain wants to renegotiate the price of the goods.'

'Does he just!' Cate leapt from the bed. 'Does he bloody well just indeed! Well, we'll see about that, won't we? Oh yes we bloody well will!'

Jack knew there was trouble brewing; his ma never cursed unless someone, and more often than not it was him, was in deep trouble.

'I've been fishing under Lennox's Bridge since early this morning. Can I go and see Cook downstairs?'

'How many times have I to tell you not to go out without having breakfast? Go downstairs immediately. Oh, and while you're there tell Cook and Dorothy that I have to go out, but I shouldn't be long. Cook's to make any big decisions in my absence.'

'Right, Ma,' Jack called back over his shoulder as he reached the main door. He knew better than to be here when his mother had the black cloud around her.

'And don't forget your schoolwork,' she yelled. 'I want it done by lunchtime.'

'Yes, Ma!' he called as he pulled the door shut behind him.

As infuriated as she was, Cate Shearley couldn't help a grim smile of satisfaction settling across her face as she strode down Swanston Street towards Flinders Street. By God, but you chose correctly, Cate, she thought as she watched the newly arrived migrant population swarming up Swanston Street against her, bound for the diggings to the west in Ballarat.

Melbourne had been a ghost town when she'd arrived. The discovery of gold in August 1851 at Poverty Point about seventy miles west of Melbourne started a gold rush, bringing thousands of prospectors to the Yarrowee Valley, which became known as the Ballarat Diggings. Every able-bodied man in the Colony of Victoria had converged on the diggings, leaving Melbourne a provincial town full of grass widows, children and the old and infirm. Land could be bought for a song and that's just what Cate had done.

Cate understood gold rushes and was a certified expert on the greed to be found in men's hearts. She knew, because she'd learned the truth in San Francisco, that when gold is discovered the nearest city invariably becomes a goldmine itself. First, everyone leaves the city to search for the nearby gold, then when they return empty-handed, they realise the property they owned and sold to go panhandling is worth ten times what it had been. Furthermore, anyone who has retained a piece of property has the wherewithal to start a business in the field of supply and demand.

She'd taken a big risk financially when she'd bought the land and ordered the building of the Golden Sheaf two years previously, two-thirds of all she possessed, but the gamble was now paying off handsomely.

In December 1851 she'd arrived in Melbourne with her son Jack and Uncle Amos, a black American man who'd been her benefactor's butler in New York and who, upon the death of the benefactor, had declared himself her lifelong servant and protector – although just who protected who remained a moot point with her.

She arrived at the intersection of Swanston and Flinders Streets and gazed across the new Lennox Bridge over the Yarra River. Like the rest of Melbourne, it contained a sea of people flowing to and fro between the city centre and Canvas Town.

Accommodation for the newly arrived was almost impossible to find, so on the south side of the river the government had laid out a grid for tents and Canvas Town soon became a bustling suburb, or in Cate's opinion a filthy, disease-ridden hellhole for thousands of displaced, poor and downtrodden souls.

To her left on the corner stood the brand-new St Paul's Parish Church, a bluestone building consecrated only the previous year. And directly opposite her to the right of the bridge was a newly built collection of weatherboard train sheds. Grandly named the Melbourne Terminus, the sheds ran along Flinders Street all the way west past Elizabeth Street. Officially opened the week before, it boasted Australia's first steam train, which operated to the port of Sandridge, south on Port Phillip Bay.

I got it right, the city's certainly booming, she thought, but she refused to let it lighten her mood. She had business to attend to, serious business, and until it was concluded she'd remain livid.

Cate strode down Flinders Street past several large tent drinking houses and Barrett's General Store, a newly constructed two-storey weatherboard building which sold everything and anything a man might need on a goldfield, until she arrived at a rugged, wooden storage shed, a gin hall and gambling house known as The Miner's Refuge.

Despite it being only ten o'clock in the morning, the thirty or more drunken, noisy men engaged in card playing and bagatelle turned their eyes as one to the main doors when they crashed open. No-one needed to ask the identity of the beautiful interloper; they knew her only too well.

Cate stood stock still, glaring at each man in turn, then she drew a double-barrel shotgun from beneath her frock coat and cocked both hammers.

Chair legs scraped and boots shuffled on the wooden floor as suddenly silent men backed towards the walls leaving her a lone figure in the middle of the room.

Cate's eyes came to rest on Uncle Amos seated at a table of card players near the back wall. Next to him sat Captain Diego Alvarez, master of the *Donna Isabella*.

'Diego,' she called through the silence that now pervaded the entire establishment. The men seated with the sea captain carefully slid out of their chairs and left him sitting alone. Cate approached the table and trained the shotgun on him. 'I heard you're unhappy with the deal we made last time you were here in port, would that be right?'

'That is not entirely correct, *señora*.' Alvarez smiled arrogantly and began to stand.

'Don't move, you fat Spanish cunt, or I'll blow your fucking head off!' Her voice was cold, hard, dripping malevolence.

'Please, *señora*,' he whined, and sat a little less sure of himself. 'You must know that the prices of commodities here in Melbourne have increased tenfold, since the discovery of –'

The boom of the gun took everyone by surprise.

Cate had aimed the shot to perfection. The majority of the pellets from the 12 gauge had entered the wall to Alvarez's right, but four of them had pierced his right ear. The seaman sat frozen, incapable of speech, as blood started running down his neck and into his collar.

'This is how it will be, *señor*,' she sneered. 'You will return to your ship forthwith in company with my man, Amos. You will give him the items I ordered from you in good faith and he will remunerate you with the amount we agreed upon, *comprende*?'

Alvarez could only nod, his fat body trembling and sweating profusely. The combination of exquisite beauty, shotgun barrels, black patch over the right eye and fierce gleam in the left had reduced him to a terrified wreck.

'Don't make me come and find you again, Diego.' Her warning was ominous. When he shook his head, she uncocked the shotgun, placed it back under her frock coat, turned and marched out.

As Cate walked back up Flinders Street the raucous, drunken laughter and rapturous applause from patrons of

The Miners' Refuge followed her all the way to St Paul's Church.

Yes, she nodded to herself, Melbourne's booming, and she laughed out loud.

She retraced her steps up Swanston Street and turned left into Collins and was struck yet again by the numbers of newly arrived that packed the streets. The lure of gold, she thought, and shook her head. It was then her attention was drawn to a mob of people gathered in front of Ryan's Butchery next to the Golden Sheaf. They were obviously being entertained, because they laughed and applauded whoever or whatever was on the raised wooden footway before them.

Cate joined the mob and pushed her way to the front. There on the built-up footpath that constituted the front of the butcher's shop was a Chinese lad doing the most extraordinary gymnastic contortions she'd ever seen. The boy stood on one hand and, as she stared fascinated, he took the entire weight of his body on the end of three fingers and held the pose for some seconds. Cate applauded along with the rest and tossed several coins into an upturned bamboo hat set on the footboards.

'He's no better than a fookin' monkey,' an Irish voice sneered. 'Hey, chinky chinky Chinaman!' the thug called as he pushed his way to the front of the crowd, shouldering Cate aside as he did so. He was followed by two mates. All were inebriated and obviously looking for trouble.

The drunk forced the little Chinese lad against the butcher's shop window, grabbed his queue – or pigtail as the long, woven plait of hair was called by the locals – then produced a knife and waved it at the crowd.

'Dis length of hair would make a fine stock whip, do youse not tink?' He and his mates laughed at the joke. ''Tis a pity it's not a few feet longer.' His mates laughed even louder as he wiggled the blade under the Chinese boy's nose.

Cate sighed inwardly. Here we go again, she thought. Where are the Victorian Police when you want them?

'Irishman,' she called to him, 'leave the boy alone and get about your business before you get into trouble.'

'Well,' the drunk exclaimed, 'and who do we have here?' He raised an eyebrow at her and grinned, revealing two rows of rotting black teeth. 'Is it a blonde-haired beauty?' he asked of his mates, 'or is it a pirate, my God! Look at that eye patch, will ya, lads?'

'I'll only say it one more time, Irishman, leave the boy alone.'

The grin disappeared from the drunk's face, replaced by a menacing glare. 'Or what?' he sneered. 'What will you do if I don't?'

Cate stepped up onto the boardwalk and produced the shotgun from beneath her frock coat. 'You're standing in my street, Paddy, in front of *my* butcher's shop, next to *my* brand-new hotel and you're threatening *my* Chinese servant. Ask yourself, is a Chinese pigtail worth dying for, because that's what'll happen if you harm the boy. I'll kill you, Paddy. I'll shoot you stone motherless dead!'

'Will you now?' The Irishman placed his knife against the Chinese boy's neck and Cate trained the shotgun on the Irishman's face in a classic standoff.

'Come on, Connor,' one of the Irishmen said. 'Stop fookin' about; the Chink's not worth it.'

'Eamon's right, Connor,' the other offered. 'Let's be goin' to Ballarat; we've got gold to find, lad!'

The Irishman smiled grimly. Never taking his eyes off Cate he lowered the blade to his side. 'All right, lads, let's be goin'.'

'That's showing some common sense.' Cate smiled back. 'Unusual for an Irishman, I must admit.'

'I'll not forget this, you bitch.' The Irishman pointed the knife at her before folding the blade away and placing the weapon in his pocket.

'You'd be a wiser man if you did, Connor,' she said, her voice full of meaning. 'People are fortunate not to know the location and time of their death, because it would be a terrible burden to live with, but I can tell you yours: it will be by my hand, if you're stupid enough to ever cross my path again.'

As the Irish trio slunk off into the crowd, the Chinese boy threw his arms around Cate's waist and hugged her. 'Thank you,' he said in very precise English.

'What's your name, China?'

'Lou . . . I mean So, my name is So Chi-ming.'

'Well, you're safe now, China.'

'Thank you.'

'Don't mention it,' Cate replied. 'I'd do the same for a black man.'

'Would you really?' Lou-shi found the statement fascinating.

'Ah kin vouch fo' dat.' Amos stood directly behind her, a cocked revolver in his hand. 'Yo' done git yo'self in trouble once again, Mistress Cate. Land o' Mercy but I kayn't as leave you alone fo' one minute.'

'I thought I told you to go to the ship with Captain Alvarez?'

'They weren't no need.' He held up a large carpet bag. 'He done had it with him all the while.'

'Is it all there?'

'Sho' nuff! I done counted it all. Every last bottle.'

'Then get it into the hotel and put it under lock and key!' She offered him a genuine smile. 'Well done, Amos.'

Sixty small bottles of the finest British-made laudanum would yield her a fortune, at least fifty times what she'd paid for it.

'Yessum! We doin' mighty fine he'ah in Melbourne. Yessum!'

'And take this China boy with you. See to the cut on his neck and give him something to eat.'

'Yessum!' Amos took the boy by the arm, but to his surprise the Chinese boy recoiled in horror.

'What's the matter?' Cate asked.

'Haak yan!' the boy exclaimed in Cantonese.

'I knows what's da matter,' Amos sneered. 'It da same thing what I seen in San Francisco. I'm a black man, da's what's da matter.'

'Haak yan!' Lou-shi repeated.

'I know what he's sayin' wid dat *haak yan* mumbo-jumbo. I dun heard it in San Fran. Black man, da's what he sayin'. Dis kid just like all Chinamen. Dey ain't never seen a black man. Dere's no black people where dey comes from. China ain't got nuthin' but yella people.'

'Listen to me,' Cate demanded, grabbing the young Chinese boy by the shirt and pointing at Amos. '*Haak yan*, yes,' she nodded, tapping her chest. 'My friend yes. Understand?'

The boy nodded, but would not let go of Cate.

'Y'all see what I means?' Amos wailed. 'Lawdy, but he most like to up and kill me in my bed!'

'Don't go overboard with the dramatics, Amos, you're not in the Deep South now.'

'What you gwine' say when I'm daid? Killed by that li'l heathen.'

'Oh, for God's sake!' Cate uncocked the shotgun and took the Chinese lad by the hand. 'Come on, we'll all go together. And, Amos, stop talking like a plantation slave!'

'I thought it suited the occasion.'

'It's undignified. Stop it.'

'Very well, madam, if you so insist, I shall desist. Your wish is my command.'

Lou-shi told herself yet again she was a smart person, a very smart person. She had reason to be well pleased with herself as she ran down Swanston Street in the early twilight towards Lennox Bridge. She had found decent lodgings for her and Master Feng and the promise of work at the one-eyed woman's hotel which would keep them from starving at least.

She and Feng had been forced to live in Canvas Town since arriving at Melbourne three weeks previously and the squalor they'd had to endure had pushed her to breaking point, hence her performance in Collins Street that morning. Her gymnastic routine for the amusement of passers-by had been netting her a few coins each day, enough to keep them in basic food, but not nearly enough to support them properly. And the tent they paid such exorbitant rent for was a piece of old sailcloth stretched between two poles, affording them little protection from either wind or rain.

Master Feng was of particular worry to her. The old man had seemed to lose his spark for life, especially over the last week. He sat about smoking and muttering to himself about the grand days in Peking and his tours with his opera company. Nothing she could do or say would drag him from his despondency and she was in fear of losing him altogether.

And then today, they had been saved by the blonde-haired woman with one eye.

Things could not have gone more badly after they'd boarded the ship in Hong Kong. She'd been confined to her cabin for most of the voyage and her rare visits on deck were invariably at dusk when the passengers and most of the crew were preparing food. To make matters worse, Stupid Ho had taken his order to infiltrate the Brothers of the Red Pavilion far too seriously, remaining below decks with them for hours at a time. Then to cap off a miserable sea journey, Mok had been taken ill with a raging fever.

Lou-shi had nursed her for three sleepless nights until exhausted by the constant effort she'd fallen asleep. When she'd been awakened by Stupid Ho the next morning it was to find Mok missing. A search of the entire ship had taken place but no trace of her could be found. It was decided she had walked off, delirious, during the night and fallen overboard.

Lou-shi had been beside herself with grief, not to mention a heavy dose of guilt for failing to keep watch on her friend. Mok had been her sister and no amount of talking with Stupid or even Master Feng could assuage her feelings of loss. She'd wept every night they'd remained at sea.

Melbourne had proved no less depressing. Upon being put ashore and making their way on foot all the way from Sandridge to Melbourne, they'd been unable to secure even the lowliest accommodation and eventually had been directed to the cesspit known as Canvas Town. There, on the third night, they'd been robbed of all they owned apart from Feng's precious trunk of opera costumes, which had been simply too heavy for the thieves to carry away.

After one week, Stupid Ho had informed Master Feng he was going to the Ballarat Diggings to seek 'their fortune', as he'd put it. He promised he would return as soon as he had enough gold to afford them passage back to China. When Master Feng had pointed out that they'd probably be murdered if they returned home, Stupid had guaranteed he would buy them a mansion in Melbourne where they could live happily and healthily into their old age.

Lou-shi had begged Stupid not to leave them, but she knew he'd been influenced by the Brotherhood and was too full of the gold fever to heed advice from anyone. And so they'd escorted him to Lennox Bridge and waved goodbye until he'd melted into the stream of hopeful adventurers making their way to Ballarat.

That very day as she watched Stupid go, Lou-shi determined to make herself useful and support her Master in his infirm state. She'd no idea what she could do; she was trained for nothing but the theatre. However, she noticed that when practising her acrobatic routines each morning, children and adults alike would gather near and applaud. Since that realisation she'd been taking her bamboo hat and upturning it on the streets of Melbourne while she performed, keeping herself in fit condition and making a few shillings each day.

Such had been Lou-shi's existence until that very morning when she'd performed in front of the butchery in Collins Street next to the Golden Sheaf Hotel, property of Cate Shearley, her very own angel. A one-eyed blonde-haired angel.

'*Wait a minute, Lou-shi,*' Master Feng called in Cantonese for the tenth time since leaving Canvas Town as he dropped his end of the trunk.

'*Stop calling me that,*' she snapped. '*It was your idea to make me a boy; at least call me by the boy's name you chose or I become confused.*'

'*I'm sorry. Chi-ming?*'

'*What is it this time?*' Lou-shi replied acidly, putting her end of the costume trunk on the ground.

Lou-shi had made two trips already that morning, to and from the Golden Sheaf, each time placing their scant belongings in the back courtyard of Cate Shearley's hotel. And now she was on her final trip, carrying one end of the hated costume trunk while Master Feng, making his first trip, brought up the rear.

'*I have been thinking . . .*' Feng began.

'*It is sometimes not good when you think,*' Lou-shi murmured.

'*Happiness is truly a state of mind.*' He smiled blissfully at her. '*I have decided this only now, after all the years of my life.*' He sat himself down on the costume trunk in the middle of Lennox Bridge and commenced to wax lyrical about his latest philosophical decision.

'*This is not a good place to sit and talk, Master.*'

'*Until this very moment, I have never been really sure, one way or the other . . .*'

'*There are big horses pulling a cart approaching us, Master Feng,*' she interrupted, '*perhaps we should not sit here at this time?*'

'*. . . but I have noticed that as I carry this load with you, I become weary quickly and my state of happiness dissolves . . .*'

'*Please, Master,*' Lou-shi begged. The large dray was nearly upon them.

'*. . . then, I stop and relieve myself of the weight and my happiness quickly returns.*' He beamed at her. '*Can you understand the clarity of mind I am experiencing to afford me such momentous insight?*'

Lou-shi was about to scream a warning when the two enormous Clydesdale horses pulling the dray halted so close to her Master they enveloped him in a cloud of their hot steamy breath.

'Get that trunk off the road!' a burly bullocky roared at them from the driver's seat of the dray, as people surged around it like a flooding river.

'I am sorry, sir, but my master is exhausted. The trunk is too heavy for us.'

The bullocky jumped to the ground and, after taking one of the huge horses by the reins, he glared at Lou-shi and the trunk.

'Where are you supposed to be taking it?'

'Up Swanston Street to Collins Street, sir. To the Golden Sheaf Hotel.'

'Cate Shearley's new place, eh?'

'Yes, sir, we are to be workers for her.'

'Well, why didn't you say so?' He gave them a wonderful smile. 'Any friend of Cate's is a friend of mine. Besides, a tiny lad like you shouldn't have to carry anything so big.' The man picked up the trunk with ease and, carrying it to the rear, put it in his empty dray. 'You and your old grandpa hop up there with it,' he indicated, 'and I'll see to it you get to Cate's place. In fact, I'll drop you right at her front door.'

As the dray made its way slowly but inexorably through the throng up Swanston Street and into Collins, Lou-shi waggled her legs off the back of the dray and listened to Old Feng describe his now nirvana-like experience.

'This morning has been truly insightful. To be relieved temporarily of a weight is a mental experience of some note, Lou-shi, sorry, I meant Chi-ming.' He patted her arm affectionately. *'But then to be relieved of the burden entirely increases the state of mental happiness exponentially. However, being transported from one place to another without expending any effort at all is tantamount to a religious experience. It puts one on a plane with the Eight Immortals and the mind into a state of ecstasy.'*

Lou-shi could only laugh out loud. *'You are saying you are lazy!'* Her dear old Master Feng was an incorrigible rogue, but she loved him more than anyone in the world.

'Hello, Bill,' Cate Shearley called as the Clydesdales halted snorting in front of the Golden Sheaf. 'I thought you were up at the Ballarat Diggings.'

'Ah, the beautiful Cate.' Bill the bullocky looked up to where she stood on the first-floor verandah. 'I took your advice and it's paid off. I'm making more money in one week operating my dray and pair between St Kilda Beach and the ports than I'd make in a year at the diggings.'

'What have you got there?' She pointed at the two Chinese figures in his dray.

'I think these little Chinamen belong to you, lass.' He laughed as he jumped to the ground and took the costume trunk out of the dray. 'I found them on Lennox Bridge, trying to get themselves killed dragging this across it.' He dumped it at the narrow side lane of the hotel.

Jack Shearley sat on an upturned apple case and stared intently at the old Chinaman smoking a pipe. With his long thin beard and moustache that dripped from either side of his lip down to his collar and his black loose-fitting coat and trousers, embroidered as they were so elaborately with birds and a tiger and even a dragon, to Jack the old man looked every inch a wizard. He has to be a magician, Jack decided. Wizards didn't exist according to his ma, but magicians did and this Chinaman just had to be one.

'Can you do magic?'

'No,' Feng replied, as he took a ring from his finger, showed it to Jack, then made it disappear into thin air.

'Wow,' Jack cried.

'I don't speak much English,' Feng Chi-pei replied in Cantonese.

'I don't understand you, Mister Feng.'

'He said he speaks very little English,' Lou-shi, who was hanging washing on the courtyard clothes line, explained. 'Only a few words.'

'I can tell by the look in his eye that the boy is intelligent. Perhaps I should teach him Cantonese. What do you think, Little Nightingale?'

'If his mother hears him speak Cantonese, she will be very angry.'

Feng smiled at the boy, touched his own chest and said *'me'* in Cantonese. Then he pointed to Jack. *'You,'* he said. Then he pointed at Lou-shi and said *'him'*.

Jack repeated the Cantonese words along with the gestures, *'Ngoh, nei, kui,'* then guessed the translation. 'Me, you, him. Am I right?'

Feng laughed out loud. *'His pronunciation is excellent. I told you, Lou-shi, sorry, Chi-ming, this boy is smart. He must share the sign of the Monkey! Tell him to avoid Tigers; he must marry a Dragon or a Rat.'*

'He's only a boy!'

'Boys are never too young to learn. This one is even smarter than Stupid Ho was when I found him in the street and taught him to be an idiot.' He beamed at young Jack, who returned the smile.

'Do not become attached to the boy, Master,' Lou-shi warned. *'He is a Western child with a very protective mother. You must not be seen to advise or educate him.'*

'China!' Cate called as she entered the courtyard. 'Have you seen . . . ah, there you are, Jack. Have you done the schoolwork I left for you?'

'No, Ma.'

'Why must I nag you every day? Get inside this instant and attend to it.'

'Yes, Ma.' Jack stood and headed for the kitchen door. 'Thanks for teaching me Chinese, Mister Feng,' he called back over his shoulder.

Cate stared at Lou-shi for several seconds. 'Did I hear correctly, China?' She pointed at Feng. 'Is he teaching my son Chinese?'

'No,' Lou-shi began in Feng's defence. 'Well, only a word or two in fun.'

'Tell him to keep it up. A second language is always a good thing to have in this world.'

'The way she wears that patch frightens the fuck out of me! From the side she looks like a pig-fucking pirate I once knew! He was known as Wang the Pig-Fucker.'

'What did he say?' Cate smiled at the old man.

'He said he would be honoured to teach Jack our language.'

'Good, now, if you've finished the washing, come with me, China. I've got some work for you in the kitchen.'

Feng Chi-pei watched the two women walk to the kitchen door and shook his head slowly at the sight of Lou-shi's buttocks. *'How is it no-one has realised she is not a boy?'* he muttered to himself. *'Her arse cheeks jiggle invitingly, like two rabbits in a sack.'*

He looked around the courtyard. It was brand new; cobblestones covered the yard and sandstone buildings filled in all three sides. To one side was a large storehouse and a laundry Lou-shi worked in each morning, to the other side a stable and blacksmith's forge, and the rear boundary of the property was two long rooms he shared with Lou-shi.

They'd been at the Golden Sheaf for a month and each morning, without fail, he thanked as many gods as he could remember for smiling on him. He thought again how lucky they had been to find this foreign woman. She'd not only supplied them with a comfortable place to live, but for a day's work they were also fed by the hotel cook and even paid a small wage – not much, but enough to keep Lou-shi content and him in tobacco.

Melbourne was no place for the Chinese; Feng had realised it the moment they'd set foot on land. Chinese citizens were regarded on a par with the poor unfortunate Indigenous tribes who had dwelt on the land for centuries before the whites arrived. He'd witnessed their plight himself. At the port where they'd disembarked a number of local black people could be seen begging. Running noses and open sores were common among them and drunkenness seemed to affect them all. The whites treated them like animals. He, Lou-shi and Stupid Ho had been similarly treated, sneered at and abused simply because they were not white.

When he'd attempted to hire transport to get them to Melbourne, he'd been refused point blank. When he'd attempted to gain accommodation for them in Melbourne he'd been refused once again because of their ethnicity. They'd finally been forced to seek refuge in Canvas Town, quite the most disgusting place Feng had ever set foot in. They'd been lucky, very lucky. Canvas Town would have seen the end of them both.

But we are safe, he nodded, reassuring himself, and for the moment that is all that matters.

CHAPTER SIX

Ballarat, British Colony of Victoria, winter 1854

John Bailleau, as John Farrington was now known to all, firmly believed the noise would eventually drive him insane. The discharging of firearms by drunken miners, the brawling that occurred all over the diggings, the screaming of women in violent domestic fights – the cacophony went on all night. And then there was the constant barking of dogs. In fact it was the barking that John hated most. Almost every miner on the Ballarat Diggings had a dog to help guard his claim. Some were savage, some otherwise, but big, fat, skinny or little, they were all trained to bark at the slightest noise or movement.

As the cold winter night crept over him, John thanked God above for the lamb's-wool-lined leather coat he'd purchased in Liverpool. Winter was well and truly on the goldfields and sullen black storm clouds threatened overhead. He sat on the edge of the small stream known as Yarrowee Creek that ran through the diggings, his Sharps rifle across his lap and his Adams revolver holstered on his hip. He was guarding 'the grand enterprise', four gold claims measuring eight feet by eight feet each, the joint property of himself, James Small, Theophilus Kittredge and Harry Foo, all former crew of the *Maid of Shanghai*. The claims stretched thirty-two feet along the creek's edge.

John smiled at the gruff voice of his friend Mister Rhodes as he complimented the cook on his excellent evening meal.

'There b'aint be no doubt but you Mongols is the best cooks in the world, Genghis, la.' He winked at Kit Kittredge.

'How many times do I have to tell you, I'm not a Mongol,' Harry Foo replied, exasperated. 'And my name is not Genghis-bloody-Khan.'

'When you took ship aboard the *Maid of Shanghai* in Cape Town, you told me your name was Genghis Khan,' Kit Kittredge continued the game. 'I signed you aboard as a ship's cook under the name Genghis Khan.'

'I was 'avin' a loan of you, weren't I, *pang yau*,' Harry whined sarcastically. 'How was I to know you was as thick as a moorin' line?'

'You looks like a Mongol, la,' Rhodes added.

'Well, I wouldn't bloody well know, would I? I ain't never bloody well seen one!'

'So what is it you reckon you are?' Kit struggled to hold back his laughter.

'My muvver and farver was Chinese, but I was born in Cheapside, London, which makes me Cockney and therefore, by geographical reckonin', more English than the lot of ya.' The two men burst into laughter and Harry realised he'd been had, again. 'All right.' He tossed aside the cloth he'd been wringing out and, taking his apron off, threw it into his tent. 'Very funny. *Veeerryy funny!* You're the funniest pair you know, aren't you? Well I've had just about enough of you two. I'm goin' for a walk!'

As Harry set off up the bank, John called after him. 'Have you got any dirt on you, Harry?' Dirt was the miners' word for alluvial gold.

'No, John. Well, yeah, just enough for a smoke or two.'

'Make sure you sleep it off, Harry, and get yourself back here in one piece. You're on watch at two am.'

'I'll do that, *pang yau*. And I've left some food for you, for when you finish your watch. And you make sure those two blighters wash up.' Harry waved and took off into the smoky evening.

Harry made a habit of using the Cantonese words *pang yau*, meaning friend, to refer to all three of his partners. He inserted other Chinese words into his conversations occasionally. It gave him a satisfying sense of identity to use words from his parents' language, but he was careful to nurture and maintain his Cockney accent, because as far as he was concerned he was English through and through. He insisted to all that he spoke no more than a word or two of Cantonese, but in reality he spoke it fluently; his mother had insisted he be raised bilingual.

John watched him disappear into the smoke from a thousand campfires, which in the absence of any breeze sat like fog over the freezing diggings. He knew where Harry was going. Harry Foo was an opium user and he was on his way to the Chinese Quarter on the edge of the diggings to inhale a pipe or two and seek escape from the dog- and mosquito-infested hellhole that was the Ballarat Diggings.

John was fond of Harry, as he was of his other two shipmates, Rhodesy and Kit. All three of them had signed off when the *Maid of Shanghai* had made Port Phillip Bay in the newly created Colony of Victoria. They'd thrown in their lot with John, deciding that time away from the sea on a goldfield adventure would be sure to spice up their lives and hopefully make them all rich. The four men had bonded like brothers on the *Maid*, as the huge ship had fairly raced across the storm-torn Southern Ocean.

What a ride it had been, he now reflected, as he sat and tried to block out the noise of far too many drunken miners, their aggrieved wives and their accursed dogs. The trip down the Atlantic had been mostly uneventful; the odd sighting of whales and dolphins and an occasional glimpse of the African continent had broken the monotony, but for the most part John had found it boring in the extreme.

Three days in Cape Town had lifted his spirits as he'd wandered the streets absorbing the local atmosphere while the ship took on supplies and a number of new immigrants, including Harry Foo, an ex-British Army cook who'd heard of the strikes in Ballarat and succumbed to the irresistible lure of gold.

But after leaving Cape Town in its wake, the *Maid of Shanghai* hoisted full sail and had taken off eastward like the thoroughbred she was, determined to reach Australia five thousand miles away, and neither rain, hail, sleet nor snow would deny her progress. Several times when she'd drifted too far south, Captain Glover had lowered the sails and used her steam engine to manoeuvre her through drifting icebergs, but once up in the higher latitudes again, she'd taken the wind full-sail and raced across that ocean wild and wide, finally sighting Australia after seventy-five days.

The Port of Fremantle in the Colony of Western Australia was where the alliance had been formed. Big James Small had approached John and asked if he could join him on his trip to Ballarat.

'Are you sure, Rhodesy?' John had been shocked that the giant second mate would even consider leaving the sea for life on a goldfield.

'I think it's high time, matey,' the big man had replied. 'I'll be fifty years and five before long and I've seen about all there is to see on the oceans of this world.'

'Well,' John raised an eyebrow. 'I can't deny you'd be worth your weight on a goldfield. A man of your size and strength would be an asset, but think hard. You may imagine life away from the water will suit you, but the call of the sea is all powerful, so I'm led to believe by Captain Glover, one seamen find it hard to resist. I wouldn't want to see you unhappy.'

'I been givin' it a lot of thought, la.' The big man shielded his eyes and gazed westward where he could just make out the silhouette of Rottnest Island in the glow of the setting sun. 'I been 'avin' a hankering for different things, like.'

'Like Eileen Maloney?'

'Well,' Rhodesy faltered like a man caught out. 'Well now, Eileen be one of 'em. She's been at me for a while now to give up the sea.'

'Tiny's a fine woman, Rhodesy, and it's obvious to anyone who cares to listen that she has strong feelings for you.'

'She's been a'rter me to live with her and be a father to her lad, Enda.'

'Are you his . . .?'

'No. No, I'm not the lad's da'. He were some young Irishman who got my Eileen in the family way then, like the rat 'e was, left her all alone to fend for herself and the boy.'

'She certainly succeeded. Her tavern is very popular.'

Rhodesy turned and, with a forlorn look, he shook his head slowly. 'That's the problem, la. She's gone so far as ta offer me a partnership in the Sailors' Retreat, you know?'

'You could do worse, man. It's a thriving business.'

'Well that's what I been a-thinkin' about, la.' The big man sighed. 'I couldn't take up her offer without I 'ad money to contribute my share in things, understand?' Before John could answer, Rhodesy went on. 'Ya see, I've never kept a single pound of my earnin's all these years. I've got nothin' ta show for meself.'

'Well –' John started to reply, but Rhodesy barged on.

'That's why I think formin' an' alliance with you in your approachin' grand enterprise could well be the answer to my predicament, la. Ya see, I'll have an 'andful o' money when I signs off and steps ashore in Port Phillip Bay, so I'd be able to contribute to the enterprise with a small stake.'

John realised he was cornered. What could he say to the friendly giant with the worried frown on his face, yet wide-eyed with expectation? He simply smiled and extended his hand.

Rhodesy seized the hand and shook it firmly. 'We have a deal then, la?'

'Yes, Rhodesy, we have a deal.'

By the time the *Maid* had crossed the Great Australian Bight and reached her final destination, Rhodesy had filled the heads of Kit Kittredge and Harry Foo with visions of himself and John setting out upon a great adventure that would equal the search for the Holy Grail. And before John knew it, they too had signed off just like Rhodesy and 'the grand alliance of two' suddenly became the grand alliance of four.

They'd pooled their money, electing John treasurer, and purchased everything they'd been told they'd need, along with two good horses, two healthy bullocks and a sturdy dray. Then, on a sunny morning in early September, they'd set off for Ballarat.

'Christ on the Cross, I'm freezing!' Theophilus Kittredge threw several logs on the fire beside John and pulled the possum skin coat he'd purchased from the local Aborigines tight around him. 'Did you know, this morning the water in the drinking buckets was frozen over?' But John appeared totally unaware of Kittredge's arrival. 'A penny for your thoughts, John.' The American threw a calico bag on the damp sand next to John, sat and placed his palms against the heat from the fire.

'Oh, Kit. Sorry, I was miles away,' he laughed self-consciously, 'trying to convince myself I've not developed a hatred for dogs.'

'Well,' Kit laughed, 'you've no need to worry about dogs in Australia, man, because there aren't any, well not local ones anyway.'

'So, what's that I'm hearing barking, kangaroos?'

'Dogs, yes, but they're immigrants just like their owners. It's the same with cattle and sheep; they don't belong here either. At least Charles Darwin thought so.'

'What about the dingo? That's a dog, is it not?'

'It's supposed to be a native dog. The dingo's been here for thousands of years, so I think it qualifies as indigenous.'

'I heard Charles Darwin speak at the Royal Society in London. Have you met him?'

'No, but I spent six years aboard the HMS *Beagle*, so I feel as if I know him.'

'The navy survey ship he sailed on that went to South America?'

'Yes, but that was a bit before my time. I served on the *Beagle* on its third expedition under Commander John Wickham from 1837 to '43 when it came here.'

'To Australia?'

'At first we surveyed the Western Australian coast from Perth right up to the FitzRoy River.' He scratched a rough map of Australia in the sand between them and indicated the north-west shore. 'Wickham named it so in honour of Captain FitzRoy, the *Beagle*'s previous skipper. Then we surveyed both shores of Bass Strait.' Again he prodded the sand map. 'The northern coastline of Van Diemen's Land and the south coast of what's lately become Victoria. I remember being in Port Phillip Bay when there was not a white man to be seen. Then we sailed back up north.' He jabbed his finger in the sand yet again. 'Right up here to the Arafura Sea between Australia and the Dutch East Indies. So you see,' he said, then destroyed the map with his knuckles, 'you might say I've seen a lot of this continent. There's parts of it I know like the back of my hand.'

'That is amazing, Kit.' John was impressed. 'But tell me, you are American born, how did you come to serve in the Royal Navy?'

'Well, it's complicated. My father was a United States Navy officer on the USS *Constitution* and fought in the War of 1812, but my Uncle Ebenezer was an officer in the Royal Navy in the same war,' Kit chuckled, 'and after that it gets complicated. Suffice it to say my Uncle Eb was a close friend of Commander Wickham and arranged for me to sail on the *Beagle* as part of the scientific discovery team. It was the chance of a lifetime for me.'

'My word!' John was impressed. 'You've truly been part of historic events, man. Why have you never spoken of this before?'

'Oh, what with your stories of India and the North-West Frontier, Harry's stories of London and Rhodesy's tales of here, there and everywhere, I've never thought the old *Beagle* stuff was worth the telling.'

'Nonsense!'

Kit did not reply, but sat silent for several long seconds, before looking John squarely in the eye. 'I've been thinking, John.'

'So have I, Kit, and I think I know what you're about to say.' John had guessed by the look he'd been given just what his friend wanted to discuss. 'Our claims are worked out, am I right?'

'That's it exactly.' Kit nodded. 'There's no more alluvial gold to be had and that's not just on our claims, but across the diggings altogether.'

'So, you want to go deep, is that it?'

'God in heaven no!' Kit's response was instantaneous.

Deep lead mining, as opposed to the simple panning and cradling they'd been doing, was a different and more complex operation that required far more skill.

Panning involved taking sand and dirt from the surface of a claim and adding water from the stream, then sifting through it to find the traces of alluvial gold. Cradling was the same exercise but on a slightly larger scale. The cradle, similar to a child's cradle, would be filled with sand and soil and rocked, then as water poured through its sieved base, the gold would be left caught up in the riffles and blankets below the sieve.

By late 1853, the alluvial gold across the Ballarat Diggings was becoming scarce. The more experienced diggers knew that gold would also be found below the surface. As a result, they formed into groups of three or four men and sunk shafts into the river banks. Then the miner working at the bottom of the shaft would fill a bucket, or kibble as the men called them, and using a windlass they would raise the kibble to the surface, take it to the stream and, by use of a cradle, sift for gold. This form of mining was known as deep lead mining and it was an operation fraught with danger, for as the shafts deepened, fresh air became an issue, as did the odds of subsidence and men being buried alive.

'I'm of the same mind, Kit; deep lead mining is beyond us. It's time to sell our claims and be done with it.'

The American nodded. 'We've managed better than most. We've made a tidy sum between us. Not enough to retire to a life of luxury, but split four ways the profits are quite respectable.'

'Respec'able? Did I 'ear you say respec'able?' Suddenly Rhodesy was towering over them, mug of tea in hand. He winked at John. 'There be nothin' respec'able about you, Kit la. You're a Yankee – they don' even know the meanin' of respec'able.'

'Sit down, Mister Rhodes.' John waved to a space next to the fire. 'We got something to discuss.'

'I don't like it when you get that sombre tone in your voice, John la.' Rhodesy sat down and eyed his mate.

'Our claims are exhausted, Rhodesy.'

'I wondered when you'd wake up to that.'

'We've a fair bit of money in the pot,' Kit added.

'We're thinking of cashing in and selling up.'

'Well,' the giant man sighed, 'I'm glad to 'ear we're sellin' and you're not gonna try a-talkin' me into goin' un'erground.'

'We don't have the expertise for that sort of operation, Rhodesy.'

'Harry reckons he can do it blindfolded.'

'Harry's welcome to try,' Kit said. 'Going underground's too dangerous for my liking.'

'Me too.' Rhodesy shook his head rapidly. 'I b'ain't be a-goin' un'erground fer no-one. Even when I die, I'll be buried at sea.'

'Then we're in agreement,' John said. 'All we need do now is tell Harry.'

'Lads! Lads!' Harry Foo hissed as he stumbled down the incline back into the campsite.

'Ah, speak of the devil,' Kit murmured.

'What is it, Harry?' Rhodesy asked.

'It's the traps!' he exclaimed, referring to the Victorian Police. 'The bleedin' traps! It's a digger-hunt.'

'Digger-hunting', as it was called by the miners of Victoria, was the much-hated exercise of spot-checking for current miners' licences. Almost immediately after the first gold strikes in 1851 the Victorian Colonial Government enacted a poll tax for which miners were required to pay thirty shillings per month for a licence to search for gold. The tax had caused widespread discontent throughout the Victorian goldfields. Miners agreed unanimously the impost was outrageous, especially the large majority of them who could not afford to pay it.

The Victoria Police didn't help matters. In his nine months on the goldfields, John had watched the odious, disreputable force of uniformed men arrive at the oddest hours, unannounced and intent on causing grief and ill-will among the miners.

When the diggers became aware there was a licence hunt on, concealment or escape were the only thoughts on men's minds. While mounted troopers and foot patrols flooded the camps, miners ran for the scrub or attempted to hide in tents, down shafts, under beds or, as some did, don women's apparel and crouch over washing tubs with wifely bonnets obscuring their faces. For most, the attempts proved futile; men were treated like animals, arrested, assaulted and marched like prisoners of war to the Colonial Administration Compound, or 'The Camp' as it was called by the miners, perched on a hill overlooking the entirety of Ballarat. Once there they were detained in appalling conditions; some, for lack of room, were even chained to logs in the open air, there to await the pleasure of a magistrate who would fine them as much as ten pounds, or imprison them at hard labour.

The law stated that miners must have the licence on their person at all times and failure to comply meant the licensed miner who failed to produce his on demand could also find himself handcuffed and before a magistrate, there to suffer the same fate as his unlicensed brothers. Instances of this were frequent.

Corruption was rife; government officials, magistrates, police and the military were all able to be bought off, and what became of legitimate government revenue raised on the goldfields was anybody's guess. No accounts were ever audited and no balance sheets ever kept. Whoever received the money kept it.

'Wha's the matter wiv you lot?' Harry Foo snapped in his thick Cockney accent, as his three companions stared at his dishevelled appearance. 'Didn't you 'ear me? There's a raid on, the bleedin' traps is everywhere.'

'You look like you've been in a fight with a box full of cats,' Kit said.

'Yeah, well, I had a bit a trouble at the Chinese temple, di'n' I?'

'What sort of trouble?' John asked. The tents at the rear of the Chinese temple on the edge of the diggings were well known to opium smokers.

'That Sergeant Harlow, the bastard, he asked for my licence and I never 'ad it on me, did I?'

'That were a foolish thing to do, la,' Rhodesy admonished. 'You know only too well what they're like. What 'appened to you?'

'He stole my pad o' black,' he whined, referring to raw black opium, 'then he run over me wiv 'is bleedin' 'orse!'

When the laughter subsided, it was John who looked at the little Cockney through narrowed eyes.

'Why didn't you have your licence with you, Harry?' All three of them had chastised him on previous occasions for not renewing his licence.

'Well . . .' Caught out, the little man could only stammer, 'I, er . . .'

'Did you renew it?' John already knew the answer, as did the others.

'Oh, no,' Kit groaned, 'not again.'

'It had to 'appen even'chally, lads,' Rhodesy added. 'It were only a matter of time afore he'd come a cropper.'

'I never 'ad the money,' Harry wailed.

'Because you spend it all on that damnable drug!' The American was livid.

'No I don't, Kit, honest,' the Cockney pleaded. 'Fings 'ave just got the better of me lately, wha' wiv the gold runnin' out. You know 'ow it is.'

'Don't blame him, Kit,' John said. 'It's an insidious thing, poppy juice. We all of us have our Achilles heel, opium just happens to be Harry's.'

'His gamblin' don't help neither.' Rhodesy cuffed Harry around the ear. 'Does it, la?'

Before any more could be said, the sounds of horses whinnying and snorting surrounded them and then the police, both mounted and on foot, appeared all about.

'Well, well, there you are, Chinaman.' Sergeant Bartholomew Harlow of the Victoria Mounted Police Contingent, quite visibly drunk, reined in his horse and sat grinning at the four miners. 'Licences please, gentlemen,' he said sarcastically. 'And you'd better have them on your person or you will be arrested forthwith and conveyed to the luxurious accommodation we keep specially for the likes of you lot.'

'You're drunk, Harlow.' John's accusation brought several sniggers from the other policemen now surrounding the four miners.

'Am I, Mister Bailleau?' Harlow grinned at his subordinates. 'Did you just hear the toffy tones of an upper-class gent, lads?' The retort brought more sniggers from his men.

'You wear the Queen's uniform, you are on duty and you are drunk!' John declared. 'If you have no respect for yourself, at least show some for your monarch, sir!'

One young mounted policeman, obviously drunk, laughed so hard he fell from his saddle into the mud.

'Get him on his horse,' Harlow snarled at his men, 'and get him out of here.'

'You're a disgrace, Harlow,' John sneered.

'Licences!' the policeman roared and pointing at Harry Foo added, 'Especially yours, Chinaman.'

John, Kit and Rhodesy, long accustomed to the police raids, produced their licences and held them aloft, but Harry Foo could only pat his pockets ineffectually then look sheepishly at his companions. 'Sorry, lads,' he muttered.

'Oh dear, oh dear,' the drunken sergeant said with unconcealed delight, 'don't tell me you're currently unlicensed, Harry.' He laughed and turning to his foot patrollers snapped, 'Arrest the Chinaman and escort him to the compound.'

Two constables grabbed Harry, now gibbering with fear, and handcuffed him. John and the others could only stand and watch, impotent to act against the law. The least opportunity to arrest them, too, would be all Harlow needed and it would not help Harry's predicament one iota.

'Chin up, *pang yau*,' John said to the terrified man.

'We'll be there when you appear before the beak, *pang yau*,' Kit added. 'We'll pay your fine, don't worry.'

'Fine?' Harlow laughed. 'There'll be no fine for this yellow rat, gentlemen. He's been in front of the bench for non-compliance before and when I've finished talking to the magistrate, he'll do six months hard or my name's not Harlow.'

'Harlot? Did you say your name was harlot, la?' Rhodesy reached out and took hold of the reins of Harlow's horse. John could sense the rage building in the big man.

'Take it easy, Jim,' John warned.

Rhodesy's other hand clamped around Harlow's boot. 'I think you should be a-showin' a bit more respect, seein' as how you be nothin' more than a harlot.'

If there was one person on the goldfields who terrified George Harlow it was James Small; the thought of ever having to arrest the man they called the Colossus of Rhodes had become a recurring nightmare to the policeman. He drew his pistol and aimed it at the giant. 'Let go of the reins,' he said, a slight tremble in his voice.

As thunder rumbled above, John drew back the side of his coat, exposing Mister Adams holstered to his hip. 'If you pull that trigger, Harlow, you're as good as dead.'

Nobody moved. A dangerous silence embraced the entire group of miners and police as John and Harlow, eyes locked, stared each other down. Then, and John wondered later if it may have been Divine Intervention, a great sheet of lightning lit up the scene, more thunder roared and, within seconds, rain of biblical intensity began to pelt down.

Harlow's horse reared upwards and broke Rhodesy's hold.

'Right,' he yelled above the storm. 'Let's get out of here, men. And bring that yellow bastard with you!'

It took three days before a magistrate could be located to sit on the bench for the morning petty sessions and hear the pleas of guilty from frozen, emaciated and utterly filthy miners. Pleas of not guilty were not tolerated by any of the circuit magistrates, and the miners knew if they dared disrupt the fluid running of the court by having the audacity to declare their innocence, they risked ninety days' hard labour on top of the heavy fine a plea of guilty would bring.

John and Kit sat in the rear of the cold weatherboard building and watched the procession of sorry souls paraded before Nathaniel Hobson JP, the magistrate presiding, who was noticeably drink-affected. To John the entire process was a farce; it made a mockery of both the criminal justice system and the newly established colonial government in Melbourne.

'These proceedings are a joke,' John said *sotto voce*.

Kit nodded furiously. 'I couldn't agree with you more. Hobson's an obnoxious drunk appointed a Police Magistrate by the local squattocracy for his willingness to do as he's told.'

John nodded his own agreement. The American was right. The squattocracy was a collective noun for the local landlords or squatters, as they were known, who, along with the Gold Fields Commissioner and a number of public servants including the Chief Police Magistrate, the Inspector of Police and the Clerk of the Courts, held the entire goldfields in an iron grip. From their collective position up in 'The Camp', they conducted their criminal activities with complete impunity.

Their behaviour in the American's eyes was unpardonable. They conspired at every given opportunity to feather their own nests with whatever corrupt scheme that came to hand. The military did likewise, throwing their considerable weight around and abusing their authority with malicious ill-will.

Kit was not without sympathy for the rank and file of both the police and military; they were treated like dirt by their officers and NCOs, their living standards were atrocious and their remuneration negligible. The soldiers in particular had it bad – virtually no accommodation, tents already two years old and useless against both sun and rain, second-hand uniforms and rusty accoutrements. Like their police contemporaries they were in the main uneducated and almost to a man alcoholics, their ranks riddled with bitterness and discontent.

It was no surprise to both men that when Harry Foo was dragged into the dock he appeared definitely the worse for wear. Three nights in the freezing cold with little or no food saw him gaunt, frightened and forlorn.

'Prisoner in the dock,' Hobson said from his position on high, 'before I pass sentence are you represented in this case?'

'Before I pass sentence?' John muttered. 'God in heaven, Harry hasn't even pleaded guilty yet.' Before Kit could stop him, he was on his feet approaching the bench. 'If it please the court?'

Nathaniel Hobson adjusted his pince-nez across the bridge of his nose in order to see clearly who had the temerity to interfere in his judicial proceedings.

'And who might you be, sirrah?' Hobson demanded.

'Your Worship,' John struggled to keep a respectful tone, 'I am here to represent Mister Foo.'

'What?' Hobson pointed at Harry. 'This damned Chinaman!'

'With all due respect, Your Worship, Mister Foo is an Englishman . . .'

'An Englishman! He's as yellow as my old mother's pound cake!' He started to laugh at his own joke and waved a hand in the air, encouraging those in the packed court to laugh along with him.

'Yellow though he may be, sir, he stands before you as Harold Foo, late of Cheapside in London. His parents were indeed Chinese, but my client is English born.'

'And who the hell are you, sir?' Hobson was annoyed.

'John Bailleau, late of Coventry Assizes, at your service.'

'Is that so?' Hobson's tone was supercilious. 'If that be the case, sir, you may tell me the name of that fair city's Chief Magistrate, for he is a friend of mine.'

'And mine also, sir. His name is the honourable Edmund Cooper.'

'Eddie Cooper, my word!' Hobson was suddenly beside himself. 'By Jove, sir, and how is dear old Eddie?'

'When last we met, some twelve months ago, he was in fine fettle. We dined in Bayley Lane at the . . .'

'The Guildhall, by Jove!'

'Yes, sir, with the Lord Mayor Samuel . . .'

'Sammy Newsome! I'd heard he was lately appointed to that august position.'

'He was indeed.'

'What joy, what joy! Oh memory, oh bliss! Newsome and Cooper were my school chums at Rugby!'

'My *alma mater* also, Your Worship.'

'Come, sir!' Hobson exhorted. 'We Old Rugbeians must dine without delay, this minute.'

John, fearing the drunken fool would adjourn the court, interrupted. 'Er . . . the matter of my servant, sir?' He offered a warning glance at Harry in the dock.

'What? Who? Oh, the Chinaman is your servant, you say?'

'Indeed, sir, a long-time family retainer, since I was a boy in fact.'

Hobson's bleary eyes scoured the courtroom until they fell upon Sergeant Harlow. He waved his gavel in the policeman's direction.

'Sergeant! Release the Chinaman.'

'But, sir,' Harlow began to protest, glaring at John.

'Are you questioning my authority?' the magistrate snarled.

'If I may be so bold,' John said, 'it was Sergeant Harlow who detained Mister Foo then urged me to come to the court and speak on his behalf. The sergeant told me you were a good and compassionate man, a man of reason who showed judicial consideration for his fellow human beings.'

'Did you really say that, Sergeant?' Hobson beamed boyishly.

'I did, Your Worship,' Harlow replied through gritted teeth.

'Well, that was very nice of you.' Hobson's tone was patronising. 'Now be a good chap and unfetter the Chinaman. And as you do so remember that all people have some good in their hearts, even our heathen brothers.'

'Yes, Your Worship,' the policeman said as, at the back of the courtroom, Kit Kittredge snorted and took off for the main doors, his hand over his mouth. Harry Foo followed Kit's example and was at the doors almost before his chains hit the floor.

'I'm most deeply grateful, Your Worship,' John stated and turned towards the exit, prepared to follow his mates.

'*Orando, laborando*,' Hobson quoted the motto of Rugby School, grinning from ear to ear.

'By praying, by working,' John translated. 'A plan for how decent men should live their lives.'

'Indeed, Bailleau, we must get together for old Rugby's sake.' Hobson was in a state of bliss. 'What say you, man?'

'Well, sir,' John said as he headed for the doors, 'I travel to Bendigo on business today and shall not return until next week. At that time it shall be my pleasure to call upon you. For now I bid you good morrow, sir.'

Outside, John's feet hit the ground running. 'Christ on the Cross, what have I done?' he muttered. He saw Kit and Harry trying to appear nonchalant as they scurried across the mud and grass towards the compound's main exit point.

'As my Chinese farver would say,' Harry gasped as John caught up with him, 'you've got "*daai chun doi*", my son.'

'What's that mean?'

'Big balls.'

'How long he keeps them is another matter,' Kit added.

'Yeah,' Harry puffed. 'Harlow won't forget this, Johnny lad.'

'Harlow won't come anywhere near us.'

'Why's that, John?'

'Because he knows full well I'll kill him.'

'Jesus,' Harry muttered. Bailleau was a cold fish, he thought, not for the first time, and hurried on.

They left the compound at speed and didn't stop until they'd reached the claims, to find Rhodesy sitting with John's rifle across his lap, grinning cheerfully.

'Everything went all right then did it, Harry la?'

'Oh yeah.' Harry fell onto the sand at Rhodesy's feet, exhausted. 'Bloody marvellous! Our goldfield's bloody lawyer here,' he wheezed, pointing vaguely up at John, 'has landed us in more trouble than a three-legged cat in a bleedin' dogs' 'ome!'

''Ow's that then, la?'

'John told the beak he was a lawyer representing Harry and then mentioned he was friends with the Mayor of Coventry.' Kit looked at John and shook his head.

'It's the truth, Kit.'

'Wha' is?' Harry asked. 'That you're a lawyer, or you're friends wiv the Mayor of bleedin' Coventry?'

'I never actually said I was a lawyer.' John held up his hands defensively. 'I simply said I was late of Coventry Assizes, which is true.'

'An' what about your pal the bleedin' Mayor?'

'That's true too. I know him quite well. He was very kind to me last year.'

'Now you've got me interested,' the Bostonian added. 'How is it you're friends with the Mayor of Coventry?'

'There be a sayin' in the colonies, lads.' Rhodesy stood to tower over them all and handed the Sharps rifle to John. 'It's "ask me no questions, I'll tell ye no lies". You've no right to ask of a man's past; it b'ain't be your business. There be many a man sent to the colonies who might like his story to remain 'is own. You 'ave to 'ave respect for that.'

'You're right, Rhodesy,' Kit declared. 'It was crass of me to inquire. You have my apology, John.'

'Your apology is not necessary.' John clapped him on the shoulder. 'However, a decision regarding our future is. Harry,' he looked down on the collapsed form of the Cockney, 'we three discussed the other night when you were incarcerated selling the claims and dividing the spoils of our hard work.'

'Well, count me in.' Harry sat up. 'And the sooner the better as far as I'm concerned. Mind you, that is after we sell the claims.'

'They be panned out, Harry.' It was Rhodesy who now spoke up. 'The claims haven't given up any gold for two weeks. They're worthless unless you be wantin' to dig down to find a lead and there b'ain't be none of us wantin' to do that.'

'I agree,' said Kit. 'Let's pack and get going.'

'Yeah,' Harry nodded, 'any more time on this bleedin' goldfield is the last thing we need, lads.'

'It's decided then?' John looked to them in turn as they nodded.

Harry stood up and shivered. 'Whoa, I fink I'll get into some warm clothes. Then I got a small errand to run.'

'I don't think it's a good idea for you to be smoking opium today, Harry. We've got some packing to do and we'll need to keep our wits about us.' Kit didn't like Harry's addiction to the drug. He'd stated often it would get them all into trouble and been proven correct.

'I won't be smokin' it, *pang yau*. I'm jus' gonna drop over to Chinatown and get some for the cold nights on the road. Don't worry, Kit, we'll be out of Ballarat by mid-afternoon or my name's not Harry Foo.'

'I thought it was Genghis Khan,' Rhodesy joked.

'Don' you start that rubbish again.' Harry grinned at the big man and headed for his tent.

By nightfall Harry had not returned. They'd scraped the claims, cleaned their equipment, harnessed their oxen, packed the dray and saddled the horses, then they'd waited for Harry, but there had been no sign of him, nor any message.

'That's it.' John jumped down from where he'd been sitting on the side of the loaded dray. 'Damn Harry for the fool that he is.'

'Wha' do we do, la?' Rhodesy, who'd been tending the oxen, came back and stood scratching his head.

Kit stubbed out a cigar he'd been smoking. 'I'll go and find him,' he said.

'No.' There was a finality in John's tone. 'I'll go.'

'He's probably smoked a pipe or two,' the American shook his head, 'damn him. You'll have to wait for him to sleep it off. It's better that I go.'

'No, I'll go and that's final.' John leapt into the saddle. 'It'll be too dark to travel soon. You two take the dray and head out onto the north road. Make camp and wait for us. I'll not be long after you.'

John kicked his mare and rode off across the diggings, threading his way among the tents and mine shafts with their windlasses, windsails, whips and whims, becoming more frequent by the day, since miners had taken to digging deep. He nodded good evening to many a man and woman set about getting evening meals and caring for their children as he nudged his mare across to the Chinese enclave.

The Chinese Village was located on the edge of the diggings. The dwellings were mostly tents; set in rows and numbered, they housed six to eight Chinese single men. Some of the tents, however, housed not only the many Chinese immigrants come to seek their fortune, but also the addicts of all races who'd succumbed to the seductive charms of opium.

John dismounted and tethered the mare to the front porch of the Chinese temple. He realised as he did so that the area was unnaturally quiet. In the months he'd been living on the goldfields he'd learned the Chinese by nature were a noisy race and the extreme quiet he was now experiencing sent a shiver up his spine. Something was very wrong in Chinatown.

Relations between the Chinese and the white population were not good at the best of times and very often incendiary; in fact, the situation had become so bad the government had placed the Chinese under an official protection programme.

John walked around the side of the weatherboard temple to the Herbalist's Hut but it was empty. Most unusual, he thought. Then, alongside it, he peered into the Scribe's Hut as it was known, but it too was empty. This was highly unusual in John's experience. The scribe was essential to the Chinese community: he translated official documents, kept accounts for diggers, wrote letters home to China and read replies for the illiterate.

Behind these huts were erected a series of tents, most of them two-man size and close together. It was the goldfields' equivalent of an opium den where the Chinese and others purchased pipes of the drug and lay down to smoke and dream.

John found Harry Foo in one of the tents. At first he appeared to be sleeping, but the blood-soaked pillow and camp bed beneath him said otherwise. Harry's throat had been slit from ear to ear.

John backed out of the tent and returned quickly to the front of the temple. He realised his situation was parlous in the extreme; his mere presence at the murder scene, given the corrupt state of the police and judicial system, could see him very quickly accused, charged and convicted.

He was about to mount his mare and get out of the place when he heard a noise from inside the temple itself. Curiosity overrode his better judgement and he entered the candlelit building.

He stood stock-still in the semi darkness and allowed his eyes to adjust. Across a row of seats at the foot of an altar to the warrior god, Kwan Gung, a figure knelt on the floor, wrapping what John recognised as packets of raw opium in oil-paper then sealing the package with a leather strap. On the floor beside the figure sat Harry Foo's very recognisable silk-embroidered money purse. The man stood and placed the package under his arm. John realised it was Sergeant Harlow at the same time the policeman became aware he was not alone.

The sergeant drew his firearm, but not having yet detected John's position in the dim candlelight, was unsure where to aim.

John drew the Bowie knife from its sheath strapped to his thigh. Unreasoning hatred surged through him. Harlow had shown himself to be a bully and a coward of the worst sort. John fought for self-control, but to no avail. His hand tightened on the knife handle and the blood rush consumed him.

'You're the lowest form of life, Harlow!'

As Bartholomew Harlow spun towards the voice and pointed his weapon, John threw the Bowie knife with all the force his anger could generate. It entered Harlow's chest and pierced his heart. He lay dead on the floor within seconds.

John approached and stood over the corpse. He knelt down, extracted the Bowie knife from Harlow's chest, then became aware he was not alone. Looking up he saw an old Chinese man with a long, stringy white beard whom Harry had called his *muk-si*, his priest. Then three young men appeared from behind the altar; bare-chested and extremely fit, they stood arms folded watching him.

'He killed my friend,' John said to no-one in particular.

'Mister Foo was my friend also,' the old Chinese man replied.

John picked up Harry's money purse and placed it on the altar, all the while keeping his eyes on the young men. 'Share that among those of your people who need it most,' he said. Then pointing to the package of opium, 'And that . . . well . . . you can do whatever you like with that.'

'What would you have us do with *that*?' the old man said, pointing at the body of the dead policeman.

'You can feed it to your pigs for all I care.' John's need to mount his horse and get out of Ballarat with all haste was beginning to overwhelm him. He would never get away with killing a policeman, no matter what the circumstances.

'I know you, Mister *Bai-lou*.' The old man moved closer and John's hand again clenched tighter around the Bowie handle. 'Mister Foo spoke of you often. He was very proud to be in your company. He said you were a wise man.'

'I'm afraid it will take more than a wise man to sort this little matter out, Mister . . . I'm sorry I don't know your name.'

'My name is Soh.'

'Well, Mister Soh, we have two dead men on our hands. If we call the police an investigation will take place and I will be held to blame.'

'We of the Chinese community did not like Harlow *Sarjin* any more than you did.'

'Be that as it may, Mister Soh, but you didn't kill the sergeant and –'

'It would seem to me,' the old man interrupted, 'your first suggestion might be wiser.'

'My first suggestion?' John was perplexed.

'It is winter, Mister *Bai-lou*, pig food is scarce upon the ground . . .' The old man let his words hang in the air.

Good God. John was shocked. Is he suggesting they really do feed Harlow's body to the pigs?

'We could dispose of it otherwise,' the old man continued. 'Down an abandoned mine shaft for instance, but that leaves to chance its discovery by some innocent and honest citizen.

The investigation you yourself suggested would then come to pass. The knife wound right through his chest would make it apparent the *sarjin's* death was not as a result of falling into the shaft by accident. Furthermore, the size of the knife wound would be noted.' Soh's eyes fell to the Bowie still in John's hand. 'A knife of such size is a rarity and . . .'

'It is wise counsel indeed that you offer, Mister Ho.' John bowed slightly and the effort was acknowledged by the old man. 'I could think of no finer destination for our sergeant's mortal remains, and as you say, it is winter . . .' John shrugged and the old man smiled.

'You are indeed wise, Mister *Bai-lou*.'

'There is, however, the matter of my friend, Harry.'

'As far as the authorities are concerned, Mister Foo will have simply disappeared from the goldfields, just like Harlow *Sarjin* . . .'

'But not in the same manner I hope . . .'

'Mister Foo's body will be looked after by my community. The See Yup Society of which I am a member will ensure his remains are buried in a place of everlasting dignity and respect.'

'You are an honourable man, sir.'

'Now,' Soh bowed, 'might I suggest that it is imperative you leave Ballarat immediately, for your own safety, Mister *Bai-lou*.'

John sheathed his knife. 'I am in your debt, Mister Soh,' he said and headed for the door. 'Please do as you will with the pads o' black and Mister Foo's purse.'

'The See Yup Society will ensure the money is put to good use. *Joi kin, pang yau*,' the old man called.

'*Pang yau*.' John paused at the door. 'Harry used to say that. It means friend, doesn't it?'

'Yes.' Soh nodded. 'And *joi kin* means goodbye.'

John rode the mare hard out along the north road towards Bendigo and it was early evening when he found Kit and

Rhodesy, the dray parked just off the road and the bullocks feeding happily on the scrub grass between assorted acacias and gum trees.

'Don't worry, John boy,' Rhodesy intoned as he poured a cup of tea from the billy. 'That See Yup Society is a good one, la. The Chinese know how to look after their own and you can trust old Soh, he's a man of honour. He'll do as he says he will, la.'

'Poor Harry,' the American said to neither in particular. He gazed at the evening stars and blew out a large breath of cigar smoke. 'No-one deserves to die like that. You did well, Johnny. Harlow was scum and the miners will welcome his absence.'

'It's a remarkable piece of steel, that knife you have, la. Went right through 'im you say, eh? I see'd a man done in once't like that with a marlinspike. Likewise, it went right through 'im it did.'

'Well, the heart is the body's blood pump after all,' Kit added. 'Once it's pierced the amount of blood it spills has to be seen to be believed. I once . . .'

'Can we skip the anatomy lesson?' John leaned back against the wheel of the dray and sipped his tea. The killing of Harlow had disturbed him. God alone knew what would result from it. He prayed Rhodesy was right and old Soh would leave no evidence of the event. If the Police Magistrate and his Inspector of Police accepted the fact that Harlow had left the goldfields for reasons of his own, all well and good; many a police officer had done so before him. And people would simply assume, when they realised the claims were abandoned, that Harry had left with his mates. John's fate, he now realised, rested in the hands of a Chinaman and, he hoped, an honourable one.

'Tomorrow we head for Bendigo, correct?' Kit looked at John for assurance.

'No,' John shook his head. 'If anything comes to light regarding today's events, the police will be looking for me and only me. You two are in the clear.'

'Wait a moment, la,' Rhodesy growled.

'Use your common sense, man,' John snapped. 'You two head for Bendigo and try your luck. I'll head east and if you're found and they ask after me, you haven't seen me since this afternoon. And,' he pointed at Rhodesy, 'Harry went with me.'

'Oh, no you don't, la!' Rhodesy growled again, preparing to make an argument of it.

'He's right, Big Jim!' Kit said forcefully. 'I don't like it any more than you do, but he's right. With the police and the judiciary being as crooked as they are, we could all three of us go down for murder as easily as that.' He snapped his fingers.

'It woul' na' be right for us to split, la!'

'It's the only sensible thing to do, my big friend.' The Bostonian looked sad.

'Good.' John rose to his feet. 'It's settled. Tomorrow morning it's you two for Bendigo and me to head east and, don't forget, Harry went with me.' He smiled at his two disconsolate friends. 'Don't worry, lads. The grand alliance is far from over. We'll meet again, have no doubts.'

CHAPTER SEVEN

Melbourne, winter 1854

In the rear courtyard of the Golden Sheaf, Jack Shearley placed his hands on the cobblestones and threw his legs into the air. Then, when he was sure of his balance, he opened and closed his legs several times before walking on his hands across the yard.

'*Mo dak ting!*' Old Feng Chi-pei called and clapped his hands.

Jack dropped back onto his feet and his eyes met the nodding, smiling face of Lou-shi. 'What did he say?'

'Master Feng described your effort as excellent,' Lou-shi answered.

'*Mo dak ting*,' Jack called repeatedly as he threw his body into a series of cartwheels across the courtyard.

'Do not use your fingers to take your body weight,' Lou-shi called after him. 'Use the flat of your palms.'

He landed upright and looked back at her. 'You use your fingertips,' he said.

'My fingers are much stronger than yours, Jack, and I only transfer my weight to them when I am stationary on a flat surface. You could snap your bones on these uneven stones; they are not safe for such exercise.'

'*The boy moves with great fluidity*,' Feng said. '*Like you, he has the grace and elegance of a girl.*'

'*What did he say?*' Jack asked.

'*How is it, do you think, Lou-shi, that he has not noticed your luscious buttocks as those of a woman?*'

'*He's only a boy!*'

'He may be homosexual.' Feng waggled a long fingernail at the boy.

'Master Feng!' Lou-shi exclaimed. She was shocked. He had used the words *tung sing luen*, meaning homosexual, once before aboard ship and when she'd asked Mok what it meant, she'd been shocked by the answer.

In the six months since Feng and Lou-shi had been at the Golden Sheaf, Jack had learned to speak some Cantonese, but he found that listening to it was far more difficult. 'Why do you Chinese speak so fast?' he complained. 'What does *tung sing luen* mean?'

'I must return to the laundry,' Lou-shi said far too quickly and disappeared through the door immediately behind her.

Jack looked at Old Feng. 'It doesn't mean that at all, does it?'

'I no speak E'lish,' Feng said and took off for the kitchen door.

Alone in the courtyard Jack shrugged and recommenced practising his cartwheels. He was determined to master all Lou-shi could teach him.

From a rear window above Cate watched her son. She was pleased with him of late; he seemed to have calmed down. She'd not given him an easy childhood so far; she'd moved from Europe to the United States and now to Australia and never offered Jack a sense of permanency. He'd not been able to call New York or San Francisco home; they'd no sooner settled than they'd been forced to move on for one reason or another. As a result he became introverted and she often saw loneliness in his eyes. But she had to admire his courage; he'd never once complained. She smiled as she watched him play. Jack was a damned fine kid.

The arrival of the two Chinese had been most fortuitous. Jack had bonded with them instantly and he'd blossomed as a result. The old man she'd analysed very quickly – she could recognise a trickster from a mile away and Master Feng was aptly named in her opinion. He was a 'master' all right, a master conman. She'd watched him hypnotise her son with cheap saloon tricks, sleight of hand, coins and jewellery that disappeared and reappeared like magic out of thin air, and card tricks that she had to admit were first class. But there was another side to the old man. It went beyond avuncular; he seemed to command respect from any who entered his space. Was it simply his age, she wondered, or his venerable appearance? She had to admit the Chinese outfits, silk long shirt with deep sleeves over silk trousers all beautifully embroidered, the cute slippers and, let's not forget, the little bobbed hat and his queue of long-plaited silver-grey hair didn't do his image any harm. He gave off the air of a wise old scholar, and yet Cate had often seen the glint of villainy, was it? Or perhaps it was glee, she could never be sure. But there was a cheerful lust for life in Old Feng. He was a rogue, of that she had no doubt, but she also knew instinctively she could trust him and, more importantly, her son would be safe with him.

China, on the other hand, was a different kettle of fish altogether. At first she'd thought the boy was stupid, for he seemed unable to cope with what seemed to her ordinary tasks, but the boy had revealed a natural aptitude for stage performance which Cate could only marvel at and she quickly put it to good use.

Cate Shearley's ability to make money had risen to new heights with the arrival of the Chinese boy. She had not forgotten the *oohs* and *aahs* of the crowd gathered round the young Chinaman when she'd rescued him from the Irish thug.

As luck would have it, the month before the Chinese duo had arrived she'd arranged the rental of a large weatherboard property directly opposite the Golden Sheaf. She'd engaged a juggler, a magician, an Italian opera soprano and a Scottish dwarf and opened Shearley's Variety Theatre.

If there was one thing Cate had learned it was that people loved being entertained. She'd witnessed for herself the success of vaudeville and burlesque in New York City and San Francisco. She had also heard that similar entertainment in London, called music hall, was the latest fad with the working classes and so she'd jumped in with her usual fearlessness and hired the warehouse, quickly turning it into a theatre.

At first, to attract the crowds, she'd had the Chinese boy perform his gymnastics out front beneath the marquee, but when she realised the crowd was perfectly happy to remain outside and watch the kid for free, she placed him in the show and ever since the money had been rolling in.

Free to perform as he pleased, China produced a range of gymnastic tricks unseen by Westerners. Apart from leaping and somersaulting through the air, the boy also walked tightrope, juggled fire and balanced spinning plates on top of thin bamboo sticks, allowing Cate to dispense with the drunken juggler she'd hired. And, almost overnight, she was turning punters away at the door. Finally, she'd been forced by popular demand to put on two shows nightly.

But the greatest surprise of all for Cate, the *pièce de résistance*, the absolute showstopper double-act that pulled the punters through the doors like a magnet, was revealed unexpectedly one Friday morning not two months after she'd started the shows.

She'd risen early, something she disliked doing, but this particular morning it had been unavoidable. She was determined to inspect the new theatre lanterns she'd had installed either side of the stage before the installers disappeared to the goldfields like everyone else. The large lanterns, six in all, which had cost her a pretty penny, arrived the previous day and workmen had toiled all night to get them ready for that Friday night's performances.

She crossed Collins Street and was surprised to find the front doors to the theatre unlocked. Entering the foyer she heard a faint whining noise coming from the stage. She opened the theatre door slightly and peered inside. There on steps at the side of the stage sat China, between his legs a single-string instrument that he was playing with a bow. The noise was entirely foreign to her, but not unpleasant, and then the kid began to sing.

Pain, desire, loneliness, joy and countless other human emotions flooded through Cate as the voice took her to places she'd long forgotten, then places she joyfully remembered and on to places she could only imagine. The voice drifted ethereally throughout the auditorium, floating on the air, magnificent in its pitch, poignant in its tone. It was glorious to hear . . . The voice was . . . she was at a loss for superlatives . . . the voice was . . . her eyes suddenly narrowed . . . the voice was *not male*.

The realisation hit like a thunderclap. Of course, she thought. Of course, how could I have been so naïve! I always thought there was something odd about the boy, something indefinable, and now the answer has been revealed. China is a girl.

Cate stepped into the auditorium and walked down the aisle. The music and singing stopped as Lou-shi saw her. The girl remained motionless and when Cate reached the foot of the stairs, she saw China was crying, tears wandering down her cheeks.

'Well, well, well, who's a clever girl?' Cate's tone was not unkind, but she was annoyed that she had been fooled so convincingly.

'I am sorry, Cate Shearley . . .'

'I've told you before, don't use my full name, call me Cate.'

'I am so sorry, Cate. I have been disguised like this since we left China.'

Cate climbed the set of six stairs, sat beside the girl and offered her a handkerchief, which was accepted. 'So, what's your real name, China?'

'Lou-shi. My family name is Chang,' the girl replied mournfully, 'my name is Chang Lou-shi.'

'Well, Miss Chang Lou-shi, I can understand the need for disguising your gender here in Melbourne at least; Chinese women are few and far between. So, what's your story?'

'My friend the Emperor became angry with me . . .'

'The Emperor of China?' Cate was taken aback. 'The *real* Emperor of China?'

'Yes, his name is Hsien-feng.'

'You know the Emperor of China personally?'

'Yes.' Lou-shi nodded, wiping her eyes. 'He used to call me his Little Nightingale. I was his favourite singer in all of China.'

'I'm not surprised. So, what happened?'

Lou-shi began to talk, hesitantly at first, but soon the whole story came bubbling from her. Master Feng, the Green Lotus Opera Company, the Taiping Rebellion, the deaths of Jiao Mun and Chou, the flight from China aboard Captain Featherstone's Yankee clipper *China Moon* and the death of Mok.

Later that morning, in the hotel kitchen, Cate had a long chat with Old Feng. With Lou-shi acting as interpreter, she had cross-examined him at length. It became clear that the girl, or woman Cate decided when she discovered Lou-shi was twenty years old, had not exaggerated her status. Feng had been a big-time impresario and had made Lou-shi the most famous voice in China until their fall from grace and subsequent persecution. Their flight from China and continuing fear of punishment had left its mark on both of them. Cate knew that if she were to use their talents, she must ensure their real identities remain secret.

'Name changes!' she declared. 'That's the first thing.'

'For me is not necessary,' Feng said in English, causing both Cate and Lou-shi to stare at him.

'I thought you didn't speak English?' Cate's eyes narrowed.

'I don't,' came the enigmatic reply. 'It is a foolish language, clumsy and, how you say . . . ambiguous?'

'It could have made things a lot easier for all of us.'

'Chinese say, "Bird that does not sing does not get shot".'

Cate laughed. 'A clever thought, Master Feng. Perhaps we should maintain the *status quo*, eh? You remain the bird who does not sing.' Feng smiled, nodding in agreement. 'Right, where were we?' she went on. 'Yes, name changes, well for Lou-shi at least.'

'You must bill her same as now, China the Chinese Circus Boy? Then when she sing, give her another name. We must disguise her.'

Yes, two performers for the price of one, she thought. 'Disguise her? How?'

'We have costumes,' Lou-shi announced. 'I could dress up and apply make-up as we did in the opera. Oh,' she clapped her hands excitedly, 'it would be just like Peking again.'

'No.' Feng shook his head. 'Chinese people hear you, they become curious. You sing Japanese, maybe.'

'I don't speak Japanese,' Lou-shi said.

'No-one speak Japanese, only Japanese,' Feng grunted. 'Just make up, sound like Japanese.'

'I've got it,' Cate began nodding furiously. 'The music. I've been thinking about that since this morning and I know who can do it.'

'Really?' Lou-shi was perplexed.

'Wolfie Bremmer, Wolfgang Bremmer!' Cate stood and headed for the door. 'A German friend of mine; he was once a great musician and conductor in Europe, now brought low by intemperance and . . . er, other vices. I'll have Amos track him down.' At the door she turned. 'And we will definitely bill you as Japanese. An international show. The customers will love it. Yes!' Cate exclaimed, warming to her idea. 'That'll throw people right off the scent. We'll bill you as Michiko, Japan's Madame Vestris.'

'Who?' Feng was utterly lost.

'Michiko was my housemaid's name in New York and Madame Vestris is the most famous woman in English theatre.' She frowned at them. 'Don't tell me you've never heard of Lucia Vestris, she's a famous contralto and she's also . . .' she suddenly offered them a radiant smile, 'a theatre impresario, just like me!' Both Chinese stared at her completely confused. 'Trust me, it'll work. Oh, I love the theatre, don't you?' Cate spun on her toes and left the kitchen with a swish of skirt.

And that's how I got two performers for the price of one, Cate thought. Lou-shi remained China the Chinese Circus Boy in Act I and Michiko Japan's Madame Vestris in Act II, and the result was spectacular.

'You've landed on your feet again, luv,' she said aloud to herself as she looked down again at Jack literally landing on his feet from a handstand. And I'm so lucky I have you, Jack, she thought; you're the reason I keep trying. Life as a mother alone had certainly had its moments over the years.

Memories of their journey made her reflect. She thought fondly of Solly, her benefactor. Solomon Shadkun, an old London Jew who'd taken her, pregnant, off the street and whisked her away to New York into a world of luxury and elegance.

And all because I helped him feed the birds in front of St Paul's, she thought. A rueful grin spread across her face. Solly, Solly, dear old Solly.

That's my mark, she decided as she crossed behind the Statue of Queen Anne and sat on the steps of St Paul's Cathedral. She watched the old man, a Jew by the look of him, walking out of Godliman Street. Now he stood almost in front of her, gazing up at the cathedral's façade.

'Designed by Christopher Wren,' she said. 'It's the tallest building in London.'

'That's only because it's on top of Ludgate Hill, don't you think, young lady?'

'Oh, know your London, do you?' She was waiting for the right moment to stand beside him, pick his pocket and then make her way, carefully, down to Limeburner Lane. Her advanced state of pregnancy made it very difficult for her to run.

'I was born not a mile from here,' he answered proudly, 'in Shoreditch. I've lived in London all my life, that is, apart from several sojourns in various parts of the world.'

'Oh, yeah?' She tried to sound interested as she got up and stood next to him. 'And whereabouts would they be?'

'Spain,' he replied. 'I like Spain. And Japan is a wonderful country; the people are impeccably polite and have the strangest customs.'

She slipped her hand into his pocket with consummate ease and immediately felt his money pouch, but when she went to withdraw her hand she could not do so. It was caught in a vice-like grip.

'Now why did you have to do that?' He spoke softly. 'I need only call for help now and the Bobbies will waltz you away to do time in the Steel,' he said, referring colloquially to Coldbath Fields Prison in Clerkenwell. 'That would be stressful indeed, given your condition.'

Fear surged through her as she tried in vain to remove her hand. 'Please forgive me,' she pleaded. 'My circumstances are desperate, sir. As you are aware, I am with child and I am also without means. Please let me go.' His grip on her hand through the fabric of his coat was beginning to hurt. 'I'll do whatever you ask of me, please, sir.'

'Would you help me feed the birds?'

'Yes, anything!' She winced in pain. 'Please, you're hurting me.'

'Oh, I'm terribly sorry.' Instantly she felt his grip relax. 'Do forgive me.'

She withdrew her hand from his pocket and stood, rubbing her wrist, unsure whether or not she should attempt to run.

'I'm sorry; I forget how much strength I have in my right hand. You can go. Please, go.'

She stood staring at him. He has kind eyes, she thought, and he's lonely. A lonely old man. 'Why do you need help feeding the birds?'

The old man withdrew his left hand from his pocket and held it up for show. It was withered, the fingers curled inward. 'I have a bit of trouble holding the bags of breadcrumbs.' He took out his money bag and offered it to her. 'But if you go to old Missus McFayden and buy me a bag, you can hold it for me, while I feed the birds.'

Is he serious? she thought. I could take his money and run. He'd never catch me. Even in my state I could outrun him. She looked down the street towards the entrance to Limeburner Lane; once she turned into that lane she'd be home safe.

'Please?' he asked again, smiling at her, and there was a twinkle in his eyes as he dangled the money bag in front of her nose.

'All right.' Is he playing some sort of game with me?

She looked to the end of the steps where Missus McFayden

sat, surrounded by birds, the bags of breadcrumbs in a tray on her lap. It was her chance. He was going to give her his entire purse and allow her to walk thirty yards or more to the old woman. More than a head start, she thought; I'll take off through Paternoster Square and be away scot-free.

'All right,' she said again and took the purse. It was heavy. She hefted it in her hand and grinned back at him. 'I'll only be a moment. You wait right here.'

She began to walk to the old woman, her heart pounding. She looked about for Bobbies, but there were none to be seen. Then she glanced back at the old man. He was standing where she'd left him and he was smiling and nodding at her encouragingly.

'Hello, luv,' Missus McFayden said as she offered up a bag of breadcrumbs. 'A penny a bag, dearie.'

She searched through the purse, finally encountering a penny coin at the bottom of a bag full of gold and silver. What are you doing? her mind screamed. Paternoster Square is only thirty more yards, right in front of you. Run!

'Thanks, Missus Mac,' she muttered, handing over the penny. Then she found herself turning back and walking towards the old man, who was beaming and nodding furiously.

'I knew you weren't a thief,' he gushed as she handed him his purse. 'I'm a very good judge of character, or so I'm told. It's in the eyes, you know?'

'What is?' She was numb. She could not believe what she'd just done, or more to the point, what she had not done.

'Character! Good character, honesty, trust, compassion and all the other wonderful human virtues. They can all be seen in the eyes.'

'Really? What about hunger, destitution, poverty? Can you see them too?'

The old man's smile disappeared. 'I once knew all three, intimately.'

'And now?'

'Ha,' he laughed, recovering his gaiety. 'Like old adversaries, they are long forgotten. Now come on, you said you'd help me feed the birds.'

She opened the bag and spilled breadcrumbs into his hand, and for the next few minutes she watched him, childlike, feeding pigeons. He talked to them as intimate friends, cooed and purred along with them, pausing only for her to refresh his palm with crumbs.

'Can you read and write?'

'Sorry?' she said. 'Are you talking to me or the birds?'

'You,' he replied, not even looking up.

'Well then, yes, I can read and write.'

When the supply of food was exhausted and the birds departed as one to seek greener pastures, he turned to her and smiled.

'Thank you, my dear.'

'You're welcome.'

'Where did you learn to read and write?'

'I taught myself.'

'Admirable,' he nodded. 'And your English, it's almost without accent; how is this so?'

'I listen a lot.'

'Hmmm, smart too, I'll warrant. Where do you live, young lady?'

'Across the river in Southwark.'

'Good grief! The devil's playground, eh? Good theatres and bad women. And whereabouts in Southwark do you reside?'

'It's not what you'd call a residence.'

'I'm intrigued.'

'I live in a brothel.' She saw the question in his eyes. 'And before you ask, no, I don't. That's why I pick pockets.'

'And is that where you'll give birth to your child?'

'Probably.'

'I see. What's your name?'

'Cate Shearley.'

'And mine is Solomon Shadkun.' He looked at her for what seemed an eternity, then he pulled a card from his waistcoat pocket and several coins from his purse and handed them to her. 'Well, Cate Shearley, go home to your bordello, gather your belongings and come to my house. I'd like to help you.'

'Oh yes,' she said sarcastically, 'and why would you want to do that?'

He stared at her again, holding her gaze. 'If you were drowning in the Thames, would you care why someone pulled you out?'

'I suppose not,' she shrugged, glancing at his card. 'You live in *Mayfair*!'

'Yes, is that not to your liking?'

Mayfair – she was impressed. God, he must be rolling in money. 'No! No, Mayfair's fine, but I would like to know what I'd be required to do, in return for your . . . help?'

'Help is precisely what I'm offering you,' he replied stiffly. 'A chance to improve your prospects and those of your child. I'm too old to play the games you're hinting at, Miss Shearley.'

'I'm sorry.' She realised she'd offended him. 'It's just that an offer of genuine help in my world is a rarity.'

'I promise to help you through your confinement, then after your baby arrives, I would require you to work for me as an assistant, for want of a better description. It would involve a lot of hard work, so if you don't think you're capable –'

'No, no, no!' she interrupted. 'I'll be there by nightfall.'

'And it was the best thing you ever did, my girl,' Cate said aloud, as she opened the window and called to her son.

'Yes, Mother,' came the reply from the courtyard.

'Have you done the schoolwork I set for you?'

'Not yet.'

'Well get on with it, my boy, or you'll suffer the consequences.'

Closing the window, she checked her appearance in the mirror and went downstairs to the front desk where Dorothy her receptionist was busy registering a number of men into accommodation. Miners from the goldfields – she recognised one as a previous customer – and they were in an ebullient mood.

'We've heard tell of your new Variety Show, Cate,' one said.

'We've heard of nothin' else but, Cate,' another added. 'It's the talk of the goldfields, it is. Everyone's sayin' the little Japanese girl is wonderful to hear.'

'I wanna see China the Chinese Circus Boy,' yet another said.

'Well,' she laughed, 'you'd better book your seats for tonight, lads, they sell out fast. Two shows on at seven and nine. Dorothy will book for you.'

'Five for tonight, gents?' Dorothy asked. 'The nine o'clock show's all that's left. Pick up your tickets here at the desk no later than seven.'

Cate took over the desk as Dorothy showed the men to their rooms. She flicked through the Receipts and Goods Received Register, checking the items off one against the other, and as usual was satisfied with Dorothy's work. The girl was good at her job and Cate knew she was lucky to have her, well, she thought, until she meets her Mister Right. Most Melbourne girls her age thought of nothing else but marriage to a rich miner and the dream of a rural idyll raising kids on a country estate, while the more impatient took off to the goldfields for the sheer adventure of it. For many of them that meant loss of virtue, prostitution and drug addiction, while for others it meant a premature death at the hands of a drunken miner or, for those lonely and abandoned few, death by exposure to the freezing winter nights or fierce heat of summer. Mercy was a rare commodity on the goldfields.

Another few months and if all goes well I'll give Dorothy a shot at managing the place, she decided, as she closed the receipt book and flicked open the Guest Register. The signature caught her eye immediately. John Bailleau, late of Coventry City and Ballarat. That's not the signature of a miner, she thought; half of them can barely write their name and the other half use a cross or thumbprint. This was the fluid handwriting of a well-educated man. What's his story? she wondered as she trailed her fingertip over the name.

'He is the man of my dreams,' Dorothy gushed as she walked behind Cate and looked over her shoulder.

Damn! There goes my manageress.

'I'm going to marry him.'

Cate smiled. 'Does he know this?'

'Well not yet, but give me time.'

'Do you know anything about him?'

'He's a real gent, of that there's no doubt,' the receptionist said. 'He's from Ballarat but originally from Coventry City.'

'Did he tell you that?'

'Well, sort of . . .' she stumbled on. 'No . . . he wrote it in the register . . . but he told me he's been staying in Collingwood! He said he wanted some hotel accommodation for a while and the Golden Sheaf had been recommended to him.' Dorothy exhaled theatrically, placing her palms on her bosom. 'He said he may be here for a while . . .'

'Do go on.' Cate turned to the girl and mocked good-naturedly. 'Is he rich? Is he tall? Is he good-looking? Broad shouldered?'

'He's all of those things,' Dorothy blushed.

'And he *told you* he's rich, did he?'

'Well, no, not exactly, but judging by what he ordered for supper he'd better be, or we'll be stuck with an enormous bill.'

'What did he order?'

'Rock lobster, sea scallops, oysters, fish roe and French champagne, to be followed by filet of beef and our best red wine.'

'Let's hope he's fresh from the fields then, with his pockets full of gold. And, by the way, does Cook have a rock lobster, or any fresh seafood at all for that matter? I would doubt it; it doesn't keep.'

'I took the liberty of asking her to order it in.' Dorothy blushed again.

'Did you now?' Cate raised an eyebrow. 'You are determined, aren't you?'

'Oh, Cate, he's so handsome!' she prattled.

'Calm down, girl.' Cate looked at the register again. 'When did he check in, by the way?'

'This morning. He pulled up out the front on a beautiful bay mare. I had Jack take her around the back to the stables and feed her.'

'All right.' Cate closed the register, walked out in front of the desk and aimed an index finger at her receptionist. 'Don't annoy him, Dot, that's an order.' She waggled her finger. 'I mean it, girl. As a guest he comes first and as an object of your matrimonial ambitions he comes last, is that understood?'

Cate left the hotel, crossed the street and sat in the rear row of the theatre. She'd taken to attending Friday morning rehearsals for the relaxation it afforded her. Her business was booming on both sides of Collins Street and required more attention each day, so whatever moments of solitude she could find she seized without hesitation.

At eleven am precisely, she watched Wolfgang Bremmer walk onto the stage and sit at the piano. He placed his music on the rest and began a five-minute finger exercise that ended in a monstrous crescendo, after which he paused for a moment before commencing Lou-shi's introduction to the finale of Act II.

Wolfie Bremmer had surprised Cate with his efforts to create the certain something special she'd requested to accompany Lou-shi's voice. He'd nodded, barely interested when she'd first told him of her plan, but when he heard the Chinese girl sing, he was instantly captivated. Cate had watched his face soften and when he closed his eyes and smiled dreamily she knew she had him, hook, line and sinker.

Wolfie had been the golden boy of European music ten years previously when Cate had met him at a Covent Garden recital, but success and money had led him from the discipline of high art into that hedonistic world shared by the very talented and their rich benefactors. Alcohol, women and gambling had seduced him in succession until first his fingers failed, then his memory failed and finally his money ran out. His self-respect and dignity were lost altogether and he sank into a life of poverty with his only escape drink and opium.

Their paths had crossed again in San Francisco three years before. Cate had employed him as a piano player in the cigar lounge of her California Eldorado Hotel. It had not been difficult for him; no-one listened, as rich men struck deals and their beautiful companions primped and preened. Then one night Wolfie had whispered to Cate of a conversation he'd overheard which confirmed her long-held suspicion.

'Your French lover is going to kill you.'

'What?'

'He needs outright ownership of the hotel.'

'It's in my name.'

'He told the O'Dowd brothers he owned the Eldorado. He staked it in a card game and lost it.'

She'd been terror struck. The O'Dowds were a very dangerous and powerful Irish family who practically ruled the world of crime in San Francisco. Fearing for her life and more so for her son's, she'd raided the hotel safe and Jean-Baptiste Le Pen had caught her red-handed. In an uncontrollable rage he'd stabbed her in the eye, but before he could do more she'd shot him in the stomach with her Derringer. Not knowing whether she'd killed him or not she emptied the safe of a fortune in black cash and with Jack and Amos in tow had disappeared into the night.

Not long after her arrival in Melbourne she received news that Jean-Baptiste had recovered from the stomach wound, but a month later a bullet through the head, courtesy of the O'Dowd brothers, had finished him off and the Irishmen had taken vacant possession of the California Eldorado Hotel.

A year after leaving San Francisco she wrote to Wolfie and it had resulted in his arrival in the Colony of Victoria.

Cate owed Wolfgang Bremmer her life and the life of her son. She saw to it he had comfortable accommodation in Collingwood and arranged for him to teach piano to the kids of Melbourne's wealthy elite. He'd managed to cling onto reality until the arrival of Lou-shi, when the world he'd thought gone forever returned with a vengeance and the music simply poured from him.

She sat in the back row and listened to him play. He'd created music that was neither Eastern nor Western, but captured the essence of each, leaving the ear to decide where the mind might wander. It was melodic and yet dissonant, bitter and yet sweet, leaving the listener undecided, until Lou-shi's voice entered the equation and his genius as a composer became obvious. Together Wolfie and Lou-shi transported their audiences to the world of beautiful long-forgotten memories.

Cate stood; she dared not listen to more. She would attend the second show that evening to listen in full and check out the new costume Lou-shi was to debut, which, according to Dorothy who had seen it, was by far the most extravagant and hauntingly beautiful costume Old Feng had ever produced.

As she crossed the street to the Golden Sheaf, to her right, trotting up Collins Street, she watched the rump and swishing tail of a beautiful bay mare. Its rider's back was upright, his shoulders broad, his hat cocked at a rakish angle. The man was definitely at home on a horse. A cavalryman, she'd bet on it. Mister John Bailleau no doubt, she thought, the cause of Dorothy's palpitating heart. She took in his polished boots, his riding crop and Lincoln green suit with burgundy trim. Well, she mused, if he looks half as good from the front as he does from the back, Dorothy may well be in for the ride of her life.

'Ha!' The thought made her hoot with laughter as she entered the hotel, attracting the stares of several women sharing tea in the foyer. 'Good day to you, ladies,' she quipped, and was rewarded with smiles all round.

'Dorothy,' she called to the desk.

'Yes, ma'am.' Dorothy was sure to always call her ma'am when other women were present.

'Reserve me a back-row seat for the second show tonight, will you, please?'

CHAPTER EIGHT

Melbourne, winter 1854

Tom Appleyard remembered, out on the wallaby track some years before, his old dog Ben had been bitten by an eastern brown, a big bugger of a snake that would have bitten Tom himself if Ben hadn't had a go at it and got taken unto the Lord for his effort. It had been a lean time that summer; water and game had been scarce because of the drought and he'd struggled for hours with the notion of eating Ben for supper. Would he get the snake's venom in his system if he ate the dog, or would roasting the carcass over an open campfire make old Ben safe to eat? Hunger had finally got the better of him, but he remembered grieving mightily, tears streaming from his eyes, as he'd chewed on old Ben's bones.

'And as you would remember, Lord,' he said looking skyward, 'I gave 'is 'ead and 'ide a Christian burial.'

That situation had presented Tom with a dichotomy and now he was confronted with another, which was fairly tearing him in half. Should he remain at his post, or should he go to the show? Cate Shearley had given him a ticket to her Variety Show starting at seven o'clock and he was very much looking forward to seeing it, but his sense of honour was telling him he should wait for the horseman. He was indeed on the horns of a dichotomy.

Tom liked the word dichotomy; in fact, over the years it had become a favourite, especially after he learned its true meaning. When he was young he'd thought the word was the second to be sung in the hymn 'Nearer Dichotomy' until the reverend had pointed out it was 'Nearer My God to Thee'. Ever since that day of enlightenment he'd recognised other people's dichotomies, but had rarely suffered them himself, until today.

Where in hell is the rich toff? he wondered. The man had said he'd be back before sunset and now here it is almost seven o'clock and there's no sign of him.

Tom Appleyard was happy with his lot. He had a fine place to sleep next door in Ryan's Bakery in the loft over the ovens and he had all his meals provided by Maude, Cate Shearley's cook at the Golden Sheaf. And all he had to do in return was keep the yard tidy, muck out the hotel's stable each morning and care for the occasional traveller's horse.

The clatter of hooves on the cobblestones snapped him from his reverie and he strode towards the bay mare and took her by the bridle strap.

'Good evenin', sir,' he called. 'I was beginnin' to think you might a' lost track o' time.'

'Oh, I'm so sorry.' John Bailleau sprang from his saddle, instantly reminded of the conversation he'd had with Tom earlier in the day. 'Of course, you're off to the Variety Show at seven, aren't you?' He checked his timepiece. 'You've got ten minutes; you'd better be going. Leave the mare to me.'

'Oh, no, sir. I couldn't . . .'

'I won't hear of it, Tom. Now off you go.' John gave him several coins. 'And take these for your trouble. Have an ale or two on me.'

'Thank you kindly, Mister Bailleau.' Tom doffed his cap. 'I'm much obliged, sir.'

As Tom made off in the deepening twilight John began to unsaddle the mare when he suspected he was being watched. He eased back his coat-tail and drew his revolver.

'It's not polite to spy on people from the shadows,' he said. 'Indeed, it's a good way to get yourself shot.'

'If my ma sees me down here I'll get what for.'

'I see.' John relaxed and holstered Mister Adams. It was the boy who hung around the hotel, the one who constantly threw cartwheels, scaring his horse. 'Did you do your schoolwork, as your mother ordered?'

'How did you know about that?'

'I was in the stable this morning when she called to you.'

'What's the mare's name?' Jack Shearley said, as he stepped into the light from the open stable door.

'What's *your* name?'

'Jack,' the boy replied, extending his hand.

'And my name's John Bailleau,' he answered, impressed with the firmness of the boy's grip.

'Well John's my name too, but everyone calls me Jack.' He patted the mare's flank. 'So, what's her name?'

'Rani.' John removed the saddle from the mare and she snorted appreciatively, nudging him with her nose. 'It's an Indian word, it means queen.'

'That's a really good name.' Jack was sincerely impressed.

'And what's your last name, Jack?'

'Shearley.'

'Ah, I assume it's your mother who owns this establishment?'

'Jack!' The strident female voice rang out.

'Oh, hail, hell and hello!' the boy muttered.

'And I assume that's her voice?' John laughed as he undid the cheek-strap and removed the bridle and bit.

'I've got to go. Nice to meet you, Rani; you too, John Bailleau.' The words came out at the speed of light as Jack took off for the kitchen door. 'Sorry, I have to go,' he called as he ran. 'Goodnight, sorry, goodnight, Rani!'

John could only laugh as he watched the boy run for his life. 'Hail, hell and hello?' he said aloud. 'I can't say I've heard that one before, Rani, how about you?' The horse snorted again. 'You're probably right, girl.' He shook his head, amused. He folded the mare's saddle blanket, patted her flank and she followed him through the stable door, nudging his back with her nose.

The curtain on the seven o'clock show came down at 8.15 and Chang Lou-shi now sat with Old Feng backstage as he ate his nightly serving of noodle soup and dumplings.

'Why do you never eat?' he asked, as he did every Friday and Saturday night between shows. *'You will become sick and die, then what will happen to me, the person who has given you a wonderful life and is now showing you parts of the world you would never have witnessed had you remained in the Middle Kingdom as the personal pet of the Ch'iang Emperor . . .?'*

'Why do you always ask that question,' she interrupted, *'when you know my answer is always the same?'* She had never been able to eat between shows because the nerves required for performance did not allow for the consumption of food. The mere thought of going on stage with a full stomach made her feel ill. And the thought that Master Feng had known this fact since she was ten years old made her irritable.

'Have you ever wondered, Lou-shi,' he lowered his voice to a conspiratorial whisper, *'how much money the one-eyed white woman makes from our theatrical endeavours?'*

'No!' she snapped. *'But I am wondering why you are speaking in a whisper, in Cantonese, in a deserted theatre, in a foreign country.'*

'Aaah,' he nodded sage-like, *'so you have noticed.'*

'Of course I've noticed!'

'You cannot be too careful. You never know who is listening.'

'Master, we are the only two people in the entire building!' Lou-shi never quite knew whether to scream, hit him, or accept his eccentricity. *'It makes you appear to be mad.'*

'Lou-shi, you should espouse the fact that madness is merely an alternate form of sanity.'

'Aaaaiiiyyaaahhh!' she exclaimed. She simply had to accept his crazy chatter without question or she would go mad herself.

'That is a most unfortunate noise. You sound like a fishwife. You will ruin your voice with such wailing. Did you know that pigs who squeal the loudest are the first to be killed?'

She loved the old man more than life and she knew he was not really insane . . . but, he conversed like an idiot . . . and he knew it . . . and he did it nevertheless.

'What do pigs have to do with our conversation? Will you please talk sense or I will leave you alone and lie down to rest before the nine o'clock show.'

'I asked you a sensible question before and you ignored me.'

'What was the question?'

'Have you ever wondered how much money the one-eyed white woman makes from our theatrical endeavours?'

'Mistress Shearley is an honest woman and she has been kind to us . . .'

'I have been making calculations in my head,' he continued as if he'd not heard, *'and I think she is making a fortune.'*

'Then that is good luck to her.' Her eyes narrowed and she stared at him. *'What are you up to?'*

'Nothing.'

'You are plotting something. I can see it in your eyes.' She waggled her index finger in front of his nose. *'When you plot we get into trouble.'*

'I have been speaking with Mister Hu Wei-long, you remember him? He has been to see your show many times. He made a fortune on the Ballarat goldfields and now lives here in Melbourne. He owns four fishing boats, two wharves in Port Melbourne and a house here in the city.'

'Go on.' She eyed him suspiciously.

'Hu Wei-long now calls himself Hugh E Long –'

'Why?' she interrupted, now intrigued and praying he would keep talking logically.

'He wants to be an Englishman.'

'He's Chinese!'

'He has decided to remain in Australia and become an English gentleman. He has adopted an English name, purchased a rural property near Geelong and even a pack of hunting hounds. And, he is wooing an English woman!'

'I have never before heard anything so stupid.' Lou-shi walked out through the wings onto the stage. She stood, hands on hips, as if inspecting the rear side of the curtain before looking back at him. *'Please tell me that whatever you are plotting has nothing to do with me? It doesn't, does it?'*

'Hugh E Long has suggested we combine as equal partners, purchase a circus-type tent and take you on a tour to the goldfields.'

'What!?' Lou-shi was flabbergasted.

'On Ballarat and Bendigo goldfields he believes we will get ten times the ticket prices the one-eyed woman is charging here in Melbourne. We would make a lot of money.'

'Would you dishonour our arrangement with Mistress Shearley after all she has done for us?' Lou-shi turned her back on the old man. *'I am ashamed of you, Master Feng. For the first time in my life, I am ashamed of you.'*

Feng Chi-pei sat shocked, as if she'd struck him in the face. Ashamed, the word rang in his head. *'Lou-shi, I . . .'* he began.

'How can you even suggest such a thing?' She took several steps away, not turning to face him. *'By doing so you insult me. For you to think I would consider joining in your shameful enterprise is an affront to my honour.'* She turned now and glared at him. *'Mistress Shearley has been a paragon of kindness to us. She took us in knowing we were destitute and has given us a life of comfort and even employed us in our cherished profession.'* Anger coursed through her. *'And you want to repay her by undermining her business and ruining what she has worked so hard to create.'* The girl shook her head and squinted as if in pain. *'Hard to create,'* she muttered. *'Hard to create! Hard to create! Hard to create.'*

Feng had never seen Lou-shi so angry and it shocked him to the core. She had thrown many a histrionic tantrum over the years, but that, he knew, was the diva's way of handling problems in a theatrical environment. This dramatic outburst, he realised, was caused by her mental problem. Her eyes told him of her disappointment and her clenched fists were evidence of her anger. He was in deep trouble and his mind searched desperately for a solution.

'Lou-shi, my angel,' he said as a light came on in his brain. *'I have hurt you and it has broken my heart.'* He went to her and stroked her arm. *'Shhhh,'* he murmured. *'I have behaved*

badly and the look of disappointment in your eyes causes me intense pain, so much so I cannot eat.' He pointed back at his chopsticks on the table. *'The one-eyed woman has indeed behaved with honour and it is I who have made the mistake . . .'*

'Oh, Master Feng,' Lou-shi interrupted. He saw the stress in her dissolve. *'I knew you would realise your error.'*

'As I was saying, Lou-shi. I have made a terrible mistake in even thinking of a joint venture with Hugh E Long. How could I have been so dishonourable, and thank you for pointing it out . . .'

'You are a good man, Master Feng,' she interrupted again, her heart going out to him.

'. . . My correct course of action should be to offer the one-eyed woman first opportunity at a joint venture with –'

'Aaaiiiyyaaaaahhh!' Lou-shi cried, exasperated, and stormed off across the stage.

'You should not make that noise!' Feng called after her. *'You will destroy your voice and then where will we be? I will tell you, we will be . . .'* He stopped. Let her go off alone and calm down so she can perform the second show. *'You are an old fool, Feng!'* he chastised himself. *'You are a fool!'* Then he shook his head, picked up his chopsticks and resumed eating his dinner.

Lou-shi, in her coolie-boy outfit, ran through the Friday night crowd congregating in Collins Street, up the side lane to the rear courtyard of the Golden Sheaf and over to the door of the stables where she paused to catch her breath before entering.

'Celestial Horse,' she said, putting her arms around the bay mare's neck. *'It is I, Lou-shi, born of your year and at your hour.'* She paused and looked up at the animal. *'But of course, you are an English horse, so I shall speak in English.* Goddess Horse,' she began in English, 'I am born within your year and your hour. I have never asked you for guidance, even though I know you help me when my mind gets upset, but I have experienced my Master Feng at his worst and must ask for you to help him.'

For the next five minutes Lou-shi poured her heart out to the animal, telling of Old Feng and her confrontation with him and his complete failure to recognise his dishonourable behaviour, as he blithely jumped from a partnership with Hu Wei-long to the idea of offering Cate Shearley the same deal.

'He lacks any moral sense,' she muttered, shaking her head. 'He needs help,' she suddenly gasped. 'He needs help, he needs help.' She began nodding furiously as her mind stalled. 'He needs help, he needs help!'

'Good evening, lad?' Lou-shi spun at the voice and was confronted by the English owner of the horse. 'I was in the harness-room and couldn't avoid hearing your conversation with Rani. It would seem you have a dilemma. I can only wish you well with it.'

'He needs help,' Lou-shi said again and attempted to get past the man out into the courtyard, but he moved simultaneously and they brushed against each other.

'I'm . . . I'm terribly sorry,' John Bailleau stammered as he felt a female breast against his arm.

'He needs . . . so sorry, so sorry!' Lou-shi muttered and took off into the night.

'Well, well, Rani old girl.' John stroked his horse's neck. 'What did you make of that? A Chinese morality play it would seem, with a beautiful heroine playing a boy, a scheming old master, an Englishman called Hughie Long, although the way she pronounced it the man could be Chinese. And it involves none other than our good lady publican, Mistress Shearley.' He paused and looked in the direction the girl had gone. Something in her behaviour had disturbed him, then he realised. 'Good heavens,' he murmured. 'Lily! My Lillypilly.'

The horse snorted as if she understood.

John nodded. 'Quite right, old girl. My sister, Lily. That girl lost control of her emotions, just as my sister does when she's upset or excited.' He stroked the horse's neck. 'What do you know about that? How strange.' He looked again out into the darkened courtyard and imagined his sister standing there, head bowed, hands folded in front of her. Then Lily looked up and smiled and his heart skipped a beat as he realised how much he missed her. 'Well now,' he coughed and straightened his hair. 'Goodnight, Rani, I'm off to the Variety Show.'

Cate entered the theatre after the houselights went down and took her seat on the end of the rear aisle. Her magician, Tommy Bartlett from Leeds, also known as Waldo the Wonderful, went through his routine producing doves from his sleeves, flowers from thin air and even a rabbit from his hat. He was roundly applauded and quickly followed by the Italian soprano who sang an aria from the English opera *Maritana* by Vincent Wallace. Cate had seen the opera performed in New York at the Astor and had to admit the Italian made a good fist of the song, albeit her voice was a little scratchy.

Scattered applause saw the soprano depart, frowning, but no sooner had she done so than onto the stage tumbled China the Chinese Circus Boy and the crowd went wild. They cheered and applauded the tumbling, somersaulting and handstands, gasped at the juggling and sat silent and awestruck as the boy walked the tightrope while controlling spinning plates on bamboo sticks with both hands. The nine o'clock show crowd of mainly miners and their women, mostly prostitutes, cheered, whistled and threw coins onto the stage, and Lou-shi, as Circus Boy, was forced to make four curtain calls to end Act I.

John Bailleau, who was sitting in the front row, stood to stretch his legs and purchase a mug of ale from one of the young serving girls from the Golden Sheaf attending the bar set in front of the stage. He had to admit he was enjoying himself immensely. He'd not seen a variety show for longer than he cared to remember and the three performers so far had been exceptional, especially the Chinese Circus Boy, who is actually a girl, he thought. She was an extraordinary performer indeed. While gazing about at the raucous audience members he caught sight of a woman exit through the rear doors some distance from him. Honey-blonde hair and a rich curvaceous figure, he noticed, then he saw the black eye patch in profile. Ah, he thought, the notorious Cate Shearley. A woman admired by one and all, or so he'd heard, for her good works with the poor and her skilful command of shotgun diplomacy. He'd heard her name bandied around the goldfields so often it was as if every miner in Ballarat knew her personally.

'What a woman she must be,' he murmured. He couldn't wait to be introduced, as he surely would be eventually. After all, he mused, I am her paying guest, am I not?

The lights dimmed and he resumed his seat. The second act took the same form as Act I; the Master of Ceremonies, a kilted dwarf named Andrew Arbuthnot McCrae, walked on stage to introduce the first performer, but before doing so he offered a poem of his own creation which John believed to be the worst verse he'd ever heard. McCrae was rewarded by a hail of abuse, but continued undaunted to introduce The Amazing Abdul the Snake Charmer, who would attempt, the dwarf said, to entice a cobra from a wicker basket by playing a flute. After several painfully unmusical minutes and with definite unrest from the audience, Abdul reached in and pulled a fat snake from the basket, displayed it triumphantly to the crowd, then let it wind itself around his body where, so it appeared to John, it promptly fell asleep.

'That's not a cobra,' a voice called from the auditorium, 'it's a bloody python.'

'Yeah,' another called. 'He won't hurt ya, he's not even poisonous. Ya oughta get yourself an eastern brown, or a tiger!'

The audience of mostly inebriated miners were all too familiar with poisonous snakes, having travelled the Australian bush in search of minerals, and they soon let their anger be known. 'Get off' seemed to be the most common advice, but there were smatterings of 'You're a fake' to 'My old woman's got a worse bite than that'd have'. And one drunken retort from the front row, 'Thommo's todger is more dangerous than that snake', which brought howls of derisive laughter, especially from the ladies.

Eventually the kilted Scottish dwarf emerged and, after calming the audience down, waved on a pair of contortionists, identical blondes billed as Anna and Lanna the Twisting Teutonic Teenage Twins. The miners fell silent, admiring the nubile young women as they contorted into every possible position, igniting the men's sexual imagination with every turn. But it quickly deteriorated into catcalling and sexually explicit recommendations and one particularly specific suggestion which threw the house into an uproar.

John had seen and heard enough and was about to leave when a man walked onto the stage unannounced, sat at the piano and began to play.

As the sound of piano filled the auditorium, Cate left her seat and stood at the side of the audience to watch the reaction. Wolfgang's playing, it seemed to her, got better with each performance. The audience realised they were in the presence of real talent, a virtuoso no less, and they fell silent, letting the music wash over them. Wolfie's playing intrigued them at first, Cate could tell by their expressions, but the faces changed as the music built. Many exchanged glances, smiling and nodding in agreement, while others merely stared at the performer now holding them captive.

Wait for it, Cate wanted to shout, wait for one more minute. Then it came on the air, a faint high-pitched voice that floated ethereally through the packed hall, right up to the rafters and across heads to the far wall. Cate watched as the frowns of annoyance, at the piano being interrupted, turned to expressions of sheer delight. Lou-shi entered from the prompter's corner to be greeted by murmurs of wonder.

Old Feng's outdone himself this time, Cate decided.

The outfit Lou-shi wore was magnificent. It was the costume, Cate had been informed, of the title role in *The Virtuous Maiden of Swatow*, a famous opera and one of the Chinese Emperor's favourites. Apparently, the women of Swatow in China were renowned for their exceptional beauty and the clothing therefore had to be spectacular. Lou-shi wore the finest gold-embroidered silk trousers and long shirt, predominantly sky-blue but with overlays of orange, pink and purple, intended to match the colours of the setting sun. Her face was perfection, a white base under rouged cheeks, orange forehead, black eyebrows and eyes painted so vividly they demanded the audience gasp in admiration. On top of her head she wore the ultimate operatic creation, a jewelled headpiece so glorious in design it brought sighs of wonder and awe. Made up of glass beads in every colour of the rainbow meant to represent fabulous gems, a silver tiara fringed with red-tasselled lace, the overall effect was one of celestial magnificence.

Soon came the closing of eyes as Lou-shi's voice and Wolfie's music, in that brilliant mixture of East and West, seized the audience and took them on a journey every single one of them would later describe differently. Some thought of home, some of friends or lost lovers, while the lucky, imaginative few felt they'd gone to heaven and back.

When the performance came to its abrupt conclusion, an eerie silence hung over the room for several seconds before the audience came back from their journeys to rise as one, cheering and whistling. Many threw coins in appreciation, while one enchanted customer threw a small bag of gold dust which was caught by Old Feng, who had rushed on stage to collect the coins. Lou-shi, as Michiko, Japan's Madame Vestris, and her German accompanist Wolfgang Bremmer, took bow after bow until Wolfie grasped Lou-shi by the hand for a final curtsey, then the curtain closed for the last time.

They stood side by side for several moments unable to move, staring at the curtain, as the realisation dawned that they had shared something wonderful, that moment experienced by very few performers when a level of artistry is reached that brings with it a complete loss of self.

'You were brilliant, unworldly, incandescent,' Wolfie exclaimed. 'I have never heard the human voice used to such effect, ever before.'

'Your music inspired me,' Lou-shi replied. Never in

her life had she experienced the musical ecstasy she'd just shared with Wolfgang Bremmer. The combination of his composition and her voice had them both lost in that world of perfect performance so rarely experienced, even by the greatest artists.

'You truly are a nightingale.'

'Shit in the rice bowl!' Feng exclaimed. He was on his hands and knees behind them still collecting the coins. *'Don't let him call you that! The Emperor of China calls you that! He'll kill us if he finds out!'*

'Isn't that already his intention?'

'What did he say?' Wolfgang asked.

'He said you are the greatest piano player in the world.'

'I did not!' Feng hissed from right behind her, then waved the little bag of gold between their noses. *'If we go to the goldfields, everyone will throw these at you. We will become richer than the Ming emperors.'*

'He said, half of that,' she indicated the bag to Wolfgang, 'is yours, as well as half of the coins.'

'Fifty percent? Fifty percent!' Feng was now beside himself. *'Are you mad? He's just a dog-fucking musician! Tell him I hope he has many retarded children, all girls, and they bring about his financial ruin.'*

'That is very generous of him.' Wolfgang smiled at the old Chinese man. 'Thank you very much, Mister Feng.' He turned again to Lou-shi. 'It is a pity he doesn't speak English; perhaps you'd better teach me Chinese.'

'He does speak English,' she replied, looking directly at Feng. 'It is just that Master Feng is such a humble man he believes his poor pronunciation of the language would offend Western ears.'

'I am German. I too have an accent when I speak English, Mister Feng.'

Feng, with both huge gown pockets stuffed with coins, began heading into the wings. *'Tell the semen-drinking runt of a sow's litter I don't care if he stutters in Russian!'* he called back over his shoulder. *'And twenty percent is all he is going to get!'*

'Wolfie!' The voice came from backstage, then Cate Shearley burst from the wings, her hands clasped over her heart. 'My God, Wolfie, that was extraordinary!'

'Thank you, Cate.'

'I mean it.' She took his hand in hers and shook it furiously. 'You created something special tonight.' Then she turned to Lou-shi. 'And you, my little Miss Japan, I have not heard the likes of your singing outside Covent Garden; even the critics at La Scala would fall at your feet. I was transported.' She hugged them both to her. 'Together you make magic!'

'And they also make much money.' During Cate's rush of jubilation Feng had walked back on stage and now stood next to her.

'They do indeed, Mister Feng.' Cate eyed the old man suspiciously. What are you up to now, you old schemer? she thought.

'You know how much money they would make in Ballarat?'

Cate's business brain switched on immediately. She paused momentarily, staring down her nose at him for effect. 'A fortune, I would imagine, Mister Feng,' she said evenly and narrowed her eyes. 'But do you know how much it would cost me to get them there?'

'Not exactly, but I think maybe we sit down and discuss, yes. We come up with budget that would ensure much profit.'

What a brilliant idea, she thought, as the possibilities of such an operation started spinning through her mind. Logistics, security, performers, the pitfalls were many, not least the gold miners themselves; full of money and drink, they would be a nightmare to control. It would be a major undertaking, but the margin for profit was crystal clear, providing nothing went wrong from within the company.

She looked at Wolfgang. 'Would you tour the goldfields, Wolfie?' Cate asked him directly. 'Or should I say, would you be *capable* of touring the goldfields?'

Wolfie looked at Lou-shi before answering. 'Of course I would. If this girl goes I'll go.' He patted Lou-shi on the back. 'Her voice is unique.'

'You'd have to stay off the drink. It would be vital that you did, or the tour would fail.'

'Have no concern on that score, madam.'

'Reduce cast,' Feng said to Cate. 'Your acts are terrible. I would not let them to perform in front of chickens.'

'Nor I, Mister Feng,' Cate said. 'Chickens have no money.' She'd had enough of business for the night. 'But, no more of this for now, two shows again tomorrow night, so why don't we discuss this on Sunday morning? Right now I'm off to celebrate the best show we've produced yet.' She looked at the German. 'Would you care to join me for dinner, Wolfie?'

'No thank you, Cate,' he declined. 'I'm tired. I will go home to bed.'

'Right.' Cate clapped her hands. 'I'm off then. Goodnight to you all. And, Mister Feng,' she pointed at the old man, 'don't forget to lock up.'

It took her ten minutes to cross Collins Street. Customers, who'd seen the show and were now in the street drinking and carousing, stopped her one after another to offer their congratulations. All the while her mind was racing. Of course, a tour of the goldfields would yield a bloody fortune! Why didn't I think of it? she asked herself. Miners starved for entertainment, well, good entertainment at least. She knew the shows that went out to Ballarat and Bendigo were second-rate at best. A top-class act like Wolfgang and Lou-shi would draw the crowds like magnets draw iron. There'd be virtually no advertising required – just Cate Shearley's Variety Show on a large banner would suffice; word of mouth had already made her acts famous throughout the colony. Finally, she pushed her way through the crowd in front of the main doors and almost fell into the lobby.

'Ma'am,' Dorothy called from the desk. 'Ma'am, could I have your assistance please, just for one moment?'

'What is it, Dorothy?' Cate crossed the crowded lobby and walked behind the desk.

'We're running out of cash, ma'am,' the girl explained as she attended to a couple wanting a late supper. 'All of the miners have been dumping dust on me for cash and we're really short of the ready stuff.'

'I've got some in my safe,' Cate assured her and headed for the office. 'Give me a minute.'

As he came down the stairs, John Bailleau saw the striking blonde fleetingly, as she disappeared into the office behind reception. She certainly appears to be a beauty, he thought again, as he crossed the lobby and entered the dining room.

'Mister Bailleau,' the waiter said, 'this way to your table, sir. And I'm to tell you from Dorothy that all the selections you made for supper have been garnered by Cook and prepared as you requested.'

'Excellent.' John sat. He was hungry he decided. He'd planned the big meal intending to indulge himself, but after the show he'd momentarily lost his appetite until that glimpse of Cate Shearley disappearing into the office had sharpened his desire in more ways than one. She was a damned fine-looking woman judging from the limited glimpses he'd had of her. Perhaps she would dine at some stage and he would be able to study her more closely. I wonder why the eye patch? he mused. Had she lost the eye, or was it only an injury, or perhaps an infection? He was intrigued. He saw her name printed on the menu and found himself reading it over and over, then the waiter arrived with his first course.

'Have you seen Amos?' Cate asked as she placed a tin of cash in front of Dorothy.

'No, ma'am, I haven't seen him all evening.'

'Damn him,' Cate muttered as she walked towards the dining room's double archway. It was typical of him to disappear just when the hotel was at its busiest. She entered the dining room and looked about but there was no sign of him. 'Damn him,' she cursed softly and turned back to the lobby. She'd try his room.

John Bailleau saw her enter the room and stand erect, hands on gorgeous hips and look to her left. The patch over her right eye is very cavalier, he thought; it makes her even more attractive. Then she turned her head to the right and revealed her left profile. John's heart leapt into his mouth. He was unable to speak. He dropped his knife and fork and stood up, but she had turned and was walking out of the room. It can't be, he thought. It can't be. He reached the archway and saw her halfway up the stairs.

'Tess!' he yelled. 'Tessa!'

She stopped on the stairway, unable to turn.

'Theresa!' John called even louder, and this time he gained the attention of all those in the lobby. Twenty or more people, standing and seated, all stared at the man and then at Cate Shearley frozen on the stairs.

She turned, and as they looked at each other the years fell away. Finally, she smiled and walked slowly down the stairs to meet him.

'You have the wrong name, sir,' she said loudly.

'But I have the right girl, do I not?'

'Oh, yes,' she walked into his open arms, 'you have the right girl.'

The kiss was full and long, so long those in the lobby began to clap and cheer, some out of embarrassment, others at the sheer spontaneity of a love obviously rediscovered.

Dorothy witnessed the whole display from behind the desk and her romantic dreams of love and marriage, like a sunset's glow, faded to twilight.

CHAPTER NINE

Melbourne, winter 1854

'Amos! Amos!' Jack yelled as he ran through the hotel searching for his mother's old retainer. 'Uncle Amos!' he called again as he burst into the kitchen and found the avuncular black man seated at the kitchen table with Cook.

'Noise, noise, lad!' Amos scowled. 'Never was there such a noisome boy! Wouldn't you agree, Maude?'

'I most certainly would, Mister Amos.' Like everyone else, Cook had no idea of Amos's surname; it had never been mentioned. 'Why all the screaming, Master Jack?'

'Mister Bailleau's in bed with my ma!'

'Oh, dear.' Cook placed her hand over her mouth and looked to Amos.

'And just how do you know that, Jack?' Amos raised his eyebrows and lowered his chin to stare at the boy over the rim of his glasses, trying to regain the air of authority that had, for once, deserted him.

'Well, I knocked five times, Amos, but Ma didn't answer so I crept in to see her.' He looked away, red-faced. 'I like watching her sleep,' he admitted softly.

'And just what did you see?'

'They were wrapped up together, just like those people in your photo book.'

'Oh, dear!' It was a squeak from Cook.

'And they were asleep, yes?' Amos wished devoutly he was right.

'Yes,' came the reply.

'Thank God for that,' Cook sighed.

'But what's he doing in my ma's bed?'

'Ah, there you are, Jack!' Cate declared as she rushed into the kitchen wrapped in a robe, her honey-blonde tresses a magnificent mess. 'I need to explain something to you.' Then, at the sight of Cook and Amos, she stopped mid-stride and her face reddened.

Amos coughed dramatically to draw her attention. 'I was just about to tell young Jack that, unbeknown to you, your old friend,' he paused for emphasis, 'your old friend John Bailleau arrived to find the hotel booked out and you kindly allowed him to share your accommodation.'

'That's right!' Cate clutched at the excuse, thin as rice paper though it was. 'That's exactly right, thank you, Amos.'

Amos had been indifferent at first when Dorothy had relayed to him that morning the story of Cate's unqualified surrender to John Bailleau in front of a packed lobby, but the more he'd turned the facts over in his mind, the more disturbed he'd become. Since arriving from California Cate had gone from success to success, as she'd done in both New York and San Francisco, before she'd fallen from grace, and both times it had been a man who'd brought her low. First it was his former employer Solomon Shadkun, who died suddenly and broke her heart, then it had been the big Frenchman Jean-Baptiste Le Pen who'd tried to kill her. Was man number three now on the horizon?

'You've never told me about any old friends, Ma. I didn't think you had any old friends, except for Amos.'

'Well I have,' Cate said. 'Mister Farrington is a very old friend indeed.'

'Don't you mean Mister Bailleau?' Cook said archly.

'Yes, of course!' Cate snapped. 'Mister Bailleau, how silly of me.' She looked at Amos in desperation.

For Amos the bells suddenly rang sweet and clear. John Farrington, her soldier boy from London. That's all they needed, he thought, an ex-lover and a refined and damned handsome man too, if Dorothy was to be believed. Cate had told him of John Farrington one night when she'd had too much to drink, which was unlike her, and momentarily dropped her guard.

'Farrington!' Amos declared. 'You got dat dere name on yo' brain, Mistress Cate,' he said in his plantation accent. 'Dat ol' bank manager you done borrowed da money of'n. Yo' all got to stop worryin' 'bout him, now.'

'Da' sure is right Uncle Amos,' Jack mimicked. Every time Amos wanted the boy to laugh he used the plantation voice and over the years it had become their personal game. 'Y'all got to stop dat dere frettin', Miss Cate, or yo' gonna fall down daid wid dat worryin'. So y'all will, yes'm'.'

'Y'all dun paid back all da money y' owes him, Mistress Cate,' Amos continued the game.

'That's enough!' Cate snapped with some severity, but her eyes thanked the old man. God, she thought, what would I do without you, Amos? 'You know what I think of that kind of plantation chatter.' She turned to Jack. 'Have you had breakfast?'

'He ate enough for three,' Cook said, getting up from the table.

'What about your schoolwork?'

'Not yet.' The boy shook his head.

'Then you better get on with it, don't you think?'

'Yes, Mother,' Jack answered smartly and seized the opportunity to flee.

When she turned back to the others, Cook was busy at the stove, but Amos stared at her unblinking.

'It's none of your business.' The warning in her voice was obvious.

'I don't want it to be.' Amos raised his palms defensively. 'But I would ask you to remember your history in these matters. New York? San Fran? Not good.'

'This time it's different,' she said as Amos gave a rueful smile. 'You know it is, Amos.'

'If you say it is, then it's fine with me.' He shrugged.

'Good.' Cate turned on her heel and left.

It was midday before Cate and John were able to get away from the Golden Sheaf. They'd planned to escape early, as they lay sated in Cate's bed the night before, but Mister Feng had been waiting for her to appear. John had hired a trap and a fine bay gelding to pull it and they'd set off down Swanston Street and over the Lennox Bridge onto St Kilda Road. And now they sat on a wooden seat overlooking St Kilda Beach and Port Phillip Bay. Anchored ships, numbered in their hundreds, dotted the bay, their masts resembling the naked tree trunks of a forest in winter.

'You didn't need to hire the trap,' Cate said. 'The Premier Omnibus Company runs a coach service twice a day from the Bull & Mouth Hotel in Bourke Street right down here to the Esplanade. It only costs a shilling each way.'

'You were so busy we would have missed the morning coach service,' John replied as he stubbed a short cigar out in the sand with the sole of his riding boot. 'Besides,' he continued, 'you have to admit the tiny trap and gelding is a far more comfortable option than those coaches. They are not made for comfort – a bit hard on the bottom for my liking.'

'I wouldn't have minded.'

'The truth is I wanted you on your own.'

'Didn't you have me on my own enough last night?' Cate said suggestively.

'I could have you on your own every night, Theresa Lacey.'

'Cate,' she retorted. 'Cate Shearley is my name.'

'Oh, come on,' he scoffed. 'It's me, John, remember? We both know it's an anagram of Theresa Lacey. It came to me this morning. I remembered the anagram game we used to play in London. Jumble, was it not?'

'Yes, that's right.'

'When I read your name on the dining room bill of fare last night, something began jiggling my memory, but then I saw you in the flesh and the thought disappeared, Tess, and I –'

'Cate!' she interrupted. 'My name is Cate. You must forget the name Theresa Lacey. That woman is no more; she disappeared from the face of the earth when I gave up the game in London. You must never call me anything but Cate, John.'

'Certainly. If that is your wish.'

'It is. It is the way it must be, for my sake and my son's. And besides,' she punched him on the shoulder, 'John *Bailleau! You've changed yours too!*'

'Fair play, my love.' He smiled at her. 'You've got me there.'

They walked on in silence for several minutes taking in the air and the magnificent vista that was Port Phillip Bay in late August with spring barely a week away. Not a cloud sat in the sky and the sun on the water was dazzling, but neither noticed; they remained deep in thought and their thoughts were very similar – London, a decade earlier.

'Tell me, Cate, whatever happened to your friend, Theresa Lacey?' John said with a grin. 'I'm sorry, I can't help but inquire. I returned to London from India and tried to find her, I owed her money, but she had indeed disappeared from the face of the earth, as you put it.'

'I never knew her very well myself,' Cate joined in the game, grateful of his acquiescence. 'I heard she was double-crossed by her accountant, a Mister Terence Charles, who robbed her of all she had . . .'

'Her houses?' John interrupted. 'She had two houses.'

'Gone, both of them,' she said. 'Her bank accounts too.'

'The swine! Why didn't she go to the authorities?'

'Ha!' she snorted. 'The authorities were in on it.'

'Oh, dear. What about her influential friends? Her wealthy admirers, her statesmen and various admirals and generals, couldn't they help?'

'Theresa found herself without means and very quickly *persona non grata*, but that's the way London is, isn't it?'

'It is indeed, sadly. It must have been a very painful time for her.'

'Yes, I'm sure it must have been.'

'Do you know how she got to San Francisco?'

'I did hear something,' Cate said as they arrived at their transport, 'but I can't for the life of me remember what it was.'

'Never mind,' John said as he helped her into the trap. 'I'm sure it will come back to you at some stage.'

'I'm sure it will.' Cate beamed at him as he climbed in beside her. 'Now get me back to the Golden Sheaf. Sunday evening is a nightmare, especially in the dining room. I must be there to supervise; Dorothy's taken the night off.'

'Your wish is my command, Cate Shearley!' John flicked the gelding's hindquarters, and the horse, only too happy to be on the move again, set off at a trot up St Kilda Road.

A combination of afternoon sun, the clip-clop of the horse's hooves and the rhythmic movement of the trap brought about a companionable silence between them and it was a silence for which Cate was particularly grateful. The past twenty-four hours had seen her world turned upside down. Never in a million years would she have dreamed of meeting John Farrington again, nor would she have thought her feelings would be precisely those she had felt in London.

I fell into his embrace, she thought, mindlessly, passionately, without giving any consideration to my circumstances, or indeed his. What if he's married? Does he have children? The thoughts had not occurred to her, in her haste to get him into bed. 'Where's your bedroom?' he'd asked when that first kiss had broken. 'Upstairs,' she'd answered and he'd whisked her into his arms and carried her upstairs to the applause of the lobby crowd.

Her face flushed red at the memory of her wantonness. Over a decade had disappeared in an instant and they'd been teenagers again in her little house in Green Street, behind London Hospital off Whitechapel Road. There'd been no conversation between them, no 'how are you', or 'where have you been'; they'd made love countless times until sleep had finally overwhelmed them.

In the morning a thousand questions had filled her brain, but before she could ask even one, Jack had walked in on them. The look on her son's face had shocked her and she'd taken off after him, desperate to explain. But what will I tell him? she'd asked herself as she'd chased him all the way to the kitchen. Fortunately, Amos had been there and got her off the hook, temporarily at least, but Jack was a smart kid and eventually she would have to sit him down and talk.

Talk! Talk! Her mind screamed the word. Talk about what? You spent a shameless night in bed with an old lover and that was all it was, a shameless night in bed. But then there's tonight? All right, two shameless nights! And that will be it! You already want it to be much more though, don't you, Tess? *Cate!* Cate, damn it! Your name is Cate Shearley. You're not that young girl in London anymore. You're a business woman, and a mother with a young son. What's the matter with you? Get John Farrington out of your system and get on with your life.

CHAPTER TEN

Melbourne, winter 1854

A most bizarre series of events was how Stupid Ho described the happenings that led him to find Master Feng and Lou-shi.

'I discovered a fortune in gold, but was robbed of it on the road to Sydney,' he wailed in Cantonese as Lou-shi gave him a cup of jasmine tea to sip.

All three were seated at the table in the 'Chinese Quarter', as Cate had christened their two-room accommodation at the rear of the courtyard.

'How unfortunate,' Feng replied with a disbelieving glance at Lou-shi. *'To be so rich and then so poor again in an instant is indeed bad luck. Tell me, why did you not put your money in a bank, Stupid? My friend Hugh E Long tells me that is what the See Yap Society of Ballarat recommends to Chinese miners who strike gold.'*

'The See Yap Society is just another triad.'

'I have been told,' Feng said, *'the See Yap Society is a very worthwhile organisation that looks after all the Chinese on the goldfields, true or not true, aaah?'* He sang the question mark in true Cantonese fashion.

'Not true!' Stupid replied. *'I would not trust them any more than I would trust the Brothers of the Red Pavilion.'*

'Ah, yes.' Feng glanced again at Lou-shi. *'The Brothers of the Red Pavilion, your friends and comrades, true or not true, ah?'*

'Not true! It was they who robbed me,' Stupid exclaimed.

'No!' Feng gasped with mock horror. *'I cannot believe that.'*

'It is true, Master. They wore masks, but they did not fool me. One of them was wearing my winter coat, which I thought I had lost.'

'So I take it you are penniless, Stupid?' Feng smiled benignly. *'And you have returned to your former family, those who once loved you, until you deserted them . . .'*

'Master Feng!' Lou-shi cried. *'How can you say that to Stupid? He is part of our family.'*

'Confucius said, once a leaf falls from the tree it begins its own journey and can never return to the tree that loved it and even if it ever did, the tree should disown it.'

'You're making that up!' Lou-shi snapped. *'Confucius never said that.'*

'He would have had he known this boy.' Feng waved his pipe at the young man. *'However, Stupid, I will offer you employment again but pay you less money.'*

'You never used to pay me anything,' Stupid replied.

'In that case I'll offer you the same wages and conditions as before.'

'Stop it!' Lou-shi stroked Stupid's arm in a gesture of welcome. *'Welcome back to the family, Stupid, and thank you so much for finding a fortune in gold to support us, even though you were robbed by your friends and you are again poor.'*

'Thank you, Lou-shi.'

'We are making good money and,' she glared at Feng, *'we will share our good fortune with you, won't we, Master?'*

'You may resume your old position as stage manager.' Feng nodded. *'But there will be added responsibilities you will have to accept on a daily basis.'*

'Thank you, Master Feng.' Stupid bowed his head.

'So, how did you find us?' Lou-shi was eager to know.

'I walked to Melbourne and returned to Canvas Town but could not find you, so I began to search the streets and it was then I saw my stolen winter coat in Bourke Street, being worn by another of the Brotherhood of the Red Pavilion.' He frowned. *'They must share its use.'*

Feng looked again at Lou-shi and shook his head sadly.

'His birth was a rare event indeed,' he muttered. *'Let us pray there are no more like him.'*

'Go on, Stupid,' Lou-shi urged.

'I followed my coat up into Collins Street and challenged the wearer to a fight.'

'By all the gods!' Lou-shi gasped.

'We were about to exchange blows when I heard you singing so I let him keep the coat and I waited outside the building opposite until you appeared.'

'Hello, my name is Jack.' Young Shearley joined the group, extending his hand to Stupid Ho.

'How do you do, I'm Stupid,' he replied, astonished at being spoken to in Cantonese by a foreign boy.

Jack looked at Lou-shi, perplexed.

Lou-shi, seeing the boy's distress, reverted to English. 'His name is Stupid Ho. Master Feng named him Stupid because he is smart.'

'Oh.' Jack seemed none the wiser.

'But you must not call him Stupid when you are speaking English or people will think you are being rude. You must always call him *Yue Chun*.'

'But *yue chun* means stupid, doesn't it?'

'Yes, but in Chinese it is all right to call him *Yue Chun*.'

'At least he's only got one name, even if it is *Yue Chun*,' Jack said. 'I have to call you China,' he turned to Lou-shi, 'or Michiko the Japanese Lady. My name is John but everyone calls me Jack. Uncle Amos told me his real name is Ngongo and his pa came from Africa, but Ma calls him Amos. My mother's name is really Theresa Lacey, but everyone calls her Cate Shearley, and even John Bailleau is called Farrington, I think, at least that's what Ma let slip. Name-changing can cause a lot of trouble.'

'If you change your name, history will forget you,' Feng offered. *'You will be safe from accusations of wrongdoing, but you will be unable to claim your achievements or successes. To change your name is a lie, but if you are in danger, it is a lie worth telling.'* He bowed in Jack's direction. *'Such is my philosophy.'*

Jack nodded, not having understood a word of the high-speed Cantonese. 'Lou-shi, you promised to teach me how to somersault in mid-air.'

'I did too.' The girl smiled at his little-boy enthusiasm. 'Let's go over to the theatre and practise on the stage mats. The stone flagging here is too dangerous.'

Upstairs in the master suite, Cate awoke and immediately reached for John, but he was not there. Perhaps it is for the best, she thought. Her appetite for the man was insatiable.

'Oh, God,' she sighed. 'Damn you, John Farrington.'

A look at her clock on the dresser told her it was ten o'clock and another glance at the chair by the bed revealed John's clothes were gone.

'What am I to do?' she asked herself. Even the simple act of taking her eye patch and putting it on made her think of him.

The first night they'd made love, she had fought with him as he'd tried to remove the patch, but he'd been insistent and she allowed him to see her closed right eye socket. When he'd finished his inspection he declared that the imperfection made her even more beautiful and he kissed the sealed eye. The simple gesture and the fact he'd not asked her how she sustained the injury had cemented his place in her heart forever.

She'd fallen in love with John Farrington in London. She remembered the precise moment vividly. She'd told him a joke or an idiotic story about one of her gentlemen friends and he'd laughed out loud; she'd watched his face light up with the joy of life and his eyes had crinkled and a tear had run down his cheek. That was the moment. Her breath had caught in her throat and her stomach spun like a wheel. Theresa Lacey, who at nineteen saw herself as a self-sufficient and experienced young woman of the world, with practically every wealthy man in London worshipping at her feet, folded and fell in love like a schoolgirl.

'With a seventeen-year-old boy,' she exclaimed. And here it is a decade on and it's happened again! She got out of bed and began to dress.

What am I to do? He's a rover, a man of the world with no intention of settling down with me or any other woman. He's also an ex-soldier, still with the blood lust in his eyes. She'd seen that look many times over the years; it revealed something in soldiers that never truly left them. John would kill if necessary and he would do it without mercy, she had no doubt. He was an adventurer with that inexplicable need to roam the earth, in search of what, he would never know until he found it.

I've got to get rid of him, she decided as she finished dressing. I've got to get him out of my bed and gone from Melbourne in order for me to stabilise my life and recover my common sense.

The solution to her problem occurred as she brushed her hair. She dropped the brush immediately and headed out in search of none other than Mister Feng.

'Where do you think you're going, young man?' Cate said as she stepped through the kitchen door into the courtyard and caught sight of Jack and Lou-shi heading off towards the side lane.

'I'm going to help Lou-shi in the theatre, Mother.'

'Are you just?' Jack never called her Mother unless he was in trouble. She looked at Lou-shi, who was nodding just a little too furiously. 'What are you up to?' She tried the suspicious tone.

'Nothing, Ma.'

'Have you done your chores?' Mistress tone.

'Yes, Ma.'

'So what are you going to help with?' Cate arched her left eyebrow.

'We're going to move the wing flats on the O P side.'

'Really?' He's learning more about theatre every day, she thought.

'Yeah, you know, the wing flats, those wooden flats with the trees painted on them that Lou-shi exits behind when she somersaults off stage on the Opposite Prompt side.' His mother was staring at him. 'Opposite Prompt is to the actor's right when he is facing the audience, Ma,' he added, thinking he needed to explain.

'I know where O P is!' Cate declared indignantly. 'It's opposite the Prompt side,' she added unnecessarily and felt utterly foolish.

'Well, Lou-shi sometimes hits them as she exits.'

'Very well,' Cate conceded defeat. 'You'd better go and help her. But make sure you're back here for lunch.'

'Right, Ma.' Jack and Lou-shi disappeared down the side of the hotel laughing at something they obviously found hilarious.

As she crossed the courtyard to the Chinese Quarter, Rani, her head extended out over the stable half-door, snorted a good morning.

'And good morning to you, beautiful,' Cate called.

'Were you talking to me?' John's head appeared beside that of the horse.

'No I was not,' Cate smiled and waved, 'but I'll need to talk to you later, over lunch.' Then she disappeared inside Mister Feng's quarters.

'Hello?' she said as she caught sight of Stupid Ho seated at the table with Feng. 'And who might this be, Mister Feng?'

'Mistress Shearley!' Feng flew up from his seat, as did a startled Stupid. 'This is Stupid.'

'What's stupid?'

'Nothing.'

'You said, this is stupid?'

'Aaaiiiyyaaahh,' the old man groaned, wishing for the second time that day he had never called the boy Stupid. But then, that had been in China where everybody understood the humour of it. How was I to know I would one day have to explain it to foreign barbarians? 'Forgive please, Mistress Shearley, this young man is *Yue Chun,* he has been member of opera company since he was a small child.'

'Like Lou-shi?'

'That is correct,' Feng sighed.

'How do you do, *Yue Chun*?' Cate extended her hand and Stupid shook it.

'His English no good, but very experienced stage manager.'

'That's excellent! Couldn't be better,' she paused, 'unless of course an actor asks him for a line prompt. That could prove awkward. But never mind that for now, sit down.' Cate sat at the table, indicating the men should do likewise. 'I have a proposition for you, Mister Feng.'

'I have a proposition for you, Mister Bailleau.'

'Is that so, Mistress Shearley?'

'They were seated in the dining room for the late session at a table for two next to the front windows. John took her hand, but Cate withdrew it.

'Oh,' John was surprised. 'You really do have a proposition for me.'

'We can't go on as we've been doing, John.' She raised her hands defensively as he started to interrupt. 'I'm a businesswoman and a mother and I have been neglecting both duties for the last week.'

'Oh, dear, this is serious.'

'Hear me out, please? Apart from our trip to St Kilda, we've spent the last week in bed . . .'

'And it's been wonderful . . .'

'Please,' she stopped him, 'let me finish. I cannot allow it to go on any longer. Dorothy is running the hotel on her own and I can sense resentment in her, and Amos for that matter. And as for Jack, God love him, he's been good, but he's only just eleven years old and he is struggling to understand what is going on.'

'I know.'

They fell silent as the waiter placed bowls of soup on the table.

Cate waited until he'd gone. 'And I don't understand what's going on either.'

'You mean between us?'

'Yes.' She sipped her wine and after placing the glass on the table dabbed the corners of her mouth with a napkin. 'But that's not what I want to discuss at the moment. As I said I have a proposition for you that will keep you busy and could, in a matter of two or three months, make us both a tidy amount of money.'

'I'm all ears.' John picked up his spoon and commenced eating.

'I've made an arrangement with Mister Feng to tour the show to the goldfields and I want you to be tour manager.'

'Ha,' John scoffed, 'I know absolutely nothing about the theatre.'

'I'm not asking you to go on stage,' she said with just a hint of exasperation.

'A little more information if you please?'

'You were an officer in the army. You know how to organise the movement, equipment and accommodation of troops, don't you?'

'Of course.' John put his spoon down and took a sip of wine. He was intrigued. 'Go on.'

'Tour management is exactly the same thing, except when you arrive at the front line you don't shoot people, you entertain them.'

'It sounds like a lot of hard work.'

'Which would do you good! And it might slow you down a bit in other areas, which would take the weight off me – no pun intended.'

'All right,' he laughed. 'Let's talk tactics, let's talk war.'

The food went untouched as the two discussed the tour in detail. Tents would be required, wagons, horses, food, the list went on. Cate ordered paper and pen from the desk and they set to it in earnest.

'Mister Feng will provide you with a list of what he thinks we will need and it will be up to you to acquire it.' Cate emptied her glass and waved for another bottle of wine. 'Thirsty work this touring business, isn't it?' She said it with all the sincerity of a drunkard, yet with the style and sparkle of a courtesan.

John smiled at her. What a magnificent woman she is, he thought. She was as beautiful as she'd been when a young woman in London. Even the eye patch did not distract from her allure; if anything it enhanced it, giving her an exotic, pirate-on-the-high-seas look.

'And I have a new stage manager,' she announced.

'Sorry?' Her voice brought him back to the present.

'A new stage manager. He is Chinese and he doesn't speak English. His name is Yue Chun.'

'He *doesn't* speak *English*?'

'He's part of Feng's family, apparently.' Cate shrugged. 'He comes with the deal I made and, so I'm told by Feng, there's nothing much he doesn't know about the stage.'

'But unfortunately he can't convey it in English.' John shook his head. 'So what's the point?'

'The point is he's free labour, which means one less labourer you'll have to hire.'

John leaned back in his chair and sipped his wine. 'Just how much is this theatrical venture going to cost you?'

Cate sniffed and looked around the room for a moment. John read it as a sign of hesitancy, but then he saw the gleam of battle in her eyes as she leaned forward over the table. 'About two thousand pounds,' she whispered.

John leaned forward now too and they faced each other, close up. 'And Mister Feng will contribute the same, I take it?' he said softly.

'No.' Her reply was so quiet he barely heard it.

'No?' John was incredulous. 'Just what sort of deal have you struck with the old villain? Because that's what he is you know, an old villain.'

'There are a few things you do not know . . .' Cate began.

'Like China the Circus Boy is actually a girl . . .'

'How do you know that?' Cate was shocked. They'd been so careful not to expose Lou-shi.

'. . . and that she doubles in the second act as the Japanese lady.'

'How did you know that? Did Jack tell you?'

'No, I felt her breasts.'

'What!'

'In the stables. She forced her way past me and they brushed against my arm.' He spread his palms outward in appeal. 'It was all perfectly innocent; she was talking to my horse and I overheard quite a tale.'

'What else do you know?' She eyed him suspiciously.

'I know Feng tried to strike a deal with an Englishman called Hughie Long . . .'

'Did he indeed?' Cate interjected. 'That would be Hu Wei-long, a Chinaman who calls himself Hugh E Long. He struck it rich in '51 on the Ballarat field and now regards himself as a wealthy English businessman, hence the name change.'

'It seems Lou-shi got very angry with Feng and refused to be involved in any deal that did not include you.'

'Well, well, well.' Cate was delighted with the story. 'That's nice to know.'

'You know she's not quite right in the head, don't you?'

'I've suspected it, but most of the time she's perfectly normal.'

'My sister Lily is the same. Well, no she's not, she's worse. She is quite the simpleton, but she has a heart of gold and I adore her.'

'Well you'd better adore Lou-shi too, because she's the secret to the deal. She pulls the crowds, she does the double act and I believed she was completely controlled by Feng. Now reflecting on the conversation I had with him, I thought he struck the deal all too easily.' She grinned at the thought of the little Chinese girl taking her side. 'So it's Lou-shi who rules the roost in the Feng family. Well, what do you know about that?' She slapped the table top.

'So what's the deal?' John said as the waiter filled their wine glasses.

'It's like this,' Cate answered, then paused until the waiter had gone. 'Feng supplies the costumes and all the sets for twenty percent . . .'

'So it's eighty–twenty your way?'

'Yes.'

'You're going to need more than two thousand pounds to fund the tour. With Melbourne prices for all that equipment, it will barely cover your initial outlay.'

'I'll manage.'

'Let me put in two thousand next to yours. Split the risk, split the profit. What do you say?'

'You've got two thousand pounds?' Cate was surprised.

'I have.' John nodded eagerly. 'The Bank of Victoria will confirm that.'

'Oh, John,' she hesitated, 'I don't know.'

'I know those goldfields and I know the miners. The tour could make a fortune and I'd like to be part of it. Come on, Cate, what do you say?'

Noooo! her mind screamed. Don't get in any deeper, Cate. It will just make things worse for you when he finally takes off into the night.

'All right, John,' she heard herself say. 'You've got yourself a deal.'

Two weeks went by in a blur as the Golden Sheaf courtyard filled with carts, drays, horses, packed canvas tents, one enormous tent for use as a performance space if a goldfields theatre was not available, horseshoes, harnesses, crates full of supplies, water containers and much more besides. The caravan – brightly painted, stickered with advertising posters and a billboard atop each wagon announcing the procession as 'Cate Shearley's Travelling Variety Show' – would be a sight to behold.

John had been right regarding the budget, Cate had to admit. She'd paid out close to sixteen hundred pounds so far. As careful as John had been, buying many items second-hand, the outlay had been considerable. The merchants of Melbourne held the citizens to ransom at every turn. Even Cate, who knew every second businessman in the city, was unpleasantly surprised by how ruthless they had been.

The relationship between John and Jack had also surprised her and offered cause for concern. The boy had accompanied John all over Melbourne as he'd put together the caravan and she'd watched as Jack's admiration became hero worship. A father figure, a male to look up to and respect, was what any boy needed, but only if the father figure stayed in the picture, and Cate knew with John that would not be the case.

She had managed to keep John out of her bed so far, but it was proving increasingly difficult to keep him at arms' length. He was an intensely virile man and the strength of her own libido was making the matter even more difficult. He'd followed her into the kitchen pantry the previous morning and pressed her against the wall and she'd been unable to resist. He'd had her, standing up, her back against flour sacks. She'd behaved like a wanton lost in the intensity of her own desire. Thank God Cook had been out of the kitchen on an errand, because once he'd seized her and kissed her throat, she'd been rendered incapable of thought.

'Lesson learned, lass,' she said aloud as she skipped down the main staircase to the lobby, 'keep him out of your pantry.' Or more accurately, she thought, keep him out of your pantalettes! She laughed out loud, but her laughter stopped abruptly when she reached the foot of the stairs. The biggest man she'd ever seen stood at the desk and he appeared to be having an altercation with Dorothy.

'What's the matter?' she asked, eyeing off the giant.

'This man doesn't seem to understand that I cannot give out information about our guests,' Dorothy explained.

'I'll attend to him.' Cate gave the man an officious one-eyed glare. 'You get on with your bookkeeping.'

'Gladly,' Dorothy retorted and headed for the office.

'As my receptionist has informed you, it is not hotel policy to give out information concerning our guests –'

'Now, you'd be the lady John Bailleau be payin' court to, or so I've heard. Am I right?'

The voice boomed around the hotel foyer like distant thunder, but as she looked into the big, bushy, grey-bearded face with the twinkling eyes, Cate could sense only warmth and generosity from the mountain of a man. Whoever he was, he was no enemy of John's.

Before she could make any more inquiries, the giant was

joined by a very handsome man, who tipped his hat to her and smiled.

'Do I have the honour of addressing Mistress Cate Shearley?'

'That's right,' Cate answered the distinctly American voice. Now who's this one? she wondered.

'My name's Kit,' he said. A Bostonian accent, she'd bet on it. 'And this is Rhodesy. We're looking for our comrade-in-life, John Bailleau. We were told he may reside in your establishment.'

So these two are Kit and Mister Rhodes? She nodded slowly at them. 'John has spoken of you both.'

'So he be 'ere then, right?' Rhodesy looked to Kit for confirmation.

'He believes you two are in Bendigo.'

'Hell-oo.' Kit Kittredge's face blossomed into a magnificent beaming smile.

Cate realised he was looking past her shoulder and when she turned, there stood Dorothy, staring in wonder, her bottom jaw practically on the floor, mesmerised by the handsome American, her dreams of marriage and children fully restored.

'So he be 'ere then right, mistress?' Rhodesy turned his attention to Cate.

'Well no, he's not at the moment, but he'll be back within the hour. If you'd care to wait, please take the table by the window and Dorothy will provide you with refreshments.'

'That be mos' kind of you, lass,' Rhodesy replied.

'Dorothy.' There was no reaction from the girl. *'Dorothy!'*

'Yes, ma'am?' The girl came back to reality with a shudder and gave Cate her undivided attention.

'These two gentlemen are friends of Mister Bailleau. You will serve them whatever they wish while they await his return. There will be no charge, the house pays.'

'Yes, ma'am,' Dorothy answered, her eyes now glued again on Kit Kittredge.

'There be no doubt about our John,' Rhodesy's voice rumbled loudly as he lumbered with Kit across to their seats, 'the woman's a true beauty, Kit, a right proper slice of 'eaven, la!'

Kit turned to her, knowing she'd heard the giant and shrugged apologetically. Cate could only shake her head and smile.

'Make sure you look after them, Dot, they're good men.'

'I will, ma'am,' the girl replied breathlessly, 'you can be sure of that.'

'And, Dot,' Cate waggled her index finger at the girl, 'a handsome man can become your worst nightmare.'

'I'm sure I don't know what you mean, ma'am.' Dorothy blushed.

Cate lay awake listening to the three of them talking fifteen to the dozen in the courtyard below her bedroom window. She glanced at the clock on her dresser. Two o'clock, she thought, and they'll be at it until daybreak.

John's delight at finding his friends in the lobby had been heartfelt and had moved her to invite them all to dine. It had been a gay old time with lots of champagne consumed, which had surprised her; she'd assumed they'd drink beer or spirits. They'd regaled her with tales of the goldfields and their journey to Australia aboard the *Maid of Shanghai*. Their deep brotherly affection had been obvious to all in the dining room.

'Shall we adjourn to the lobby, gentlemen?' Cate stood, making any reply to her question unnecessary. The men stood respectfully and all four left the dining room. Cate indicated a table by the window then went to order brandy and cigars.

'You'll have your 'ands full wi' that one, la,' Rhodesy declared as they sat. 'You b'ain't be tellin' 'er what to do, John boy.' He gurgled with amusement, his huge frame shaking. 'You'll get short shrift if'n you do, or a crack around the ears.'

'I must agree with Rhodesy, John, your Cate is a formidable woman, to put it mildly.'

'She has a way about her,' John replied.

'She's got brains, that's what she 'as.' The big man nodded furiously, agreeing with himself. 'Women with brains is marvellous things.'

'Like your Tiny Maloney in Liverpool?' Kit winked at John.

'Aye,' Rhodesy agreed, 'like my Eileen Maloney, a woman who lives in a man's world and she's as tough as any of 'em, and smarter than most.'

'Cate's wealthy, too.' Kit's eyes wandered the elegant foyer and returned to John. 'You could do worse, shipmate.'

'Will you be going back to the fields, gentlemen?' she asked as she joined them. 'Or has the gold fever deserted you?'

'Like we was sayin' at dinner, there be no easy pickin's no more, Mistress,' Rhodesy intoned as the three men sat after Cate indicated John take the seat next to her. 'Especially in Bendigo. Ballarat's still the place, but only if you dig deep, lass. Pan handlin's a thing of the past; you 'ave to be a real miner to find gold now.'

'Rhodesy's right, Cate,' Kit agreed, 'the alluvial gold has been harvested once and for all. Ballarat's having bigger strikes than ever, remarkable finds worth tens of thousands of pounds, "jewellers' shops" they call them, but they're all from deep leads, some as deep as a hundred feet and more.'

'Diggin' down into the earth like a badger b'ain't be natural for a man,' Rhodesy commented, shaking his shaggy bearded head.

'I've no stomach for being underground, I must say,' Kit concurred. 'The very thought of it terrifies me.'

'An' I don' fit down the shafts!' Rhodesy added, trying to make light of what was becoming to him a very boring repeat of the conversation they'd had over dinner, but Kit went on.

'There are more people than ever in Ballarat and when you combine their disappointment at not finding gold with the outrageous price of the miner's licence and the appalling treatment they receive from the police and soldiers, you get discontent.' He looked at John. 'Extreme discontent.'

'Are you saying it's worse than it was when we were there?' John was surprised.

'I thought that things were on the up and up since our new Governor visited the fields?' Cate supervised the arrival of the brandy as she talked. 'I heard he had a love affair with the entire mining population. He's being heralded as a saviour here in Melbourne.'

'It was hardly a love affair,' Kit snorted. 'It was more a quick dance around and it wasn't our dear Lieutenant Governor Hotham who danced, it was his good lady wife.'

'Aye,' Rhodesy nodded. 'Lady Jane 'ad 'em eatin' out of 'er 'and, she did!' All she 'ad to do were walk through the mud in 'er dainty shoes and eat a bit o' damper and every woman on the fields was 'er sister, like.'

'The men too,' the American added. 'Lady Hotham is beautiful woman, fair hair, blue eyes, an English rose if ever I've seen one.'

Kit looked at John and shook his head sadly, before continuing. 'Then, just as his bride had them eating out of her hand, guess what our new Governor did? In an act of *breathless* stupidity, he increased the licence hunts to two a week, "or as many more as it takes", he's supposed to have told Robert Rede, the new Goldfields Commissioner.'

'He be a bad man that Robert Rede,' Rhodesy growled.

'As many as it takes!' John was incredulous.

'Believe me, John,' Kit continued, 'licence hunts have become a daily humiliation. Worse than ever.'

Cate placed her brandy on the table. 'Hotham's situation is desperate, after the disastrous efforts of Governor La Trobe's administration. The colony is in debt to the hilt. Hotham has pledged to restructure the economy. He's promised to take a knife to spending, especially in the public service. He's got to maintain the government coffers with income from somewhere,' she shrugged. 'All he's got are liquor excises and mining fees.'

'The police and the soldiers are worse than ever.' Rhodesy addressed John through a cloud of cigar smoke. 'They be takin' honest people's money and spillin' their blood. There'll be a reckonin' soon, la.'

'Rebellion?' John scoffed. 'I don't think it will ever come to that, my giant friend.'

'He's right, John.' Kit finished his brandy and extinguished his cigar in the ashtray on the table. 'The situation, especially in Ballarat, is deteriorating rapidly.'

'But surely not as Rhodesy's suggesting, to the point of insurrection?'

'There are over one hundred thousand souls out on the western goldfields, who were looking forward to the arrival of the new Governor after suffering the ruinous administration led by Charles La Trobe!' Kit warmed to his theme. 'There are thousands of men out there with wives and children who long to settle permanently in Victoria and take up farming and other worthwhile pursuits.'

'Just as people have done in the other colonies,' Cate said.

'Exactly,' Kit nodded. 'They see a future for their sons and daughters here in Victoria, but can they secure land? No! Most of Victoria is owned by a handful of money-hungry squatters, the squattocracy as they're known, who offer it for sale at prices that exceed the bounds of propriety or reason.'

'That's not quite correct, Kit,' Cate suggested. 'Last year Governor La Trobe approved the sale of over half a million acres across the colony –'

'Yes,' the American interjected, 'but who bought it, Cate? The squattocracy and corrupt public servants, that's who, and the price of an acre of dirt has increased thirty-fold, far beyond the expectation of any working man.'

'It's up to the Legislative Council to sort that out,' Cate said.

'But there's the rub! Many of these land-grabbers are actually members of that very same Legislative Council.'

'You're sounding like a bit of a Chartist to me, old chap,' John said in an off-handed fashion. 'Universal suffrage eh, Kit? Not your cup of tea I'd have thought.'

'I'm an American!' Kit snapped. 'Where I'm from, universal suffrage is an inalienable right. I have not been home for many years, but my country, to quote Francis Scott Key, is "the land of the free and the home of the brave".' He glared at John. 'And that freedom was duly paid for in blood.'

'I'm sorry, my friend.' John suddenly became aware the American was angry. 'I never realised you were quite so politically inclined. Do forgive my flippancy. Your concern for the plight of the miners is noted and admired.'

'It's all right, John.' Kit softened his tone, then shook his head and laughed humourlessly. 'It's not just the plight of the miners.' He paused to gather his thoughts. 'You English are a strange lot, are you not? Australia is three million square miles in area. It's a continent, for God's sake. This Colony of Victoria alone is the size of the United Kingdom and every man here could live on his own fifty acres of land and provide his family and all of his kith and kin with a very healthy and prosperous existence. *Liberté, egalité, fraternité,* as the French espouse so passionately, is entirely possible here. But what do I see? I see the English class system beginning to flourish as it has done since the Norman Invasion. The landowners will become the lords, barons and earls, the Australian aristocracy, the owners of all they survey, the merchants, public servants, magistrates and local government officials will be the middle class, the owners of all they're allowed to survey, and the people who work like dogs to enable the classes above them to exist will remain at the bottom of the social structure, the lowest of the low.'

'But that won't happen, Kit, la,' Rhodesy said forcefully. 'Those men out there on the fields, they can see the light o' paradise right in front of their noses. They can smell freedom an' prosperity an' they won't put up with bein' talked down to, 'specially by those who see 'emselves as better 'n others!'

'He's right,' Kit declared to John. 'My argument precisely. Ballarat's a volcano waiting to explode and one day soon, you mark my words, the miners will take matters into their own hands and insurrection will be the result.'

This remark brought the conversation to an abrupt halt and each man retreated into his own thoughts.

Cate stared at them in turn before standing. 'If you will excuse me, gentlemen, I'm off to bed. Don't get up,' she held her hands out in front of her, 'I bid you all goodnight.' She pecked John on the cheek and left them to their thoughts.

At the top of the stairs she paused and looked down, pleased to see they'd resumed their conversation with Kit, smiling and gesticulating avidly.

Cate had taken turns at feeling happy for the good fortune they'd had to meet and unite as friends, and envious of the relationship they shared. She'd never known real friendship with her own sex. Of course there'd been times back in London when she'd shared heartache and sadness, interspersed with the rare happy moment that even the worst existence can bring, but true friendship with members of her own sex, she'd never really known. Her only friends had ever been men, and one in particular, Solly.

Solly had been a true friend. Solomon Shadkun, the wealthy Jew from Mayfair, had taken her into his house and into his life. When Jack had arrived Solly had arranged a full-time nurse to care for the boy and put Cate to work as he'd promised. She'd worked diligently, learning not only a great deal about Solly's world of commodity trading, but about business in general, until the old man had let her manage his books and even trade occasionally on his behalf.

Then he'd announced he was off to New York City, which he called his hometown, and Cate's hopes had crumbled just when life seemed so rosy. She'd managed to save some money, a goodly sum in fact, but a life outside Solly's world filled her with trepidation.

'What are you weeping for?' he'd asked her the following morning at breakfast. 'Not going!' he'd bellowed when she'd told him. 'Of course you're going! You and our dear Jack, we are a family, are we not?' And before he could continue she'd flown from her seat and thrown her arms around his neck.

'Did you honestly believe I would go off and leave you both behind?' he asked when she'd calmed down and resumed her seat. 'You and little Jack mean the world to me.' He shook his head then frowned at her. 'You're my daughter as far as I am concerned and Jack is my grandchild,' he said. 'I won't have it any other way.' He picked up his knife and fork. 'You'll love New York.'

And indeed she had loved the city at the bottom of Manhattan Island. Solly owned a three-storey house with a brownstone façade on 14th Street just off the Broadway, ruled and run by his black butler and confidant Amos. The ensuing three years had been happy ones for her. She'd worked hard for Solly, sometimes toiling late into the night on his financial books and ledgers, and she'd overseen at various times the management of his Grand Hotel on Broadway. But she always found ample time to spend with Jack, and their Sunday morning walks in the park with Solly and Amos were her favourite occasions.

Theatre, in all its various forms, flourished in New York and Cate had found herself caught up in a whirlwind of local productions and grand shows imported from Europe. She had led the life of a princess, wanting for nothing. Then in 1847 Solly had died, just like that, peacefully in his sleep, and Cate's world had collapsed.

She looked at the clock, three am and Rhodesy's attempt at whispering had to be keeping half of Melbourne awake. She got out of bed and opened the window, causing all three men to look up.

'Ah, what light from yonder window breaks . . .' John slurred drunkenly.

'Shut up!' she silenced him. 'You're drunk, all three of you! Get to your beds!'

She had to smile at the haste with which they disappeared, scurrying off like boarding school boys caught chattering after lights out.

CHAPTER ELEVEN

The Road to Ballarat, spring 1854

John and Cate had planned for the caravan to reach Ballarat on Wednesday 11 October, giving the company time to set up and rehearse for their first double shows on Friday the 13th, a good omen for Cate, who was born on that very date.

'A bad day for most, but a good-luck day for me,' she laughed when they'd decided upon the date of departure. 'What a pity I won't be there to share the opening night with you all.' She patted John's shoulder.

'I don't see why you can't be there,' John said, just a little miffed at her reticence to leave Melbourne.

'Don't be like that, John,' she said softly. 'I can't just drop the running of the hotel in Dorothy's lap.'

'What about Amos? Surely he can help her.'

'He will, but I feel I must stay to oversee her efforts for a couple of days at least.'

'All right.' John kissed her cheek. 'But you will come as soon as you can, won't you?'

'Of course. I'd like to see anyone attempt to stop me.'

Not two days before the caravan had departed Melbourne, Cate had been informed that one James Ludlow, a self-described goldfields entrepreneur, had been incarcerated in Melbourne Gaol Debtors' Wing for defaulting on outstanding loans with the Bank of Victoria.

'He's only just finished building a new theatre. He's called it the Paragon and it's in the very heart of Ballarat, near the Adelphi,' Cate, breathless with excitement, had announced to John and Kit, who'd both stared at her perplexed.

'Is that good news?' John had asked.

'For God's sake, man,' she'd wailed in exasperation, 'I just told you he's in gaol! What good's a theatre to a man who's in gaol?'

'I'm afraid I can't answer that.'

'Nor I,' Kit had added. 'I have no experience of theatre in any shape or form.'

'He owes the Bank of Vic three thousand pounds,' she declared, staring at them as if they were simpletons. 'Does that little scenario ring any bells with you?'

'Ah.' The glow of enlightenment appeared in John's eyes. 'We give him three thousand pounds and he gives us the theatre . . .'

'Wrong!' The force of the exclamation hurt Cate's throat and she coughed. 'He's incarcerated, remember? We offer him fifteen hundred, which, if he pays it back to the bank, will reduce his sentence by half.'

'So he stays in gaol?' Kit pretended to understand.

'Of course!' she exclaimed. 'We don't want him back in Ballarat creating competition, do we? We'll get enough of that from Sarah Hanmer.'

'The actress?' Kit asked.

'Not anymore,' Cate said. 'Apparently she now owns the Adelphi and runs it with an iron fist, but we'll draw so much business from her we'll shut her down.'

'You're a hard woman, Cate,' John murmured.

'Business is business.' She waved a wad of pound notes under his nose. 'Fifteen hundred for the Paragon and not a penny more, providing Ludlow signs over ownership immediately, what do you say?'

'About what?'

'We're in a joint venture, remember, John?' She was finding them both exasperating. 'You invested two thousand pounds into a travelling show which is going, coincidentally, to Ballarat. We have the chance to buy a theatre there for next to nothing . . .'

'I'm not a child, Cate!' John snapped. 'I understand and the answer is yes.'

'Good!' She slapped the money against his chest. 'Now get over to Melbourne Gaol as fast as your horse will carry you.' She pointed a thumb at Kit. 'And take him with you.'

Cate Shearley's Travelling Variety Show left Melbourne on 5 October.

The procession of brightly painted wagons, drays and carts caused considerable excitement from the minute it made its way down Collins Street. People waved and cheered, children ran alongside the wagons and dogs barked excitedly until it passed through Flemington, the last of the outlying suburbs, and snaked its way onto the flat expanse of plains to Keilor.

To the east, behind John's caravan, people on foot, in carts and on drays and horses stretched back along the road like a human ribbon to the horizon, while all around the grassy plains shimmered golden in the morning sunlight.

My God, what a land, he thought, and not for the first time. Australia was claiming him. The spring had brought with it that zephyr of hope and energy that inspires the hearts of men to heed the call of the wild and John had willingly succumbed. With Rani beneath him and the blue sky above he felt the urge to fly. He nudged the horse then dug his heels into her flanks, commanding her to run. And run she did. Like a wild west wind Rani flew out across the sun-washed plain, nostrils flared, filled with the joy of the gallop. John leaned over her flanks, head down, legs straight to the stirrups, knees caressing her sides, feeling the rush of air through his open-necked shirt. Freedom was the only word his mind could entertain.

He hauled Rani in and horse and man stood sentinel still in the rippling waves of grass.

He looked back at the road, now a mile or more away. The gaily painted wagons of the travelling show were no more than bright dots on a flat horizon. He closed his eyes and breathed deeply, savouring the fresh morning air and allowing the joy of being alive to wash over him.

'Come on, princess,' he sighed finally, contentedly. Rani snorted her agreement and the two moved slowly back through the undulant ocean of golden grass.

At Keilor John had called a halt and they'd made their first camp. He had sent Kit on in advance with saddlebags full of posters to announce their arrival and inform the public of the intended location of the soon to open Cate Shearley's Paragon Theatre.

Cate became aware of a rumbling sound as she allowed her gelding to shuffle gently through the casuarina trees up a steep incline. As she climbed the hill in the gathering dusk the noise grew louder, reminding her of the crowd when she'd attended Ascot Racecourse many years before. Is it some sort of dispute, she thought, or a heated quarrel between some of the many travellers ahead? As she neared the hilltop it became far more audible. It's human voices, she realised, but they were mixed with other sounds, many of which her ear was beginning to isolate and identify. She determined gunshots, musical instruments playing various dissonant tunes at odds with each other, horses whinnying, cattle lowing, the solitary scream of a distressed woman and something else, harsh and jarring. Dogs, yes that was what she could hear above all else – the barking of dogs, hundreds of them by the sound of it. And intermittently kookaburras laughed, announcing as they do the end of day, or was it their complaint about the unholy racket?

'What's that noise, Ma?' Jack spurred his mare past a wagon and pair struggling to get up the hill, its owner on foot, holding the reins, encouraging his horses to a greater effort on the appalling excuse for a road.

'That's Ballarat, laddie,' the Scottish wagon driver called.

Jack reined in his mare alongside his mother's horse as Cate stared down into the vast plain below.

It was dusk and the sight that met their eyes was one neither would ever forget. The twinkling of ten thousand campfires seemed at first like all the stars in the heavens reflected in a vast lake. Ballarat and its goldfields lay spread before them, stretching into the twilight distance like a fairyland.

But this is no fairyland, Cate thought, this is a goldfield just like any other anywhere in the world. A place where fortunes can be discovered overnight and poor men turned into instant millionaires. But they were the rare few, she knew. Goldfields for most people were dangerous, desolate places shared by the poorest of humanity, the have-nots, those destined to find little or nothing and continue to suffer the hard knocks and disappointments that real life regularly dispensed them.

Immediately below the steep decline they must now descend lay Ballarat East, the scene of the diggings. Main Street, or Main Road as it was also called, was obvious even in the gathering dusk. It seemed to bisect the entire area, running pretty much north to south. To the east of it and closer to the ridge she stood on, Cate looked down on the now famous Eureka Lead, which ran vaguely east and north-east from Main Street. Beyond Main Street, further distant and running parallel with it, she could make out what had to be the original Yarrowee Lead along Yarrowee Creek, where John and the boys had panned for alluvial gold. On a small hill to the north, along the Yarrowee Creek where Main Street turned sharp left and crossed it, stood the Camp. Cate had heard much about Ballarat from travellers and she was aware that the Camp housed the military, the police and the public servants whose job it was to oversee the running of the goldfields. It was renowned as a hotbed of vice and corruption.

'So that's the infamous Camp,' she muttered as she nudged her horse forward.

'What did you say, Ma?' Jack spurred his horse to follow suit.

'Never mind,' she called back. 'Let's get into the town before it gets dark.'

In the deepening twilight they made their way down the hill and followed the Melbourne Road along the Eureka Lead until it met Main Street, a street of stores and houses. Most, Cate was surprised to see, were made partly from timber, many with canvas roofs.

'From tents to timber it must be
Tis mankind's great philosophy
To make then break a goldfield down
And build another Christian town.
Where righteous men live righteous lives,
The light of freedom fades and dies'

Cate sang the song softly and smiled at the memories it invoked. *From Tents to Timber* was a song of the California goldfields she'd heard sung on many an occasion by miners – or '49ers as they were known – in her California Eldorado Hotel in San Francisco. It was a lively reel that rattled along in duple time, but in truth it was a lament, sung by free-spirited, adventurous men, pioneers mourning the encroachment of civilisation upon their wild frontier.

'Remember what you're seeing, Jack,' she said to her son. 'Places like this don't last long.'

'Why not, Ma?'

'Civilisation catches up with them.'

Cate noticed the build-up of shops and stores on either side of her as she entered the street. The noise was at its greatest here and the atmosphere carnival-like. It was Wednesday night, but no different to any other. In Ballarat, according to the locals, every night was Saturday night and despite the fact there'd been a major riot involving thousands of locals the previous afternoon, the street was well and truly alive. Any number of drinking tents dotted the street, several bed-and-breakfast establishments offering 'a wooden stretcher and morning tucker for gentlemen only', a butcher's shamble or slaughterhouse, three barber shops with signs that read 'free bath to them whats paid in advance', several tailor shops and a dressmaker with the unnecessary sign 'females only' and next to it a millinery with a window full of women's hats and the same pointless 'females only' sign over the door. A number of tented brothels were obvious to Cate's experienced eye and all the while buskers performed with hats at their feet, and wild, feral-looking children ran shouting and screaming between drays, dogs and horses. But it was Sarah Hanmer's Adelphi Theatre which caught Cate's eye. Ballarat's most popular theatre was packed out judging by the crowd lined up at the ticket office.

'Wow, there it is, Ma!' Jack exclaimed, pointing beyond her.

Three doors up the street from the Adelphi on the opposite side of the road stood the Paragon. A large, commodious, wood and sod-walled construction with a canvas roof, it was lit up like a Christmas tree with a huge banner across the top announcing 'Cate Shearley's Travelling Variety Show'. The crowd inside and spilling onto the street declared it was open for business and thriving.

'Cate!' John Bailleau exclaimed as she and Jack entered through the rear stage door. 'What are you doing here?'

'I'm very well,' she replied sarcastically. 'Thank you for asking.'

'I'm sorry, I mean . . . I wasn't expecting you. I take it Dorothy's doing well?'

'She's a natural hotelier. So good at it I've officially made her manageress. And Amos will keep an eye on her for me, until she's used to it.'

'Hello, Captain Bailleau,' Jack saluted.

'And hello to you, Lieutenant Shearley.' John returned the salute and entered into the military routine they'd developed. 'Is the guard set, Lieutenant?'

'The watch is secure on the square, sir.' The boy beamed.

'Do we hold a clear field of fire, Lieutenant?'

'We do, sir.'

'Well done, Lieutenant. Stand easy.' John ruffled the boy's hair and looked at Cate.

Jack tapped his mother's arm. 'Can I go and watch the show?'

'Yes, but don't leave the theatre.'

'I'm glad to hear you've had no trouble at the hotel, lass.'

'I had one minor problem caused by a friend of yours.'

'Oh, really, a friend of mine? And who might that have been?'

'Nathaniel Hobson,' she smiled. 'A magistrate who holds you in the highest esteem.'

'Oh dear me, no.'

'He booked into the hotel for two nights. He had nothing but praise for you. Said you were an English gentleman of the finest quality.'

'Ha,' John laughed. 'Good old Hobbo.'

'He said he knew you from Coventry.' She stared at him warily. 'If he knows you so well, why doesn't he know your real name is Farrington?'

'I don't know him from Horatio Nelson,' John declared, palms raised. 'We both apparently went to Rugby School, albeit thirty years apart. That's our only connection. He's a silly old thing, but he's harmless.'

'Harmless!' Cate's eyes widened. 'You think so, do you?'

'Why, what did he do?'

'The dirty old bugger did everything but drag me into his room.'

'Sssssssssssstt.' It was Stupid Ho. John turned to see him waving frantically.

'I've got to go, Cate. I'm the stagehand tonight. It's my turn. I've got to help with the costume changes and sets.'

Cate could only nod before John disappeared through black curtains.

She had to admit she was impressed with the set-up. Four mud-brick and bark walls with a foyer and theatre space all with floorboards; the rear six foot of space behind the stage stretched across the entire width of the building affording room for sets, make-up and costume areas, all separately curtained off.

Definitely a good buy, she thought, looking at the canvas roof, unless it rains heavily. Yes, she nodded, a bargain it would have been at twice the price. A proper roof of bark secured by bush poles would give it that sense of permanency and double the price yet again. Well done, girl, she congratulated herself.

It's a tight fit though, she thought, looking around again. When you consider there is a cast of, let's see, Tommy Bartlett the magician; Adelina Panotti the Italian 'Soprano from Milano' who was actually Adalina Vasquez, a Spaniard from Madrid; Master of Ceremonies Andrew Arbuthnot McCrae, the kilted Scottish dwarf; identical blonde contortionists billed as Anna and Lanna the Twisting Teutonic Teenage Twins; Wolfie Bremmer the musical director; and last but not least Lou-shi with her two characters, China the Chinese Circus Boy and Michiko the Japanese Songstress. Seven performers, then Mister Feng and Yue Chun, the stage manager who doesn't speak English – she raised her eyes to heaven – then John as manager and Rhodesy and Kit, all three of whom acted alternately as stagehand and Front of House manager. That's twelve in all, she thought, and now Jack and I make fourteen.

'A big family indeed,' she muttered to herself.

'Well, well, well, now! If it b'aint be the beautiful Mistress Cate!'

'Hello, Rhodesy.' She smiled at the big man grinning at her from outside the stage door. 'You're a sight for sore eyes.' She went to him, stood on the topmost step, tugged his beard and kissed his cheek.

'What you be thinkin' a' the place? Grand, ain't it?'

'I was just wondering where everyone sleeps.'

'We ain't had no trouble there at all.' He pointed at one of the various caravans and wagons on the block behind the theatre. 'Adelina and the twins share the Costumes caravan right there and they seem to manage all right. Then you got Tommy the magician and Wolfgang the piano player in that there long cart, that be the Sets and Props wagon. Me and Kit shares that light blue wagon over there.' He pointed into the darkness again. 'Mostly we sleeps under it unless it be rainin' and John sleeps in the Manager's wagon, that big 'un there.'

'What about our Chinese friends?'

'They sleeps in the back in there,' he said, pointing past Cate's shoulder. 'In them little curtained stalls like, where they seem very happy.'

'And Mister McCrae?'

'Ah, yeah, little Dafty Boy as I calls 'im. He's got 'is own 'ouse, ain't 'e.'

'Indeed?' Cate was surprised. 'And just how did that come about?'

'Well, lass, seein' as he's only four foot 'igh and the stage is five foot 'igh, he's made 'imself an 'ouse under it. 'Ow's that now?' He laughed.

Cate laughed along with the gentle giant. 'Ah, Rhodesy, as I said, you're a sight for sore eyes.'

'An' you might be jus' what the doctor ordered.' He nodded, suddenly serious.

'Meaning?'

'That man of yours, John, he could do with the likes o' you right about this time.'

'Oh really?' She leaned against the doorframe and breathed in the smoky night air. 'Why is that, Mister Rhodes?'

'Did he tell you about 'Arlow, the police sergeant?' Rhodesy leaned into her. Even standing three steps below on the ground, he was face-to-face with her.

'No.'

'Well, I can't say as I blame 'im, but now we're all 'ere in Ballarat, you should know about 'Arlow.'

'Should I?'

'Aye, lass, but you must never let on I told you.' Rhodesy raised his index finger to emphasise the seriousness of their discussion. 'What I tell you now, be our secret. You must never mention it to anyone, especially John la. Swear it now!'

'I swear.'

'Orright, 'Arlow were a police sergeant who was the worst type o' scum. Last time we was 'ere, 'e killed a friend of ours name of 'Arry Foo.' Rhodesy took a look about him before continuing. 'John caught 'im red-handed goin' through 'Arry's stuff. 'Arlow pulled a gun and John ran 'im through with that knife 'e carries what's more the size of a sword.'

'Heavens!' Cate was shocked. 'Didn't the authorities have anything to say about it?'

'They don' know it 'appened, girl. They think 'Arlow just left the diggin's like a lot of men do.'

'John's not capable of killing someone like that.'

'Now that's where you be wrong, lass.' Rhodesy lowered his voice. 'You gotta understand, 'e's got the soldier's disease, girl. The blood rush some calls it. Comes o' fightin' in wars and the like. Too much blood and guts. 'Opefully it'll leave 'im one day, it does with most men, but in the meantime it's violent places like these 'ere goldfields what brings it on. You wait an' see. If he's threatened, or worse still, someone threatens you or that boy o' yours, he'll explode. And you'd better get used to it. Do you understand?'

'Yes, I do,' Cate answered, nodding furiously. 'Yes.'

'And make sure you carry a gun.'

Cate flexed her arm and instantly a double-barrelled Philadelphia Derringer appeared in her hand. 'I always do, Rhodesy.'

'Oh,' the giant was surprised, 'a sleeve holster, eh? That be the ticket, Cate. My word, but that be the ticket indeed!' He raised the lantern he was carrying and the silver barrel of the percussion cap pistol gleamed brightly. 'A gambler's gun, eh, lass? You need to be at close range, yeah?'

'It's a big bullet, .41 calibre, but yes, the closer the better.'

There was a determined note in her reply that pleased Rhodesy. 'Spoken like my Eileen,' he declared. 'Now I best be on my way. Between shows I'm to do the perimeter inspection, as it be called by them what was in the army, to make sure there be no blackguards nor 'eathens lurkin' about like.'

When he'd disappeared around the side of the building Cate remained leaning against the doorframe taking in the night air, flavoured with the smell of cooking meat and smoke from a thousand campfires. The worry in her deepened. What had she got herself and Jack into? Who was John Bailleau? Where was John Farrington? Who did she love? And more importantly, was she loved in return?

From behind, John's arm slid around her waist and he pressed himself against her back. 'I've got red wine in the main wagon,' his breath was hot against her ear, 'and talking is the last thing I have in mind.' He tried to kiss her but she slipped out of his grip.

'It's what we have to do above all else, John.' She looked him straight in the eye. Then the promise she'd made to Rhodesy silenced her.

'How so?' He drew back and stared at her in turn. 'We've been open for a week and everything's going along nicely.'

Until you lose your temper again and kill someone else, she thought. 'I just meant I need you to familiarise me with the state of our business affairs,' she said weakly, wishing already the conversation with Rhodesy had not occurred. She looked into John's smiling face; God Almighty how she loved him, but where would her love lead her?

He put his arms around her again and she allowed herself to be cuddled. 'Don't worry, Cate, everything's going along perfectly.'

How I've missed those arms, she thought. Damn it, he's my addiction. She felt her stomach muscles clench as desire surged through her.

'I'd really like that drink of wine. How about you?' he whispered in her ear.

'Where's the wagon?' she stammered breathlessly.

'Right out the back.'

'Quickly!' Her response to his touch had been so fast she thought she would faint.

His arms took her body weight and he carried her over to the management caravan. No sooner had he shut the door than he tried to force her onto the bed.

'No!' she gasped. 'Standing up! Hurry!' The thought of the way he'd taken her in the pantry at the hotel overwhelmed her. He'd already lifted her skirts and found his way. 'Quickly, John . . . Oh yes!' He was suddenly there, deep within. Reason failed her as she was swept away in a flood of desire.

The following morning, reason returned with a vengeance. Cate was furious with herself for giving in to her body. She avoided the company and took a walk down Main Street, ostensibly, she convinced herself, to see Sarah Hanmer's theatre and make herself familiar with the street's other inhabitants.

Thursday morning was no different to the previous evening when she'd ridden up the street with Jack; the activity was just as intense, with people bustling from side to side and door to door. Children were even more in evidence, out of control and intent on larceny. Men were already drunk, one lying unconscious in the dusty road and others staggering about soon to join him, she imagined. Coffee houses and barber shops were equally packed and doing a roaring trade. Only the brothels were inactive. Cate noticed a number of good-time gals enjoying the morning sun and the chance to relax well-worked hips and buttocks.

She stopped in front of the Adelphi Theatre and saw a tall elegant woman on the first-floor balcony. Sarah Hanmer no doubt, she surmised. The two women nodded politely. Then as they stared at each other, Cate noticed a smile spread across Sarah Hanmer's face. Was it superiority? Confidence? Adversity? Or was it a genuine greeting? Cate chose to believe the latter. Oh you're my sort of woman, Sarah, she thought as she smiled back. I think I'm actually going to like you.

The bustling street and the appearance of Sarah Hanmer had relaxed her, but it was only short-lived. John's face came to mind again and her concern began to grow once more. Did she really know him? Could she trust him? What could she do to bring about a confirmation of their love for each other? And is that what she really wanted? She had one card left to play, but again, she wondered, should she play it?

Cate began her trek back up Main Street to the Paragon. She had made a date with Mister Feng to inspect the books.

Mister Feng, who kept meticulous records, sat next to her nodding with each page she turned.

'What's this?' Her finger tapped the page she was reading. 'Gold Field Regulations Fee fifteen pounds? We don't mine for gold; why should we pay a fee?'

'Everyone on fields must pay fee, not only miners. We operate business so we must pay! Fifteen pounds for three months. Only priests and children no have to pay.'

'That's daylight robbery! No wonder the miners are up in arms; it's nothing more than a poll tax.'

'Every man and woman must pay one pound every month, no matter they find gold or not.'

'It's disgusting.'

'Licence fee was thirty shilling every month, but is more now.'

'It's no wonder there is such ill-feeling. Living in Melbourne I never realised it was so bad.'

'There is much hatred for the government.'

'And what's this?' She crinkled her brow as she tapped the next entry in the ledger. 'God, that's a lot of money to pay for horse feed, isn't it?'

'It is Ballarat. We give our supplier free tickets to show or we pay much more,' Feng said defensively. 'Also, cast and crew eat vegetables only. Meat very expensive. Vegetables are very good for them, but they are not Chinese people. English people must have meat. So they complain all the time.'

'Who complains?'

'*Fei-jai*, mostly,' the old man answered automatically.

'And just who or what is *Fei-jai*?'

'*Fei-jai* means fat boy,' said Jack who'd walked in on the conversation.

'Ah, I presume you mean Mister Rhodes?'

'Please don't confuse meaning, Miss Cate,' Feng said. '*Fei-jai* is friendly meaning.'

'I'm glad to hear it.' She looked at her son. 'Do you want something?'

'Can I go exploring with Lou-shi?'

'Yes, of course, but don't get into mischief.'

'Thanks, Ma,' Jack replied and was gone in a flash.

'An extraordinary boy,' Feng offered.

'Yes he is.'

'Where his father is?'

Cate turned her attention back to the ledgers. 'Long gone,

Mister Feng, long gone and forgotten.' He would have to mention that. 'Shall we continue with the audit?'

'*Bai-lou* should be his father. I will negotiate marriage for you, yes?'

'You most certainly will not!' Cate was appalled at the thought.

'It is custom in China to arrange marriage.'

'Well it's not the custom here! Now, can we get on with it?'

'The boy likes *Bai-lou*.' Feng would not be put off.

'Mister Bailleau is not the marrying kind, Mister Feng. He is a soldier and . . . you know . . . an adventurer.'

'I understand. In China we say *daan long*, the single wolf.'

'Yes a lone wolf, that's him exactly.' She wanted desperately to tell Feng to shut up, but she knew he was only being polite, in his own strange way. 'So, let's have no more talk of marriage, arranged or otherwise. Mister Bailleau will leave one day and that will break my son's heart.'

And not only your son's heart, Feng thought, as he pointed to the ledgers, deciding it was time now to change the subject. 'Despite being here only one week, Miss Cate, I feel sure . . .'

'Sure?' Cate interjected. 'How can you be sure of anything in this Godforsaken place?'

'I talk only of business.' Feng bowed his head slightly. 'Ballarat is no good place otherwise, but never mind.'

'Never mind?' For Cate the subject was not yet closed. 'What about the riot last week? I heard over ten thousand people were involved.'

'It was very bad, mistress. The people show their anger. They burn down Eureka Hotel because Bentley, the owner, is found not guilty of murder.'

'The Scobie murder. A miscarriage of justice if ever there was one by the sound of it.' Cate shook her head. 'I can't believe the miners could go berserk like that and then attend a variety performance the same night.'

'But they did! They come and spend money.' Feng indicated the ledger again. 'Figures very satisfactory, yes?'

'More than satisfactory, Mister Feng.' She smiled at him, forcing herself to, yet again, dismiss thoughts of John from her mind. 'We're sitting on a goldmine.'

'In the middle of a goldfield,' he added. 'Is that not the strangest of things to wonder upon? *Bai-lou Saang*, he say so too.'

'People are paying ten shillings a time.' Cate frowned. *Bai-lou Saang*, the name rang in her ears. She really wanted Feng to shut up.

'That is the average price, but *Bai-lou* insists he, Mister Kit, or *Fei-jai* ask how much money people have when they come to door.'

'What for?'

'To some people, mostly poor women, he let in for free. Mothers and little children he let stand at rear of theatre for Act I, so they can watch Lou-shi tumble and juggling.'

'Really?' Cate was taken aback. 'He lets them in without charge? Are we talking about the same man?'

'Yes, *Bai-lou*.' Feng nodded solemnly. 'But men with big money, he make pay five pounds or admission refused.'

'Five pounds! Each?'

'Very small amount for a rich man.'

'I must admit,' she tapped the page with her finger, 'the money for the sale of grog is excellent.'

'People of Ballarat dependent on alcohol. People of China dependent on opium. Is essential to them, it make poverty bearable. Alcohol what bring extra money to shows.'

'Which brings me to my next question, Mister Feng.' She looked into his eyes. 'Where's the money?'

'That a good question.'

'That is *not* a good answer!'

'Is OK, mistress,' Feng raised his hands defensively. 'The money I put in the bank.'

'What! Where?' Cate's voice was a terrified squeak. 'When!?'

'Monday morning.'

'Mother of God!' Her hands flew to her mouth. 'How much?'

'Two thousand guineas.' Feng smiled.

'The Ballarat branch of the Bank of Victoria was robbed on Monday afternoon. Haven't you heard? Four armed men wearing masks stole fifteen thousand pounds in cash and gold dust.'

'Not our money,' Feng tried to reassure her.

'Of course it was our money! It was everybody's money! They took the lot!' Cate was on her feet, pacing backstage. 'And nobody's got a clue who they were, or where they went!' She turned on the Chinese man, nose to nose. 'They've disappeared without a trace, *with our money*!'

'What's all the noise about?' Kit Kittredge came from behind the curtains. 'Are you all right, Cate?'

'No I'm not all right!' Cate turned on him, nostrils flaring. 'This idiot,' she pointed at Feng, 'put two thousand guineas into the Bank of Victoria on Monday morning, just before it was robbed!'

'Not our bank!' Feng exclaimed loudly, finally gaining Cate's attention. 'Only a *gwailo*, a Western person, would put money in that bank! That bank is a wooden box on edge of forest behind the town. Only idiot put money in that bank. Your son Jack could rob that bank.'

'So where's our money, Mister Feng?' the American asked.

'I gave our money to the See Yup Society . . .'

'What in God's name is that?' Cate snapped.

'All Chinese in Ballarat use See Yup Society to transfer gold and cash to main branch of Bank of Victoria in Melbourne.'

'You gave two thousand guineas to a group of Chinamen?'

'See Yup Society is safest way to send money. *Bai-lou Saang* agree with me.'

'Did he just!' The mention of John fired her up again.

'Cate,' Kit said calmly, 'I believe the See Yup Society is a reputable organisation.'

'Our money is safe.' Feng's voice pleaded. 'It is already in Melbourne. You are angry for no reason. Money is safe.'

'It had better be, Chinaman!' Cate growled. She would not allow the wind to be taken out of her sails so readily.

'Well, that settles that matter,' the Bostonian offered a little too jovially. 'There's no need for you to be angry, Cate.'

But I *am* still angry, she thought. *Why* am I so angry? I'm so angry I'm getting angry with myself for getting angry. She knew John Farrington alias John Bailleau was the source of her anger, or was he? Does the problem lie with me? She thought briefly. No, John was a threat to her future and far more so to the future of her son. In John's world, Jack would be carrying a gun before he knew it.

As temper overtook her she commenced a diatribe about the danger of irregular banking practices, which slowly evolved into a volcanic tirade about everything from the appalling condition of the road from Melbourne, to the filthy state of the diggings, to the uncontained, lawless behaviour of the rioting locals.

The company, attracted by her shouting, began filling the backstage area. The contortionist twins arrived sleepy-eyed, wearing colourful dressing room robes; Adalina the soprano, similarly attired, positioned herself inside the door. Tommy the magician and Wolfie Bremmer, Rhodesy and Jack and then little Lou-shi came next, until the backstage was full. When John finally arrived he was forced to push his way into the centre of the mob only to be confronted by the enraged Cate.

'What's going on?' he demanded.

At the sight of him Cate became incandescent. 'And as for you!' Cate flexed her arm and the Derringer flew into her hand. 'You son-of-a-bitch!'

John grabbed her wrist and the lethal weapon discharged into the wooden support beam above their heads. Pandemonium broke out among the cast and crew and within seconds the two were left alone in a thick cloud of black gunpowder smoke.

As she struggled to free herself from his grip, Cate's face was a twisted mask of anger, her good eye glared at him and, as she realised he was indeed the source of her pent-up hostility, her nails reached for his cheeks.

'What on earth's got into you, girl?' He grasped her other wrist.

'How dare you!' Cate growled, increasing her effort to escape. 'You . . . you . . . you come to Melbourne! You seek me out!'

'I did no such thing. Our meeting was one of pure chance.'

'Oh, yes,' she laughed humourlessly. 'So you say!'

'Cate, please.'

'You've taken my affection for granted! And this time you'll hurt Jack as well.'

'Cate!'

'You've destroyed my life yet again!' she screamed like a banshee.

'Contain yourself, madam!'

Grunting, Cate redoubled her effort but it was to no avail; he had her in a vice-like grip. Then something burst within her, the fight left her limbs, a last angry tear rolled down her cheek and she exhaled, surrendering.

'That's better,' he murmured, releasing her. 'Stay calm now and tell me what on earth has reduced you to such a state.'

'Everything,' she said finally. 'Everything.' She sunk to her knees and placed her hands in her lap, heedless of her wet cheeks and running nose. 'London, New York, San Francisco, everything . . .' Her voice faded off. She looked up at him and shook her head despairingly.

John knelt and offered her his handkerchief. 'Here,' he said. 'Wipe your nose and dry your cheeks. Your face is as red as a beetroot.'

She took the handkerchief and did as bidden, then she stared at the wall for some seconds and made a clinical decision.

'Damn it!' she snapped and got to her feet. 'I'm not this sort of woman! Never have been! I'm tougher than any man I ever knew!' She planted her hands on her hips and looked down at him. 'Including you!' She began to pace the room. 'I've been on my own for as long as I can remember and I've never needed anyone. Yes, I fell from grace on more than one occasion, but I always got up and got on with life!'

John got to his feet. 'Go on,' he urged her, 'spit it out, whatever your problem is, get it off your chest.'

'It's *you*!' She paced back and forth. 'You are my problem! Damn you!'

'Me?'

'I fell in love with you in London . . .'

'As did I with you,' he interrupted. 'When I came back from India I tried –'

'It's my turn to talk! Shut up and listen, because I'll never explain myself to you again.' She raised her chin and looked him in the eye. 'I suffered the pain of lost love when you went off to India. I never, ever got over it and twelve years later you simply walked into my life and all those feelings came rushing back.'

'As did mine, Cate.'

'Shut up! This is my story,' she continued. 'I got lucky; I met an old man who virtually adopted me and Jack. He took us to New York and he gave me a father's love. Then I lost love again. I finished up in San Francisco and discovered love again, the love of my son. I made a lot of money in San Fran but I got mixed up with a bad man, a Frenchman and a bastard named Jean-Baptiste Le Pen, and had to run again.' She tapped her eye patch. 'He's how I got this. I learned from Wolfie, of all people, that Jean-Baptiste was planning to murder me for my property, a very valuable business. He stabbed me in the eye so I shot him and ran like hell with Jack and Amos.'

She sat on the steps that led down to backstage and John joined her.

'Then I arrived in Melbourne at the bottom of the world and began again, but this time Jack came first. I determined to give him a good life and lots of love and attention.' She looked at John. 'And what happened? You appear! Let me finish,' she said as he opened his mouth to speak. 'You were a *boy* in London, John. A baby. I know now the affair we had would not have lasted three more months. But you turned up in Melbourne a fully grown man and I couldn't resist you. I fell in love with you all over again, but it was selfish of me. I didn't consider Jack. I didn't take into account the effect you would have on that young, impressionable, fatherless boy.'

'He's a fine boy.'

'And he needs a father!' She looked at him again. 'A real father. Not a man like you, John, an adventurer, a man who wanders the world tilting at windmills. Don't you understand? I can't be in love with you!'

'But we make a good team, Cate.' He tried to take her hand but she pulled away from him.

'No we don't.' She wanted to throw the killing of the police sergeant at him, but could never do so, because of her promise to Rhodesy. 'Your world is a sea of troubles, John, brought about mainly through your own efforts. I can't possibly let Jack be drawn into it.'

'I've been trying hard, Cate. We could get married and . . .'

'Don't be ridiculous!'

'But, we could . . .'

'It's not about *we*! It is not about *you*, or *me*! It's about Jack! I've dragged that little boy all over the world and I owe him, John. I owe him a good life. I'm not going to entrust his future to a man who could run off, to whatever Godforsaken place, on the spur of the moment. And,' she finished, 'probably never come back.'

'Is that what you really think of me?' John stood and walked across the floor and stared at the piles of Chinese costumes spread out in the far corner.

'There, you see?' Cate waved her hands in the air, exasperated. 'That's exactly what I'm talking about. You're a fully grown man with the intellect of a spoilt boy. *"Is that what you really think of me?"*' she mimicked him in a childish voice. Cate got to her feet and pointed an accusing finger at him. 'It's not about you! You stupid man! It's about Jack and *only* Jack!'

Cate braced herself for a resumption of the fight, but instead watched as John frowned at the multi-coloured pile of costumes for some seconds. Then his expression cleared and he pointed a finger at her.

'Is Jack my son?'

'Of course not!' Cate scoffed sarcastically. 'Where on earth did you get that idea? *Work it out, idiot!* We haven't seen each other for twelve years and I have an *eleven*-year-old son and his name is *John*! How could he *possibly* be yours?'

'But . . . wait a minute.' John began counting with his fingers.

'Stop that!' She wanted to hit him. '*Of course he's your son!*'

'Really?' His voice was full of wonder.

'Have you looked in his eyes, John?' She spoke softly. 'Have you noticed his smile? The way he tilts his head slightly when he laughs? How his chin comes up when he's angry? *Oh, shit!*'

'What?' John followed her stare.

Jack stood in the doorway looking at them in turn, his eyes as wide as saucers.

Cate was first to recover. 'Did you hear what was said, boy?' Jack nodded. 'Well it's true. He's your real father and his name is John Farrington, not Bailleau. So you'd better come inside.' She turned her attention to John. 'I'll leave you two to sort it out, shall I?'

'But . . .?' John's eyes appealed to her.

'Get your priorities in order, Johnny m'lad.' Cate paused in the doorway, her number-one priority suddenly crystal clear. As the weight of the world lifted from her shoulders, she looked at her son, then looked again at John. 'And if those priorities don't suit us you can go to hell. Get out of Ballarat, get out of Victoria, but most importantly get out of our lives once and for all.'

She left them, John staring up at the canvas ceiling and Jack gazing down at the floor.

John finally looked at the little boy standing with his hands at his sides, staring at his boots. Come on, Farrington, he urged himself, break the silence. He's your son, for God's sake! Say something!

'Right, Jack,' he began haltingly, 'where do we go from here?'

The boy shrugged and continued to gaze at the floor, but when John reached out and touched his shoulder, Jack wrapped his arms around his father's waist and clung like a limpet.

'Well, I suppose that's a start,' he said softly and ruffled his son's hair.

CHAPTER TWELVE

Ballarat, October 1854

The winter had proven to be the wettest on record; the rain had arrived in May and continued throughout the season. Aided by howling winds and freezing temperatures it had turned Ballarat into a quagmire. Mining in its variant forms practically ceased owing to the inability of man or beast to negotiate the swamp that the goldfields became. Then spring had arrived with a vengeance. Hot northerly winds dried the diggings in a matter of days and where once families had huddled, shivering in their flimsy sodden tents, they now sat in any shade they could create, suffering the stultifying heat of the southern sun.

Just as Ballarat's weather was a case of extremes, so too was its cultural sphere. The town and diggings had polarised into two competing ideological positions. On the one hand were the miners, the shopkeepers and other business people, in fact all men and women who chose to live at Ballarat and were forced to pay outrageous licence fees for the privilege. On the other hand was the 'Unholy Trinity', as the citizens called the officials of the Gold Commission, the British Army and the Victorian Police Force.

Corruption, not uncommon in the fledgling colony, was utterly rampant on the goldfields. Anyone with the slightest influence was dishonest and those with real authority – especially Robert Rede, the Goldfields Commissioner, and his assistants – were drunk on the power they wielded. Abuse of such power was blatant and autocratic misrule the standing order of the day.

In mid-October, just before Shearley's Travelling Show arrived, an incident occurred that inflamed the Catholic population in particular. Johannes Grigorius, a servant of Father Smyth, the young Irish priest who had recently inherited Ballarat's ten thousand or more Catholics, had been challenged by a drunken police trooper to produce his licence. Grigorius, a crippled Armenian with limited English, tried to explain he was exempt from needing a licence, which indeed he was as an employee of the Catholic Church, but the mounted trooper had trampled the man with his horse. The incident had been witnessed by James Johnston, an Assistant Commissioner of the Goldfields Commission, and the crowd watching presumed the trooper would be, at the very least, publicly admonished. But Gregorius was ordered to appear the following day before the Police Magistrate John D'Ewes, also an Assistant Commissioner of the GFC. James Johnston appeared as a witness for the prosecution and incredulously he accused poor Gregorius of assaulting the trooper, despite a wealth of witnesses prepared to swear otherwise. D'Ewes concluded Johnston's evidence was true and duly fined Gregorius five pounds on the charge of being unlicensed, despite his legal exemption, and a further five pounds for assaulting the police trooper.

Such treatment of people and the flagrant disregard for their constitutional rights was so commonplace that petitions claiming offence and victimisation demanding redress by law flooded the bureaucratic halls and offices of the Victorian Government. But it was all to no avail and as the turbulent days of October became the tempestuous days of November, the bureaucrats kept their heads buried in the political sand, some unaware of and others indifferent to the anger they were fuelling, anger that had been brewing since 1851, anger that would turn to hatred and eventually armed rebellion.

'Licensing fees have been law since the beginning, since the Gold Field Regulations came into effect back in September

'51. They've caused nothing but heartache and grief. Except for the damned ruling class of course – all they do is benefit from them.'

It was Kit Kittredge, the avowed republican, who spoke. He, John and Cate sat around the glowing embers of a campfire outside the door of the Management wagon, cups of rum in hand, the remnants of a late-night supper evidenced by tin plates and forks piled on the steps that led up into the wagon.

John gave a snort. 'Spoken like a true Chartist, Kit, my lad.'

'Universal suffrage is the inalienable right of all men and here on these very goldfields men have the chance to achieve it. They could break free from the yoke of British imperialism and fight for their freedom as we did in America.'

John's smile disappeared. 'That's dangerous talk, my friend,' he said firmly. 'Let's not forget why we are here. We're in the entertainment business, that is all, and it wouldn't do for certain people to hear you expounding your political expectations.'

'I must say I agree with Kit,' Cate offered. 'I feel for the miners. I've gathered from those who patronise the Golden Sheaf that the licence fees have been a bone of contention for a long time, but I never realised how iniquitous the situation had become . . .'

'Don't poke your nose into things that don't concern you, Cate,' John warned. 'We stand to make a fortune here in Ballarat and we should be seen to stick to the apolitical business of theatre management.'

'Don't be so condescending!' Cate snapped. 'I'm not your lackey to be spoken to like that. I'm a citizen no less than you and I've a right to express my opinions.'

Damn it, John thought, what's got into her now? 'I'm sorry,' he said.

'Accepted,' she answered abruptly and returned her attention to Kit. 'Go on, man,' she said, 'I'm interested in what you have to say.'

'Things will only get worse until Governor Hotham and his cronies put the people before their own self-interest.' Kit drained his cup. 'They don't seem to realise the situation they could find themselves in. The trouble has been on the horizon for two years and the last several months have seen it intensify greatly. Yet they continue to ignore the signs. Rebellion is imminent.'

'If we're going to speak seditiously,' John chimed, 'I must say I agree with you about the ignorance of the government concerning the licence fees, but I don't believe for one minute there will be any form of rebellion.'

Kit poured himself another tot of rum. 'There were riots at the Ovens field and Reid's Creek as far back as eighteen months ago, remember? And the Bendigo miners' Red Ribbon movement was formed to demand a reduction of licence fees. And what was the result of that? A Select Committee was formed stacked with government cronies and their report only inflamed the miners even more.'

'They did suggest the fees be lessened,' John said, pouring himself another drink and offering one to Cate, who declined with a shake of her head.

'To what?' Kit exclaimed. 'One pound for one month, two pounds for three, three pounds for six and five pounds for twelve months! And then what does the government do? They amend the proposal to four pounds for six months and eight for twelve, then pass it as law! It's outrageous!'

'It's disgusting,' Cate added, 'that's what it is.'

'And look at events this year,' Kit went on, warming to the subject. 'Robert Rede succeeds James Clow as Goldfields Commissioner, a disastrous occurrence. Rede is a contemptible creature. Then we finally get rid of Governor La Trobe, an incompetent, who is succeeded by a military idiot in Sir Charles Hotham, a man who knows nothing of colonial government and who orders licence inspections twice weekly instead of once a month! And I've no doubt he gets a slice of the takings,' Kit finished with a sneer.

'I'm quite sure you're right.' John nodded. 'But it's not out of the ordinary for British colonial authorities to obtain personal benefit while remaining within the letter of the law.'

'Do you call what happened to James Scobie "remaining within the letter of the law", John?' Cate challenged.

'No, but that's a different kettle of fish.'

The Scobie affair was the talk of the goldfields. On the night of 6 October James Scobie, a young Irish miner, and his mate Peter Martin had too much to drink and Scobie banged loudly on the front door of the Eureka Hotel to demand entry, even though it was well after midnight and the hotel was closed. When no-one responded, he smashed a pane of glass in the front door of the premises that were owned by James Bentley. Scobie and Martin ran off, but were pursued by Bentley, his wife, Catherine, and two employees named Hance and Farrell, who soon caught up with the drunken revellers. In the ensuing scuffle Scobie was hit on the head with a shovel and fell down dead. Martin, who later claimed it had been too dark to see which of the group of pursuers had wielded the shovel, ran off to get help.

A coronial inquest was conducted the very next day and the weight of evidence certainly pointed to charges being laid, and on the 9th Bentley and his two employees were arrested and charged with murder. However, on Thursday the 12th and Friday the 13th an official inquiry into the alleged murder, presided over by none other than John D'Ewes, Robert Rede and James Johnston – all members of the Gold Fields Commission – heard the evidence, deliberated for thirty minutes and ruled there was no case to answer. All charges were dropped.

'A different kettle of fish, John?' Cate's tone was a little incredulous.

'Yes,' he answered, his voice hardening in response to her aggressive tone. 'Although I feel only sadness for James Scobie and nothing but contempt for D'Ewes, Rede and Johnston. Especially D'Ewes. I've heard it said lately that he owed Bentley quite a lot of money.'

'Good God!' Kit exclaimed. 'Well, there's a conflict of interest if ever there was one. If it's true, D'Ewes should never have presided over the inquiry. Ha,' he scoffed humourlessly, 'what am I saying? Would it have mattered who presided over the inquiry? Of course not – all the officials in Ballarat are as bad as one another.'

'It's no wonder the miners rioted and burned down Bentley's pub,' said Cate.

'Well, I don't agree with what they did,' John said with conviction. 'It makes them no better than the corrupt officials they hate.'

'But it raised the stakes all round.' Kit stood. 'It showed the powers that be how people denied justice can exert their strength. And what better example than the gathering on Bakery Hill a few days later. Ten thousand people turning up to hear Peter Lalor, John Humffray and young Henry Holyoake and others demand action from the government to right the wrongs being inflicted on ordinary citizens.'

'And thereby get innocent people shot in the process!'

'"Government of the people, for the people and by the people"; it's a wonderful phrase, is it not? I heard it echoed up on Bakery Hill. It describes democracy as it should be.'

'It's beautiful,' agreed Cate.

'But it's not about democracy!' John said forcefully. He was annoyed. Why couldn't Kit, and Cate for that matter, keep their noses out of the political struggle occurring on the goldfields? We're in Ballarat on business, for God's sake, he wanted to shout at them. Miners' rights are not our concern.

He stood up and drained his cup. 'The miners' rights are the last thing I want to be caught up in. I think Lalor and Humffray *et al* should keep their seditious mouths firmly shut! Now I'll bid you both goodnight!'

On Monday morning Jack sat on the stage steps backstage and assisted Mister Feng counting the week's takings. Mister Rhodes stood over them like the colossus he was named after, while Stupid Ho sat in the backstage doorway on the lookout for the See Yup Society men, who would escort him and the money to the Chinese Village for onward transfer to the Bank of Victoria in Melbourne.

'My coins add up to seven hundred and twenty-five shillings, Mister Feng,' Jack declared at the conclusion of his count. 'That's thirty-six pounds and five shillings.'

'Very good, Master Jack.' Feng looked up from the piles of notes he was counting and smiled at the boy. 'You will remove, please, one pound and five shillings and put in petty cash tin. Put remaining coins into this.' He handed the boy a cloth moneybag.

'They are here,' Stupid said to Feng in Cantonese, as four young and very fit-looking Chinese men arrived and positioned themselves outside the stage door.

'What did he say, la?' Rhodesy asked of Jack.

'He said they are here.'

'An' just who be they?'

'The men to take the money to . . .'

'Good!' the giant declared. 'That's my job done. I'm off up Main Street to the Empire Bowlin' Saloon to give them there ninepins wha' for!'

'Can I come?' Jack asked.

'No, la! Your ma would gi' me what for if I took you up *there.*' He moved to the stage door, where he paused in the doorway and looked down on the four awestruck Chinese men staring open-mouthed at his mammoth frame. 'How you be, lads?' he said as he stepped down between them. 'The money now be yours for the guardin', gents.' He gave them a mock bow and walked off around the side of the theatre.

'Go and fuck your mother!' one of the men declared loudly in Cantonese. *'He's the biggest person I've ever seen.'*

'Imagine the size of his turds!' another exclaimed. *'They would block the Yangtze River.'* All four burst out laughing.

Jack watched the young men enter backstage where Mister Feng handed each of them a bag of money, which they placed in shoulder bags.

'As usual my assistant, Mister Ho,' Feng began, indicating Stupid, *'will accompany you to Golden Point and report to me when the money has been delivered to Mister Soong of the See Yup Society. May I say, gentlemen, what an honour it is for me to have the support of such noble men as you are.'* He bowed to them. *'My admiration for Shaolin-si and what it stands for is infinite.'*

The young men before him bowed in return before filing out of the door, followed by Stupid Ho.

'*What is Shaolin-si?*' Jack asked in his chirpy Cantonese.

'*Shao* is name of place and *lin* mean forest. *Shaolin-si* is a Buddhist temple built many, many years ago in Song Mountains in province of Henan,' Feng explained in English, as he sat on the step next to the boy. 'Is a very famous place, Little Jack. Young men you just see are monks from *Shaolin-si*. They train since they are boys in the way of Shaolin.'

'So they're like priests?'

'That is correct, but they are very special priests, because much of their training is martial arts.'

'What's that mean?' Jack stood and went to the rear door.

'The arts of war. They are warrior monks. If bad men challenge them for that money they transport for us, bad men would not succeed. That is why our money is safe with them.'

'But they don't have any guns or swords, or anything.'

'They no need weapons,' the old man answered. 'Their fighting skills legendary in my country. If attacked they very dangerous.'

'Right, I have to go now.' Jack jumped off the steps and ran around the building where he saw the men walking down Main Street. He watched them turn and disappear behind the Hope Bakery and decided to follow them. If someone tried to take the money, he wanted to witness the outcome.

He scurried past the bakery, downhill past a stable and onto the beginning of the Eureka Lead where the digging took place. He followed their route around open shafts with windlasses and windsails over them, jumping small hillocks of discarded earth, scrambling beneath a wooden water channel several feet above his head and weaving between tents, making his way towards the Chinese Village one hundred yards distant.

'Well, well, if it isn't Master Jack Shearley,' a woman called as he moved carefully between an open shaft and tent flap. 'Tell me now, what's your ma thinkin' of bringin' you here to this Godforsaken goldfield?'

'Hello, Missus Hunter,' he responded to the dowdy red-faced woman smiling at him from inside the tent. 'Ma came west for business.'

'What be you doin' out 'ere on the Flat, Jackie? You mind you don't fall down a shaft now.' She came from the tent and took him firmly by the arm. 'Shouldn't you be a-schoolin' or somethin' or other?'

'Mondays I don't do school because I do lessons on Saturday mornings and work in the theatre on Sundays, so Ma lets me have Monday off.' He tried politely to free himself from her grip, but she was having none of it.

Nellie Hunter was a tough, no-nonsense mother of eight and wife to an unsuccessful miner. In Melbourne the year before, she'd occasionally done laundry work for his mother's hotel. Nellie was a big, warm-hearted woman, with a kindly nature, until she was crossed. The day before, Jack had seen her flatten a drunken miner for using bad language in front of her kids. Before he could free himself and continue the chase, she'd dragged him into her tent and virtually rammed a biscuit in his mouth.

'There you go, lovey,' she boomed, picking up her youngest from a crib. 'You eat that up and tell me all about your mum and the show, while I clean up this little one 'ere.'

'I'm in a hurry, Missus Hunter,' he cried as he smelt the mess contained in the baby's nappy. 'Mum sent me to fetch Mister Ho from the Chinese Village,' he lied.

'You shouldn't oughta be goin' to the likes of that camp, Jack,' she said, trying to wipe the struggling child's bottom. 'It's full of heathen Chine'e, lovey.' She eyed him meaningfully. 'I've 'eard as 'ow they eats young 'uns like you.'

'I've got to be going, Missus Hunter, or I'll get what for from Ma.'

'All right, lovey.' She offered him the folded, shit-filled nappy. 'Put that in the washing pot over the fire on your way out, will you? There's a good lad.'

Jack gagged as he took the nappy and rushed out of the tent, spitting the biscuit on the way.

'Give my love to your ma when you get home, Jackie,' he heard her yell as he dropped the nappy in the pot and frantically wiped his hand on his shirt. The men carrying the money were nowhere to be seen, but he caught a glimpse of Stupid Ho entering the red-painted Chinese Temple not fifty yards in front of him and set off in pursuit.

He came to a grinding halt outside the entrance to the little temple. He couldn't afford to let Stupid see him; he'd rather no-one, and especially his ma, know he'd been in the Chinese Camp, so he slipped around the back of the building looking for the priests.

He hid behind the Scribe's Hut and watched them walk past, obviously after delivering the moneybags they'd received from Mister Feng to Mister Soh of the See Yup Society. Through a crack in the wood-slabbed wall he watched as the scribe, who everyone called *Daan Tau*, which meant egghead, finished making notes in his ledger, throw his quilled pen on the table and began responding angrily to an old man with a long thin beard who was asking questions way too fast and complicated for Jack to understand.

He watched the four young Shaolin monks, now divested of their moneybags, walk to the small clearing behind the temple and to his amazement they lined up and began what he could only guess was a dance.

'Jack!' It was Stupid Ho, right behind him. 'Wha' you do he'ah?' he wailed in Jack's ear in barely understandable English. 'Missy Cate no like you he'ah!'

'*Yue Chun.*' He grabbed the Chinese man by the shoulder and pointed to the four Shaolin monks. '*What are they doing?*'

'*Shaolin,*' was Stupid's response.

'*Is it a dance?*'

'*Kung fu.*' Stupid shaped up as if to fight.

'*Kung fu,*' Jack murmured. He knew *kung fu* meant to do work, but the way Stupid sang the words wasn't the same tune Mister Feng used when he would wave Jack away telling him to get on with his work. This *kung fu* had a different meaning. He shaped up as if to fight Stupid, punching the air as the monks did and repeated the phrase with the same tune Ho had used. '*Kung fu?*' he asked.

'Yes!' Stupid grinned, nodding his head furiously, happy that Jack had understood.

'Shaolin kung fu?' Jack punched the air again. So, the monks are practising the arts of war Old Feng had spoken of.

'Yes, yes.' Ho grinned, delighted, then frowned and switched to English. '*Shaolin kung fu* very . . . *ngai him* . . . how you say . . . danger . . . you un'erstan?'

'It sure looks dangerous,' Jack replied as he watched the monks go through the 'kung fu dance', as he decided to call it.

The men moved in complete unison, their fists and feet striking imaginary targets, and they hissed and grunted with each strike. They look like animals, Jack thought. Yes, they move like animals. One moment they were tigers, the next monkeys and then birds flapping their wings; the dance was mesmerising. They wheeled and swung in the bright morning light, limbs flashing, muscles straining to the limit and sweat pouring in rivulets down their bare chests. On and on they went without let-up.

'Mista' Jack.' Stupid tapped him on the shoulder. 'You go home. Here no goo' for you.'

'OK, OK.' Jack pulled his attention away from the monks' dance and nodded at Stupid, but he had no intention of going home until he'd watched the kung fu dance to its very end. He remained behind the Scribe's Hut and watched Stupid Ho head back across the diggings. Then, as he was about to return to watch the dance, a very heated argument started up inside the Scribe's Hut.

'You cannot touch the girl!' he heard exclaimed in Cantonese. *'She is an innocent!'*

He placed his eye against a crack in the bark wall of the hut and saw the agitated old man with the beard chattering aggressively to the Scribe and another young man in Cantonese. He knew some words they used, not enough to understand the gist of the conversation, but one phrase the old man used a number of times registered in his mind, *gwok wong dik yeh gang*. It seemed to be the central point of the argument and he decided he must ask Feng what it meant.

Then he heard the grunt of a man in pain. He looked through the crack again and saw the old man with the beard slump to the floor. There was blood coming from his nose and, as his gaze focused on Jack's eye staring through the crack in the bark, he raised a withered hand and pointed a gnarled finger.

That was enough for Jack. He'd had his fill of the China Camp for one day. He ran for all he was worth, stopping only once outside Missus Hunter's tent to check he was not being followed, then he headed across the diggings for Main Street like a homing pigeon.

'And now, ladies and gentlemen,' Andrew Arbuthnot McCrae, the kilted Scottish dwarf, roared from centre stage, 'at great expense to the management, all the way from ancient Cathay, Cate Shearley Productions proudly presents that tumbling ball of amazement, that Oriental spinning top, that juggling genius, that unparalleled phenomenon of . . .'

'Shut up and get on with the show!' a drunken voice called from the audience.

'Yeah,' another howled, 'you little Scottish piss-ant, bring on the China Boy.'

The late show crowd of mostly drunken miners all hissed and booed in agreement and several threw food scraps onto the stage causing the little Scot to exit posthaste to the shelter of the wings.

With Cate's appearance on stage the food throwing stopped and the booing turned to lascivious whistling and calls to 'take it off, Catie girl', which also stopped when Cate produced a shotgun from the folds of her skirt and discharged both barrels into the canvas roof.

'I'm tired, lads,' she said, opening the breach and reloading both barrels. 'I've had a long day. So I'll tell you all only once, if you don't shut up and stop throwing rubbish, I swear I'll shoot one of you. I don't much care which one of you it is, but be it known that whoever it is will be dragged from the theatre out onto the street and he'll die in the dust and horseshit and the stray dogs will eat his remains.'

The silence that followed was palpable. All in the theatre knew of Cate's ability with a shotgun, they'd all heard of her performances in Melbourne dealing with drunken louts and scoundrels, and not a man among them doubted her capability to carry out the threat.

'Good.' She smiled at the house. 'Now I have your undivided attention,' she let the open shotgun rest over her forearm, 'we'll get on with the show.' She slammed the breech closed and gave them a wink with her good eye. 'Shall we?'

'Good on ya, Cate! Too right, Cate, m' beauty! You bet!' came the replies.

'Then without further ado,' she yelled bawdily, 'put your filthy paws together for the one and only China Boy!'

The applause became deafening as Lou-shi somersaulted onto the stage and Cate stepped into the wings.

'That was a stupid thing to do.' It was John standing backstage.

'Well, I had to do something! They were getting out of hand and you were nowhere to be seen!'

'One of these days, Cate!' John shouted as he snatched the shotgun from her and threw it across the backstage area into a pile of costumes. 'One of these God-damned days one of those drunken fools is going to take umbrage at what you say! Then what will you do?'

'Shoot him!' Cate glared at him. 'Like I ought to shoot you.' She pushed past him, picked up the shotgun and glared at him. 'You should decide who you are and what you want or you'll end up with nothing at all!' She went out the stage door, shoving Rhodesy aside as she did.

'What in God's name's the matter with her lately?' John sat dejectedly on the backstage steps.

'For a smart man you be fairly dim-witted, John la.'

'And what's that supposed to mean?' John looked up at his giant mate.

'She be wantin' a weddin' ring, la, and she won't settle for nought else.'

'A wedding ring?' John was genuinely shocked. 'No she doesn't. I already asked her to marry me and she said no,' he scoffed.

'She b'ain't of meant that, la. Women is fickle.'

'She's not that sort of woman.'

'What sort of woman is she, John *Saang*?' asked Feng. He had been sitting on a stool in the corner throughout the whole conversation.

'Well,' John stumbled, caught out. 'She's . . . well . . . you know . . . she's Cate!'

'All women are same, John *Saang*,' Feng said. He stood, folded his hands into his wide sleeves and walked over to stand by Rhodesy. 'Missy Cate no different to other women, except perhaps,' he reconsidered, raising his long index fingernail in the air, 'the Christian women called nuns. They believe they must only fuck the one true god, yes? Women need marriage and the father of their children must be honourable, you know, make a family, with a house and rice and noodles, you understand?'

'Now Old Feng there,' Rhodesy said, clapping his hands together, 'he's 'it the nail right on the 'ead, la! Cate, she bin both mother and father to young Jack now for years an' more. She wants a man to help her raise that boy. Someone who'll help carry the weight and not run off when the goin' gets tough.'

'I'd do that!' John exclaimed loudly. 'She knows I'd do that. I love her.'

'Ah, but John *Saang*, Mistress Cate must know you will love her son and be honourable father.'

'I would do that.'

'Have you tell her this, John *Saang*?'

'She won't let me near enough to tell her. I don't know what's wrong. I would not be surprised if she pulled a gun on me.'

'She's already done that, la.'

'Don't remind me.'

'You must try harder, *Bai-lou Saang*.'

'She won't sit still long enough for me to tell her.'

'Here's what you do, la.' Rhodesy placed his huge paw on John's shoulder. 'Tomorra mornin', you get down to the Hope Bakery and buy her a cake . . .'

'A cake?' John asked, doubtful.

'Or a pastry, you know,' the giant wiggled his fingers in a very fussy gesture, 'one of them fine tarts with cream in it and jam an' . . .'

'How could that possibly help?'

'She'll 'ave to be quiet while she sits down and eats it and that's when you ask 'er to marry you.'

John stared at the giant, incredulous. 'Are you serious?'

'Ladies don't talk when they eat, it's not polite, la.'

'Christ on the cross!' John exploded and stormed out through the stage door.

Rhodesy shrugged. 'I thought it were a good idea, Mister Feng, didn't you? I mean, she gets somethin' nice to eat an' 'e gets to talk to 'er, like.' He sat on the stage steps John had vacated and shrugged again. 'When he gets a bee in his bonnet about somethin' there's no talking sense to 'im.'

'John *Saang* is not wearing bonnet.'

'It's just a sayin'.'

'What is?'

'A bee in your bonnet.'

'It sound like unpleasant experience.'

'What I meant was John's upset and not thinkin' straight.'

'Ah, yes.' Feng nodded, sage-like, and squeezed himself onto the stage steps next to the big man. 'John *Saang* in love with Mistress Cate. Any man who lusts after a woman is a fool.'

'Now, 'ow can you say that, Feng me hearty?' It was Rhodesy's turn to look puzzled. 'A man a' your years must 'ave 'ad many a romantic tryst, as they say, in his life.'

'Only one.'

'Well now, I find that hard to believe!' The giant gave Feng a friendly nudge with his elbow that all but sent the old man off the steps to the floor. 'A man who's spent his life in theatre, I mean . . . if Chinese theatre be anythin' like the theatre where I come from, there must have been no end a' beautiful young women to be 'ad.'

'She was the daughter of a third-ranked Mandarin . . .' Feng began.

'Wha's a Mandarin?'

'A senior court official.'

'I see. And what 'appened?'

'He discovered our relationship and had me emasculated.'

'You don't say? Emasculated, eh? And wha's that?'

'His servants captured me and cut off my testicles.'

'Whoa! Now, now!' Rhodesy flew to his feet unnerved. 'Wait just a minute! Hang about now, la!' He looked, wide-eyed, at the little Chinese man. 'Do you mean to say 'e 'ad 'is men cut off your tackle! Your whatsits, like?'

What's it like? A strange question, Feng thought. 'It was not a pleasant experience.'

'You can say that again!' The big man waved his hands in front of Feng. 'No, no, I mean don't say it again.'

'Do you have a bee in your bonnet, Rhodes *Saang*?'

'Now don't start up with that again either!' Rhodesy headed for the stage door. 'I gotta be off now; I've got to do me rounds of the premises, like. I'm on guard duty, so I'd better get about it. G'night, Feng . . . and . . . I'm sorry . . . about your testicles!'

It was Lou-shi, the following day, who was first to notice the change in Jack's demeanour. At the evening meal, the usually ebullient boy was quiet and withdrawn and he played with the Chinese food he normally gulped down like a greedy piglet. Since being introduced to it he adored Chinese food and not an evening went by that she would not find him loitering at the stage door awaiting an invitation to join her, Feng and Stupid in a bowl of Cantonese cuisine.

She caught Feng's eye and realised he too was aware of the boy's subdued manner. With a nod of his head he encouraged her to question Jack.

'Do you like, or not like the fried rice, Jack boy?' she asked in Cantonese.

'What?' he asked back, distracted. *'Sorry . . . eh . . . what?'* he mumbled, as he attempted to dissect the simple Cantonese question. *'Like,'* he finally replied with the verb, *'like very much.'*

'When people do not eat food it means they are sick,' Feng said.

'I am not hungry this evening, Master Feng.'

'A boy who is not hungry is sick,' the old man answered. *'Boys eat like pigs until their stomachs burst, true or not true?'*

'I do not know.' Jack placed the unfinished bowl of rice on the floor in front of him. He was bursting to unburden himself of what he'd witnessed in the Scribe's Hut, but knew he could tell them nothing of what he'd seen. If the Scribe were to find out he saw the old man with the bleeding nose, he might send the Shaolin men to kill him. And they might also kill his mother and father John, and Lou-shi, and Feng and Stupid. The panic began to rise in him and he got to his feet.

'I have to go,' he said rapidly and took off through the stage door.

'He is worried about something,' Feng said.

'The death of Old Soong, the Scribe's father, yesterday at the Chinese Camp,' Stupid said matter-of-factly. *'Maybe he knows and it has upset him.'*

'How could Jack know what happened in the camp?' Lou-shi asked. *'He is not allowed to go there unless I accompany him. That is Mistress Cate's order.'*

'He followed me down to Golden Point, so maybe he . . .'

'What!' Feng interrupted. *'You let him go into the Chinese Camp? Alone?'*

'I did not know he was in the village until I saw him behind the temple,' Stupid howled.

'You're an idiot, Stupid!'

'I kept my eye on him!' the stage manager asserted. *'I let him watch the Shaolin monks go through their disciplines, then I sent him straight home. That was well before the old man was found dead, so Jack boy could not possibly know of it, true or not true, aaahh?'* The question mark was a defensive, elongated, Cantonese plea.

Feng sighed, placed his empty rice bowl on the floor and leaned back against the wall. *'Something is wrong with that boy. I do not like to see him unhappy.'* He looked at Lou-shi. *'Go and talk to him, perhaps he will confide in you.'*

'How did Old Soong die?' Lou-shi asked of Stupid.

'The Scribe's apprentice Leung-jai found him in his tent; he apparently died of a heart attack.'

'So it was a natural death?'

'Yes.' Stupid shook his head. *'He was an old man and he died. That is all.'*

'Why would you ask such a question, Lou-shi?' Feng asked.

'I don't know,' she shrugged.

'It would be ill-advised to suggest otherwise,' Feng said. *'Soong the Scribe, the one they call Egghead, is the trusted accountant of the See Yup Society. He is held in high regard as an honourable man.'*

'*Daan Tau* is not honourable. He is a bad person, he hit an old man.'

All three looked to where Jack stood, framed in the stage doorway. The boy was visibly upset; his lip was quivering and his hands trembling.

'Come and sit down, Jack.' Lou-shi spoke in English and patted the floor beside her. 'Tell us what has upset you.'

Jack quickly took up her invitation and when Lou-shi put her arm around him he informed them of what he'd observed the previous day.

'You are sure you see blood, Jack?' Feng asked softly when the boy finally fell silent.

'Yes,' Jack sobbed. 'The old man had a bleeding nose.'

'Was he alive?'

'Was he alive?' Jack repeated the question. It had unnerved him. He looked at Feng with startled eyes. 'Yes, he was alive. As I told you, he was lying on the floor with a bleeding nose. Then he saw me looking through the crack in the wall and he pointed at me. That's when I ran off.'

'Did anyone see you, Jack?'

'No, Lou-shi. Only the old man and he could only see my eye.'

'Are you sure there was no-one else?' Lou-shi hugged him.

'Yes, I'm sure.'

'Who was the other man with the Scribe?' Feng asked.

'I don't know. I only saw *Daan Tau*. I saw his bald head.'

'Who hit the old man?'

'I don't know. I only heard him get hit. I thought it must have been *Daan Tau*, because he was very angry.'

'Will he send the fighting priests after me?'

'No,' Lou-shi said, reassuring him.

'Did you understand what they were arguing about?'

'No,' Jack shook his head, 'not really. Some words, not enough. But I heard one phrase said a lot.'

'Really?' Feng felt a shiver run up his spine.

'Yes, the old man kept saying it.'

'And what was the phrase?'

'Gwok wong dik yeh gang.' Jack registered Lou-shi's shocked intake of breath. 'What does it mean, Mister Feng?'

Feng looked at Lou-shi and Stupid Ho in turn before answering. 'It means "The Emperor's Nightingale".'

'Do you mean the *real* Emperor of China?' John looked up from where he sat by the morning campfire.

'Yes, *Bai-lou Saang*.' Feng tucked his hands into the sleeves of his long robe. 'Hsien-feng is his name. He is very powerful. He would pay much money for her.'

'Who would pay much money for whom?' Cate stepped down from the stage door, sat next to John, took his cup of tea and sipped it.

'Feng is saying there may be a plan afoot in the Chinese village to kidnap Lou-shi and sell her to the Emperor of China.' He raised an eyebrow at Cate. 'I must say it sounds highly fanciful, to say the least.'

Cate looked at Feng. 'Does Lou-shi know of this threat?'

'Yes, Mistress Cate. She is very frightened.'

She nodded. 'I just left her in the theatre. I wondered what was bothering her.'

'Well now you know,' John grunted. 'Being kidnapped is not the sort of thing anyone wants to contemplate, I'm sure.'

'Lou-shi told me, back in Melbourne,' Cate continued, 'about the Green Lotus Opera Company and the . . . um . . . Taiping Rebellion, was it?' Feng nodded. 'And the deaths of her friends. Apparently, this Emperor fellow believes she is a traitor.'

'She is not traitor.' Feng shook his head. 'Emperor make big mistake.'

'Well can't you tell these Red Pavilion people that?' John shrugged at Cate. 'Maybe that will put a stop to it all.'

'Brotherhood of Red Pavilion is very powerful. They will take her to Emperor. This is certain!'

'Forgive me,' John raised his palms, 'but Peking is ten thousand miles from here.'

'Do not doubt the Brotherhood, *Bai-lou Saang*. They just like 14-K of Hong Kong and Green Pang of Shanghai; they have influence across the world. London, San Francisco, Peking, Singapore, you find triads. Melbourne, too, no different. They will steal her.'

'Don't you think in this instance they may be behaving a little obsessively? I mean, Ballarat to Peking. Surely not?'

'*Bai-lou Saang*, Chinese Emperor represent Celestial Kingdom of Heaven here on earth. Citizens of the Middle Kingdom regard Hsien-feng as a god. Is our patriotic duty to ensure Emperor remain forever happy and content; therefore, the return of his nightingale would be good for all Chinese people.'

John raised an eyebrow. 'Are you saying this Brotherhood lot really are doing it for love of their Emperor?'

'No,' Feng replied, remaining expressionless. 'They just do for money.'

John stared at Feng for several seconds before deciding the workings of the Oriental mind were beyond his comprehension. He looked at Cate and shook his head in exasperation.

'We have to protect her, John.'

'Why don't I simply go to the Chinese Village and have a word with these people . . .'

'Nooo!' Feng wailed. 'Brotherhood very bad men.'

'Feng's right, my love.' Cate put her hand on his shoulder. 'That would just invite trouble. And more importantly, it would make them aware that we know of their plot.'

John's face broke into a smile. 'You are not just a pretty face, are you, my pet?' He patted her hand. 'Very well, I'll inform Kit and Rhodesy of the situation and have them go armed at all times. We'll look after our little Chinese princess and make damned sure no-one takes her anywhere.'

CHAPTER THIRTEEN

Ballarat, November 1854

Two weeks had passed since the Bakery Hill meeting when fifteen thousand angry miners had established the Ballarat Reform League. The Goldfields Chief Administrator, Commissioner Robert Rede, had continued to ignore the warning signs and allowed the political situation to deteriorate to such an extent that open rebellion was all but assured. Furthermore, he had persisted in ignoring the behaviour of the military and his policemen, many of whom were ex-convicts and drunkards, and their appalling behaviour and wanton cruelty had fuelled the hatred of the miners to a fever pitch. His chief cohort, Police Magistrate John D'Ewes, had been sacked from his post on 4 November, a week before the Bakery Hill meeting, but his replacement, Police Inspector Gordon Evans, was a man of even worse character than D'Ewes and he openly disliked Rede.

British military class to his bootstraps, Commissioner Rede firmly believed the Irish and Americans were inciting sedition among law-abiding British subjects and were bent on bringing about rebellion and eventually a republic free from British control. An insufferable, bureaucratic snob, swollen with a sense of his own social importance, Robert Rede was universally despised.

Shearley's Variety Shows had increased to four a day and played to packed houses. The money was rolling in.

'The ledgers are a sight to behold, Mister Feng,' Cate said as she perused the books backstage. 'Indeed they are works of art.'

'Even the Dynasty of the Ming could not create such beauty,' Feng added, nodding at his one-eyed boss. He tried at all times to retain his inscrutable Oriental mask of disinterest, but inside he smiled with the joy of a birthday child. He would be rich beyond his wildest expectations when they returned to Melbourne and divided the spoils.

Feng deeply respected Cate Shearley; the Englishwoman had all the attributes that brought about greatness: intelligence above all and wit, strength of will, an innate capacity for organisation and the intrinsic ability to bind people to her. Yes, Feng thought as he looked at her examining the accounts, her good eye following her flickering fingers across the paper, Mistress Cate was a woman to be admired. *Bai-lou Saang* obviously found her irresistible judging by the interminable rocking of her caravan every night, which kept Feng awake.

Feng had not needed to sexually evaluate a woman for many years, ever since an irate Mandarin had relieved him of his testicles. His eyes examined her breasts, desperately pressing to escape the confines of her dress, but nothing sexual stirred within him, only the faintest desire for opium, for the juice of the poppy had been the closest experience to love he'd ever known.

'Tell me, how is Lou-shi coping?' She was suddenly standing, staring at him.

'Why you ask?' He looked up at her, frowning. It had been two weeks and nothing had occurred. He no longer feared the Brotherhood had any interest in his nightingale. They would have acted by now.

'It's just that we are now doing four shows a day and I know she's been stressed. I hope the increased workload is not too hard for her.'

'Lou-shi is very happy. Four shows okay.'

'I'm pleased to hear it.' She smiled at him. She enjoyed her conversations with Feng. 'Should we continue to expect trouble from those Brotherhood men?'

'No. No more trouble. I no think so.'

'Your compatriots in the Chinese Village, are they coping with all the troubles Ballarat is having?'

'Chinese same as all miners. Chinese do not like licence law, but they will do nothing. Nothing is best thing to do. But government will cause some trouble.'

'Is that what you think?'

Feng produced a fan from the folds of his sleeve and fluttered it rapidly under his chin. 'Government will make trouble between whites and Chinese. The Commission men, Rede and Johnston, will do this, so they can say Ballarat people is racist, not a political matter. Is better for them to say this. Then they can say trouble in Ballarat not their fault.'

She looked at him, her eyes revealing concern. 'Are we really treading that close to the abyss, Mister Feng?'

'Since murder of James Scobie last month and riot and burning down Bentley's Hotel. Trouble must come!' He thought suddenly of Lou-shi and the Brotherhood. Despite the fact they had not acted, he could not trust the triad society. He really should get the girl out of Ballarat just to be on the safe side. 'Mistress Cate, I think we end tour and return to Melbourne. We make much money, far more than I think possible to do.'

'Yes, you're right. Ballarat will explode sooner or later, if not this year then certainly next.' Cate began to pace back and forth. 'What's today?'

'Sunday, twenty-sixth day of November.' Feng was meticulous with calendars.

'We'll see out the month, Mister Feng,' Cate decided, turning to him. 'We'll re-evaluate in December,' she ticked off days on her fingers, 'a week tomorrow, Monday the fourth. If things have deteriorated further by then we'll pack up and go.'

'That is wise, Cate Shearley.' Feng nodded.

'Yes. Yes it is, isn't it?' She suddenly felt happy. Melbourne was home. Melbourne meant safety and security for Jack.

'What's wise of Cate Shearley?' John said as he burst through the backstage door, his arms full of pink flowering bushes.

'Boronia!' Cate declared and thrust her nose into the plants. 'Oh, do they not have the most divine scent.' John pulled away from her and threw the bushes through the wings onto the stage. 'They are not for you. I had them gathered to alleviate the overwhelming smell of urine, vomit and dog shit!'

'Perhaps just one small sprig,' she pleaded with a glint of humour in her eye.

'Of course, my dear.' He picked up a small branch from the floor and thrust it at her.

'Oh, Romeo,' she sighed theatrically, clutching the plant to her bosom. Her histrionics brought a rare smile to Feng's face.

'Now, what did you say that Feng thought so wise?' John asked, brushing leaves and blossoms from his clothing.

'He's of the opinion Ballarat is soon to be consumed by the flames of rebellion and I'm inclined to agree with him. I've decided . . .'

'Rubbish!' John snorted. 'The miners are angry, you'll get no argument from me there, but the vast majority of them are decent law-abiding men. Those who would push matters to the point of revolt against the Crown are a mere handful of troublemakers.'

'A handful of troublemakers!' Cate couldn't believe her ears. John's grasp of the matter was, to say the least, disingenuous, bordering on naïve. 'Half the population of Ballarat was at the last meeting on Bakery Hill and you're saying that constitutes a handful of troublemakers?'

'There *will* be trouble, *Bai-lou Saang*,' Feng interjected. 'The hotel man Bentley is on trial in Melbourne for murder of Scobie, and the three miners on trial for riotous behaviour. If outcome not favourable, miners will rise up.'

'Any violence whatsoever and the miners would be despatched instantly!' John scoffed. 'Why, a single troop of dragoons would sort them out in no time at all.'

'Get your head out of the ranks, John!' Cate snapped. 'We're not talking about war. We're speaking about civilians who believe unjust authorities are persecuting them.'

'Nonetheless,' he replied, 'the outcome will be the same: they'll be decimated.'

'Stop thinking like a soldier,' Cate groaned in frustration. 'It matters not one whit who wins; what matters is the result and how it will be perceived.'

'It will be regarded as an act of treason.'

'Put yourself in their place, John,' she said. 'You've experienced it yourself, having to produce a licence on demand. Just imagine you're out on the flats panning for gold, with a family by your side, living in a tent. You're having no luck and you have little money, yet you're constantly trying to pay an outrageous licence fee and still keep enough money to feed us all. Would you put up with it?'

Before he could respond Kit Kittredge burst through the stage door, his arms also full of flowering boronia bushes.

'Odds bodekins, Bailleau!' the American growled through the plants obscuring his vision, 'I'll stink like a French cathouse if I don't divest myself of these damned things.'

John laughed. 'Throw them on the stage to Rhodesy; he'll spread them around the theatre.'

Kit heaved the bushes through the wings onto the stage, stood back brushing himself down and suddenly became aware of Cate's presence.

'Oh, I'm so sorry, Cate.' His faced reddened. 'Do forgive the intemperate language; it's just that the scent of flowers and I don't get along. And I must say forest boronia has the strongest and sweetest scent I've ever experienced.'

Cate smiled. 'You've spent quite a bit of time in cathouses, have you, Kit?'

'Oh no!' he gasped, not knowing where to look. 'It's just a saying.'

'I did once,' she said, looking at John, 'but that's another story, isn't it?'

'Um . . . er . . .' Kit stammered, '. . . right.' He looked at John. 'News in from Melbourne: Bentley was convicted of the manslaughter of that miner Scobie –'

'That will make the miners happy,' John interrupted.

'Not for long.' Kit shook his head. 'McIntyre, Fletcher and Westoby were convicted of riotous behaviour.'

'Oh, no!' Cate's hand flew to her mouth. 'That will cause trouble.'

'Straw that break camel's back,' Feng announced. 'Is what you say, I think.'

'I don't believe there will be violence,' John said firmly. 'Governor Hotham's announcement last week that he's ordered a Royal Commission to inquire into the goldfields should keep a lid on things . . . well, for a while at least.'

'Hotham is an idiot!' Cate exclaimed. 'The Commission will appease no-one. There'll be blood on the wattle before they even announce who the Commissioner will be.'

'Don't worry, Cate,' Kit waved at her, 'the Commission will never happen. And if it does it will be a superficial, highly theatrical affair and they'll find some gigantic clown or other to stage-manage it.'

'Orright, orright!' Rhodesy burst through the wings from the stage. 'I'm the stage manager and you lot'll 'ave to get out of 'ere or be very quiet.' He stood blinking in amazement as they all began laughing. 'Shut up!' he cried. 'There's payin' customers enterin' the 'ouse.'

'Sorry,' was all Cate could manage to squeak as she imagined the bearded giant overseeing the Royal Commission. She took a handkerchief from her sleeve and wiped tears from her eyes.

'I'm the stage manager!'

This statement set Cate off anew.

It was at that precise moment Lou-shi and Wolfie Bremmer entered. Lou-shi went immediately behind a black curtain to don her China Boy costume and Wolfie went through the wings to the stage and began playing the house piano to welcome the 'bums on seats', as Cate called the customers.

'Is everyone ready to go?' It was Andrew the Scottish dwarf followed closely by Adelina the Italian who was actually Spanish, and Anna and Lanna the contortionist twins chattering madly in German, then finally Virat, the Indian snake charmer, the newest member of the troupe.

Cate collected herself. 'The entire cast is present, Mister Rhodes,' she said in her most professional tone. 'You may give them their five-minute call.'

Cate had insisted on 'the calls' before each show. A tradition in British theatre, the 'half' call is given to all performers to alert them that the first act will commence in thirty-five minutes. The five-minute call is then given five minutes before curtain up.

'Right now, you lot!' Rhodesy bellowed.

The entire cast turned to him as one.

'Consider yourselves called, or whatever,' he whispered. 'You,' he pointed to the boy billed as Virat the Indian Snake Charmer. 'You're first up so be ready when Dafty Boy announces you,' he pointed at the diminutive Scot.

'I'd rather you didn't call me that,' the dwarf snapped.

'The music's stopped, Dafty,' the giant growled at the little man. 'You're on, la!' He pointed to the steps leading up to the wings. 'Get out there and introduce the darky!' He turned to the supposedly Indian snake charmer. 'Have you got your snakes, la?'

The 'darky' was in fact an Aborigine of the Tooloora clan, a branch of the Wathaurung people, who had resided in the Ballarat area for tens of thousands of years and now found itself – thanks to the British Empire, European diseases and a gold rush – on the verge of extinction.

One month before while out riding, Cate had discovered the boy, whose name was Djali, on the flat beyond the diggings playing with several venomous snakes and handling them with complete disregard for his welfare. When asked why he appeared unafraid, he said snakes were his brothers and would never bite him. Djali, or Charlie as he became instantly known, had no home, no family and no future as far as Cate could determine. Therefore, she'd contracted the lad to the Variety Show and taken him under her wing.

'Have you got your snakes, la?' Rhodesy asked again in what he believed was a whisper.

'I got 'em, boss.' Charlie grinned and waved a calico bag at the big man while the whole cast gathered in the confines of backstage, shivering at the sight of the snake bag.

'Good morning, ladies and gentlemen,' the Scottish dwarf was heard announcing from centre stage, 'and welcome to

Cate Shearley's Travelling Variety Show. And now, without further ado, please welcome to the stage, all the way from India, that Regent of Reptiles, that Saint of Slippery Snakes, that Virtuous Vendor of the Venomous, the one and only Virat of Varanasi, the Indian Snake Charmer!'

'That means you, la,' Rhodesy smiled at the young Aborigine.

'I'm not Indian, boss, I'm Koori.'

'That's close enough. On you go now, there's a good lad.'

Despite half the audience being drunk and boisterous at ten o'clock in the morning, the show went off without a hitch.

It was two o'clock when the afternoon show began and from the outset things did not run as smoothly as the morning.

'I'm authorised,' Andrew the dwarf bellowed in his thick Glaswegian accent, 'by none other than the Queen of Melbourne herself, Madam Cate Shearley, to pay fifty pounds to anyone who'll step up here and pull a snake from the bag being held by Virat, the Indian Snake Charmer.' He waved his hand theatrically at Djali, who was shaking his head at the stupidity of the offer, while placing a brown snake back in the calico bag.

Cate had never authorised such an offer be made, but Andrew knew no-one in their right mind would ever accept the challenge, so he'd made it his party piece during every performance. He was about to dismiss Djali and bring on Tommy the magician when a voice called from the back row, 'Oi'll be havin' that fifty pounds, if you don't moind.'

'Christ and Saint Michael save me from the fucking Irish,' Andrew said from behind his hand. But before he could dismiss the drunk, who was already halfway to the stage, the audience, mostly drunk themselves, began cheering and howling encouragement to the idiot, who was grinning stupidly and waving to them as he mounted the stage.

'Get the money ready, little man,' the Irishman said with a wink, then without further invitation thrust his hand into the bag full of snakes. His drunken grin disappeared immediately; he screamed, pulled his hand from the bag and, clasping it to his chest, fell onto the stage. 'The fookin' thing's bit me!' he screamed. 'I'm gonna die, for fook's sake!'

Djali looked at the bite on the man's index finger and shook his head. 'You're one lucky white-fella today. You got bit by that red-bellied black snake I got livin' in there. You won't die today, white-fella, you'll just be sick and tomorrow you'll be all right.'

'Are you sure, Charlie laddie?' It was Andrew Arbuthnot McCrae who asked the question, not the Irishman. Andrew was already envisaging Cate Shearley pointing her shotgun at him.

Djali thrust his hand in the bag and pulled out another snake – it was an eastern brown, the snake feared above all by Australians. Fast-moving, aggressive and bad-tempered, the brown snake contained enough venom to kill everyone in the place.

'If this bloke bit you,' Djali said good-naturedly, waving the animal in the Irishman's face, 'I'd be sayin' hoo-roo to you right now.'

'Fook, fook, fook!' the Irishman groaned. He got to his feet, walked to the edge of the stage and vomited on the fresh boronia.

'Get outside if you're going to do that!' the little Scot yelled and the Irishman staggered up the side aisle and out through the doors.

Things did not go according to plan with Adelina's performance either. The 'Soprano from Milano' was halfway through a Verdi aria when a series of guttural remarks in her native Spanish came from the audience. Without hesitating, or indeed even stopping the song, she leapt from the stage, waded through the first five rows and punched the heckler senseless. The eighth punch, which rendered the man unconscious, coincided with the final note of the aria and Adelina used it most theatrically in a blazing display of bravura. The audience applauded with gusto as Adelina walked back onto the stage in a highly dignified manner, bowed to the drunks and exited stage right with an aristocratic toss of her head and a swish of her voluminous dress.

Sudden piano chords pounded out the entrance of China Boy, and Lou-shi tumbled across the stage in a series of handstands synchronised with high-speed arpeggios by Wolfie Bremmer. She was met with cheering and loud applause from the audience, all of whom had obviously seen the show on more than one occasion. More musical somersaults followed then she left the stage momentarily to reappear with two thin bamboo rods atop of which porcelain saucers were spinning at high speed.

It was at that moment her eye caught movement at the rear of the theatre. Four Chinese men, all wearing red bandanas, entered and sat themselves in the back row. Lou-shi's involuntary reaction saw both saucers crash onto the stage, splintering and spraying into the audience.

The spectators were taken aback by this rare mistake from their favourite performer, but Lou-shi, the consummate professional, recovered herself quickly and began to juggle six silver balls with great skill.

Mister Feng, who'd heard the saucers smash, came to the wings. Wolfie caught his eye then transferred his gaze to the back row. Feng's eyes followed and his reaction was similar to Lou-shi's, an involuntary spasm of the abdominal muscles. He took a deep breath, nodded to Wolfie and disappeared.

Lou-shi managed to end Act I without further incident and when she looked back into the theatre from the wings, the four men had gone.

Feng grabbed her and ushered her into the corner of the backstage area.

'They were just boys, Lou-shi,' he said, reassuring her in Cantonese. *'We should not worry. It was a foolish act of bravado. If their master knew he would punish them severely.'*

'They are looking for me! They know I am the nightingale. Remember what Jack heard.'

'Tell no-one,' Feng interrupted as he saw Wolfie Bemmer approaching. *'All will be well, princess.'*

'What did you make of that, Mister Feng?' Wolfie placed his hand on Lou-shi's shoulder.

'They were stupid boys,' she tried to reassure him, but her voice wavered. 'Just stupid boys, just stupid boys, just stupid boys.'

'Hush now, Lou-shi.' Feng used the soothing tone he reserved for her when she became agitated.

'They looked very serious to me,' Wolfie said. 'Shouldn't we tell John Bailleau, or Cate?'

'No need, Bremmer *Saang*,' Feng cooed. He turned to Lou-shi. 'You must get dressed, Lou-shi. You, Bremmer *Saang*, you first on stage to open Act II. Hurry, hurry,' he went on, reacting to her anxious expression, then he changed again to Cantonese. *'And the show must continue, Lou-shi. The show must always continue, true or not true, ah?'*

'They will take me back to China!' The girl began humming and rocking back and forth. *'To China, to China, to China.'*

'Don't concern yourself with those triad boys.' He tenderly stroked her shoulder, recognising the peculiar mental state she sometimes entered into. *'You are all that matters in my life, Lou-shi, I would never let any harm come to you.'*

The girl calmed down but he saw the beginning of tears in her eyes.

Act II began well; Adelina sang the Verdi aria *'Ah fors' è lui che l'anima'* beautifully, but unfortunately her Spanish heckler had regained consciousness and took up where he'd left off. However, Adelina had no need to leave the stage as three other miners sitting nearby rendered him insensible again.

The German girls also exchanged blows with several drunken miners who climbed onto the stage to grope them, but years of touring with obscure, second-rate companies on the less salubrious theatrical circuits of Europe had served them well. Both girls could fist-fight like men and did so whenever the chance arose. Feng was convinced they enjoyed it.

Act II continued to the finale and Lou-shi, now as Michiko the Japanese Lady, went on stage in her Virtuous Maiden of Swatow costume of gold-embroidered silk trousers and a long shirt that was predominantly sky blue, but with overlays of orange, pink and purple, intended to match the colours of the setting sun. Her make-up was superb and the magnificent jewelled headpiece her crowning glory. However, no sooner did she begin to sing than the four young Chinese men in their red bandanas entered from the street and again sat in the back row. They were clearly targeting her performances.

Lou-shi sang on, but her rapid glances at Wolfie and to Feng in the wings told them she was unnerved. No sooner had she completed her songs than she fled into the wings and refused to go back on to take bows, despite the audience's standing ovation.

'If you don't tell Bailleau, I will,' Wolfie snapped at Feng backstage. 'They terrified her.'

'I agree,' Feng replied. 'I have sent little Jack-jai to bring *Bai-lou Saang* here immediately.'

Lou-shi was shaking so badly the twins Anna and Lanna had to help remove the elaborate Chinese costume, and then she refused to come out of the costume alcove.

'What seems to be the problem, Mister Feng?' John entered the backstage area. 'Jack says we've got trouble.'

'Four young Chinese men enter theatre for Lou-shi's performances, *Bai-lou Saang*,' Feng began.

'Who are they?'

'They are Brotherhood of the Red Pavilion. Bad men. Criminals.'

'Did you know about this?' John demanded of Rhodesy.

'No.' The big man shook his head. 'I don't look at the audience when I'm stage-managerin', I only look at 'em when I'm securityin'. Today I'm stage-managerin'.'

'You should have been aware of what was occurring.'

'That's Security's job,' Rhodesy growled.

'Well, who was on Security?'

'You,' the big man said. 'But you 'aven't done a bit of it all day.'

'Oh, dear.' John looked at his giant friend. 'I'm sorry, Rhodesy. I've been attending to contractual obligations with businesses around the town.'

'They entered the theatre during both acts,' Wolfie contributed, 'but only during Lou-shi's performances, then left immediately after she had finished. They were clearly sending a message.'

'What do you have to say about all this, Mister Feng?'

'Simple. Brotherhood will take Lou-shi.'

'What do you mean, "take her"?'

'English word is kidnap.'

'Not if I have any say in the matter.' He looked at Rhodesy. 'Find Kit and have him report to me. We three will commence guarding Lou-shi on a rotating four-hour watch. And Mister Feng?'

'Yes, *Bai-lou Saang*.'

'You will assist Yue Chun with all stage management duties. Another pair of eyes won't go astray. Between us we'll inform all the cast members to remain inside the compound between shows and report anything they may consider even remotely suspicious.'

'What shall I do, Father?' Jack desperately wanted a role.

'The most important job of all, son.' John ruffled the boy's hair. 'You must ensure that your mother is safe at all times.'

'Aaaaw!' Jack scowled. 'That's not a job.'

'It is essential everyone obeys orders, Jack.'

'Can I have a gun?'

'I don't know. Ask your mother.'

It was almost midnight when John met Kit outside the stage door to take over guard duty.

'Where's our little Chinese miss?'

'Safely in bed,' Kit replied, tilting his head to indicate backstage.

'Good. I'll take over now.' John placed his Sharps rifle against the door jamb and checked the cylinder of his revolver. 'Otherwise all quiet?'

'Well, as quiet as Main Street can get, I suppose, given the theatres are closed and the bowling alley.' The American raised his eyebrows and shrugged. 'But the beer tents seem to be operating as usual and those damned dogs keep up their infernal barking no matter what the time.'

John laughed. 'Add to that barking the noises of children crying and women screaming, interspersed with gunfire and foul-mouthed abuse, and you have what Cate calls the "Nocturnal Symphony of Ballarat".'

'Yes,' Kit nodded. 'And add to that the stink of unwashed bodies and human waste carried in the smoke of ten thousand campfires and you have what I would describe as "Dante's Inferno".'

'Very apt, Mister Kittredge,' John said. 'The Nine Circles of Hell and all to be found on one goldfield, eh?'

'And I believe the Seventh Circle will soon raise its ugly head.'

'The Seventh?' John shook his head. 'Remind me?'

'Violence, the Seventh Circle of Hell is Violence, John.' He sniffed the night air, as if suddenly aware of it. 'My word but the smoke is incredibly thick tonight.'

'Yes, I must agree.' John pulled back the curtain that acted as the stage door and smoke billowed forth. 'God in heaven! Fire! Fire!' he called, noticing the glow from behind the curtains, as Lou-shi and Feng sat up in their backstage bed. Lou-shi screamed and, pushing past the two men, rushed out through the stage door. 'Christ alive, Kit, the theatre's on fire! Get him out of here.' He pointed at Feng as he rushed through the wings. 'And find Lou-shi. She'll be the one they're after.'

There were five men in the theatre, all wearing red headbands and each brandishing a blazing torch. He drew Mister Adams and shot one who was standing on the stage. The remaining four threw their torches into the mass of boronia branches scattered between the pews and made for the front doors. John chased them out into Main Street where he took aim and fired, hitting one man in the back of the knee, as the others disappeared.

He looked back at the Paragon. The fire was taking hold of the theatre. The wooden structure was starting to flame.

'John la,' Rhodesy called as he came around the side of the theatre. 'Where be Andy boy?'

'Who?'

'Andy, the little Scot. All the other cast be out in the back, but I can't find Andy.'

'I haven't seen him.'

John watched in horror as the giant ran in through the box office and foyer, directly into what was now a blazing inferno.

'What's he doing?' Cate yelled at John over the roar of the flames as she ran into the street.

'Good God!' John realised the giant's intention. 'He's gone to get the dwarf.'

They could only watch as flames and sparks leapt into the night sky.

Inside the theatre Rhodesy made his way through the smoke to the stage. He burned his hands on the wooden structure as he knelt and reached beneath it. He dragged the unconscious Scot out and lifted him. He turned as burning pain struck his forearms and he staggered towards the front of house.

John and Cate saw Rhodesy walk from the flames with Andrew Arbuthnot McCrae in his arms. He placed the little man on the ground as John and Cate smothered the giant's burning clothes.

'Christ alive, man!' John roared at his friend. 'What were you thinking!'

'I couldn't leave Dafty Boy to the flames, la! No-one deserves to die like that.'

'Is he dead?' Cate stared at the little Scotsman's body.

'Aye,' Rhodesy nodded. 'He be dead orright! Dead drunk. He'll sleep it off – he'll be fine in the morning.'

'Have you seen Lou-shi?'

'She be orright, Cate. Don't worry yourself. Kit's got her well guarded, but he had a bit o' trouble. Two of them Chinamen came fer 'er. Kit shot 'em both, but your little stage manager man Ho, he got hurt tryin' to 'elp the lass.'

The street was already filled with people organising buckets of water from the creek below. Within several minutes buildings and tents were being drenched either side of Cate's theatre. But there was no saving the Paragon; once its canvas roof took flame, the wood and sod walls quickly followed and the theatre was done for. Thankfully the Shearley travelling caravans and wagons had been preserved, due mainly to the efforts of the entertainers who had quickly and effectively organised themselves into a fire-fighting crew.

In Main Street the angry crowd now encircled the man John had shot in the knee. They fell silent, staring at the wounded Oriental, allowing their rage to foment. Then a woman's voice screeched, 'Kill the Chink! Kill the heathen bastard!' and the crowd acted as one, stomping and kicking the man to death.

John looked on dispassionately, caring not one iota for the Chinese man's fate. Then he chanced to look to his left and there, in front of what had once been the main entrance to the Paragon, he saw his son Jack staring, horrified, at the sickening violence of the crowd.

John leapt among the riotous mob, several of whom were inciting the crowd to kill all the Chinese in Ballarat, and fired his revolver three times in the air. It brought him the mob's attention and he stood in the middle of them and stared at the mad-eyed crowd, his expression daring anyone to defy him.

'Has there not been enough killing tonight?' He turned full circle, glaring at men, defying them to refute his statement. 'Well?' His voice rose. 'Has there not been enough killing for one night?' He turned again, seeking any eyes that would challenge him. 'You're being watched by children, for God's sake, one of whom is mine! You should all get home to your beds.' He glared at the now silent men and women, then heaved a sigh and continued. 'On behalf of Cate Shearley I thank you all for your speedy response to assist us in our misfortune. We may not have saved the Paragon, but your efforts to do so were noble in the extreme.' He looked down and pointed at the dead Chinese man at his feet. 'There must be no more of this; it serves no purpose. Five young men set fire to the Paragon tonight and two have paid with their lives, so let's have an end to it.'

With the fire now out, slowly but surely the crowd began to disperse, and as the street cleared he felt Cate's arm thread itself through his.

'That's what I call being a father.' She looked up at him, then they both took in their son standing alone in the deserted street. 'I especially liked, "You're being watched by children, for God's sake, one of whom is mine". Most impressive, delivered with biblical intensity, I do believe you are maturing at last. There could even be a career for you on the stage.'

'Are you being facetious?'

'Not remotely.'

'No-one his age should have to witness such animal behaviour.' He turned towards the pile of ashes which had been the Paragon Theatre and she turned with him. 'There goes your theatre, my dear. But look on the bright side – at least none of our people were hurt.'

'Rhodesy, but his burns are superficial. He'll be all right. And didn't he say little Yue Chun was hurt?' Cate released his arm. 'I can't speak for the others.' She began to make her way across the smouldering ashes – all that remained of her theatre. 'We'd better check on them.'

She stopped momentarily and stared down on the wet, burnt, dead body of a Chinese man in the ashes.

John came up behind her and placed his arm around her shoulders. 'I shot him in the head. He wouldn't have felt any pain.'

'That's a pity,' Cate replied. Then she stepped over the body and kept walking.

'How is everyone, Kit?'

'This one's pretty shaken up,' Kit called from where he was seated on the Management caravan steps, his firearm still in his hand and his arm wrapped around a terrified Lou-shi. 'And the little fellow copped it trying to defend her.'

Beside the caravan steps next to Kit's feet lay the lifeless body of Stupid Ho, one hand still clasped over the gaping knife wound in his stomach.

'Anna and Lanna both got burns on their feet,' Rhodesy added. 'Adelina too and she twisted 'er ankle to boot.'

'Anyone else hurt?' John asked.

'I don't think so.'

'Jack,' Cate said, then held out her arms to Lou-shi who entered them all too willingly and clung to Cate like a limpet. 'You'd better get the bandage box and the jar of unguent from next to the dresser.'

'What?' Jack dragged his gaze from the little Chinese man's dead form. 'Oh, right, Ma.'

'And get one of the phials of laudanum from under the bed.' She turned to John as the boy obeyed. 'A sip or two of laudanum for everyone might not be a bad idea.'

She caught her breath at the expression clouding John's face. He was staring, frozen at the sight of Stupid Ho's corpse. 'John?' she said softly. 'Now, John,' she warned, 'don't get upset.'

The anger rose in John faster than the flames that destroyed the Paragon. He looked at the body of the Chinese man who had given his life for his friend and the rage descended. 'Someone should pay for this fellow's life.'

'*Bai-lou Saang*,' Feng said. 'Enough killing already. You say so yourself. No good to kill anymore.'

'If you have an infestation of rats, Mister Feng,' John began, his voice cold and even, 'you don't kill three or four as it does not solve the problem. However,' the smile he offered was devoid of humour, 'if you eradicate the lot, the problem ceases to exist.'

'My people not rats, *Bai-lou Saang*. They human beings just like Englishman.' Feng looked at Kit. 'Just like American.'

'I beg to differ, Feng!' John snapped. 'This Brotherhood you speak of is a criminal organisation and nothing less. I intend to shoot every single one of them for the rats they have proven themselves to be.'

'You will kill everyone?' Feng shook his head sadly. 'How you know who is Brotherhood, who is not Brotherhood?'

'Feng's right, John.' It was Kit. 'You can't go to that village and shoot people indiscriminately. Most of those people are decent, hard-working men and women no different from us.'

John pointed at Stupid Ho's body. 'Who pays for this!' he demanded.

'No-one!' Cate yelled at him. She'd heard enough. 'No-one pays.' Her eyes bored into his. 'Good God, man! Have you forgotten already, the look on your son's face as he watched a wounded man trampled to death? Have you forgotten the words you said to that murderous mob of drunks? If so you're no better than them.'

Cate's tirade hit him like a shower of cold water. His rage subsided and his anger dissolved. His shoulders slumped.

'That's better.' She said it soothingly, lovingly, causing Kit and Rhodesy to exchange a look. 'Now come along, there's work to be done. We'll tend to those who are injured. James?' She pointed at Ho's body.

'I be right 'ere, Cate.' The big man waved his giant paw at her. 'I'll take care of the little fella's body. But I'm worried about Dafty Boy. I think he still be out in the street sleepin' it off.'

'Oh, hell!' Kit pulled a face. 'I'll get him.'

'Thank you, Kit.' Cate looked at John, who seemed dazed. 'Come along, John,' she ordered. 'Look after Lou-shi for me. She trusts you.'

CHAPTER FOURTEEN

Ballarat, Friday 1 December 1854

In the days following Sunday's fire events in Ballarat slowly, but very definitely, escalated to the point of no return.

On Monday in response to the conviction of the three miners in Melbourne a delegation from the Ballarat Reform League was dispatched to a meeting arranged with Governor Hotham to demand their release. The meeting was a failure with neither side backing down. Even as it took place Hotham approved the transfer of another one hundred and fifty men from the 40th Regiment to Ballarat Camp.

On Wednesday, another monster meeting of the Ballarat Reform League took place on Bakery Hill where, it was rumoured, a formal declaration of independence would be made. On a hot and windy day fifteen thousand men and women stopped work, shut stores and attended to hear impassioned speeches, while angry men burned their miners' and storekeepers' licences. Rumours abounded: revolution was at hand, government officials had been shot, military property had been destroyed and soldiers had joined forces with the Reform League.

Thursday 30 November, the fourth Thursday in the month and traditionally Thanksgiving Day in the United States, was celebrated by the hundreds of Americans in Ballarat. There were dinners and feasts all over the fields and a grand ball was held at the Victoria Hotel. James Tarleton the American Ambassador attended as did Robert Rede. Anthems were sung, whisky was downed by the bucketload and raucous good spirits held sway. But when the official toasts began, Rede was called away urgently.

A small contingent of the 12th Regiment delivering several wagons full of ammunition had been ambushed by a group of diggers. It was not uncommon for soldiers to be jeered and spat upon and even stoned by angry residents. But this particular incident had quickly descended into a gunfight.

The following morning at the Shearley allotment on Main Street, John and Kit sat by the campfire sipping breakfast tea when Rhodesy walked in across the ashes eating a muffin.

'I just heard from the bakery that there were trouble out on the Melbourne Road last night. A troop of soldiers from the 12th Regiment drove some wagons in across the diggin's and the lads was waitin' for 'em.'

Kit frowned. 'It's not uncommon to stir up the military. A bit of hooting and jeering and the odd rock gets thrown, but that's about all.'

'Not this time,' said Rhodesy. 'This time it got nasty. As the army wagons crossed Eureka there was real fightin' an' a young drummer boy got shot in the leg an' some of the horses got shot too.'

'Hell's teeth!' John exclaimed. 'Was there any retaliation?'

'Not yet there ain't been, but an awful lot more soldiers marched in 'ere last night from Geelong . . .'

'That'd be the 40th Regiment.' Kit looked at John. 'They've been expected.'

'And they're not 'appy,' Rhodesy went on. 'There's five hunnert or more of 'em now, soldiers and police that is, jammed together in the Camp.' He thumbed towards the hill behind them. 'That there compound's s'posed to hold no more 'an one hunnert. They're living cheek by jowl in filthy conditions and from what I 'ear they're as angry as 'ornets.' He looked at John meaningfully. 'An' there's nothing more dangerous than angry soldiers, as you would well know, John la.'

'I think trouble is now inevitable,' Kit added.

'Trouble?' Rhodesy said. 'That's 'ardly the word I'd use to describe what's gonna 'appen.' He gazed intently at John. 'People . . . and I don't mean just the miners . . . people of all trades and industry be talkin' open-like of revolution. Wednesday on Bakery Hill a crowd of fifteen thousand of 'em. They lit bonfires and burned licences. The police was about but they was outnumbered by a hunnert to one at least.'

'The miners raised their own flag,' Kit said. 'It certainly was a grand sight.'

Rhodesy nodded. 'The noise on Bakery Hill when it were hoisted was deafening. Enormous it be, blue with a silver cross an' five stars. Mark my words, lads, there's gonna to be a war, an' I don' reckon the troupe orta be 'ere when it happens.'

'Cate was right,' John said to himself more than the others. 'She said the troupe should leave some days ago.'

'They can't leave straight away,' said Kit.

'Why not, la?'

'Wagons are not ready. Three new wheels and one new axle needed. And the blacksmith can't come until tomorrow.'

'Then they should leave on Sunday,' Rhodesy said. 'Less traffic on the Melbourne Road. It being the Sabbath an' all. People choose not to travel on the Lord's Day.'

'Sunday it is then!' John agreed, then announced it loudly across the entire allotment. 'Everybody, you leave for Melbourne on Sunday at first light.'

'It can't come too soon for 'em, I reckon,' Rhodesy grunted as he stood.

'By the way,' John raised a hand. 'Where is our little Chinese princess?'

'In Feng's wagon as far as I know,' said Kit. 'I've not actually seen her this morning.'

'Knock on her door, Mister Rhodes. We must be sure of her whereabouts.'

'Aye aye, la.' The giant headed for Feng's wagon.

'I don't suppose you seen young Jack this morning? I have a little job for him.'

'I saw him,' Kit said, watching Rhodesy pull back the flap of Feng's wagon.

'There's no-one 'ere, John la!' Rhodesy called, his voice suddenly full of concern.

'Didn't Jack say he was off to the Gravel Pits?' Kit asked the big man.

The Gravel Pits was a very successful goldfield, running east around Bakery Hill then parallel with the Melbourne Road at the foot of Black Hill.

'Not to me, but I saw Old Feng.' Rhodesy returned to the fire. 'And 'e 'ad 'is leather bag full of laud'n'm over his shoulder. I'll bet the old villain's off to sell it all before we pull out on Sunday.'

'Christ on the Cross,' John said, getting to his feet. 'Jack will be with him! And Lou-shi I'll wager. She follows Feng like a puppy dog. Come on, Kit, to horse! We must find them quickly.'

'Good morning, gentlemen,' Cate said as she emerged from her caravan and took in the windy, overcast day. 'Another day of relentless heat to look forward to, wouldn't you say?' She kissed John on the lips. 'Who must you find quickly?'

'Apparently Jack's at the Gravel Pits,' John said lightly.

Suspicion darkened her brow. 'Go on.'

'The lad be with Old Feng,' Rhodesy let slip and received a glare from John.

'Old Feng?' She looked at John. 'Did you know this?'

'I found out but a minute ago.'

'Feng will have him toting his laudanum satchel.' Her voice was icy. 'I've warned Jack before and I've given Feng strict instructions that Jack is not to be involved in his double-dealing schemes!'

John held his palms out in a pacifying gesture. 'And we think Lou-shi's with them.'

'What!' she roared. 'Well don't just stand there!' She punched John in the shoulder. 'Go and get them! Now!'

Both men ran to their horses and flew into the saddle as Cate continued to rant. 'There are people on those diggings who would kill for one sip of laudanum, let alone an entire satchel full of it, and Lou-shi will be exposed to those damned Chinese,' she called and as they galloped off she turned her focus onto Rhodesy. 'When I get hold of those three I'll . . .'

'Whoa!' The roar of a bullocky's voice cut her off in full flight. Cate turned as two enormous Clydesdale carthorses halted at the command. 'Good morning, Missus Shearley,' the blacksmith called from his wagon seat. 'I got three new wheels and an axle shaft in the back.' He tilted his head to his wagon load. 'I'm 'ere to repair your wagons.'

'Right,' Cate called. 'Some good news at last.' She waved her hand towards the rear of her caravan. 'Get your wagon up to the back of the allotment behind the others and I'll point out the ones to be repaired.' She then pointed her finger at Rhodesy. 'You get down to the Gravel Pits, too.'

'The Gravel Pits, did you say, missus?' the big bullocky asked. 'I wouldn't be going over there right now. I just saw that bastard Commissioner Johnston leavin' the Camp at the 'ead of troopers and them new mounted soldiers what's just arrived last night. They're 'eadin' for the Pits and I'd say they're gonna run a licence hunt most likely.'

'They wouldn't dare do that!' Cate exclaimed with deep concern. 'Surely not after Wednesday's events on Bakery Hill; they'll start a riot.'

'That's exactly what the government wants, I reckon,' the blacksmith nodded furiously. 'Don't ya see? It's a show of force.'

Cate clutched Rhodesy's arm. 'Go and help look for Jack and the others.' The fear in her voice was palpable. 'Hurry, go and help find them. Now!'

On the goldfield known as the Gravel Pits, windlasses, wound by lean, strong men standing over open shafts, creaked painfully with the weight of the earth-filled buckets being slowly hauled to the surface. Children screamed and darted about among the hillocks, dogs excited by the constant activity set to barking madly, women chattered and scolded infants while labouring at their daily chores. Shopkeepers from their tents scattered intermittently across the diggings, shouted prices and announced their latest wares while flies buzzed, mosquitoes hummed, horses whinnied and flicked their tails and flags flapped in the strong wind. And all the while tents, the canvas castles of the poor, baked in the relentless summer heat.

Lou-shi, in her boy's disguise, saw none of it as her eyes searched the landscape for her master and his companion Jack Shearley.

'Get thee away from 'ere, you ungodly heathen!' a miner yelled as she passed his hillock.

'Aye!' another man growled and wielded a knife blade at her. 'Be gone, Chinaman, lest you be gutted.'

Lou-shi, disturbed by the threats, wandered aimlessly, her eyes searching continuously for her master and young Jack. 'Mister Feng, Mister Feng,' she chanted over and over. 'Mister Feng.'

'Lou-shi! Lou-shi!' It was Jack's voice.

She saw him away to her right, waving, hat in hand. She increased her speed, weaving deftly between shafts and hillocks until she saw Old Feng seated at a table beside a tent, sipping tea, completely unconcerned by the industrial chaos around him.

'Lou-shi,' he said calmly, 'you're supposed to stay at the camp.'

The young Chinese girl was trembling as she knelt beside the only father she'd ever known. She said nothing, but clung fiercely to his arm.

'You should be at home with my ma, Lou-shi,' Jack continued.

'It is all right, my little princess.' Feng continued in Cantonese as he placed his teacup on the rickety table. *'I understand the depth of your worry. But I do not think the Brotherhood of the Red Pavilion will give us any more trouble. The burning of the theatre and the deaths will have put an end to it all.'* He placed his arm around her shoulders

and with his free hand indicated Jack should pass him a bottle of laudanum.

'It is the last one, Mister Feng.' Jack too adopted Cantonese as he handed the old man the vial from the satchel.

The old man removed the plug and placed the bottle against her lips. *'Sip this, my little princess. It will relieve your concerns.'*

'Will it make her a drug addict?' Jack stared, suddenly horrified, at the miner and his wife standing by the table sharing a bottle of the drug Feng had sold them not minutes before.

'No, Jack-jai,' Feng reassured him. *'It must be consumed regularly and often, such as these two do,'* he waved airily at the man and his wife, *'for the body to become dependent upon it.'*

'So these two people are drug addicts?' The boy continued to stare at the couple then he looked back at Feng. *'But they have children, true or not true, ah? How can they look after their children if they are drug addicts?'*

'It is a sad fact of life that addiction to pleasure forms part of the human condition, Jack-jai.' Feng was about to expound on his theory when Jack interrupted him.

'Yes, but should she be drinking all *of that?'* he asked, pointing towards Lou-shi.

'Aaaaiiiyyaaahh!' Feng cried and slapped the bottle from Lou-shi's hand. The miner's wife dived headlong towards the bottle now emptying onto the baked earth.

Suddenly the cries of terrified men and women rang across the diggings. 'Joe! Joe! Joe!'

Whenever a police or military presence was spotted, people called out 'Joe! Joe!' – the nickname for the police. Diggers would disappear down into mine shafts or run for the bush, women would scurry about frantically ushering their children into tents or behind hillocks or windlass uprights, for they knew only too well of the merciless, drunken brutality of the troopers who, when they caught diggers without licences, would tie them to trees or chain them together like dogs. Then when the hunt was over the unfortunates would be taken back to the Government Camp to be fined five pounds, or if they did not have the money, imprisoned for as much as a year.

'Joe! Joe!' the cries continued across the diggings. A tremendous uproar commenced and panic quickly took hold of all.

Jack saw the military extended in a line all the way from the Camp gates to the edge of the Gravel Pits, then as one, they turned and began the hunt for the unlicensed. People ran every which way, but some angry miners stood their ground and threw bottles, rocks and anything else that came to hand. Police under the protection of their mounted unit swept the field, forcing many to crowd at the bottom of Bakery Hill.

Then the unthinkable happened. Police opened fired indiscriminately at a crowd of mostly women and children. Bullets ripped through tents and even pierced several ladies' dresses, but by the grace of God, no-one was hit. Those civilian men still on the field reacted furiously; several troopers were unhorsed and beaten like rag dolls. Though no sooner had the civilians' retaliations commenced than an officer, a major from the 40th Regiment, ordered his soldiers to drop to one knee and raise their rifles at the main crowd.

'Take aim!' the officer ordered from horseback.

'Wait! Wait!' The Goldfields Chief Commissioner Robert Rede rode through the lines to the front of the riflemen. He quickly unrolled the paper scroll he was waving about and read it aloud. 'Our Sovereign the Queen chargeth and commandeth all persons, being assembled, immediately to disperse themselves, and peaceably to depart to their habitations, or to their lawful business, upon the pains contained in the act made in the first year of King George the First, for preventing tumults and riotous assemblies. God Save the Queen!'

Never had the Riot Act of 1715 been invoked so quickly. The terrified Rede had gabbled it with such rapidity that most on the field failed to understand what it was he'd said.

The major ordered the riflemen to stand easy then drew his sword and raised it above his head. 'To all of you assembled,' he called in stentorian fashion, 'by order of the Riot Act you have been ordered to disperse; therefore, I warn you to do so immediately, or suffer the consequences.' He looked at Robert Rede. 'Do I have your permission to clear the field, sir?'

'Yes, yes,' replied a shaken Commissioner Rede. 'By all means, do whatever is necessary.'

'Number 1 Troop!' he called to his mounted men. 'Number 1 Troop will advance in order abreast!' He pointed his sabre horizontally and nudged his horse with his knees. 'At the canter, forward, ho!'

Even the bravest of the Gravel Pits inhabitants now fled the cavalry advance, while those already hiding down shafts trembled in silence, listening to the horses pass the windlasses above, snorting and stamping, anticipating the order to charge at the gallop, which was of course impossible given the mineshaft-riddled terrain.

In the middle of the madness the major noticed a young Chinese boy standing motionless between a tent and an upturned table. Beside the table a white boy knelt next to the body of an old Chinese man. Neither of the boys appeared to be aware of the chaos around them. The Chinese boy stood staring vacantly at the horizon, while the white boy did not move as he held tight to the old man's hand.

The major of the 40th halted his mount and stared, mesmerised by the scene before him. The young Chinese boy did not flinch; he simply stared as if in a trance while the boy cried silently. Now he was nearer, the officer noticed the old Oriental's clothing was drenched in blood. Something stirred within the major's memory. He looked again at the Chinese boy. His eyes focused on something on the back of the boy's right hand, between thumb and index finger. It was a tattoo of a blue nightingale. His pulse rate quickened and his mouth went dry, then he pointed his sabre at two uniformed policemen.

'You two men,' he snapped. 'Take this Chinese boy to the Camp. He's to be held in custody for the murder of the old man.'

'Yessir,' the taller of the two policemen mumbled.

'Keep him separated from the other prisoners.'

'Yessir,' the man mumbled yet again.

'And stand to attention when you speak to a senior officer!' the major roared.

'Yessir!' both men replied and snapped to attention.

'That's better.' The major offered them a pleasant smile, which faded rapidly to an icy stare. 'I've given you an order,' he said softly, menacingly. 'Disobey it, or fail to carry it out, and I'll have you both stripped bare and publicly flogged. Do you understand me, sirs?'

'Yessir,' they replied in unison.

'Good. Now get on with it.' He pointed his sabre at the girl. 'Take him!'

As the two policemen seized an unresisting Lou-shi and led her away, the major stared at the young white boy beside the Celestial.

'You, lad,' he called to the boy. 'What's your name?'

'Jack Shearley, sir,' Jack answered, sniffing and wiping at the wetness on his cheeks.

'Are you mourning over that Chinaman, or robbing him of his purse?'

'He was my friend.'

'Really,' the major was intrigued. 'And was the Chinese boy your friend too?'

'No,' Jack lied instantly. Warning bells had been set off by the suddenly gentle tone in the soldier's voice. He sensed at once the man was not to be trusted. 'No, sir, I don't know him at all.'

'All right,' the man snapped. 'Well you can think yourself lucky a stray bullet hit the Chinaman and not you. Now get off the field at once or you'll be arrested too.'

'Can I stay with him?'

'Don't be ridiculous, boy, the man's a heathen Chinese, no better than a dog. Now pick yourself up and get off home to your mother.' The soldier spurred his horse and moved away.

Jack watched the animal trot off amid the chaos that was the Gravel Pits Lead then he reached into Feng's blood-soaked coat as the major's words came back to him, 'Are you mourning over that Chinaman, or robbing him of his purse?' He removed the large wad of money from Feng's inside pocket and stuffed it inside his shirt. He would keep it for Lou-shi.

He stood as the foot soldiers marched past. He looked at his old friend and a new tear trickled down his cheek.

'Goodbye, Mister Feng,' he whispered in Cantonese.

Then he set off for home.

'What have you done with Jack?' John asked as Cate emerged from her caravan and came to his side.

'He's asleep.' She took his arm and they stood staring into the campfire. 'I gave him some laudanum in sugar milk.' She squeezed his upper arm as his body stiffened at the mention of the drug. 'It will do him no harm!' she said sternly. 'He's seen enough mayhem and murder for one day. He needs to sleep.'

'Yes,' John conceded. 'Nature's soft nurse, eh? You're right of course: sleep is probably the best thing for him, considering what he's been through.'

'Poor Mister Feng, what a tragedy. And Jack had to witness it.'

'Yes,' John patted her hand clutching his bicep, 'a stray bullet from a drunken policeman, a most undignified death.'

'We must retrieve his body and ensure he's buried, or whatever it is the Chinese do with their dead.'

'I'll get Rhodesy onto it as soon as he returns. He'll take the body to the temple in the Chinese village and make inquiries.'

'More importantly,' Cate drew away from him, folding her arms across her chest, 'what are we going to do about Lou-shi?'

'I don't see what we can do at the moment, given what's transpiring out on the diggings. No-one with the authority to discuss prisoners will be in the Camp. There's going to be even more serious trouble and very soon, I'm beginning to think.'

'Trouble b'ain't be the word for it, John la,' Rhodesy exclaimed as he joined them, huffing and puffing from his rigorous trek back through the increasingly hot and windy morning. 'The word 'as spread like wildfire, there's people from all over the diggin's headin' for Bakery Hill and they mean business, my word they do. There'll be thousands of 'em up there a'fore long. They've got the Eureka flag 'oisted 'igh in this 'ot wind an' they're armed with everythin' from picks and shovels to shotguns an' pistols.'

'You see?' John shrugged at Cate. 'With that sort of thing going on there will be no-one in the Camp with the authority to deal with Lou-shi's detention.'

'But . . .' Cate's attempt to reply was cut off.

'All we can do is wait until things calm down and the officers resume their administrative duties!' John snapped. Then seeing the hurt in her eyes he softened his tone. 'Believe me, my love,' he smiled reassuringly, 'I know how the army functions. And look on the bright side: locked up, she's safe from those Chinese triad fellows.'

'But that girl is all alone up there and she'll be grieving for Mister Feng. Heaven knows what condition she's in, or indeed under what conditions she's being detained. They could have her in a dog kennel for all we know.'

'Cate, for the last time, going up to the Camp now would be a waste of time. I've no doubt tomorrow everyone will have calmed down, and for the army that will mean business as usual. That's when I'll go and get Lou-shi and not before.'

'Then I'll go myself,' Cate said firmly, placing her clenched fists on her hips.

'Fine! Fine! By all means go. In the meantime, Mister Rhodes and I will help the blacksmith repair the wagons.' John too placed his hands on his hips. 'Because I believe, given the mood you're in, the quicker you get out of Ballarat the better off things will be!'

'Right!' Cate roared and the finality in her voice resonated between them.

'Right!' he replied then watched as she gave him one last defiant stare and stormed off to her caravan.

CHAPTER FIFTEEN

Ballarat, Friday 1 December 1854

Commissioner Robert Rede was a tall, skinny man about forty years of age with a pointed and pronounced nose and a set of muttonchop whiskers that ran from his ears to the tip of his chin. A former medical student who had renounced academia for colonial service, he found himself, in very quick time, in a position of power for which he was not sufficiently experienced or suited.

Now, as the summer heat threatened to singe his scalp, he scurried towards his quarters across the dry, windblown earth of the Government Camp, dragging with him a tiny bedraggled figure.

The name Cate Shearley rattled through his brain. He'd seen her on several vice-regal occasions in Melbourne, but had never actually made her acquaintance until now. Even with the famous black patch over her eye she was still strikingly beautiful. And a most formidable Melbournian he'd been assured, with money, property, power and even a shotgun, which she apparently used to persuade people to her way of thinking.

She had burst into his private quarters like a charging rhinoceros not twenty minutes before and demanded an explanation regarding one of her Chinese performers. When he'd informed her the boy was being held by the military on suspicion of murder she'd become positively incandescent.

'Don't be ridiculous, Mister Rede! The boy was on the diggings with his guardian, Mister Feng Chi-pei, who was shot in the back – by your men I might add – during this morning's very ill-timed licence hunt.' She twisted her head, aiming her good eye at him. 'Was that your idea, by the way?'

'Was what my idea?' The woman's eye patch was most unsettling, or was it the steely glint in her good eye, he could not decide.

'The licence hunt,' Cate snapped.

'No,' he cried defensively, then wondered immediately why he'd done so. He was a highly placed government official; he was unused to people, especially women, addressing him in such an aggressive manner. 'No, it was Commissioner Johnston's idea; he's rather keen on stamping his authority . . . that sort of thing . . . you know,' he finished weakly.

'When I heard there had been a licence hunt after yesterday's heated display of unrest, I was left gasping at the stupidity of such an action.'

'Yes, well, it did cause a bit of trouble.' The woman was really unnerving him.

'A bit of trouble!' Cate's voice rose an octave. '*A bit!* My business associate Mister Feng is dead and you have his ward, Lou-shi, under arrest for his murder. The situation is utterly ridiculous. The two were on official business under my instructions when they were caught in a hail of bullets, fired – *I must reiterate* – by your drunken troopers. And you call that *a bit* of trouble!'

'My dear Mistress Shearley –' Rede began in an effort to placate the woman.

'Don't you dare deny it, sir!' Cate exclaimed. 'My son is able to verify the fact, as he was with them. He witnessed the entire tragedy. And,' she waved a finger at him, 'you can thank your lucky stars he was not shot in the Chinaman's stead or, as the persons ultimately responsible for the carnage that occurred, you and your fellow Commissioner, that idiot James Johnston, would be facing a charge of murder yourselves!'

'Madam –'

'And don't think I would not be capable of inveigling wealthy friends of mine in Melbourne to bring such a charge against you both. People far more powerful than you, to whom even your precious Governor Hotham would willingly bow down, await my bidding, sir.'

'Mistress Shearley, let me tell you –'

'No!' Cate interrupted. 'Let me tell you! We are in a colony of the British Empire, which is blessed with an abundance of gold.' She pressed home her advantage. No man had ever been her match when she really wanted to win. 'Here, money talks!' She stood and glared at him. 'Or would you care to deny that?' She continued to challenge him for several more seconds. 'I didn't think so.' Then she smiled radiantly. 'My dear Commissioner,' she intoned sweetly, 'I'm on your side, believe me. I hope you sort these rebels out once and for all. But my Chinese boy has done nothing wrong, I assure you.' She let her smile fade. 'And I want him returned to me *immediately*.'

'Well,' Rede said clumsily, 'I'll talk to the major about it and –'

'One does not *talk* to soldiers, Mister Rede!' Cate announced imperiously. She didn't quite have him where she wanted him. One more slap should do it, she thought. 'One gives *orders* to soldiers!' Her voice bounced off the wall behind him. 'You are this major's superior, are you not?'

'Of course.' Rede was wishing he was anywhere but where he stood. Cate Shearley was reminding him of a schoolmistress who had bullied him constantly as a boy. Now he stood equally terrified of the one-eyed virago berating him.

'Tell the man his act of arresting a tiny, unarmed Chinese theatre performer for the murder of the person he loved more than life was an act of such stupidity that he should, for his own dignity's sake, pretend it never occurred and get on with the more pressing matter of subduing Ballarat's rebels before Britain has another colonial war on its hands!'

'Quite so, quite so, Mistress Shearley,' Chief Commissioner Robert Rede capitulated. He was totally out of his depth. He'd been expertly manipulated by a woman who knew more about men than could be found in all the books of the Bodleian Library. 'I will liberate the boy immediately.'

Now he stood outside the door of his inadequate accommodation. He straightened his coat and tie and pushed the young Chinese boy he'd dragged across the compound, into the room.

'Mistress Cate,' Lou-shi gasped and fell onto her knees, wrapping her arms about her employer.

'Good God!' Cate gasped. 'He's filthy! What have you done to him?'

'Me?' Rede was horrified to think Cate Shearley had the impression he'd harm anyone, Oriental or otherwise. 'I haven't done anything to him. He's merely been locked up in the stables. Apparently, the major ordered him kept in solitary confinement and it was the only spare bit of space to be had.'

'She is a defenceless girl!'

'Girl?' Rede frowned.

'Boy, I said, a defenceless boy!'

Cate reached down and drew Lou-shi to her feet. She glared at Rede again, only this time the pretence was over; she really was incensed. However, after her slip of the tongue she was mindful of departing and decided it was better not to bully the man any further. 'That is no way to treat another human being, Mister Rede. I know this mistreatment was not of your doing,' she offered a patronising smile, 'but your men should be ashamed of themselves. There is no other word for it.'

'I quite agree with you, Mistress Shearley, but in their defence, the men are tired and somewhat frustrated at the attitude being adopted towards them by their own countrymen.' He glanced disdainfully at Lou-shi. 'And others.'

Cate raised her chin haughtily. 'That is entirely a matter for your concern, sir,' she said with a regal air.

'Oh, but of course,' the Chief Commissioner of the Goldfields mumbled and buckled forward in a deep obeisance.

At that moment a soldier burst through the door. 'Sorry to interrupt you, Mister Rede, but there be trouble startin' up on Bakery Hill.'

'Not again,' Rede groaned.

'Right!' Cate placed an arm around Lou-shi and began walking her towards the door. 'I have what I came for.' She paused, looked back at him and smiled graciously. 'I thank you for your magnanimity and for showing a great deal more common sense than your subordinates, Commissioner. Now I bid you good day.'

It was late afternoon of what had been a momentous day on the goldfields of Ballarat when Kit returned to the allotment. His horse kicked through the ashen traces of the Paragon Theatre and came to a grateful halt. He dismounted, tied the mare to the rear of Cate's cabin and sat heavily on the steps leading up to her door.

No sooner had he done so than he heard the creak of the latch and leapt to his feet, barely escaping the swing of the caravan door, which would have hit the back of his head.

'Oh, I'm sorry, Kit.' Cate noticed the American's weary dust-blackened face. She stepped down from the caravan, took his arm and sat him back where he'd been. 'You look exhausted; sit there and I'll get you a cup of tea.'

She took the billy kettle from over the perennial campfire and busied herself making a brew.

'I've been up on Eureka Flat, Cate. The miners gathered on Bakery Hill in their thousands and then we all moved over to Eureka. What transpired today will be remembered long after we've departed this mortal coil.'

'It is one I shall remember with great sadness,' she called back to him.

'John got Jack home safely, didn't he? The last time I saw him was on the Gravel Pits. He had Jack up on his horse and they were heading this way.'

'Oh, yes, they're fine; Jack's asleep.' She approached and handed him a cup of tea. 'Are you aware of what happened at the Gravel Pits?'

'Of course I am. The police opened fire on innocent civilians. I saw it with my own eyes. Fortunately no-one was hit.'

'That's not entirely true, Kit.' Cate nudged his shoulder with her hip, forcing him to move, and she sat beside him on the caravan steps. 'Mister Feng was hit . . .'

'Oh my God,' Kit gasped. 'How is he?'

'He's dead. A stray bullet from a drunken policeman and our dear Mister Feng is gone from us.' Cate felt tears begin and rubbed her eyes.

'And what of Lou-shi? I searched all over for her to no avail.'

'That's where the story becomes even more tragic,' Cate replied and went on to tell him of the morning's events.

'It is indeed a sad affair,' the American said. 'I was very fond of Mister Feng.'

'As was I, Kit.'

'What possessed them to think she killed Old Feng?'

Cate shrugged. 'She's Chinese. She was there. And according to Jack, she was particularly distressed. You know how she gets agitated and confused? After losing little Mister Ho last Sunday, the sight of Feng lying dead at her feet would have been simply too much for her to comprehend. And what's more, she'd had laudanum.'

'Laudanum?' Kit was surprised. 'Surely not?'

'Feng gave her a vial of laudanum to sip in order to calm her, but she drank half the bottle. Then the police opened fire and the dear old chap was mortally wounded. Jack said an army officer ordered the police to seize Lou-shi and she was taken away.'

'So what do we do about her?'

'Nothing. She's safe in my bed.'

'Are you saying Lou-shi is here?' Kit pointed his thumb over his shoulder at the caravan door. 'You said she'd been arrested. How on earth . . .?'

'Cate went up to the Government Camp, on her own, and threatened no less a figure than the Chief Commissioner of the Goldfields,' John said loudly as he came around the corner of the caravan. 'It was a very stupid thing to do.' He glared at Cate, but a faint smile crossed his lips. 'At first I was angry with her, but if one is to believe the alarming stories of violence and disorder spreading across the diggings, it might be just as well we have Lou-shi with us.'

'Oh, you can believe the stories, John.' The American's voice quivered with excitement. 'This afternoon's confrontation finally lit the fuse of revolution.'

'I saw miners heading for Bakery Hill when I left the Camp,' Cate said, 'but I've been busy keeping an eye on Lou-shi. What happened up there?'

'The miners are furious. There'll be a clash of arms, I've no doubt.'

'Oh, no.' Cate gave John a worried look.

'Well, there is one remaining hope. It was decided to make one last effort at reconciliation. Lalor intends to send a delegation to the Camp to debate terms with the authorities, but no-one expects it will do any good.'

'I take it you mean Peter Lalor?' John asked. 'The young engineer? Irish chap?'

'The very man,' Kit declared. 'He took charge on Bakery Hill.'

'How so?' Intrigued, John sat on an upturned bucket next to Cate.

'Because "the Hour's come, and the Man", to quote Sir Walter Scott.' Kit got to his feet and placed his teacup on the steps next to Cate. 'There were thousands on Bakery Hill from all over the diggings, including women and children. Peter Lalor was amazing!' Kit waved his arms, painting the picture. 'He stepped forward, raised his clenched fist to heaven and roared the word *"Liberty!"*.' The American's face shone at his recollection of the historic moment. 'The approval of those present reverberated across the diggings and they unanimously chose him as leader.'

'What happened then?' John asked; Kit's excitement was infectious.

'They've moved over onto Eureka Flat. Lalor and the others had a meeting in Annie Diamond's store.'

'Which others?'

'There was no shortage of them I can assure you. And from so many countries. The Brits for a start led by George

Black, Irishmen Pat Curtain and Johnny Manning, Frederick Vern the Hanoverian, plus several Canadians, the Scotsman Kennedy and of course James McGill from the dear old US of A. That's when they decided to send the deputation to see Commissioner Rede. By God, John, but it was inspiring and . . .' Kit saw the warning look on Cate's face and stopped mid-sentence.

'And? And what?' John could feel the blood rush consuming him. 'Come on, man, tell me! What's afoot?'

'. . . er, well, they've decided to drill and oppose the police and military by force.' He saw Cate's shoulders slump.

'Have they, by God! And I can't say I blame them.'

'They've raised the Eureka flag and they're building a defensive wall, a stockade I suppose you'd call it,' Kit finished.

'Well done, those noble souls!' John exclaimed, leaping to his feet. 'To the ramparts, eh, Kit, and the devil take the hindmost!'

Cate reacted to her lover's tone of voice. She saw the blood rush in his eyes and her heart sank. 'John, my love,' she said softly, 'it's no concern of ours what the Reform League and others do. We have a responsibility to our troupe to get them safely away from here as soon as the wagons are ready.'

'It's taken me a while, Cate,' his eyes gleamed, 'but I am now compelled to stand with the Reform League. For the first time in my life I am ashamed to admit I was once an officer in the British Army.'

'You have responsibilities, John.' Cate's voice held a warning. 'Our troupe, or what's left of it, is at risk here. We agreed to go to Melbourne –'

'They are minor concerns, Cate. I've tried to ignore the business entirely, but we are talking about the rights of downtrodden fellow Britons and I cannot stand by and see them abused, especially by lackeys supposedly representing our Sovereign.'

Cate, too, now stood and planted her clenched fists on her hips. 'Never mind Queen Victoria – what about the welfare of our son? He could have been killed this morning just like poor Mister Feng.'

'Yes, and by whom? I'll tell you, the drunken lackeys of petty bureaucrats employed by an oppressive government that has the temerity to sell freedom to its citizens in the form of miners' licences!' John's face was now flushed with anger. 'I have witnessed oppression as one of the oppressors, I've watched it work, I've seen the tears it creates and the anguish it brings to those who are not free.'

'My, my!' Cate intoned. 'From soldier of the Queen to wild-eyed revolutionary in one extraordinary leap.' Anger flared in her eyes. 'You've changed your tune rather suddenly, wouldn't you say? What happened to the unflinching Royalist? And more to the point, what happened to the father who decided to take his son away from what will very soon be a bloody battlefield?'

'All right. All right. I admit I've been a hypocrite,' he looked into the distance, searching for words, 'but I've learned quite a bit about myself in these last few days and I am forced to say, I never believed Ballarat would come to this, but now it has I refuse to stand idly by and watch my own countrymen oppressed. I would be of no value as a man were I to desert my friends when they are in danger.' He looked into her eyes. 'And I would be undeserving of you and your love if I conducted myself so. Freedom is the one right that must be defended above all else, because without it there is no life for any of us!'

'Very well,' Cate's voice shook. She was caught between two shores; on one stood the man she loved and on the other her only son. 'I can understand your concern for your friends, in fact I find it commendable, and I would never doubt your honour.' She paused and made her decision. 'But my concern must be for my son and I warn you, John, if you fail in your duty as his father and protector, I will take him away and you will never see him again.'

'No you won't, Mother.' All three responded to Jack's voice as the caravan door opened and he stood on the steps. 'I am not important. Not today. Father must go and help the miners. Mister Kittredge and Mister Rhodes are going and I'm proud that Father will go with them.'

'From the mouths of babes,' Kit murmured.

There came a long pause after which Cate sighed; the fight had drained from her. She looked at John. 'There's no doubting whose son he is.' She smiled weakly. 'He's right of course. You must go even if only to protect your friends. Forgive my outburst. I was wrong to speak as harshly as I did.'

'You said no less than a mother would.'

'But I am going to take him and the troupe to Melbourne by Monday at the latest. I should rather leave this minute, but I've promised performances from Adelina and Lou-shi tonight at Sarah Hanmer's fundraiser for the Reform League. But rest assured we'll be gone by Monday.'

'You don't expect Lou-shi to perform tonight, do you?' Kit asked.

'Of course not. She'll remain here in the caravan with Jack. Mister Rhodes will guard them both, but Adelina will sing. I promised Sarah.'

'Well, we haven't much time, we'd better get ready for tonight.' John tried to sound enthusiastic. 'But I must say, an evening of gaiety, even including a theatrical piece by Sarah Hanmer, is hardly what I'm in the mood for.'

It was 7.30 pm when John saw Cate enter the Adelphi Theatre and the transformation from the stressed woman of the afternoon to the beautiful sophisticate present in the canvas foyer was sensational. Her golden-blonde hair was drawn back, middle-parted and braided into a bun at the back with clusters of curls to either side and covered with a sheer frill trimmed with matching blue ribbon. But it was her crinoline gown that drew the admiring looks, pale blue silk with delicate lace and ribbon trim that left her neck and shoulders completely exposed, allowing her alabaster skin to highlight a diamond necklace, tasselled earrings, and glittering bracelets on each wrist. Even her eye patch was bejewelled, which heightened the dazzling effect. The fact that the jewellery was costume, from Feng Chi-pei's Chinese theatre collection, remained Cate's secret.

There was an audible gasp from several ladies standing by John and Kit as Cate entered the enormous canvas tent that was Sarah Hanmer's performance space.

'My God,' Kit said softly, 'I've yet to see a more breathtaking sight. You surely are the luckiest man in the world, Mister Bailleau.'

Cate smiled radiantly and, inclining her head slightly, she offered her hand, which John hastened across the room to accept.

'Ravishing,' John muttered as he kissed her hand. 'You have never looked more beautiful.'

She let her smile travel the room as she replied, 'Oh God, look at them, Victoria's privileged, all medals and make-up. The sooner I'm gone from Ballarat, the happier I'll be.'

'Let's get tonight out of the way first. Shall we?' He took her arm and guided her to where Kit stood smiling.

'You have outdone yourself this evening if I may say so, Mistress Shearley.'

'You may indeed, Mister Kittredge.' Cate offered him her hand and he kissed it reverently.

Everyone with any influence in Ballarat was in the Adelphi, John realised, as his eyes wandered the room. Cigar smoke and perfume filled the air and there was a sense of heightened expectation as if something momentous was about to occur, and he was sure it had nothing to do with Sarah Hanmer's performance, as brilliant as it would no doubt be. The intense awareness was brought about by the presence of certain men, some of whom were military, including the newly arrived Major-General Sir Robert Nickle and other army officers. James Johnston attended, representing the Victoria Police, along with a number of government representatives from various departments. However, others in the room represented polite, gentlemanly opposition. Some were from the business section of Ballarat who believed they had been persecuted along with the miners. And others mingled, like John Basson Humffray and Charles Evans, both of the Reform League, who still clung to the hope of reaching a peaceful outcome with the government.

'I can smell the blood,' Cate said as if reading his mind. 'There's no going back for any of these men.'

John was about to answer when they were interrupted by none other than their hostess, Sarah Hanmer.

'My dearest Cate,' she began in regal fashion. 'How lovely of you to come, and you too, Mister Bailleau, welcome to our little offering.' Sarah Hanmer was a statuesque woman, tall and solidly built, with a smile fit to illuminate a cathedral. She and Cate had formed an unlikely alliance, considering their business rivalry. They were genuinely fond of each other.

'Delighted, I'm sure, Sarah,' Cate replied. She deeply admired the woman's ability to exist so successfully in the world of men by constantly playing one off against the other. Sarah Hanmer was a very clever woman. 'We're looking forward to your performance tonight.'

Sarah half-turned and seized the arm of the man accompanying her. He was a grey-haired old soldier, his red tunic festooned with medals and badges of rank and honour. 'Do let me introduce you to Major-General Sir Robert Nickle, commander-in-chief of our British forces here in Victoria, just arrived with his advance party. He has more troops on the Melbourne Road, apparently.' Her eyes flicked between Cate and John. 'Sir Robert, this is Mistress Cate Shearley and Mister John Bailleau . . .'

As the general gave a stiff, courtly bow to Cate, John extended his hand. Then his whole body froze as Sarah concluded the introduction.

'. . . Oh, yes,' she added theatrically, 'and let me not forget our dashing officer from the 40th Regiment, Major Roger Bingham, recently arrived from British Hong Kong.'

General Nickle shook John's hand, but John could do no more than stare into the eyes of Roger Bingham, as his mind flashed back to that foggy London morning in St James's Park.

Five seconds became ten, as the two men stared icily at each other.

Bingham finally broke the silence. 'I'm sorry, for a moment I thought you were someone I once knew.'

Sensing John's reluctance to reply, Cate thrust her hand out to Bingham. 'How do you do, sir?'

'Mistress Shearley, the pleasure is mine,' Bingham replied. 'I've heard so much about you. It is indeed an honour . . .'

As Roger Bingham was about to take Cate's hand, John thrust his arm into the mix and shook hands with his enemy. The thought of the man even touching Cate was anathema to him. 'Major Bingham,' he managed to say stiffly.

'Mister Bailleau.' Bingham's smile was forced, his eyes cold.

Sarah Hanmer put an end to the impasse. 'Well, gentlemen,' she said stridently, 'and ladies, why don't you take your seats?' She indicated the break in the curtains leading into the theatre proper. 'I must get backstage; it is curtain up in ten minutes.'

'What on earth just took place?' Cate asked as they filed into the theatre. 'Do you know that soldier?'

'No I don't,' John said bluntly as they took their seats.

To open the show, Adelina sang a 6/8 cavatina '*O, mattutini albori*' from Rossini's *La Donna Del Lago* and received very deserved applause, then followed the first act of the play entitled *Money* starring Sarah Hanmer and her daughter Julia Hanmer. It was received with great gaiety by all but two of the audience, John Bailleau and Roger Bingham, both of whom sat through the amusing farce stiff-backed and grim-faced.

Cate was well aware of the tension in John; his jawbone clenched periodically and his fists remained taut, causing his knuckles to whiten. He stared unblinking at the stage and seemed only vaguely aware when the interval arrived. Cate remained in her seat for the short intermission and John sat beside her, morose and uncommunicative.

Prior to the curtain going up on the second act was when Lou-shi was to have performed as Michiko, Japan's Madame Vestris, and Cate realised, despite the fact she'd informed Sarah of Lou-shi's unavailability, no announcement had been made to the public. The entire audience returned to their seats in order not to miss her entrance. Expectation was high; all had heard of or seen Michiko before and the crowd was reduced to puzzled murmuring when China the Chinese Circus Boy entered from the wings and stood centre stage.

Lou-shi wore her everyday China Boy clothing, black cotton pants and coat and little black slippers. She stood for several seconds until the murmuring ceased, then she began to sing.

Wolfie Bremmer, sitting at the piano, had no idea of the song. He stared at Cate and shrugged helplessly.

The song was the lament of the maiden, Ho Chow Yu, one of grief in which a young woman laments the loss of her father and brother. Lou-shi fed off the lyrics as she thought of Feng and Stupid Ho. She transmitted her own pain to the audience, ensnaring their attention.

The sad young woman imagined her master standing in the wings smiling just for her. She watched Feng's right hand gently conducting her, as he so often had done. His arm rose, taking her voice with it, up and across the high canvas roof, then out into the heat of the night and over the diggings caressing all it reached, before returning to her like a long-lost friend. The final note arrived and the enraptured audience tensed with expectation. Lou-shi turned to them, took a deep breath, but no note arrived. She froze, staring across the heads of the audience to the back of the theatre and a deep frown distorted her face. Then she ran from the stage.

Cate was the only one with the presence of mind to turn and seek the cause of Lou-shi's consternation. And her eyes found Roger Bingham. The soldier stood, arms folded, at the rear of the audience, staring, his expression one of pure evil.

An hour later, Lou-shi sat on Cate's bed trembling and clutching her knees to her chest as she remembered the Canton Opera House and the officer of the Imperial Forces and an Englishman in the bright red coat and white trousers of the British Army. But this time it was not the recurring nightmare that dissolved when she awoke.

She remembered watching in horror as the British officer took his pistol and held it to the props manager's head then put a bullet through the man's skull. He'd then pointed the gun at Chou, one of the chorus girls who helped her dress.

'Where is Jiao Mun?' the Chinese officer of the Emperor called out over the crowd. *'I want the revolutionary called Jiao Mun . . .'*

Lou-shi's body flinched as if she'd been struck. The realisation that her recurring nightmare was not a dream at all, but a memory of an event she had witnessed in Canton, struck her like a fist. Jiao Mun and her companion little Chou had been shot and the man responsible was the English army officer she had seen in the Adelphi Theatre not one hour before. Terror gripped her. She was all alone. Master Feng was dead. Stupid Ho was dead. The Englishman had come to get her.

'The English army officer,' she murmured in Cantonese. *'The English army officer.'* The soldier had hunted her all the way to Australia. *'The English army officer,'* she said again and then it became a mantra. *'The English army officer, the English army officer,'* she repeated as terror consumed her.

That was how John and Cate found her, in the caravan huddled on the bed and with young Jack sitting on his bunk watching her.

'I told you to stay here with Jack,' Cate said, but the girl did not respond.

'I tried to stop her,' Jack said defensively. 'So did Mister Rhodes.'

'Ying gwok gaau wai, Ying gwok gaau wai, Ying gwok gaau wai,' Lou-shi intoned in singsong fashion as her mind floated outside the burning theatre in Canton.

'Is she saying "go away"?' John said. 'Is that what she's saying? What on earth is the matter with the girl?'

'She's frightened,' Jack said. 'Something terrified her.'

Cate sat and placed her arm around the trembling girl.

'It must have been a soldier,' Jack said, 'because she's saying, "English army officer". She keeps saying it over and over.'

Cate looked at John. 'It has something to do with that major Sarah Hanmer introduced us to, what was his name? Bingham. When Lou-shi froze on stage she was looking directly at him.'

'Don't be foolish, Cate.' John wanted to avoid at all cost any conversation concerning Roger Bingham. 'That's pure supposition. How on earth would Lou-shi know that man?' He was even careful not to mention the man by name.

The brow above her eye patch creased into a frown then her visible eyebrow rose in realisation. 'Didn't Sarah say he was late of Hong Kong? Yes, he recently arrived from the new British colony, Hong Kong, that's what she said. Lou-shi could have met him there.'

'That is fanciful to say the least,' John replied.

Lou-shi sat upright, startling them all. 'Not Hong Kong, it was in Canton at the opera house,' she began. 'He killed Jiao Mun and also my friend Chou. Jiao Mun used a dragon to fill the theatre with smoke.'

'Good God, she's lost her mind,' John muttered.

'Right, you two,' Cate snapped at John and Jack, 'outside, stoke up the fire and make us all a late-night cup of tea, while I get to the bottom of this.'

It was ten minutes before the two women emerged from the caravan and sat themselves around the campfire.

'Lou-shi is convinced Bingham is after her,' Cate began. 'She believes he wants to return her to China where he has powerful friends . . .'

'I know,' John interrupted. 'The Viceroy of Canton for one.' Both women stared at him.

'How did you know that?' Cate frowned.

'Bingham served as the British Army Liaison Officer to the Viceroy of Canton.'

Lou-shi was nodding furiously. 'Yes, Viceroy is Ye Ming Chen . . .'

'Just a moment!' Cate held her hand up to silence the girl then looked at John. 'You told me you didn't know Major Bingham.'

'I don't,' John lied again.

'Are you sure?' she replied suspiciously.

'Of course I'm sure.' He saw no sense in Cate knowing that Bingham was the man with whom he'd fought the duel. She had enough to be concerned with already. 'I merely know of him. He was universally disliked within the army. I heard he was posted to the Far East, to Canton in fact.'

'He saw this.' Lou-shi pointed to the little blue nightingale tattoo on the back of her right hand. 'He has seen it before in Canton. He will take me back there to the Viceroy to collect the reward. The Viceroy will gain great face by making a gift of me to the Emperor in Peking.'

'And what would become of you?' Cate asked.

'Remember I told you of the Taiping Rebellion in the south of China when our opera company was caught in the rebel city of Tianjing?'

'Vaguely,' Cate nodded.

'We could not leave Tianjing for many, many months and the rebels used my name to recruit people to fight for their cause. The leaders told everyone I was committed to the rebellion, but I was not. The Emperor declared me a traitor and if I am taken to Peking he will execute me.'

'Surely not,' Cate tried to reassure the frightened girl. 'You said once that the Emperor was your friend.'

'Once yes, but not now. He thinks I betrayed him. But I did not!'

'Well don't you worry, my dear,' Cate put her arm around the girl, 'neither Major Bingham nor anyone else will be taking you anywhere. We'll see to that, won't we, John?'

'Yes, of course we will.' John nodded furiously, hoping his enthusiastic response would hide the concern he was sure Cate suspected.

Hell's bells, he thought, to say the appearance of Roger Bingham was inopportune was putting it mildly. There was a time, a year ago, when John had dreamed of nothing but confronting the man again and putting a bullet through his head. But that was a year ago and in the intervening months his life had altered dramatically.

A change of name and a change of scenery had given him cause to re-analyse his life and expectations. He had forged strong new friendships on his voyage to the bottom of the world and found life in Australia much to his liking. And the rediscovery of his one true love and the son she had borne him had made him happier than he had ever been. The reappearance of Roger Bingham was a threat he could not afford to ignore, not merely for his own sake, but for Cate's and Jack's. And now there was Lou-shi's predicament to consider. With the deaths of Ho and old Master Feng she was alone in a foreign land and she too was his responsibility.

'Right,' John barked a little too militarily, 'the first thing we must do is get Lou-shi out of Ballarat.'

'My thoughts exactly.' Cate stood. 'Should I awaken the girls and get the wagons hitched? They're all repaired.'

'No!' John got to his feet. 'We must not let Bingham know we are aware of his intentions. If he's informed the whole troupe has packed up and taken off for Melbourne . . . The wagons must remain where they are and the normal day-to-day routines must be observed so he suspects nothing. You must take her and Jack. Right now. Tonight.'

'Wait, John.'

'Jack, get the two young mares that draw the props wagon and start saddling them up. I'll be along in a minute.'

'Yes, Father.' The boy began to move off.

'Wait!' Cate exclaimed. 'Wait.' Things were suddenly happening too fast for her. 'There must be a . . .'

'You must get Lou-shi as far from Ballarat as you can before first light, my love. Lou-shi and Jack will have to share a saddle.'

'I have it,' she snapped. 'Jack!' she called, stopping the boy in his tracks. 'Set the mares to the props wagon. Wake Tommy and have him help you. Tell him he's driving to Melbourne tonight.' She turned to John. 'He's been whining about wanting to leave Ballarat, so he can take Lou-shi to Melbourne tonight. Just an old man travelling the highway. Nothing could draw less attention.'

'With a Chinese princess hidden in the back,' John nodded, 'brilliant, but what about Jack?'

'Jack stays with me.' Her statement brooked no argument. 'He's the least of our problems. Major Bingham is our more pressing concern. He'll no doubt be well aware that Lou-shi was released into my company by Commissioner Dewes.'

'He'll come after her, Cate, and when he does we must keep our story simple, look him in the eye and say she ran off and you have no idea where she went.'

'And strictly speaking that would be true.' She sighed. 'Do you really think he would try to take Lou-shi back to China? I mean, it's an enormous undertaking, more than a bit fanciful, wouldn't you say?'

'Believe me, Cate, I know Bingham . . .'

'But you *don't* know Bingham.' Cate stared at him. 'You said you merely knew of him by reputation.'

John shrugged. 'I honestly believed I'd never see him again, especially here, in Australia . . .'

'So you lied to me?'

'I didn't want to give you any more reason for concern, God knows you've got enough already.'

She took some moments to reply. 'All right, tell me who he is.'

John sighed. 'Remember the duel I told you about . . .'

'Is he the man who shot you in the back?'

'He's the one.'

Cate considered the information and slowly her brow creased into a frown. 'Bingham? Bingham?' she murmured. 'Good God!' She stiffened. 'Not *the* Binghams, he's not one of the Binghams of London, is he?'

'Yes, do you know of them?'

'Know them! Lady Catherine Bingham, when I knew her, was the most dangerous woman in England, a capricious schemer and manipulator. A she-wolf who destroyed people's lives on a whim.'

'That's his mother.'

'Good Lord.' She shook her head. 'They're a treacherous family, John. And powerful. I knew Sir Horace Bolitho too, he's one of the Bingham clan.'

'That's his uncle.'

'I knew Horace very well.'

'Oh no,' John groaned.

'Not like that,' she exclaimed in reaction to his startled expression. 'He was Private Secretary to the Chancellor of the Exchequer. He hired me to attend social functions and play his mistress, while he feigned the *roué*. The truth was he had no interest in women. He was obsessed with young men.' She stretched her arms above her head and yawned. 'Come on, we've more to do yet.'

'No, no, no.' He took her arm. 'Sleep is what you need at this moment. Why don't you prepare yourself for bed?'

'Oh no you don't.' She pulled free of his grip. 'You won't get rid of me that easily. I must get Lou-shi ready to travel. You go and tell Tommy to get a move on. And warn the rest of the troupe that if asked, they have no idea of Lou-shi's whereabouts. And,' she pointed a warning finger at him, 'you go to the Stockade at first light and stay there.'

'Now just one moment,' John adopted his best officer voice.

'Don't you "just one moment" me,' Cate snapped back as their noses almost touched. 'You're the loose cannon in this entire scenario. If anyone ruins things it will be you.'

'Steady on, Cate.'

'If Bingham does come here you'd last two seconds before you lost your temper and destroyed any plan we may have in place.'

'You have no idea what you're talking about.'

'You cannot control your anger, John; there is a blood rush that comes over you which you cannot control. You know it and I know it. And I'm sure Roger Bingham knows it, too.'

'That's rubbish!'

'Is it?' she queried knowingly. 'I take it that it was *you* who challenged *him* to the duel, was it not?'

'I did indeed! He besmirched the honour of my family!' The anger in his voice was obvious. 'And the swine shot me in the back. The man's a coward, Cate, a craven coward.'

'And what will you do when you see him again?'

'I'll tell you precisely what I'll do,' he growled. 'I'll . . .' He paused, suddenly aware she was provoking him.

'Go on,' her voice had a mocking tone. 'You'll do what? You'll explode, that's what you'll do, and jeopardise not only your own future but mine and Jack's as well. If indeed we have one!' He did not answer. 'Leave him to me, John. I beg you, leave him to me. He may not even come here, but if he does I'll handle him and I'll get the troupe packed up and on the road home. Your place is at the Stockade with your friends.'

John considered her words for some moments before finally nodding. 'You're right as usual. You're a wise owl, Mistress Shearley,' he said affectionately. 'I'll leave for the Stockade at first light.'

'And we'll see how it pans out, as they say on the diggings.' Cate smiled but her eyes told a different story.

CHAPTER SIXTEEN

Ballarat, the morning of Saturday 2 December 1854

First light found John on the diggings, his horse picking its way gingerly through abandoned shafts, as he began the long slow ride between Pennyweight and Specimen hills, navigating the Eureka Lead.

It's a cemetery, was all he could think as he looked about. The shafts were open graves surrounded by hills of mullock to serve as interment dust, the windlasses nameless crosses already in place. All that was needed to complete the depressing scene were corpses to bury and widows to grieve.

Robert Rede and Charles Hotham have brought this about. The thought angered him. The Chief Commissioner and the Colonial Governor had caused such damage to the relationship between the Crown and its citizens that armed confrontation was inevitable.

He felt the pinprick of fear, not for himself but for the safety of others, stab his gut. He realised how desperately he wanted to spend his days with Cate and watch his son grow up to be a good and honest man. He wanted to contribute to Jack's upbringing, to see him properly educated and positive in outlook. *The lad will one day inherit Farrington Vale and it is incumbent upon me to prepare him for life as a Squire, if indeed that is the path the boy chooses to walk.*

He looked up the gentle slope that was the north-east part of the Eureka Diggings to the Stockade. 'It's a bloody joke, Rani,' he said to his horse as he looked at the forlorn defensive redoubt. 'It couldn't resist a decent gust of wind.

Trained soldiers will make short work of the structure, if it comes down to it.'

The Stockade was a ramshackle affair of upturned carts and wagons, trunks and branches of trees, wooden barrels, sacks of grain and flour, fence posts, rusting buckets and wooden slabs, once the walls of mine shafts and anything else that might stop or even slow the passage of a bullet. The rickety wall was not even a complete enclosure, with the trees and scrub of Brown's Hill making up the rear wall, if it could be called such, and another part of it edged the Melbourne Road. As a fort it was, in John's opinion, more akin to a children's playpen and would be treated as such by any trained military force advancing upon it.

The Stockade covered roughly an acre or two of ground and enclosed about a dozen or so miners' tents with their accompanying sinkholes, Diamond's Store – the home and general store of Martin Diamond and his wife, Anne – and several sly-grog tents all unfortunate enough to have been surrounded by the hastily built wall. But outside the barricade there were hundreds of canvas dwellings, sinkholes and windlasses. This area was still crawling with people who thought it safe enough to keep mining, knowing they could run into the Stockade if trouble arose.

The mare snorted and pawed the ground.

'Yes, Rani, you're right. People are going to die here.'

He turned in the saddle and gazed again at the cemetery in the making. 'Ashes to ashes, dust to dust, eh, girl?' he murmured. He nudged the mare gently with his knees to begin the walk up the rise to the Stockade.

'Eh, John la!' Rhodesy's voice boomed across the stockaded ground as the mare made her way through the gap in the fortification that represented the front gate.

John waved at the giant and steered Rani towards him. He was surprised by the number of people inside the Stockade. It was in the hundreds, the majority of men marching to and fro under the command of instructors hastily appointed to teach them basic drill and musketry. Some were armed with flintlock rifles in various stages of repair, some sported pistols, while others marched with pick-axe or shovel on their shoulder. John could only shake his head in dismay. A little knowledge was a dangerous thing, especially in the game of war. Training was all well and good for keeping discipline and good order in the ranks, but when these men were confronted by professional troops the harsh reality of killing would cause them to falter and flee. Good Lord, a dozen mounted men from my old 3rd Dragoons Regiment would set the lot of them to running in all directions.

Rhodesy held the mare's reins as John dismounted.

'Good to see you, John.' It was Kit who emerged from beneath a canvas shelter strung between the side of Diamond's Store and two saplings recently cut and embedded in the hard ground.

'We thought you b'ain't be comin', la,' Rhodesy boomed. 'Mind you, I'd not 'ave blamed you, what with Cate and your lad Jack and the troupe dependin' on you.'

'I could never countenance my friends fighting for my rights with me not at their side. Unthinkable.'

'That's the spirit I'm searching for!' The voice, an Irish voice, came from under the canvas awning. Then a tall, blue-eyed, fair-haired man emerged and offered his hand to John. 'Good to have you on board, Mister Bailleau, I'm sure we can put your military knowledge and experience to good use.'

'Have we met?' John asked as he shook the Irishman's hand. He knew precisely who he was shaking hands with, but could not remember ever having been introduced.

'Not officially.' The man offered a winning smile. 'Peter Lalor, late of Queens County in the Province of Leinster, Ireland.'

'Ah, yes, and currently the voice of Bakery Hill. I must say I admire your principles, Mister Lalor. But,' he looked around the compound, taking in the activity, 'surely you will not encourage these civilians to engage in armed conflict?'

'I don't believe we'll be offered a choice in the matter,' Lalor replied. 'The bureaucratic indifference shown by Hotham, Rede and others towards the genuine grievances of the people, not to mention the drunken lawlessness displayed by the police and military, has created a situation from which the government will have difficulty retreating.'

'I agree with you. Johnston's idea to launch a licence hunt at the Gravel Pits on the very morning after the diggers had burned their licences was an act of stupidity . . .'

'The police opened fire on women and children!' Lalor interrupted.

'I reckon they done it deliberate, like,' Rhodesy growled. 'That Gov'nor 'Otham, 'e wants an end to this 'ere miners' mutiny before 'e gets blamed by the Parliament in London for bein' 'opeless at his job. I can 'ear 'im now crowin' to them powers that be in London, "Them miners was a violent mob of revolutionaries. We opened fire on 'em at the Gravel Pits, bein' careful not to 'it anyone, mind, but they didn't take 'eed o' the warning and the next time they started up we 'ad no alternative but to shoot 'em for the rebellious dogs they was." That's what 'e'll say and 'e'll get away with it, won't he, 'cause 'e's a toff, a British Gov'nor no less.'

'I believe Rhodesy's right,' Kit said. 'The Gravel Pits shooting was planned. It gives the government *carte blanche* to create another confrontation then use lethal force to quell what they'll claim was an act of revolution.'

'We can only hope that Hotham is a man incapable of such behaviour,' John countered. 'I mean to say, it was only two weeks ago he appointed a Royal Commissioner to investigate the grievances here on the goldfields; surely that says something of the man's character.' Then a thought struck him. 'But Rede is a different kettle of fish,' he added. 'I wouldn't be surprised if he conspired with Johnston to bring about what happened at the Gravel Pits.'

'Well,' Lalor said, 'whether it's true or not is immaterial. All I'm sure of is another confrontation is inevitable and it will be sooner rather than later.'

'How soon do ya think, la?'

'As early as Monday would not surprise me.'

'Why not tomorra'?'

'Tomorrow is the Sabbath, Mister Rhodes,' Lalor reminded him. 'Not even Rede would have the temerity to engage in military shenanigans on the Lord's day of rest.'

'That's what I make of it too. So it be orright for me t' step outside a' the Stockade for an evenin' a card playin' and the like?'

'"And the like", Rhodesy?' Kit laughed out loud.

'Well,' the big man growled defensively, 'a man can't play cards all night without a drink or two and somethin' t' eat.'

'And let's not forget "and the like"!' Kit repeated.

On Saturday morning Cate had awoken to the realisation that John was gone. He'd left at first light without waking her as he'd said he would when she'd lain in his arms several hours before. She was satisfied with the way things had worked out. The previous day had been a momentous one to say the least, but at least things had been decided and they had a plan in place.

She rose, washed her face and dressed hurriedly, desperate to be out in the morning air.

At first, when Cate had stepped from the caravan, she'd been unaware of the change that had fallen across Ballarat. It was still very early and none of the troupe was yet about, so she stoked the remnants of the campfire, resurrecting a flame, and listened to the beautiful warbling of magpies in the lone wattle tree behind the allotment. As the sun rose across the diggings a family of kookaburras briefly added their insane laughter to the morning chorus then fell silent, satisfied their efforts had been recognised, and she was left with the sound she'd learned to love, the magnificent morning-song of the Australian magpie.

Usually her ears were greeted by the barking of dogs, the racket from Main Street and the loud profane language of miners already hard at work, but this morning she smiled contentedly and let the avian symphony wash over her.

'Good morning, Ma.'

'Good morning, son.' She noticed the frown on his face. 'What's the matter?'

'Something's wrong. There's no-one anywhere. Everybody's gone.'

'What do you mean?'

'There's no-one in the street,' Jack said, pointing across the piles of ashes where once the Paragon Theatre had stood, to the street beyond.

The boy was right, she realised.

She walked across the allotment through the ashes and looked left and right along the street. 'How odd.' Together they walked up the main street to the bowling alley and gazed out across the diggings, west across Yarrowee Flat to the Camp and east to Specimen Hill.

The tent stores on the diggings were shut and the storekeepers had vanished; not one call of the price of wares was to be heard anywhere. Both east and west of Main Street windlasses were still and the few miners to be seen were huddled together smoking and furtively glancing about. Gone were the women and children too, even the dogs.

The entire goldfields had stopped functioning.

Out beyond Specimen Hill, a mile distant to the east, there was activity on the Eureka rise. Men and women were fortifying their Stockade and above their activities, on a tall pole, flew the Eureka flag. But as for the rest of Ballarat there was only silence and a sense of ominous foreboding.

'We'd best be getting back, son.'

As they re-entered the allotment across the scattered ashes it was obvious to both that the remainder of the troupe, now gathered together around the campfire drinking tea, were patently aware of the situation and all were expressing their concerns. John, Kit and Rhodesy, she knew, were at the Stockade.

'I zink ve all in trouble.' It was Anna, elder by ten minutes of the Twisting Teutonic Twins. 'Every vun who haz der shmartz,' the German tapped her forehead with an index finger, 'has leaf dis place already in der nacht.'

'Ja,' her sister Lanna added. 'Listen to Anna. Ve who don't leave last night, we going to get caught in der mittle of zings!'

Cate raised her hands to signal a halt to the squabbling. 'All right, all right,' she said, staring at each individual face. 'That's enough. You sound like a gaggle of geese. Let us talk quietly and sensibly about our situation. We decided to leave for Melbourne on Monday morning at first light.'

'Top o' da mornin' to yez, ladies.' It was a deep, aggressive and very Irish voice. Cate turned to find three men, obviously miners and all carrying firearms. The spokesman grinned, showing two rows of rotten teeth.

'Can I help you, gentlemen?' Cate knew this man. She could not immediately remember where or when they'd met, but she definitely knew him.

'Well, Cate,' began the spokesman, 'it's like this, we be on official business for da Reform League Committee. We're on a gun gatherin' mission and need yez all to hand over da firearms you have for use at da Stockade.' The Irishman nodded with a grin to his companions. 'Oh, yeah,' he added, 'an' any food you have in your possession.' He and his mates had decided to scour the diggings, ostensibly in search of firearms as a number of groups of miners had been ordered to do by the Reform League. The Irishmen, not so ordered, thought it a smart way to make a bit of profit on the side and even above gold and guns, food was the most valuable commodity to be had.

Cate placed her hand on her son's shoulder. 'Get into the caravan, Jack.'

The boy responded like a puppy to its mother's growl and went straight into the caravan and closed the door.

'Now, gentlemen,' Cate said evenly, 'the request for firearms I can understand, not that we're going to give you any, but food? I can't believe the Committee would ask people to surrender their food; many don't have enough to survive on as it is. I think you three are up to no good.'

'You can think what you like, Cate . . .'

'It is my opinion,' Cate interrupted, her voice smooth and even, 'that you three are committing the crime of robbery under arms and for that,' she turned her good eye on each of them in turn, 'I can shoot you dead where you stand.'

The laughter ceased, smiles disappeared and the spokesman bared his rotten teeth. 'Firearms and food, Cate, dat's da deal. Hand 'em over.'

'I won't do that,' Cate continued. 'What I will do is ask you to leave my property.' She paused and her voice went icy cold. 'Or face the consequences.'

Silence reigned for a good ten seconds. The three men shifted uneasily as they weighed up the threat. They were all aware of Cate Shearley's reputation and had witnessed first-hand her ability with a shotgun.

'C'mon, Connor,' another man, also Irish, said, 'it ain't worth it. They're just show people.'

'We're on official Reform League business, lads,' he growled.

'No we're not!' one of them replied.

'We're under orders!' He took a Colt revolver from his hip holster and held it, barrel pointing downward by his side. 'We was sent by Lalor himself and so we was.'

'Connor, of course,' Cate said as she eyed the revolver. 'Now I remember.' It was the rotten teeth. 'You're the three Irish pigs I met in Collins Street. You threatened the life of my young Chinese acrobat.'

'Dat's right. You had the upper hand then, Cate, but now it's my turn.'

She looked again at the leader. 'Well, Connor, I seem to remember predicting the time and place of your demise.'

The Irishman did not detect the threat in her voice. He laughed humourlessly. 'Oh yeah, remind me joost when and where was dat supposed ta be?'

'Right here, right now, if you're not careful.'

'You're full a' shite, Cate. I can see both your hands an' dey 's empty.' She watched his knuckles whiten on the revolver. 'You're blooffin'. You ain't got your shotgun. Like I said, it's my turn dis time.'

'I'm warning you for the last time – leave my property or face the consequences.'

For one brief moment, doubt appeared in the man's eyes then he offered a broad black-toothed grin and slowly shook his head. 'You're blooffin', Cate.' He raised the pistol. 'I know you's blooffin', you ain't got a gun.'

'Oh, but I have, Connor.' Cate raised her arm and pointed her index finger directly at him; then flexed muscles activated the spring-loaded sleeve holster and the double-barrelled Philadelphia Derringer appeared instantly in her hand. She didn't hesitate, she aimed instinctively, pulled the trigger and the big .41 calibre bullet hit the Irishman in the forehead and he fell to the ground lifeless. Her good eye glared at the other two through the cloud of gun-smoke filling the air in front of the Derringer. 'One shot left, boys. Who's next?'

Both men – young men behind thick, bushy beards – turned and ran.

'I want you all to listen to me carefully,' Cate said sternly, drawing the shocked performers' attention from the dead Irishman. 'Well, if we wanted proof that Ballarat is no longer safe, that was it. Start preparing to leave for Melbourne immediately.'

'Not possible at the moment, I'm afraid.' It was the Scottish dwarf Andrew McCrae. 'Well for you anyway, mistress.'

'What do you mean?'

'We still need some running gear. John said last night he'd find what was needed.'

'Running gear?' Cate frowned.

'Aye, lass,' the little man said, 'for your wagon. We need a bolster plate and a flange, or you'll never get out of here.'

'Are you saying my wagon's *not* repaired?'

'That's right, Cate. The smithy took off to the Stockade and left us two parts short. John said he'd find them.'

'What about the others?'

'The other wagons are ready to go.'

'Well, that's it, everyone. You heard Mister McCrae. You will all leave today.'

'But what about you, Señora?' Adelina asked.

Cate shrugged at the troupe. 'I won't be far behind you all. Now, you two,' she scowled at the German twins, 'can busy yourselves making breakfast. And the rest of you can start packing. I want you all fed and ready to go at a moment's notice.'

'McCrae,' she snapped at the Scot. 'You and Adelina, hide the Irishman.'

'Where?'

'I don't care! Just hide him!'

Her tone drove them in all directions and she stood alone by the fire for some minutes staring into the flames, slowly adjusting her mind to the situation.

Finally she went to the caravan, but Jack was not there. She walked across to Main Street and saw, a hundred yards down the street, her boy talking to a lone mounted soldier. Just then the man leaned down and hauled the lad up onto the horse's back.

'Dear God,' she murmured, 'let it not be Bingham.' She only had the Derringer with one bullet in it and the distance between them would allow the man to ride off before she could even begin to cover the ground.

The redcoat nudged his mount, a grey cavalry horse, and it began to walk up the hill towards her. As he came nearer, her fear eased. The man was not Bingham, neither was he a major, or even an officer; his forearm sported the three chevrons of a sergeant.

'There you go, lad,' the man said, lowering Jack to the ground.

'Get back into the caravan, Jack. Now.'

'Yes, Ma.' Jack knew his mother's tone would brook no argument and he scurried across the dusty allotment.

'Good day to you, Mistress Shearley.' The voice was deep and rich. 'Sergeant Geary of the 40th Regiment at your service, ma'am.'

'Good day to you, Sergeant.' She squinted up at him, shielding her good eye from the sun. 'I assume you are here on business?'

'I am, mistress.'

'If you were sent here to recover the Chinese boy, you're too late. He ran off.'

'I know nothing about any Chinese boy.'

'Really?' Cate sneered.

'It is imperative that I speak with Captain John Farrington, late of Her Majesty's 3rd Dragoons, on a matter of the utmost urgency.'

Her face lost all expression. 'I know no-one of that name.'

'I do, ma'am. I fought in the Sikh Wars on the North-West Frontier of India with Captain Farrington.'

'I know no-one of that name.'

'I rode alongside him at the Battle of Gujrat when his bravery inspired the entire regiment and he was promoted in the field to brevet major by General Gough.'

'Well good for you, Sergeant. I can only repeat I know no-one of that name.'

'And I saw him yesterday, from a distance.' He looked down at her and paused for a moment. 'I need to speak with John Farrington, ma'am, urgently. I saw him yesterday riding across the Gravel Pits. I was told by two of my men who spoke to him that the man identified himself as John Bailleau.' He offered her a wry grin. 'But you and I know better than that, don't we?'

'If you'll excuse me, Sergeant, I'm busy.' Cate waved her arm in the general direction of the allotment.

'I've taken a risk coming here, Mistress Shearley. If word was to get back to the 40th that I was seen –'

'Fraternising with the enemy?' she interrupted, holding up her hand. 'I understand, Sergeant.'

'Please, ma'am, let's have done with the charade. Tell Captain Farrington that Sergeant Geary said he must be on the alert, because Major John Bingham's here in Ballarat. That's all you need tell him. He'll understand.' He straightened in the saddle. 'My respects to the captain, ma'am, and good day to you.'

Cate was forced to take a step back as the soldier spurred his mount into a reverse turn and trotted off down Main Street.

She stood watching and wondering until horse and rider disappeared. What should I make of that exchange? Should I inform John of Sergeant Geary's visit? It would confirm Geary's bona fides if John recognised the name, but then no new information had been forthcoming from the soldier. John and Bingham had met face to face last evening in the coldest of meetings. It had been obvious to all present that they shared a profound dislike of each other. Mind you, she thought, Geary was not an officer and was probably unaware of the awkward confrontation at the Adelphi.

'Who was that sergeant, Mother?' Jack joined her in the middle of the street.

'I'm fairly sure he was a friend of your father's.'

'What did he want?'

'Never mind.' Cate turned. 'There's stew in the pot over the campfire and fresh damper. Go on now, help yourself.'

The boy shook his head. 'I'm not hungry.' He remained standing beside her, head down and scuffing the dust with his toe.

'What's your problem, son? Come on, out with it.'

'When I came out of the caravan I saw Andrew and Adelina dragging that Irishman up the allotment. He was dead, wasn't he?'

'Yes. Did you see what happened?'

'No.' He scuffed the dust again. 'But I heard a gunshot. I reckon it was your Derringer.' He looked up at her. 'It sure sounded like it.'

'You're right. It was the Derringer.' She shook her head and sighed. 'I had no alternative but to shoot him, before he shot me.'

'Or someone else,' he added.

'Yes. Had he fired he may well have hit any one of the troupe. He was a bad man, Jack.' She looked up the now deserted street. 'And Ballarat's a bad place.'

'It's a goldfield, Ma.' The boy squeezed his mother's forearm. 'It's like Mister Rhodes says, "There's some what finds gold, but most just gets old and not many makes it to heaven."' He gave her a reassuring smile and squeezed her arm again. As he walked off he called back over his shoulder, 'But you'll make it, Ma. You're the best there is!'

She remained standing in the middle of the street watching the boy kick up the sooty dust as he ran across the allotment. The love he stirred in her breast was overwhelming. Then an image of John crept into her brain and she wanted to cry out in protest at her predicament. Why can't I simply have my son and the man I love somewhere safe? Is it too much to ask?

Cate looked through the narrow gap between the blacksmith's and the hat-maker's shop and she could just make out, over a mile away to the north-east, the smoke from the campfires of the Eureka Stockade.

'God watch over you, John Farrington, and see you home safe to your son.'

John returned to the allotment at around three o'clock that afternoon, accompanied by Kit, both looking the worse for wear.

'You two look like something a cat would drag in,' Cate commented as they dismounted.

John frowned. 'Where are the wagons? Where is everyone?'

'They've gone. I sent them all back to Melbourne this morning.'

'And Jack?'

'He's here with me, of course.' She decided not to tell him about the killing of the Irishman. 'They're show folk, John. They'll be better off in Melbourne.'

'You should have gone with them.'

'We would have had this wagon been serviceable. I sincerely hope you found the *running gear* you failed to tell me we needed?'

'We've been helping construct the walls of Lalor's Stockade,' replied John in a very sarcastic tone, as he led his horse to the trough to drink.

'That's wonderful news for Mister Lalor, but what about the wagon parts?'

He splashed his face with water and gave her a world-weary look. 'And just where do you think every known piece of wagon, sulky, dray, cart, trolley, surrey or buggy is to be found at this particular time?'

'I don't know, John,' she said temperately, 'but I've no doubt you'll tell me.'

'They are all to be found as parts of that blasted stockade wall Peter Lalor ordered built, that's where!' He began to pace back and forth as he expounded upon his frustrating afternoon in search of wagon parts. 'I scoured the entirety of Ballarat and could not find one single piece of undercarriage in any direction.' He stopped and threw his hands in the air. 'So where did I find this, you may well ask?' He held aloft an axle flange. 'In Lalor's damned wall, half of which is constructed of upturned wagons and undercarriage iron.'

'Calm down, John.'

'Calm down be damned, madam! I spent four hours helping build that wall, which I might add will collapse if charged by a herd of mice, before I felt I'd earned the right to souvenir this from it!' He shook the round flange like a tambourine.

'Mischief,' Cate said softly.

'I beg your pardon?' He frowned, utterly perplexed.

'It's a *mischief* of mice, not a herd.'

'Really?'

'She's right,' Kit nodded knowingly. 'Mischief is the collective noun for mice.'

'Well I'll be damned.' John's face broke into a smile.

'Now that you've calmed down,' she continued smoothly, 'perhaps you can set about finishing the repairs to the wagon.'

'Of course, Kit's offered his help. With a bit of effort we'll have it ready in no time.'

'And then you're straight back to the Stockade.'

'Yes, of course.' He gave her a quizzical stare. 'Why, did something happen in my absence?'

'No, no.' Her face gave nothing away.

'Bingham didn't turn up, did he?'

'No.' She shook her head.

'Right.' He squinted. 'Well, we'll get on with repairing the wagon. And as soon as it's done you and Jack are off to Melbourne.'

'No.' Cate shook her head. 'We'll leave on Monday as decided,' she said, hoping against hope he may join them.

'I don't like the thought of you staying here on the allotment alone,' Kit said and looked at John. 'Not a good idea.'

'I'll return tonight and tomorrow night and stay with them.'

'Your place is at the Stockade, John.'

'No, Cate. Not if you and the boy are here alone.'

'There's no need . . .'

'Then you'll leave when the wagon is repaired, right?'

'No.'

'Then I'll be here each night. There's no more to be said. Come along, Kit, let's get on with the repairs.'

Peter Lalor had stood on a tree stump earlier that afternoon and given one of his most inspiring speeches to two thousand or more people gathered in the Stockade. John and Kit now found him seated upon that same stump, outside Diamond's Store, drinking tea and in deep discussion with George Black and Raffaello Carboni, two of the more vociferous pro-republican members of the Reform League Committee, and a Catholic priest, Father Smyth. The three had been used by Lalor the previous night to approach Commissioner Rede in a last-ditch effort to negotiate the release of prisoners and perhaps finally defuse what had become a highly explosive situation. Rede had dismissed them out of hand.

'The men are leaving the Stockade in droves,' John heard Lalor complain.

'Because they're convinced, as I am,' George Black said, 'that nothing will happen today or tomorrow. Can you ever remember a licensing raid being conducted on a Saturday afternoon or on a Sunday?'

'George is right, Peter,' Father Smyth agreed. 'The authorities would never dare start trouble on the Sabbath. That's why I've urged my flock to get home to their wives and prepare themselves for Sunday Mass, which I'll conduct here in the compound.'

The group dispersed and John and Kit settled down outside their canvas extension of Diamond's Store. Kit soon had a brew up and the two partook of tea with a dash of rum.

'I can smell the blood already,' John said darkly, looking around the Stockade. His concern was well founded. On a tall pole in the centre of the Stockade flew the Eureka flag, blue silk with a silver cross and five stars attached. It fluttered defiantly in the late-afternoon breeze.

He then looked west to the Government Camp with the Union Jack fluttering above it about a mile and a half distant. 'Combining the military and police personnel there must be several hundred men under arms on that hill,' he said to himself more than to Kit.

Kit sipped his drink. 'What do they think is going to occur here, another Battle of Waterloo? They're dealing with irate miners, not the French Army. I've heard tell,' he went on, 'that disharmony within the ranks at the Camp is causing more trouble for Commissioner Rede than the miners themselves. The hunger, crowded compound and unsanitary living conditions the soldiers and police have had to suffer, when added to the months of insults and abuse from the miners, have created a rare atmosphere indeed. Rede himself never goes anywhere unattended, because he's terrified of violence from his own disgruntled men.'

'Rebellion in the ranks, eh?' John raised his eyebrows. 'I've seen it before; mutiny is not an uncommon occurrence in the British Army.'

'What is your real name?'

The question hung in the air. John looked at Kit but did not answer.

'Rumours have been pouring out of the Camp over the last several days, since the 40th Regiment arrived. They say you are the famous Captain John Farrington, the Hero of Gujrat, and the revolver you carry was given to you by Prince Albert himself.'

Still John did not answer; he stared intently into his tea and rum as if an answer might be found there.

'Normally I would not ask, but given the situation we find ourselves in, I would like to know.'

'My name is Farrington, John Farrington,' John said quickly. 'Bailleau was my mother's maiden name.'

Kit drained his cup and took John's from him. 'Go home to Cate and Jack, John. Go now, before night sets in. Go home and tell them you love them. You may not get another chance.'

'Half the population of Ballarat suddenly knows my real identity.'

It was midnight and Cate and John lay in each other's arms, Jack asleep in his single bunk and the light of the rising moon shining through the small window at the side of the bed.

'Secrets don't last, my love,' Cate whispered. 'They never do.'

'It was the arrival of the 40th Regiment that let the cat out of the bag. Apparently several members of it were once in the 3rd Dragoons and fought with me in India.'

'Would one be named Geary?'

'Geary, yes, there was an Edward Geary in the 3rd, a sergeant and a damned good soldier he was too.'

'He came here this morning.'

'What? Here to the allotment?'

'Yes. He asked to speak to Captain Farrington, but I told him I knew no-one of that name. He said he wanted to warn Captain Farrington that Major Bingham was in Ballarat and that the captain should watch his back.'

'He's a good man, Geary. Oddly enough, he was actually present at the duel I fought with Bingham, he drove the hearse . . .'

'The hearse?' The words horrified her.

'That's what they call the cart that carries away the dead or injured from a duel. It's considered amusing in military circles to refer to it as that.'

'They may consider it amusing, I'd call it macabre.'

John sighed. 'Well that's it, my love, my identity is revealed. I am undone, madam. The thing now is, what do I do about it?'

'More importantly what are you going to do about Roger Bingham?'

'I'll take care of the Bingham business when, or indeed *if*, he confronts me. Until then I'm not going to let it be of concern.'

'He's a dangerous man, John. Promise me you won't do anything foolish.' The fear in her voice was unmistakable.

'I promise.' He stroked her arm to calm her, surprised by the depth of his reaction to her concern. 'I have too much to lose.'

'Yes you do.'

'Earlier today at the camp, Kit told me to come and say goodbye to you both for I may not get another opportunity. His words made me think and riding down the Eureka rise on the way back here, I came to a decision.'

Cate waited for him to continue, then finally asked, 'And?'

'I'll go back to the Stockade tomorrow, but if nothing happens by Monday we'll leave this place. We'll take Jack and go home to Melbourne. We'll marry, Cate. And I will devote my life to my family.'

CHAPTER SEVENTEEN

Eureka Stockade, Sunday 3 December 1854

Jack ran fast all the way across the Yarrowee Creek and up the hill to Main Street, but his speed was failing him, his lungs heaving. He knew his chances of making the caravan were slight, but the image in his mind of his mother grieving at his graveside spurred him on.

'Front rank load!' he heard a voice behind him call. 'Front rank take aim at the retreating boy!' He knew who called the order; it was Sergeant Geary of the 40th. 'Fire!' the voice screamed.

Jack heard the musket volley and braced himself for the bullets to strike his back.

Suddenly he was sitting up in his bunk with sweat pouring down his face. He looked about the caravan to reassure himself it was only a dream, but then he heard another volley.

'Father!' Jack leapt from his bunk and shook John's arm. 'Father, listen.'

John and Cate sat up simultaneously. 'The Stockade!' they exclaimed in unison.

John dressed hurriedly. 'Surely they wouldn't dare?' he muttered, strapping on his knife and pistol. 'It's Sunday, Cate! It's the Sabbath!'

'I'll saddle Rani,' was all Cate replied as her heart sank. She seized the horse's bridle from a hook on the wall, thrust open the caravan door and stepped out into the darkness wearing only her nightgown.

Now, as the first hint of light threatened the night sky, she could hear more clearly the screams of men and women among the increasing rapidity of musket fire.

At the caravan door, John turned to his son and raised a warning finger. 'You stay put, young man,' he ordered. 'I hold you responsible for your mother's safety.'

'Yes, sir.'

'Under no circumstances approach the Stockade and, more particularly, make sure your mother doesn't either.'

'Yes, sir.'

'Good man, Lieutenant.' He tousled his son's hair. 'You are Officer of the Day and the watch is yours.'

'Yes, sir.'

John reached the mare as Cate flung the saddle onto its back. He seized the girth strap, tightened it and in an instant he was mounted.

'Be careful, my love,' was all Cate could say.

'I'll be back. Don't worry, just keep Jack safe.' And with that he spurred Rani and was off at the gallop.

By the time he got down onto the flat to set off across the diggings, the mare could only walk, picking her way, in darkness, through the sinkholes and windlasses and the men, women and children, who were rushing towards high ground to view what was obviously a full-scale military attack. It took him twenty minutes to get onto the Eureka rise that led up to the Stockade, and by then the shooting had all but ceased, except for the odd shot here and there. But all about he could hear the screams and groans of the injured and the wailing of distressed women. His blood ran cold.

Theophilus Kittredge came out from under the canvas shelter strung along the side of Diamond's Store. He breathed deeply, taking in the fresh air with its hints of eucalyptus and wood smoke. It will be dawn soon, he thought, as he stoked the embers of his campfire. Then a shot was fired and the hairs on his neck stood on end. The shot seemed to come from near the guard tent on the western side of the Stockade not fifty yards from where he stood.

'Joe!' someone yelled. 'It's Joe!' Other men on the night watch began calling the word that warned of the presence of troopers and police.

Before Kit could make any decisions, he heard a loud volley of musket fire; bullets smashed into the flimsy Stockade walls and a man to his right screamed in pain.

'It's Joe! It's Joe!' someone else screamed. 'We're surrounded, the Stockade is surrounded.'

Within seconds of the first volley from beyond the wall, the Stockade became a madhouse. Men burst from tents and rushed about, unsure of what to do. Lacking order or discipline, those with firearms ran towards the western wall, while others, unarmed, stumbled over each other in panic. Women gathered their children in arms and hustled them back into tents. Terrified horses whinnied, dogs barked and all about was chaos.

Peter Lalor appeared beside Kit. He leapt onto the stump he'd used the previous day and tried to call order. 'Gather to your commanders, lads!' he called across the compound. 'To the walls, men! For liberty!'

Inside the Stockade men found places against the walls and opened fire on the government forces. The air was filled with lead, but the military advance on the Stockade continued unabated.

'It's no use,' someone called. 'They'll have us in no time.'

'They're all around us!' shouted another over the crack of rifle fire.

Next to one of the many tents and fifty yards from the Stockade entrance John saw a mother on her knees sobbing and holding at her breast a boy no more than eight years old. The lad was bleeding from a stomach wound. John had no sooner decided to stop and help the mother when he saw, just to his right, the prone body of Irish Annie the prostitute. She was lying on her back outside her sly-grog tent and there beside her lay James Small.

John leapt from the saddle and knelt by the bodies. Annie was dead, but not from rifle fire; she'd been bayoneted, as had Rhodesy. Beside her tent lay a dead policeman and inside there was another. Both had their eyes open but their heads were at unnatural angles, signifying to John their necks had been broken.

'James!' he hissed and shook his giant friend. 'James!'

The big man's eyes opened. 'John, la!' Rhodesy tried to sit up but blood oozed from a bayonet wound in his side.

John forced him back down. 'Lay still, man, while I tamp you up.' He took a handkerchief from his pocket and stuffed it into the wound.

'They was at 'er, John,' Rhodesy managed to rasp. 'Outside 'ere, they was at Annie when I woke up. Like dogs they was, la, so I done for 'em both.'

'All right. Lay still and don't talk.'

'There was soldiers everywhere. Marchin' in lines right past 'ere an' on up the hill. Firin' and screamin' they was, like animals.'

'I'm going to roll Annie on top of you to conceal you, James. She's gone, man, so there's no harm and she just might save your life. Don't strain your stomach muscles or you'll increase the bleeding. Lay still until I get back. I've got to find Kit.'

He looked up the hill and saw the wall had been well and truly breached and the government troops were inside. He assumed they had won the battle, but the screaming from within was horrendous. My God, he thought, what's going on in there?

Inside the Stockade Kit knew that all was lost. In a matter of fifteen minutes from the first shot the miners had thrown down their arms and surrendered, but it seemed the government troops were not satisfied with mere capitulation.

Kit had been at the western wall when it had been breached. He'd fallen beneath a wooden slab and the military had stormed straight over him. Now playing dead, he watched horrified as police and soldiers vented their months of pent-up hostility on anyone and anything. He saw four policemen with rifles surround a tent and thrust their bayonets repeatedly through the canvas. Screams from within were from the throats of children, then a mother crawled out to beg for her family's lives and was viciously stabbed several times in the stomach. The fact she was heavily pregnant brought forth pointing and howls of maniacal laughter from the men.

Bodies were strewn all across the Stockade. Pandemonium reigned as soldiers and policemen bayoneted dead and wounded alike. Blood lust took over and Kit could only watch dumbfounded as the so-called colonial authorities murdered and butchered with gun, sword and bayonet.

Women threw themselves over their wounded men and begged for their lives. Miners, fearful of the insanity of the troops, threw themselves into mine shafts, some full of water, as others, dragging their women and children, ran from the Stockade through the rough scrub onto Brown Hill and disappeared into the trees.

Kit lay unbelieving at what then occurred. He heard troops given orders from none other than Major Roger Bingham to destroy the entire Stockade.

'Burn it to the ground!' Bingham ordered from horseback. 'I want no sign left that this place ever existed. Kill every pig in the sty,' he sneered. 'Leave no-one alive!'

It was at that moment a miner ran past Bingham's horse chasing a small, terrified boy.

'Come back, Georgie!' the man yelled angrily.

'Allow me!' Bingham called, drawing his revolver, and shot the child in the back. Then as the shocked father fell next to his child and took him in his arms, Bingham fired again and the man collapsed upon his dead son.

Before John could make it to the Stockade it was a raging inferno. He watched in horror as soldiers and police spewed forth from it with flaming torches and began setting fire to every tent on Eureka Lead. Men, women and children, totally innocent of any insurgent thoughts or actions, ran for their lives as their tents and meagre belongings became part of the scorched earth policy adopted by the authorities. Some women were caught and subjected to the ultimate humiliation at the hands of men gone mad. Several women went so far as to lift their skirts and offer themselves in order to allow their families to escape.

He returned to Annie's tent and, with superhuman strength brought about by pure adrenalin, he managed to get Rhodesy onto Rani's back and led her down the slope away from the Stockade.

Behind him the flames leapt higher and the screams of women and the groans of the wounded and dying filled the air, making him hurry all the more. His mind was suddenly filled with the childhood memories of the Book of Genesis when Lot's wife looked back on the city of Sodom. It seemed that all the devils of hell were roaring immediately behind him. Don't look back, his mind shrieked, don't look back. He concentrated on getting Rhodesy and the mare down off the rise and over the diggings.

John Farrington did not look back.

'How on earth did you ever get him over the saddle?' Cate grunted, as she and John managed to get Rhodesy from Rani's back to the ground, but even with their combined strength they could not get him into the caravan. They were forced to lay a blanket beneath the undercarriage and drag him onto it, where Cate inspected his wound.

'You're lucky, man,' Cate assured him. 'The bayonet went straight through your fat. I don't think it got your kidney; we'll have to wait and see. If there is blood in your urine you're in trouble, but I think not.'

'I caught 'em havin' their way with Irish Annie, Cate,' Rhodesy said through gritted teeth as Cate re-tamped his wound.

'You stay quiet now.'

'They killed 'er.'

'It would seem they've killed quite a number of people.' She looked at John. She had never seen him so lost. 'You rest now, Mister Rhodes, and keep warm. Whether you like it or not keep the blanket on you and keep yourself full of this.' She handed a vial of laudanum to him. 'A sip every hour or two, but no more than that, mind!'

'Right, Cate,' the big man grunted.

She sat on the caravan steps next to John and took his hand.

'I tell you, Cate,' John shook his head, 'never, even on the North-West Frontier of India, did I ever see British soldiers act with such utter barbarity.' He was in a state of shock. What he had just witnessed had left him sick with disgust. 'God alone knows what occurred inside the Stockade, but what I saw on the Eureka rise was enough. Butchery is all one can call it and by those who are sworn to preserve the peace and protect Her Majesty's citizens.' He stared at her and she flinched at what she saw in his eyes. The blood rush was well and truly on him. 'For what occurred up there,' he pointed towards the distant plumes of smoke rising from the Stockade and its surrounds, 'someone must be held to account.'

He tried to stand but Cate clung tightly to his arm, forcing him to remain seated. 'You have responsibilities, John.' Cate chose her words carefully and delivered them meaningfully. 'You are accountable for your actions. I thought you'd finally realised that, but I can see the madness in your eyes. You can't simply charge back up that hill like an enraged bull and wreak your personal justice upon anyone you may think guilty. That would be the John Farrington I have no use for. Think of the consequences if you were killed. What of me and Jack? What of Rhodesy?' She could see her words were sinking in so she played her ace. 'What of Kit? He's still up there, somewhere.'

John's shoulders slumped. 'Of course, you're right. It's Kit we must be concerned for.'

'Judging by the lack of gunfire and screaming, whatever took place in the Stockade is now finished. We should give it a while for things to calm down, then we'll go up to the Stockade and discover his fate.'

'What about our boy?'

'I'll order him to remain in the caravan and,' she took a deep breath and exhaled, 'I'll give him my Derringer.'

It was midday when Cate and John set off. They went down Main Street and turned right onto the old Melbourne track and headed east towards the Stockade. Twice they were forced off the track only to sit and watch as armed police escorted arrested miners to the west for imprisonment at the Camp. One of those in shackles was Raffaello Carboni. He looked up as he shuffled past them and shook his head, warning John not to acknowledge him.

As they moved along the track evidence of the massacre, for they agreed it could be called nothing less, became more evident. The air was full of the smoke from burning tents and possessions, and carried with it the once-experienced never-to-be-forgotten stench of burnt flesh. Men and women, their arms full of whatever valuables they had managed to save, and urging children in front of them, scurried across the Eureka Lead in the direction of Brown Hill and the forest they hoped would offer protection.

With the sun now well into the sky, the hills around were filled with hundreds of ghoulish sightseers. On the slope of Eureka Lead, grieving relatives hovered over dead loved ones while policemen were supposedly searching for insurgents. In reality, they were looting from the pockets of corpses.

'It's a scene from hell,' Cate murmured. 'Dear God, can this be happening?'

They reached the smouldering Stockade walls and made their way inside. As with the case on the surrounding hill, civilians were working to get their dead and injured loved ones away to safety. However, they were being impeded by a sergeant and a working party of policemen who, having been told to arrest insurgents, were rolling bodies onto their backs seeking to identify anyone involved in the rebellion.

Several men attending their injured mates made complaints and were instantly arrested and shackled. Even a woman who tried to intervene on her husband's behalf was assaulted, put in chains and marched off at the point of a bayonet. Around the burnt remains of the Stockade women grieved as their husbands' corpses were roughly manhandled and thrown into a wagon.

Cate and John moved slowly around the compound, offering what little help or consolation they could. Diamond's Store was nothing more than a pile of smouldering ashes and the married couple who owned it were not in evidence. The blacksmith's forge next to it was completely destroyed and on the flag pole nearby flew the Union Jack where once, briefly, had fluttered the flag of Eureka with its emblem of the Southern Cross. The ramshackle homes of the Shanahans, Quins and Curtains, meagre tented properties unfortunate enough to have been encircled by the Stockade wall, were also no more and the occupants had fled or were dead.

Cate could only wonder why they were not being challenged by authority, then she glanced at John's right hip. On it was slung Mister Adams, with its side plate above the trigger guard and the royal coat of arms on the grip, glittering golden. And beneath the revolver on John's thigh was the Bowie knife, in Cate's opinion the very essence of evil. The men in uniform moving around the compound are frightened of him, she thought. Even as they bully others they cast furtive glances in his direction. Captain John Farrington of Her Majesty's 3rd Dragoons is a man they fear and, judging by the occasional look and nod offered by one or two soldiers, a man many respect.

'Cap'n Farrington,' a soldier hissed from the side of his mouth as he walked by, 'your man Kittredge is under a slab by the burnt-out guard shed.'

It took them two minutes to find Kit and get him to his feet. Apart from a gash over the eye he appeared unharmed and only too ready to talk.

'By all that is holy, John, I've never seen such brutality.'

'Not now, Kit,' John urged him. 'We'll talk later.'

'That Major Bingham shot a small boy, no older than four or five, in the back!'

'Shhh!' Cate shushed him. 'Let us get you out of here first.'

They went unchallenged all the way back out of the Stockade with one soldier even giving Cate a knowing wink as they passed.

It was early afternoon, around the campfire with tea and damper, when the stories of the Stockade began to filter in. Main Street was filled with horrified inhabitants and the rumours began to spread. Peter Lalor had been shot and killed, one said. Peter Lalor had been wounded, said another. Peter Lalor had been smuggled out of the Stockade. And so it went. Anne Diamond had escaped but her husband, Martin, had been hacked to bits by troopers. A young miner had been stabbed and shot then trampled to death under the hooves of troopers' horses. The wife and children of John Sheehan were all burned to death in their family tent, set fire to by police. Stories of rape were common. People who had fled the neighbourhood at the time had returned to find their entire belongings burnt and looted. Worst of all were the rumours that miners were still being hunted down and killed on Brown Hill.

'I shall never, for my entire life, forget the image of that child being shot in the back,' Kit said as he sipped his tea.

'And you say it was Bingham?' John asked.

'I saw him do it with my own eyes. And then he shot the child's father.'

'Let's just pray that everyone remains calm.'

'You can't expect them to remain calm, Cate,' Kit offered. 'The military and police have been let off the leash by their masters and no-one is safe, especially women.'

'Kit's right.' John, who had been staring off into the middle distance for some time, finally entered the conversation. 'In the last twelve hours Ballarat has cemented its spot in history. It will forever be known as the place where the British massacred their own. And,' he looked directly at Cate, 'the place where Major Roger Bingham committed his last act of treachery.'

Cate's stomach lurched. 'Oh, John, no, my love. What are you contemplating now? Let's hitch the horses and leave! Please!'

He continued to stare at her for several seconds then shook his head slowly. 'I must go to the Camp.'

'Oh no! Let's take Jack and go. Please!' Her heart sank as she registered the determination in his eyes.

'He murdered a child, Cate! He shot a little boy in the back, for God's sake! And then he shot the father!'

What can I say? she thought, as all hope drained from her. He'll probably be killed, but he's determined to do whatever it is he has decided to do and there is no way I can stop him. At least she could see no evidence of the blood rush in him. He seemed calm and collected.

'What do you intend to do?' she asked.

'I'm going to see his senior officers and demand they take action against him. And if they refuse I'll tell them I'll take the story to London and Queen Victoria herself.' He stood. 'Kit, will you attend with me? I will need you to testify as an eyewitness.'

'It would be an honour, John.' Kit placed his tea mug on the firestones and got to his feet.

'Good,' John said and looked down at Cate who simply nodded in defeat. 'And there's no time like the present! Shall we go?'

Cate watched them mount up and trot across the allotment into Main Street, her dreams of a secure family life in tatters.

John did not slow the mare until he neared the entrance to the Camp, then he brought her down to a trot. The Camp was an area of three or so acres surrounded by a high picket fence and at its main gate stood two soldiers on guard duty.

'Who goes there?' declared a soldier of no more than fifteen or sixteen as he pointed a rifle at John.

'Captain John Farrington late of the 3rd Dragoons, to see the 40th Regiment Officer of the Day.'

The boy was lost for words. He'd recently heard the stories about the famous captain and found himself unable to say anything.

'Captain Farrington,' a deep voice said and John watched as a sergeant and four soldiers walked out of the gates to surround his mount. 'You've saved us a long walk to your allotment, sir.'

John studied the man closely. 'Geary?' he said. 'Edward Geary?'

'The very same, sir,' Geary saluted. 'Late of the 3rd Dragoons and sergeant now to the 40th.'

'I remember you well. Gujrat of course. Good to see you, Geary.'

'I'm afraid I can't say the same, sir.'

'And why not?'

'I'm under orders to find you and place you under arrest. So, if you would dismount, sir, and follow me, I'd appreciate it.'

John and Kit dismounted and a young soldier took the mare's reins while another relieved John of his pistol and knife.

'I'm afraid your friend will have to remain here at the gates, Captain.'

'It's all right, Kit,' John said as Kit prepared to intervene. 'I'll send for you when I need you.'

As Geary and his detail of men escorted him through the compound he was shocked to see the behaviour of some soldiers. Any number of them were drunk and several were playing a game with the remnants of the Eureka flag they had souvenired that morning. They were bundling it up and throwing it to each other while another of them tried to spear it with a bayonet.

The Camp was a disgrace. On John's right and against the tall picket fence, he saw a row of tents with sod chimneys, obviously for officers and government employees, while on his left were even more tents barely fit for human habitation, which he assumed housed the rank and file of the army.

There were several wooden buildings central to the compound, newly built by the look of them, and beyond stood a line of commissariat stores, the courthouse and a long low building of logs, which had not been in existence on his last visit a year ago when he'd defended Harry Foo the Chinese Cockney. Members of the Victorian Police Force, in various states of undress almost to nakedness, lay in the dirt among the tents insensibly drunk. And flying proudly above the scene was the Union Jack of the British Empire. It made John feel physically sick to witness it all.

Rather than march directly to the military office, they continued on towards the courthouse then veered left and marched behind the long, low prison building, where Geary ordered them to stop.

'I'm here to see Major Bingham's commanding officer, Geary.'

The soldier ignored his demand. 'May I have your word that you will remain here unescorted until I return, sir?'

'Of course.'

'Thank you, sir.' He saluted. 'Right, you lot, let's move it.'

John was left alone in what could only be described as a corridor of grass some thirty feet wide. He stood with his back to the log prison wall and in front of him was the high picket fence of the Camp perimeter. After several minutes he heard the sergeant's voice again.

'Left wheel,' Geary's voice snapped and John's attention was drawn to a file of six riflemen with arms shouldered who marched to a point in front of him and against the perimeter fence, where Geary halted them. A cold shiver ran through him as he realised they were a firing squad. My God, Bingham has ordered my execution, was all he could think as sweat broke out on his palms.

'What, no trial, Geary?' he sneered. 'So the military has sunk to performing execution without trial, has it?'

Geary did not look at him, but stood facing the front alongside his file of riflemen.

Then, from the corner of his eye, John sensed movement and turned his head right to see the arrival of a half-dozen military officers, a major, two captains and three lieutenants. They lined up at right angles to the firing squad and stood silently.

'You might have the good grace to get on with it, Geary,' he sneered again, with false bravado.

'We're waiting for Major Bingham, Captain Farrington.'

'I'm here, Geary.'

John looked left and saw Bingham, accompanied by another soldier he recognised from India, Godfrey Jenkins, formerly Regimental Sergeant Major of the 16th Queen's Lancers.

'Well, well, well, this is a pleasant surprise, Farrington,' Bingham purred upon approach. 'And not before time, eh?' Then he looked at the officers from his regiment lined up at right angles to him. 'Francis,' he asked of the major, 'what on earth are you doing here? And you too, George?'

Major Francis Watt looked towards RSM Connor. 'Can we get on with it, Sarn't Major?'

'Yes, sir,' the RSM growled, looking at Bingham. He flipped open the holster on Bingham's waist and removed the firearm from it. 'Major Roger Dalkeith Bingham, this morning during the planned attack on the insurgents' stockade, you did commit murder so foul and heinous as to shoot a child and his father, killing them both.'

'What the hell are you talking about?' shouted Bingham.

'Shut up, man!' Captain George Carrick yelled in return. 'Show some grace for once in your miserable life.'

'In a meeting of the officers and NCOs of the 40th Regiment,' the RSM continued, 'it was decided that your action, if ever it were to become common knowledge, would bring such public shame and dishonour upon the regiment that anything less than your death will not suffice. Therefore under the Queen's Regulations, as you have been found guilty by your peers of conduct unbecoming an officer on the field of battle . . .'

'Are you serious?' The question was rhetorical. Roger Bingham was suddenly more than aware of how dire his situation was.

'The entire regiment will keep the matter a secret, Roger,' Major Francis Watt said. 'No-one will ever know what you did.'

'You can't do this!' Bingham screamed as his panic rose. 'You have no authority . . .'

'Think of your family, man!' Watt snapped. 'Think of the shame they would suffer if ever this matter became public knowledge!'

'Francis, wa– wait a minute,' Bingham stammered as he noticed RSM Connor unload the firearm he'd taken.

Watt held his hand up. 'All that remains for you to do is the right thing, for yourself and the regiment.'

'But, but . . .' Bingham was now terrified. 'What do you mean?'

'Take a minute to compose yourself, Major,' the RSM said as he offered Bingham his firearm back, now loaded with one bullet. 'Because if you don't do it like a gentleman should, the RSM will do it for you.'

Bingham went to water. 'No, no I can't,' he sobbed, pushing his revolver back into the RSM's hand. 'Francis, George, gentlemen,' he pleaded to his fellow officers, 'I have a family, children.'

John suddenly remembered the same plea Bingham had made to him on that winter morning two years ago.

'He doesn't have it in him, Francis,' Carrick said to Watts.

'A coward to the last,' uttered one of the lieutenants.

'And a killer of children,' sneered another.

'Sarn't Major,' Watt called and nodded at the RSM. 'Do it.'

'Yes, sir,' Connor replied. He pointed the firearm at Roger Bingham's temple and pulled the trigger.

Silence followed for some seconds as the echo of the gunshot faded.

'Military justice has been done,' Major Watt announced. He took a step forward and inspected the corpse. 'It shall be reported that Major Roger Dalkeith Bingham, taken with a bout of severe melancholy over this morning's events and using his army issue revolver, tragically took his own life.

What occurred in that Stockade and here will remain a regimental secret never to be revealed.' He stared into the eyes of every man present, including John. 'Now let that be an end to it.'

All of the soldiers moved off in their own time until only Geary remained.

John looked down at the shattered head of the corpse. Then he felt a hand on his shoulder. 'Geary,' he said as he turned. 'I'm . . . er, sorry I didn't show more faith in you. I . . . er . . .'

'It's all right, Captain Farrington. You weren't to know. Take your one-eyed beauty and go home, sir.' He saluted. 'And may God be with you.'

'What took you so long?' Cate asked as he dismounted and embraced her.

'Everything's been sorted out. There'll be no more trouble with Bingham.'

'Really?' She sensed something strange in him. 'Are you sure you're all right?'

'Couldn't be better, my love,' he replied.

The look in his eyes says different, she thought. 'Are you sure?'

'Positive.' He smiled softly. 'Come on, girl, let's get ready to go home.' Home, Cate thought. He said home. 'Is Rhodesy right to travel?'

She laughed, so suddenly it shocked her. 'Yes. He's so full of laudanum he could probably pull the wagon.'

'Kit,' he called, 'let's get this wagon hitched and our gentle giant into it and head for Melbourne.'

'Right you are, man!' Kit smiled.

Finally, when they were ready to travel, with Cate on the seat of the wagon and Jack next to her, John walked up, leading his mare.

'Right, are you ready, Lieutenant?'

'We're ready, sir,' Jack replied with a smile.

Cate looked down at a world-weary face. 'What happened at the Camp?'

'Nothing of any consequence.'

'I'm worried. Tell me you didn't kill Bingham.'

'I didn't kill him.'

'Swear it to me, John.'

'I swear by all that I love, which is you and Jack, I did not kill Roger Bingham.' He remembered the moment he had looked down upon the corpse of Roger Bingham, the man he had despised above all men on earth. Initially, in that moment of Bingham's death he'd felt deprived, then to his surprise a rush of sadness had taken him. It's over, he thought. It's finally over.

He mounted Rani and tugged the reins. 'Now let's head for Melbourne. We've got a theatre to run, a wedding to arrange and a son to raise.'

'That sounds good to me,' she called as he took Rani in front of the wagon. 'You're a good man, John Farrington.'

'And you're a fine woman, Theresa Lacey, the finest in the land.'

EPILOGUE

Melbourne, 16 April 1855

In the aftermath of that fateful morning of 3 December word of the atrocities spread like a virus. Almost the entire population of Victoria fell solidly and instantly in support of the miners and widespread demonstrations resulted, particularly in the streets of Melbourne where groups of ten thousand and more were reported as gathering in protest by the newspapers of the day, especially *The Age* and *The Geelong Advertiser*, both suddenly advocates of male suffrage.

Any public servants who saw themselves as even remotely connected to acts of corruption or misfeasance departed for parts unknown. Soldiers, many from the 12th Regiment, discarded their uniforms and deserted like the cowards they had shown themselves to be.

Of those who were forced to face public scrutiny, Gold Commissioner Robert Rede and fellow Commissioner James Johnston, like many historical villains before and since, escaped scot-free. Rede was transferred from Ballarat to the position of Sheriff of Geelong and Johnston married, took up farming and sired fifteen children in twenty years. Governor Charles Hotham's post was raised to a full governorship on 3 February 1855 and the Imperial Government commended him for suppressing the rebellion at the Eureka Stockade, as the incident had become known. He failed to see the year out, dying on New Year's Eve. Of any other officials who could be held accountable for the wrongdoing in Ballarat, none were ever held to account and in the minds of honest men British justice reached its nadir.

Of the approximately one hundred and twenty men arrested at Eureka only thirteen, considered ringleaders, were put on trial for treason and they were quickly acquitted by juries of their peers.

How many died at Eureka? No-one seems to know. That's the way with revolution – nobody counts the dead. First reports claimed sixteen 'rebels' and five soldiers, later revised to twenty-eight and six respectively. Many accounts gave figures in excess of thirty-five dead bodies counted on the Eureka Lead that fateful morning, but still others say the slaughter continued further into the day as unhinged soldiers and policemen chased and killed men, women and children sought refuge in the forests, and the estimates rose to sixty or more. Others died of wounds or heartbreak in the following months, so the actual death toll question remains forever unanswerable.

Life at the Golden Sheaf hotel went on and those involved in the Travelling Show slowly recovered. Cate named her theatre opposite the hotel the Eureka Theatre in honour of those who died at the Stockade. Amos, Cate's trusted retainer, took over management of the company and the shows went from strength to strength. Andrew Arbuthnot McCrae continued as Master of Ceremonies, never denying, or confirming, the rumour started by Rhodesy that 'Dafty Boy' had sustained the burns to his arms and neck while defending the miners' rights at Eureka. The dwarf subsequently became the toast of Melbourne's theatre set. Anna and Lanna, the German twins, in the absence of Lou-shi, extended their contorting to include juggling and tumbling and proved to be quite proficient, although not a performance passed without an audience member asking after China the Circus Boy. Adelina sang operatic arias in Act I and filled in for Lou-shi in Act II with a display of Spanish dance at which she proved quite proficient. She lost weight and fell madly in love with her flamenco guitarist, a failed gold miner from

Barcelona. Tommy the Magician claimed he had purchased a half-share in a hotel in Geelong and disappeared from the scene, while Djali the Snake Boy returned as a star attraction along with six new snakes including a western taipan and his newest addition, Albert, a large, aggressive, yellow-tailed black cockatoo who sang 'God Save the Queen' interspersed with obscene, racist remarks about white people. The audiences cheered the bird and sat in silent terror of the snakes.

Lou-shi failed to return to the stage. The loss of Stupid Ho and especially her master, Feng Chi-pei, had delivered the girl into the depths of depression and no amount of effort from Cate, John, Jack or any of the cast could draw her out of it.

It was Wolfgang Bremmer who slowly but surely drew her back from the brink, and he achieved this success by appealing to her innate sense of musicality. Every morning Wolfie would play the onstage piano in the Eureka Theatre, feigning rehearsal, knowing the sound of music would draw her near and in due course Lou-shi came to sit at the back of the auditorium and listen. Eventually she came closer and they conversed as he played. He would tell her of the great Western operas and play some of the arias and eventually she related the stories of China's most famous. Then one morning at Wolfie's request she hummed the song she'd sung that night in Ballarat when Roger Bingham had become a reality to her.

'It is the lament of the maiden, Ho Chow Yu,' she said softly when she finished. 'It is a song of grief in which a young woman laments the loss of her father and brother.'

'Could you sing it to this?' Wolfie, consummate pianist that he was, began to play the Oriental melody in an elaborate Western manner and Lou-shi nodded. 'Then why don't we start together?'

That was how it began. They kept their early-morning performances a secret and within a month they had a repertoire of ten magnificent arias based loosely on the tunes and lyrics of Chinese operas.

When Cate and John announced their plans to marry in a simple ceremony in the foyer of the Golden Sheaf, Lou-shi agreed to Wolfgang's suggestion that she sing at the wedding.

And so it came to pass that on 16 April 1855, in the foyer of the hotel beautifully decorated by Dorothy and the German twins, John and Cate took their vows and Lou-shi stood on the grand staircase and sang 'The Ode to Constancy', from the *Yue* opera of the same name, to a magnificent Westernised composition by Wolfgang Bremmer.

As her final noted faded to silence, all of the women and several men in the audience were wiping tears away, despite not having understood one word of the Cantonese lyrics, when a voice called excitedly from the front doorway.

'*Aaaaaiiiiyaaaahhh!* I fink is time for all new special opera tour of goldfields!'

Master Feng Chi-pei stood, arms outstretched in declaration, and everyone was suddenly struck dumb.

'*Aaaaaiiiiyaaaahhh!*' It was none other than Lou-shi who broke the silence. 'Master! Master!' she screamed and charged through the crowd of guests to throw her arms around him.

'I thought he was dead,' Kit said to Rhodesy.

'He was,' Rhodesy said when John and Cate gave him quizzical looks. 'I gave 'is body to Mister Soh, that there See Yup Society fella. I said to bury 'im, not make 'im better!' He stared wide-eyed at Cate and said sagely, 'Chinese medicine, see. There's some what swears by it!'

Many of those gathered together in the foyer joyously hugging Feng and each other had decisions to make regarding their futures, but for the time being they could wait. The harmony and friendship shared at that moment was overpowering.

ACKNOWLEDGEMENTS

Firstly, thank you to my wife, Judy Nunn, for her love and encouragement, especially when my brain drifts into day-dreaming mode as it sometimes does. Her strident order to re-focus comes at me like an approaching freight train.

Thanks once again to my publisher, Beverley Cousins; editor Brandon VanOver; and the Princess Royal of Public Relations, Jessica Malpass PR, for their support and advice, but more importantly their friendship. And to Annabel Adair and Tom Langshaw, and all the other cheerful, hardworking people at Penguin Random House from reception to the book warehouse, thank you so much.

Thanks to my dear friends and agents, James Laurie and Susan Greaves, who, despite having had a difficult year on a personal level, continued to smile and urge me to the finish line.

Thanks yet again to my mate Colin Julin, who understands computers and regularly assures me that I do too, despite the fact he knows full well I don't and never will.

A big thank you to the historians and employees of the Sovereign Hill Museums Association, who welcomed me so warmly, and to the ladies at the Ballarat Historical Society, who showed me sketches of the Stockade and the goldfields. Thanks also to those at the Ballarat Archives Centre, Ballarat Library, the Ballarat Fine Art Gallery and the chaps at the Eureka Centre for their help and advice. And my thanks to all those kind citizens of Ballarat who welcomed me during my several research trips to their fine city.

Finally, to all those with opposable thumbs . . . *Wassail!*

BIBLIOGRAPHY

Soldier Sahibs: The Men Who Made the North-West Frontier. Charles Allen, Abacus, 2001.

Discovering Costume. Audrey I. Barfoot, University of London Press, 1959.

Eureka Rediscovered: In Search of the Site of the Historic Stockade. Jack Harvey, University of Ballarat, 1994.

Letters of Rachel Henning. Angus & Robertson, 1986.

Gold Fever: Voices from Australian Goldfields. Nancy Keesing (ed.), Angus & Robertson, 1989.

Chinese Opera: Images and Stories. Wang-Ngai Siu with Peter Lovrick, University of British Columbia Press, 1997.

Women of the Diggings, Ballarat 1854. Dorothy Wickham, Ballarat Heritage Services Publishing, Ballarat, 2009.

The Forgotten Rebels of Eureka. Clare Wright, The Text Publishing Company, 2013.

THE TIME OF THE
Dragons
BRUCE VENABLES

THE TIME OF THE DRAGONS
Bruce Venables

For the first time in 3000 years no emperor sits on the Dragon Throne. China is a seething cauldron of vice and corruption. Soon the Japanese will invade, and China will bleed like never before. In the eye of the storm sits the British Crown Colony of Hong Kong, jewel of the South China Sea.

Like Hong Kong itself, Inspector Richard Brewster, an idealistic young Englishman, struggles to survive in the maelstrom of war and political upheaval that is China in the 1920s and '30s.

Pirates and triad societies risk the wrath of the Kuo Min Tang army in a murderous hunt for a fabled treasure. Within the very ranks of the Hong Kong Police Force itself, desperate young men form a triad for their mutual protection. The illegal secret society becomes a malevolent dragon, spreading its wings to cast a shadow of evil across half the world.

From the pirate enclaves of the South China Sea to the opulent mansions of Victoria Peak; from the Japanese invasion of Shanghai to the vicious aerial combat of the Battle of Britain; Richard Brewster's life spins out of control in a world of passion, corruption and intrigue.

***The Time of the Dragons* is a gripping story of passion, corruption and intrigue, spanning generations and set between Hong Kong, China and London.**

AVAILABLE NOW IN EBOOK

TWO
TIGERS
One Mountain
BRUCE VENABLES

TWO TIGERS, ONE MOUNTAIN
Bruce Venables

'Two tigers cannot live on one mountain' – *Chinese proverb*

There can only be one winner in a battle. A truce, the Chinese say, merely delays the inevitable. In Korea, two brothers fight on opposing sides in a war where black market profiteering is rife, and patriotism and honour have lost their meanings. When they depart the battlefield, one is a hero, the other a traitor.

One brother, General Lee Kwan Man-hop, returns to the volatile political climate of Beijing and an uncertain future in the communist People's Republic of China. The other, Wing Commander James Merchant RAF, goes home to Hong Kong to restore a family business. Through China's turbulent years of the 1950s and '60s, Lee Kwan fights to protect his family from brutal oppression, while in Hong Kong, James Merchant's family empire is in danger of disintegrating.

Strong women, the lovers of powerful men, join in the fight for its preservation, and indeed their own, as the Noble House of Merchant becomes a house divided. A house plagued with treachery and haunted by tales of a long-lost fortune in gold, supposedly the bequest of an illegal, secret, triad society.

From the Korean War to the Cultural Revolution, *Two Tigers, One Mountain* is the long-awaited sequel to *The Time of the Dragons* and a dramatic story of a family dynasty on a violent course to destruction. From Hong Kong to London; from the foreign embassies of war-torn Seoul to the far-east elegance of Singapore; from the narrow lanes of Bejing slums, to the famous banking houses of Geneva, *Two Tigers, One Mountain*, like an opiate dream, is a fabulous tale of the Orient.

AVAILABLE NOW IN EBOOK

Scattered
MONKEYS
HONG KONG, 1976. A FAMILY AT WAR, AN EMPIRE THE PRIZE.
BRUCE VENABLES

SCATTERED MONKEYS
Bruce Venables

Hong Kong, 1976. A family at war, an empire the prize . . .

Brendan Murray arrives in the British Crown Colony of Hong Kong in 1976 to serve in the Royal Hong Kong Police Force. Despite five years' experience as a cop in Australia, he discovers he has much to learn, especially when faced with three formidable women linked by both business and blood . . .

Jenny Woo, once a street urchin and now the owner of an infamous nightclub, seeks Brendan's friendship – something that does not go unnoticed by his scheming superiors in search of a high-level informant . . .

Kwan Su-lin, a dedicated doctor who suffered horrifically at the hands of MaoTse-tung's infamous Red Guard, has allowed her remarkable martial arts skills to lie dormant. Until now . . .

Georgina Merchant, CEO of the most powerful company in Asia, a striking beauty, a ruthless adversary, a woman not to be crossed . . .

When the mighty Merchant Corporation comes under threat, Brendan and his colleagues in the RHKP are drawn into a web of intrigue, with the stakes climbing higher at every turn.

From Hong Kong's glittering mansions to its shady opium divans, from its wealthy elite to its brutal triad societies, from warrior monks to merciless politicians, *Scattered Monkeys* is a heart-stopping, exhilarating thriller.

AVAILABLE NOW IN PRINT AND EBOOK